THE FINDER OF THE

LUCKY DEVIL

— Top-Shelf Edition —

BOOK ONE OF THE LUCKY DEVIL SERIES

THE FINDER OF THE LUCKY DEVIL

— *Top-Shelf Edition* —

MEGAN MACKIE

Books

PENNSVILLE, NJ

PUBLISHED BY
eSpec Books LLC
Danielle McPhail,
Publisher
PO Box 242,
Pennsville, New Jersey 08070
www.especbooks.com

ISBN: 978-1-949691-21-4
ISBN (ebook): 978-1-949691-20-7

Published in an earlier edition by
Mystique Press, an imprint of Crossroad Press.

Copy Editor: Greg Schauer
Interior Design: Danielle McPhail,
Sidhe na Daire Multimedia
www.sidhenadaire.com

Interior Graphics: www.fotolia.com
Firewall Tattoo Tribal Pattern © Diverser
Tribal flames and elements © Seamartini Graphics

Cover Art and Design: J. Caleb Clark, jcalebdesign.com

To my grandmother, Anna, the librarian

ACKNOWLEDGMENTS

Thank you first and foremost to my mother, Connie, for my entire life in general and for proofreading my book three times specifically.

Thank you to Jenna, my editor, for guiding me through this process, as well as Jay and Michael, for being my mentors.

Thank you, Andrew, for always dropping everything to come over and help me figure out what was wrong with my book.

Thank you to Frank for being my life-affirming snowman.

Thank you to Caleb for working with me tirelessly on getting my cover art exactly right.

Thank you to my husband and friend, Paul, for supporting me unwaveringly. I love you with all my heart. Thank you to Byron and Alaina for leaving mommy alone for five minutes so she could finish her book.

For whatsoeuer from one place doth fall,
Is with the tide vnto an other brought:
For there is nothing lost, that may be found, if sought.

Edmund Spenser
The Faerie Queen, 1590

PROLOGUE

The door shut heavily behind the prisoner, slamming in a way that had become too familiar over the past six months...or was it a lifetime? It was hard to tell anymore. The room never changed. The bare white walls, the gray round table, with two rounded chairs. The same horrible woman sitting on the far side, smiling like she ate the cat that ate the canary. She sat upright, her hands folded before her. She wore another perfect business suit; this one a dark green that complemented her blonde hair and matched the green-rimmed glasses sitting smartly on her nose.

The prisoner wore the same bright-yellow jumpsuit she had worn every day she had been in this hell, her own brown hair unstylishly short, hacked and kept that way since she first arrived. Her tormentor did it herself whenever she took a fancy to, like a child playing hairdresser with her least favorite doll, cooing how it was for her own good. Short hair so much easier to manage. Wouldn't want the guards thinking she was too beautiful to resist. What would Justin think of her now?

'Her doll' dreaded this place, dreaded it with every step away from the cell. It had been two weeks. She counted them on her cell wall. Two weeks since she last entered this awful room. Since she faced this awful woman with her cruel, smiling face. Heard her fake words. Always said pleasantly, but containing three different meanings. It had been too much to hope that her tormentor had forgotten her; that the torture and interrogations were over.

"Oh, you don't look happy to see me. I'm hurt," the well-dressed woman said, feigning a pout. The prisoner's face remained dispassionate as she took the open seat, like the well-trained dog she was. Her tormentor looked at her expectantly, but the prisoner just laid her hands one on top the other on the cold table's surface and waited. Any move she made ended in her suffering, so she had learned to just stay still and wait. They each waited for a response from the other.

"I'd think you would miss me a little bit, seeing as I am your only friend in the world," the well-dressed woman pushed.

The prisoner swallowed a dry lump in her throat. God, she hated this woman. "How are you, ma'am?" she asked, her voice dry and creaky.

"Oh, dear, you sound parched. Here, have some of this," she said and fetched a plastic bottle of liquid from the leather satchel next to her chair. The prisoner noticed how she avoided identifying what 'this' was. Just as likely, it wasn't water at all, but some medicinal concoction or tasteless poison designed to make her suffer or be more compliant. If she didn't take the bottle, she would suffer either way and, at that moment, thirst overwhelmed her.

She took the bottle, cracked the seal, and downed the whole thing. It was room temperature, mineral-rich and delicious. While she guzzled her "probably water," her interrogator busied herself setting out papers in a neat little stack in front of her prisoner, followed by two pens that she aligned perfectly with the top of the papers. Her prisoner eyed the symmetry warily.

"No need to look like that. This won't be too strenuous today. Just a little paperwork, and then it's all over." She uncapped one of the pens; it was the flowy quill type.

"You mean this is it?" the prisoner asked, not really believing what the well-dressed woman was saying.

"Well, I can bring back the car battery if you like, but I think you'd rather just sign my papers. Am I right?" the well-dressed woman said as if she was trying to make a joke.

The well-dressed woman was right, and the prisoner knew it.

Bitch.

Yet, the prisoner knew she would sign anything the well-dressed woman ordered. The momentary resistance sparking within quieted.

Then the well-dressed woman slammed something into the surface of the table, forcing her prisoner to flinch and recoil. It was the pair of dull scissors, the point not dull enough to prevent it from sticking out of the table's surface. She stared at it in horror, before lowering her head forward, to offer her hair to be cut. The move was so automatic, her hands resting on the table, her fingers pointing to the ceiling like a supplicant.

"Tell me again, why are you here?" the well-dressed woman asked, pulling the scissors out of the table and setting them aside. This, too was part of the ritual, a sign that her prisoner responded correctly.

"Because my husband, Justin Masterson," a catch in her throat forced the prisoner to pause. No matter how many times she repeated these words, it hurt as freshly as the day they were arrested. The sight of Justin's eyes as he stared at her across the floor, his hands pinned behind his back by men in body armor. They were doing the same to her, and her heart broke as she looked into those perfect, beautiful eyes. But her suffering and continued longing for him wasn't what the well-dressed woman wanted to hear. "He embezzled money and betrayed his loyalty to the company," the prisoner recited. "I did not report my suspicions to the company, thereby enabling and abetting him in this crime."

"And you admit this freely?" the well-dressed woman asked.

That made the prisoner pause. The question was a deviation from the usual ritual.

"Am… am I supposed to?" she asked softly.

The well-dressed woman huffed out a harsh breath before sliding the first piece of paper before her prisoner. "This document is your confession to your crimes, listed below. Take some time to go over them. Make sure I didn't miss anything. Then sign it that you agree."

The prisoner double blinked at the page. Sign it? With her name?

She didn't know why any of this was necessary but had stopped asking why a long time ago. It was what her tormentor wanted. There was no getting out of it. Nobody was coming for her, nor was anyone looking for her. She was going to die very soon, and no one would know what had happened to her — or to Justin, whatever they had done with him.

The prisoner closed her eyes and tried to picture him again, his dark hair and wicked smile. The way his blue eyes twinkled and the way his hands felt on her waist when he pulled her close while he told one of his great stories to her — his rapt audience. She held the memories tight. No matter what they did to her, she wouldn't let them truly take him from her.

"Will you hurry up," her interrogator ordered, snapping her back to the present moment. She slid a single page across the table to the prisoner. "Sign this next, attesting that you are alive and in reasonable health."

The prisoner picked up a pen and uncapped it. The quill mesmerized her. It was so pointy. So sharp. She could easily visualize it piercing flesh. Never before had they given her anything that came even close to a weapon. How easy would it be to just stab her tormentor with it? She didn't believe she could escape, but maybe for just a moment, she could strike out at this person. Get a little of her own back. Make this bitch bleed like she had bled. Show her that she wasn't broken. Didn't she have a reason to want revenge, the best reason?

"Hurry up, I don't have all day," the well-dressed woman snapped.

Quickly, the prisoner complied, signing on the line at the bottom. Her hand seemed to know what it was doing, though she barely remembered her own name anymore; it had been something pretty, something she had loved once.

Once the paper was marked, her interrogator took it, stamped it, and then signed it herself. They repeated this sequence five more times. The prisoner didn't bother to listen to what her interrogator said about each page and what it was for. She just signed and signed. Finally, they reached the last little stack of pages that were stapled together.

"Last but not least," the well-dressed woman declared and slapped the papers in front of the prisoner, who blinked at the words scrawled across the top.

"Dissolution of marriage?" The prisoner read the top aloud, and only then did the words make sense. The prisoner looked at her interrogator feeling lost and numb. "I don't understand."

The well-dressed woman did something surprising. She reached across the table and squeezed the prisoner's hand. "I'm sorry, dear." Somehow, her kindness hurt worse, as if the small bit of sympathy made what she was saying more real. The gentle touch was more painful than a slap. The prisoner wanted to shake her hand off, itched to do it, but she didn't dare. Instead, she picked the pages up and looked at them closer.

There in the first space of every set of two was his name, his signature, in crisp, ugly, thin letters: *Justin Masterson. Justin Masterson. Justin Masterson.*

"He already signed them?"

The prisoner shoved the pages away like they were acid. "No!" Her throat closed, and her hands shook. "This is a trick," she argued as panic rose to fill her up.

"No, you stupid little bitch, this is very real," the well-dressed woman said, her voice now the cold familiar one the prisoner knew too well.

"But I don't understand. Why is he doing this?"

Suddenly, her interrogator slapped her hand on the table, and the prisoner jumped reflexively. "You're whining again. I don't like it when you whine."

The prisoner flinched. Cowered. "I'm sorry!" Her hands shook even worse now. Her interrogator pulled the pages back toward herself and tidied them up in an exaggerated show of irritation.

"I would think it would be obvious why this is happening. Your husband accepted our offer, you did not. Now he will be rid of you once you sign those papers." The well-dressed woman's eyes gleamed the corners of her mouth upturning into the threat of a smile.

"I … I want to see him," the prisoner requested, knowing it would be denied. She had asked every day to see her husband, her Justin. She had called for him. Cried his name in pain and fear. Clung on to any tiny shred of hope that he was somewhere in this place, like her, and that maybe they would both survive it. The lie that they were in this together kept her going like nothing else had. "I need to talk to him."

"That's not going to happen, you pathetic idiot child. Sign the papers." It was an order, not a request.

"But I … I don't want to divorce." She did sound like a child, even to her own ears.

"It's not a divorce. It's a dissolution of marriage. There is a difference. Sign the papers," the interrogator repeated, her voice growing even colder, even quieter.

The prisoner looked down at the documents, and her eyes filled with tears. Her hands came together, the right one fiddling with the wedding band on her left ring finger. She never understood why they let her keep it. Her last link to Justin. It was a plain band, no jewels or anything; just gold with white-gold running through the middle. She had twisted it a million times until it had left a red dent in the flesh of her finger. She could barely see it now through her tears. She let them trickle down her face, not bothering to wipe them away. Her grief flowed free as she realized he had abandoned her as she feared he would. She signed one line after another until the dissolution decree was completed.

"Truthfully, I'm not sure what he saw in you, to begin with," her interrogator said as soon as the prisoner finished signing. "It must be a relief, I'm sure, to be rid of a worthless piece of garbage like you." She said it so matter-of-fact. No malice, or hate, really, just as if it were a simple, undeniable fact. The moment the prisoner's last signature was in place, the well-dressed woman snatched the page out from under her pen and stowed it with the rest. Then she stood, plucked the prisoner's pen from her weak hands, placed it in the satchel, and slung the whole thing over her shoulder.

"Goodbye," she said, the mask of pleasantness reasserting itself over the well-dressed woman's face, contrasting her words "I never did find out what secret you're still keeping, but oh, well. I will never see you again," she declared, with happy relief, as if she were the one who endured months of torture. Then she walked out the door just as two burly men entered.

The hairs on the back of the prisoner's arms rose as she realized the implications of the things her tormentor, her *former* tormentor, had said. It was over.

These men weren't her escort. They were her executioners.

The minute the first meaty hand wrapped itself around her wrist, something snapped inside her. She screamed her rage at the top of her lungs. She kicked and clawed and bucked, not caring that she might also hurt herself in her struggle to get away.

It took both the burly men to secure her. One tried to bear-hug her. The other wrangled her legs. Together they got her out the door. Once in the hall, they managed to carry her a short distance. Her struggles freed one foot. She kicked off the ground, partially breaking the hold on her upper body.

"Goddamn bitch!" one of the men yelled. He swung back to slap her across the face. The blow didn't connect. She scrambled up, out of his range, and tried to run, but one of them caught her feet again. The other caught her by the hair, and that was how they dragged her down the hall, through clinical double doors.

The moment they passed those doors, she gave up. She couldn't see where they were going anymore.

"Unhand her!" snapped a voice, filled with eerie power. Or rather, there was a snap. Something crackled through the air. The burly men dropped her, each of them arching their backs as they writhed in pain. Softly, the young woman floated like a feather to the ground while they both fell hard. Some force seemed to fling the men back through the doors they had just entered.

She laid on the cold tiled floor, collapsed onto her knees, breathing hard, her face covered in sweat. She stayed that way for an eternity, but no one touched her.

No one was touching her. That was strange. Why wasn't she being hauled to her feet and strapped into some horror device out of a dark nightmare?

"Anna?"

She looked up, startled at the sound of the gentle voice. The gentle, *familiar* voice.

Anna? She was Anna, and she lay on the floor of what looked like a visitor's room. So disturbingly ordinary. Comfortable, even, with its sofa, a side table, and two armchairs. On the wall hung a painting of a gentle landscape. In the middle of the room, looking down at her, stood a small, old woman. Her features were soft. In fact, everything about her was soft, from her pink sweater to the curl of her snowy white hair, to the hand reaching out to Anna, palm open in invitation. Anna remembered those eyes, blue and clear as the sky. She remembered that wrinkled face. The one that smiled even when the lips did not. Anna knew her. She knew her!

"Aunt Maddie?" Anna dared to ask, dared to hope.

"Yes, darling Anna. I'm here. I've come for you," Aunt Maddie said, as she knelt beside Anna, tears glittering in her eyes.

Anna started crying as she was wrapped into the older woman's arms. Aunt Maddie was here. Anna breathed in the scent of cinnamon, cream, and old lady. They rocked for a long time, until Anna's tears stopped. Then Aunt Maddie brushed an invisible hair away from Anna's face and looked at her with so much love.

"My poor, sweet, little Rune girl. Let's go home. I swear by every ounce of magic in me, no one will ever hurt you again."

CHAPTER 1

Six Years Later…Chicago

The bar was overcrowded. After the third tray of glasses crashed to the floor, Rune seriously considered the legal ramifications of whipping out her great aunt's old shotgun and clearing the room.

It all started when the bachelorette party exploded out of the back room and into the quieter sanctuary of the Lounge Bar. Alf, the bar's general manager, made her book the Quintet of Stupid, reminding her that the mortgage bill was coming due in less than a week. Not that she needed reminding. Grumbling under her breath about selling him to the lollipop guild, she had confirmed the date and time. The way the maid of honor had been talking, one would think they were having an entire party of twenty or more people. Rune was irritated beyond belief when they showed up with only five, all wearing bedazzled shirts designating them as princess bride, maid of dishonor, the rebel bridesmaid, the fat bridesmaid, and the replacement bridesmaid.

"Exactly, how much are they going to drink if they're already drunk?" Rune grumbled under her breath at Alf, after she had led the small party to their private room in the back. She attempted to retuck a long strand of her hair back into her braid, but she would probably have to simply redo it. Her hair was starting to get too long, but cutting it always gave her the creeps.

"They've prepaid the room and the drinks, so stop your bitching." Alf slapped his damp shoulder towel onto the bar to swipe peanut shells into an empty trash bin that floated up on its own next to him. "And where are all the bottle openers?"

Rune didn't need to look; she never did. She just reached back behind herself and swiped the green one from next to the cash register to hand to the little man. Though Alf only reached about mid-waist, he gave her an intimidating glare. He was a dwarf, but not *that* kind of dwarf, and he would be the first to kneecap anyone for making that mistake.

"Hey Alf, the bathroom cleaning spell is wearing off in the men's bathroom," one of the regulars, a vampire named Morlock, informed them as he swiped up the shot and blood chaser waiting for him. "Smells like something died in there."

"Now, if you could just do some actual magic, and not just find things," Alf said at Rune.

"You can't do magic? Whoa, wait, weren't you Maddie's apprentice?" Morlock asked, tapping his shot glass on the bar for another hit.

"If she could, do you think I would be heading off to manually clean the bathroom?" Alf groused as he hopped down from his literal soapbox.

Rune made a face at her bar manager when his back was turned and opened the register with a quick, muttered spell word. She touched one finger to the crystal set at the top to activate the "unlock" magic. It wasn't that she couldn't do magic. She had a magical Talent, it was just for Finding things, which was a pretty passive, quiet magic. She sighed to herself, knowing they were going to have to pay for someone to recast the "auto-cleaning" spell for them, and that was going to be pricey.

Rune tucked the party deposit under the tray in the register, annoyed that they were so late with it. She should have just given the room away, but they kept promising to bring it in, only to do so the night of the party. Yet, she knew Alf was right about booking the bridal party despite the risk. It irked her just the same. While the deposit went a long way, Rune was still $2500 short on the mortgage. Getting the rest of the fee would be its own nightmare and far too late to help with this month.

"If we hadn't booked it out, we could have opened it up for more game patrons," Rune argued to herself, but she wasn't buying it.

The Lounge Bar was moderately attended for a Wednesday night, mostly working couples looking to unwind in the dimmer, calmer atmosphere. By contrast, the Main Bar was overly full as the Chicago Cubs were playing the New York Mets. From the sounds in the next room, Chicago was doing pretty well. That was when the first tray of glasses crashed in the Main Bar. Alf hurried past from the bathrooms to see what happened, leaving Rune alone to run the Lounge.

"Hey, Rune!"

She looked over her shoulder at the centaur sitting at his usual place at the end of the old stained bar. He was slovenly dressed in a disheveled business jacket, with his tie mostly undone around his neck and his sleeves rolled up in a way that Rune didn't think the suit was ever designed for. He wore a matching, gray, formal apron, cut much like a horse blanket, sitting askew across his horse-like body. Rune thought the idea of a formal apron was silly looking but dared not say that to a centaur. He smiled at her warmly, the smile cracking across his brown face and enviably perfect white teeth. His mane and tail were done up in dreadlocks, the neatness of his hair making an odd counter to his rumpled clothes.

Rune pushed off the back wall and made her way unhurriedly down the bar, smiling. All the other patrons seemed satisfied enough at the moment, so she grabbed up a bottle of ginger ale and cracked it open to drink and enjoy with her friend.

"Are you sure you need another, Franklin?" she asked, teasingly, trying not to sound too motherly, while the effervescent bubbles burned up her nose.

"No, but I'm sure you need one. Have a drink with me, Rune." He folded both his arms onto the bar and leaned as far forward as he dared, making the whole bar creak as he gave it his weight. Franklin was a regular customer, and the large centaur knew his limits. Even when he didn't, he never caused a scene.

"I can't have a drink with you, Frankie. Not tonight. Things are a bit on edge. Baseball next door," Rune said politely enough, as she pulled him another beer from the tap, a craft IPA from Wisconsin. She set the tall glass on a cardboard coaster and slid the whole thing toward his big meaty hands. Instead of the beer, he caught her hand, folding her fingers over the top of his larger, longer ones, pinning the tips with his thumb gently but firmly.

"Go out on a date with me, then," Franklin said, doubling down and tugging her a bit closer, to bring her knuckles up so that his breath rolled over them as he spoke.

"Sorry, but no. I'm not your type," she said, then amended, "I don't mean that how it sounds…which just makes it sound worse, I know." This was not the first time Franklin had asked this question, but it didn't seem to stop him when he'd had a few. Rune just never could figure out how to put him off for good without hurting his feelings. He loosened his grip on her fingers just enough for her to snatch them away before he could lay a big, old, sloppy, wet kiss on them. Instead, he groaned melodramatically.

"Oh, Rune, please. What do I have to do?"

"Stop being a cliché when a girl tells you no?" she quipped.

"I just want a real woman, and you are really a woman," he said, following his own drunken logic.

"You mean all plus-size of me?" she threw back at him.

Rune was feeling a bit cheeky that night. Being considered plus-size didn't bother her much; in her opinion, it was in all the right places. That night she wore one of her taper-cut blouses, her dark brown one that emphasized her bust, cinching her much smaller middle before flaring out again at her hips. She had taken to wearing skinny jeans again after a long stint in boot cut. Skinny jeans tucked better into the knee-high brown boots that she favored at the moment. She loved earth tones and real clothes made from cotton, leather, and metal, having spent too much of her previous life in synthetics. Apparently, Franklin loved it too.

"Girl, what hot-blooded male doesn't want a woman of substance?" Franklin asked, and she flashed him a shameless smile. Luckily for her, she got another hail from back down the bar allowing her to make a smooth, tasteful escape.

"To be continued. I'll be right back, Franklin."

"Let them wait. Come on. Why don't you ever say yes?"

"Franklin, you're a nice enough guy, but I am just not interested, really." Rune hoped this came off as letting him down gently but firmly.

"What? What is it, Rune? What is wrong with me? I'll change, I promise. I'm not like those other males who can't be changed. I'll change for you all day long! I promise," he begged, sliding his arms across the bar so that he was lying on it, the picture of dejection.

"Sounds like a lot of work. It's easier to give up on dating altogether. It just doesn't work out for me," she laughed. "You know the saying, right? I got baggage you don't want."

"Rune, you should have more confidence in yourself," Franklin said as if he thought he was being helpful.

Rune faltered and then forced her smile again. "Sorry, but I'm feeling the pressure from needing to serve those other patrons. I'll be back, I promise." As she turned, she saw Alf intercept them, after giving her a dirty look.

"What kind of guys do you go for then?" another voice asked.

Normally, Rune would have noticed the newcomer when he slid up next to her on the other side of the bar. It was an instinct developed by years of looking over her shoulder, but this gentleman had appeared almost like magic, which was likely to be more literal than metaphorical. Rune still found it unsettling and irritating, though maybe not as strange as it would have been at one of the more hominal-only bars in the city.

What did unsettle her was how he stared directly at her with intense green eyes rimmed with blue. Being the focus of his stare made her trip, trapped in his gaze as if she was locking eyes with a wolf. He was dressed in a fine suit, charcoal gray and three-piece, with a matching fedora and a stench of money about him. He was also unfairly handsome, with an angular face and cheekbones that could cut glass. The edges of his hat showed dark hair, and the cut of his suit suggested a man who did a lot of swimming; all lithe strength without the bulk from weight-lifting. She would even bet he had suspenders on, though that thought only lived in her imagination. Rune loved men in suspenders.

Then that arresting gaze softened so quickly, Rune wondered if she had misinterpreted what she had seen. He smiled broadly as the wolf faded back, and he gave her a charming wink that warmed her insides against her will.

"Clever like a jackrabbit," she muttered under her breath. He blinked and cocked his head to the side.

"Sorry?" he asked, blinking twice more before leaning on the bar top and wrapping his hands around the opposite elbows.

"Uh, it's just a saying of my great aunt's. The charming ones are by far more dangerous than the handsome ones; just ask anyone who's gone up against the jackrabbit," she explained, rubbing at the top of the bar with a damp cloth to cover up her embarrassment at being overheard. She kicked at the magically sentient garbage can that tapped eagerly at her legs, like a dog looking for crumbs.

"Then which am I? Charming or handsome?" the jackrabbit man asked, a wicked, knowing gleam in his eye that now looked wolfish again.

"Hmm, neither," Rune said like a smartass with a hint of flirt.

"What kind of guys do you like then, Rune?" Franklin interjected, obviously concerned that she was paying attention to another male.

"I suppose someone interested in starting a conversation with me that doesn't include my dating preferences. Maybe a conversation about the feminine mystique or the nuances of British Parliamentary procedure. You know, the usual, because we're an advanced society and all," Rune said in a syrupy-sweet voice accompanied by an acrid smile.

"Ah, a progressive woman, I see. That's refreshing in a bar," the mystery man said.

"And why is that?" Rune asked, drawn in, in spite of herself.

"I would think it would be more advantageous to you to play dumb and smile a lot to increase your tip count. Isn't that the usual, smart business plan for a female bartender?" he asked so pleasantly that it almost took away the edge in his words.

"Do you often get away with saying rude, sexist things by being dark, handsome, and mysterious?" she shot back, her eyes and her smile widening like a cat before she pounced. This was getting fun.

"Ah, so I am handsome then?" he countered, smirking even harder as if he won.

Both males stared at her, but it was the stranger who captured Rune's gaze again. Under his unwavering smile, she felt her cheeks flush bright pink like she was in high school. Franklin looked back and forth between them, not liking that their gazes were locked or what it might mean.

"Hey, Rune. Is this guy bothering you?" Franklin asked, using the old cliché instead of coming up with something original to say. It was enough, because the stranger broke their connection to smile at Franklin as some sort of gear shifted between himself and Rune.

"I'll have a vodka tonic and another beer for my new friend here," he said, inclining his head toward Franklin, "and whatever you want for yourself. I have some more questions for you about dark, handsome, mysterious men. And also I have..." he reached into his jacket's front pocket. Before Rune could see what was inside, Franklin shoved himself up to his hooves.

"None for me, thanks. I need to piss like a racehorse," Franklin said, digging up another bad taste cliché, obviously irritated as he pushed away from the bar, unsteady on his hooves.

"Franklin, are you alright?" Rune asked, feeling unsure about his sudden departure. He waved her off.

"I'll see you tomorrow, Rune. I should be getting home," he said and clomped his way to the front in a mostly straight line.

"Uh, yeah, see you later, Franklin," Rune called after him, trying to sound cheerfully nonchalant to mask her worry.

He paused at the sound of her voice, but his shoulders slumped noticeably when he heard her words. She received a backward wave as he trotted out the door, instead of to the restrooms.

"Ah, geez," she said to herself under her breath and opened the cooler in front of her to toss the ice in irritation. "Sorry, what was it you ordered again?" she asked as she tried to refocus and push down the sad feeling in her stomach. Before the stranger could speak, one of the Back Bar bartenders came up behind Rune, making her jump a little.

"Hey, boss, sorry. I think we're out of the cherry liquor and I can't find any more in the back."

Rune blinked at her as if she couldn't comprehend what she was looking at before nodding. "Cherry liquor? For the bridal party from hell?"

"Yeah, they're burning through Tainted Virgins like they're mineral water," the bartender complained.

Rune stepped back and reached up to slide the bottle of cherry liquor off the shelf and handed it to her bartender. "You're doing a good job, just hang in there," Rune said.

"Wow, I should have you come to my apartment and help me find my lost keys. At this rate, I'm going to have to marry a locksmith," she said, bubbly, and then headed toward the Backroom Bar.

"So, you're the owner of this place?" the stranger asked.

"Uh, yeah. Yeah, I am now. The original owner died recently." The knot appeared again, threatening the back of Rune's throat, but she managed to swallow it down. "And she left everything to me! So, here I am, trying to run a bar. Speaking of, you said vodka tonic, right?"

"Or a beer if that's easier," he answered.

"It's up to you. I can try either," Rune answered back.

"You know what? Let's just forget about the drink. If you're the owner, you might be exactly who I am looking for." He slipped his hand back into the front pocket of his jacket.

And then a woman hailed her just a few feet away at the far edge of the bar. She was so loud that by reflex, they both looked at her. It was one of the bridesmaids, drunkenly leaning against the bar, looking like she was a lost contestant from some slutty beauty pageant. The bedazzled shirt that proclaimed her the maid of dishonor was missing a few gems.

"Hey! Bartender!" she shouted too loudly for the easy conversational atmosphere of the Lounge Bar.

"Um, excuse me," Rune said and picked up the rag she had been fiddling with as she walked down the bar to meet the loud woman. "Can I help you?" she asked as she approached, pitching her voice pointedly low in an attempt to get the maid of dishonor to do the same.

"Hi. So, we were supposed to have the devil in our room. What's going on with that?" the maid of dishonor asked, in a pissy tone, completely ignoring Rune's subtle hint to bring it down a notch.

Rune blinked at her for a second and glanced over at Lucky Devil in his booth.

Lucky Devil and the bar that was named for him were both icons of Chicago and the bar's biggest attraction. The Lucky Devil figure sat in the only booth in the whole bar, smiling a wicked smile to the delight of tourists, and was an icon of pride for regular customers as well. He was made out of the same plastic and wood hodgepodge that carousel horses were made of, the inside completely mechanical, except for a couple of magical modifications to prevent rot from various libations of spilled drinks. Yet, the most powerful spell on it was designed for one purpose: to grant wishes.

To look at the Devil himself, one would think he belonged in a lost attraction on Coney Island or a freak show that traveled along back roads. He sat with one arm resting along the back of the booth, alert yet relaxed at the same time. He was jauntily dressed in an old-fashioned yellow suit and bowtie with the standard pointed, black devil beard, and eyebrows arching sharply on his bright Tabasco red skin. Perched on his head was a matching fedora, sitting at an angle amongst black curls so that one of his horns arched free around the brim. The booth and table were raised up on their own dais, so patrons had to step up to sit across from him. Only then could they see his goat furred legs, one black cloven hoof crossed nonchalantly over the knee of the other leg. His other hand rested on the table, a lowball glass gripped in his fist, waiting to be filled. When patrons sat across from him, he stared at them with wicked, smiling eyes and an equally wicked grin that showed a little bit of sharpened tooth.

At that moment, Lucky Devil was entertaining a pair of customers; two young men who were obviously on a first date and seemed to be having a really good one at that. The Latino boy, with long clever hands and a bright, white-toothed smile, pulled a tab on the old-fashioned cigarette machine that had been repurposed to dispense souvenir coins, each stamped with the bar's logo on one side and a smiling Lucky Devil winking on the other side. The Latino kid had chosen a silver coin, worth about $10, to make his wish with. Apparently, the date was going very well, but not well enough to warrant a $100 coin, which was a combination of gold, silver, and platinum. Most people who purchased those coins never gave them to the Devil to make their wish but would pocket them as souvenirs to take home. Then there were the jade coins, only twelve ever made, and they always found their way back to the Devil eventually. This kid had no jade coin, those were $1,000 apiece, nor did he intend to pocket the coin he had purchased. Instead, he slipped back into the booth next to his date, showing him the coin. The other Filipino-looking young man was filling out a slip of paper with a small pencil. They giggled as the Filipino kid folded up the paper, presumably his wish, and tucked it into the front pocket of Lucky Devil's jacket. Then the Latino kid dropped the silver coin into the lowball glass, per the instructions left on the table. Both waited, watching the mechanical devil, eager eyes filled with child-like anticipation. It was so cute that Rune couldn't help but wish she had a camera or imaging crystal to capture it with.

Then the Devil came to life, or so it appeared. The mechanical arm lifted the glass and drank the coin, the mouth dropping open to swallow it. The young couple squealed in delight, grabbing each other's hands in their excitement. Once the Lucky Devil had "emptied" the glass, he set it down and gave a merry, menacing chuckle. Eagerly, the Latino kid checked the pocket only to exclaim in shock to his date, that the slip of paper was gone, and that the wish had been "granted."

As she watched, Rune felt the paper appear in the front pocket of her button-up shirt. Though the paper itself didn't weigh much or have much mass, the magic always made her skin tickle when the spell dropped the wish from Lucky Devil's pocket to her own. Or if she didn't have front pockets that day, the spell would redirect to the inside of her bra strap, tingling her skin like the end of a battery.

"Is that the Devil there?" the maid of dishonor demanded.

"Yes, he is." Rune fished the slip of paper out of her front pocket and looked at it. "Hey, Liam!" she called over her shoulder. From around the separating wall that led to the Main Bar, a Shiva appeared.

The kid was tall, with nice brown skin and darker hair, dressed in a polo shirt with the Lucky Devil logo over the heart. Rune had to special order the shirt for him with four sleeves, but he wore it religiously when he worked, so she concluded it was worth it. "We need two double-sized frozen Margaritas and some supreme nachos at Lucky Devil's table."

"Put it on his tab?" Liam asked with a wry smile, folding his lower set of arms across his extra-long chest.

Rune nodded and put the piece of paper back into her front pocket. The maid of dishonor eyed both of them with judgmental disgust. Liam's face fell a bit as he turned to head toward the kitchen in the next room.

"Are you listening to me?" the maid of dishonor asked shrilly, making Rune wish a little bit harder that the floor would open up and swallow the woman, complete with licking fire and a nice refreshing sulfur smell. "Hey! Hey! I asked you a question. We're supposed to be in the room with the devil."

"That would be this room." Rune dug deep for friendly professionalism and gestured over to Lucky Devil. The young couple at the table squealed again in delight as their drinks appeared with amazing haste. Liam's four fast hands pulled off that miracle, as well as an order of the bar's famous spicy nachos, probably stolen from another order to pull off the Lucky Devil's trick.

"No, no, I was told there is a devil. We want to take pictures," the maid of dishonor snapped again, pulling Rune's attention away from enjoying the couple's delight.

"Yes, there is. You can come out here and take as many pictures as you want," Rune tried again, her irritation evident in her voice and through her smile.

"Look, this is obviously over your little head. I'd like to talk to your manager," the maid of dishonor declared regally.

Before Rune could say something even more unwise, like something degrading about her customer's intelligence, which was too wordy for good banter, Alf shoved Rune out of the way. She gave a little puppy yelp as she went flying behind the bar, landing on the cushy mats that helped prevent sore feet. Rune cussed under her breath as she rubbed the spot at mid-thigh that Alf had bumped. For a dwarf, or little person, or whatever, he had a very sharp hip bone.

"I am the general manager. How can I help you, ma'am?" Alf said with a sweet, congenial smile as he stood on the built-in step that had been installed along the bottom of the bar just for him.

"I can't believe we're being treated this way," the maid of dishonor repeated in the exact tone she had used on Rune and then launched into her litany of woe again.

Rune started to pick herself off of the floor when she looked up to see the charming man, leaning forward on his elbows to look down at her. Quickly, Rune mimed a "bada bump ching" on an invisible drum set. The charming guy's grin cracked fully into a smile. "One of my more graceful moments," Rune added as she pulled herself up.

"I can't believe he bumped you like that. Aren't you his boss?" the stranger asked, nodding his head at Alf, who was working full tilt to soothe the maid of dishonor's hurt feelings.

"Depends on the day, I guess," Rune said. "Do you still want that beer... or was it a vodka tonic? Or gin and tonic? Something tonic. I'm almost 90% sure."

"Vodka tonic," he said, and gave her another wink like he was sharing a secret with her.

"Sure, coming right up, I promise." Rune pulled out the tall glass she needed to mix the drink.

"I must say he's very spritely for a dwarf," the stranger said, nodding in Alf's direction. That brought Rune up short.

"Excuse me?"

The stranger shifted a little, his grin fading just a bit as he tried to figure out what he had said wrong.

"Alf is not a dwarf. He's a hominal person just like you and me, Buddy. The correct term is little person." Rune set the glass down on the bar.

Sure, she thought of Alf as a dwarf, but that was in her own head and only when she was mad at him. This guy was a stranger.

"Hominal?" the stranger asked. Something about him seemed to tense, though he hadn't moved a muscle. In fact, he seemed just as relaxed as ever, yet Rune couldn't shake the feeling that he was about to spring into action.

"Human being. We serve a lot of different peoples here at the Lucky Devil, but don't go making assumptions about any of them, if you please," Rune said. Alf may not have been Rune's favorite person in the world, but he was one of her people.

"I meant no disrespect. It's just not a term that comes up often for me, or the term dwarf. Is that a derogatory word or something?" the stranger asked, his head tilting to the side just a little, his hat casting a shadow across part of his face.

"He's not a dragon-killing enthusiast or a really good mining/witch-slaying aficionado from the folk tales. There is a big difference," she said.

"I apologize for my ignorance," he conceded, taking his hat off so that light shined on him again. He held it against his chest as he bowed his head in apology.

That took the wind out of Rune's sails, and she started mixing the drink again.

"I'm sorry. I'm just a little on edge tonight." She shoveled ice into the glass.

"Why is that?"

Rune eyed him for a moment with a soft smile as she set the glass onto the bar before him and pulled out the pop hose, pushing one of the many buttons on the back to dispense the tonic water.

Before she could answer, Alf appeared like an insistent itch at her elbow. "Jasper and Calvin are here," he growled.

Rune's head shot up to glance sideways over Alf, and sure enough, the Tigerman and the hominal man waited like bad habits at the end of the bar. They were both dressed in slick, high-corporate suits. Rune snorted at the sight of Calvin, who still wore his sunglasses, heedless of being indoors.

"They want their money," Alf said indelicately.

"I got 'til Monday morning. It's only Wednesday. Just ignore them," Rune said in a hushed, confidently defiant voice, just before she flooded the drink with too much tonic water.

"No, you just ignore them." Alf pushed Rune out of the way to swipe up the drink and slap a cloth on the bar to sop the excess liquid spilling to the ground. Rune managed to release her thumb from the button, but the damage was done. Her antics caught Calvin's attention apparently because he looked at her over his stupid sunglasses. Their eyes met as she glanced nervously back at him, cursing herself silently for looking. Jasper just smiled a toothy grin and continued to munch on the free, shell-on peanuts.

"If you would just attend the Magic Guild summons instead of only paying your dues..." Alf continued to grumble.

Avoiding that sore subject again, Rune apologized to the stranger and handed over the vodka and tonic to Alf, so she could make her way to the corporate thugs waiting for her.

"Aren't those bad for you?" Rune asked Jasper when she approached.

He continued shoveling peanuts, grinning grossly as he snapped them into pieces in his sharp feline teeth. "Lots of things are bad for you," the Tigerman answered.

"Like not making your mortgage payments on time, for example." His associate lifted the glasses up off his face to reveal ghostly blue eyes.

"Last I checked my due date is Monday, Calvin," Rune answered innocently, wiping the counter clear of peanut refuse into the eagerly waiting magical bin that had taken up residence at that particular edge of the bar, trying to catch the random bits that came its way. "Do you need help finding a calendar?" On reflex, her senses stretched out to pull her toward every available calendar in the room, but Rune ignored it and flashed Calvin a cheeky smile.

That earned her a furrowing of eyebrows and a quiet stare. "Look, we get it, don't we, Mr. Locke? This old place, it's got sentimental value for you. The old lady took you in off the streets after all, but Rune, this does not make good business sense, holding onto this money sink of a place."

"Money pit or sinkhole," Jasper corrected, cracking another peanut.

Calvin shot him a look. "Really? You do this now in front of the client," Calvin said under his breath.

"And yet my bar isn't empty. Funny that," Rune cut in, not wanting to wait for them to resolve their little spat. She eyed the near-empty bowl Jasper was eating out of. "Do you want something to drink with all those peanuts, Jasper?"

"Mr. Locke," the Tigerman corrected, narrowing his feline eyes at Rune, which were plenty intimidating.

"We both know..." Calvin started again before his partner cut him off.

"I'll take a Bailey's," Jasper said, "no ice." His partner pursed his lips together and turned his head to his partner in a disapproving manner before swinging it back to Rune and continuing, "We both know that your old boss didn't make her mortgage payments on the proceeds from this place."

"She was a woman of many hobbies." Rune smiled as she brought up a lowball tumbler from under the bar and set it on the counter before fishing around in the little fridge near her foot for the open bottle of Bailey's Irish Cream. "I suppose being a cat person, this makes perfect sense," she said, pouring the tumbler a quarter full.

"We're prepared to make you a really good offer, Rune." Calvin pushed the glass away before Rune could pour any more. Jasper growled a little, and Calvin gave him a chastising swat on the arm, which completely undermined Jasper's menace. "You can walk away from all this and start a better life."

Rune really didn't know what to say to that, so she just stared him down and hoped it came across as unfazed.

"Or if you want to stay here, a salary can be arranged, but either way, we can take this burden off your hands and make that mortgage just go away."

"I'll have the payment for you on Wednesday morning. Do you want me to come by the office or are you two going to come to pick it up again in person?" Rune answered evenly, hugging the Bailey's bottle against her shoulder.

"We're losing our patience, Rune," Calvin warned.

"Do you need help finding that too?" she asked.

That's when the bridal party and a bar fight exploded out of the back room.

CHAPTER 2

Rune barely registered the shouts and whoops coming from next door, until the moment someone's backside crashed through the glass-block divider between the peaceful, serene Lounge Bar and the Main Bar.

The whole room erupted into chaos. Rune was already moving toward the fight when she spotted Liam. The poor kid struggled to break up the two fighters who were both trying to get chokeholds on each other. Unfortunately for Liam, someone spun him around from behind with a haymaker punch straight to his left cheek. More people poured through the hole and Rune spotted the bridesmaids mixing in, cheering and whooping at the fighters on the floor.

Before Rune was even halfway down the bar, Liam pulled himself back up and tried again to get in between the fighters, only to be interfered with by the bridesmaids as two grabbed one set of his arms, tripping him up. Rune shoved Alf out of the way, who stood stunned with a look of horror as if he was watching a church being defaced.

"Hey! Hey!!" Rune shouted as she plunged into the fight.

One of the bridesmaids egged the fighters on. Another grabbed a bottle of champagne and shook it up before spraying it all over the combatants as she screamed in Bacchic ecstasy.

"That's right, big boys! Fight over us!" she screamed as a third one gave a wild-woman, banshee scream and laughed. "I love a good bar fight!"

Rune barreled into one of the guys who was throwing wild punches, trying to channel "linebacker" as her smaller frame hit his larger one, intending to knock him off balance. Sadly, it only managed to shift him a bit. Even worse, it put her face in the pathway of the opponent that had just swung at him. She closed her eyes and braced for the pain as she saw the bottle coming. Instead, she heard a crash, and her eyes snapped open. An arm filled her vision, blocking the bottle. The bottle itself shattered against the arm, sending shards of glass and wine pelting around her. Most of it went into her hair, while she and the arm were drenched with what smelled like a pinot grigio.

At a grunt from behind her, Rune became aware of the body pressed against her back. Before she could turn, the man snaked his other arm — the one not protecting her face — around her middle to haul her out before she could do much more than protest. She landed upright a few feet away and stumbled as she was partly tossed. Rune managed to spin back around to catch sight of the stranger's back as he returned to the fight to help Liam. The stranger stepped elegantly through the fray, shifting amongst the chaos in such a way that it seemed like he existed in his own bubble of air that repelled everything around him. He avoided punches and kicks. Then he caught one arm and tossed the opponent over his shoulder, away from Liam's unprotected chest. A path cleared, and the stranger grabbed Liam by an upper arm and spun him out of the fight. Using the momentum from the maneuver, he turned and deflected a bigger, rounder bar patron away before he could land a blow on the back of Liam's head. Liam stumbled in her direction, and Rune caught him, steadying the kid back to his feet.

"Call the sheriff and stay clear!" she shouted at him.

The kid swallowed and nodded, heading to the far end of the bar where Alf was already on the phone.

"Right." Rune turned back to the fight, but fewer punches were thrown as the stranger dodged the sloppy, tired swings of the last two men still on their feet. The bridesmaids were suspiciously absent.

That was when Rune felt a familiar tingle on the side of her face. Call it magic or intuition, Rune turned to the left in the direction of Lucky Devil. All five of them were over at the bar mascot, lounging over him like a five-woman cabaret. They were taking pictures as if they hadn't started the raging violence over in the corner. To Rune's horror, the bride-to-be, wearing a too-short mini skirt that did not cover anything, had climbed up onto the bench to put her crotch right in poor Lucky Devil's smiling face.

"Hey! Stop that!" Rune shouted, appalled.

These five had met and exceeded her limit of tolerance, but the bridesmaids' laughter and hooting drowned her out.

Growling in frustration, Rune hurried over to them. "Get off of him now!" she continued to shout as she grabbed the bride by the waist, to haul her too-skinny behind down. Her legs kicked out as Rune pulled, like a five-year-old kid being yanked off the monkey bars.

"What the hell is your problem?" snarled the fat bridesmaid as Rune tried to put the fighting bride on the ground.

"She's bumping and grinding so hard the paint is going to come off!" Rune shouted back

"Get your hands off of her!" someone else shouted in her ear, as sharp-nailed fingers clawed painfully into her upper arm before she could let the bride go safely. Rune dropped her instead.

"You can't do that," Rune tried to say, meaning the bumping and grinding in Lucky Devil's face, but she found herself standing in the middle of the group of angry, drunk women. Before she registered what was happening, someone pulled her hair with a tight, scalp-wrenching grip.

"Do you know who we are, bitch?" the fat bridesmaid spit into Rune's face. Flashbacks of another time, when a well-dressed woman did something very similar, flashed through her mind. The fat bridesmaid, who was still skinnier than Rune by two dress sizes — though they probably shopped for bras in the same letter — twisted Rune's scalp a little harder as she said, "We work for the Kodiak Company."

Oh great.

As if she read Rune's mind, the maid of dishonor pointed at the bride. "Yeah, and she's marrying a guy in the Acquisition Department."

Oh, double damn in a handbasket.

"This is a Magic Guild affiliated place," Rune said, swallowing down the bile coming up her throat. She had to keep it together. "I am well within my rights to ask you not to hump the furniture. You have no more rights in here than any other corporate patron."

She might as well have been talking to Lucky Devil's wooden ears for all the comprehension she got from this group. The hand in her hair tightened even more painfully and she felt a couple of strands pull free. She whimpered a little. She couldn't keep it in. Her legs shook.

"Bindi, I wanted to have a good time," whined the bride-to-be, who was wavering on her stilt legs. That was all Rune needed, for the bride to throw up right in the middle of the confrontation and all over the wood floor.

"Let her go already," said the one with the replacement bridesmaid shirt on.

Out of the whole group, she looked pretty sober and still put together, dressed in a nice skirt that seemed to go with the t-shirt.

Suddenly, Rune's hair was released, and she was able to stand all the way up again. The women around her continued to stare daggers and Rune was still very much surrounded with no place to back down. She folded her arms to hide how badly they shook, begging herself to keep it together. To not show fear. To not be the weak and stupid girl from six years ago.

"I apologize if there has been some misunderstanding..." she started, but her voice trembled, which was just blood in the water to the maid of dishonor. Her eyes flashed with vicious excitement.

"Oh, you'll be more than sorry. I'm going to see to it you get fired. Tonight. I have never had such a horrible customer service experience in my life," she threatened triumphantly.

"I seriously doubt that," Rune said out loud in challenge. She didn't mean to, it just happened.

"That's it! What is your name? I want to talk to the owner!"

Rune cocked her head, and for one suicidal moment, she almost laughed. "I am the owner," she said. The maid of dishonor looked taken aback.

"I don't know what kind of establishment you think you're running here, but this is no way to run a business," the maid of dishonor finally sniffed, and the fat bridesmaid muttered a few derogatory terms at Rune's back.

Abruptly, a tray appeared amongst them, cutting its way through the circle around Rune. A half dozen champagne glasses winked in the low light, each filled with a bubbly tan liquid.

"I understand that someone is getting married!" said the stranger, his charm on at full blast as he offered up the tray to the gaggle of bimbos. They all melted at the sight of more booze and the handsomeness of the man in his suit and fedora. Rune glanced over at the bar and saw Alf giving her the stink eye. He shook the last drop from the last bottle of the really good champagne at Rune as if it was her fault he had to empty it. Liam was propped up on a barstool next to him, a bag of ice held over his eye. A pair of bartenders and the doorman blocked the exits, not letting anybody leave before the authorities arrived.

Sensing her opening, Rune extricated herself from the space and retreated to safety back behind the bar.

"What happened to Calvin and Jasper?" she asked, stepping up beside Liam.

"They left when the fight started," Alf answered her, chucking the bottle into a bin to crash sharply. "I called the sheriff's office. They said they'd be here in five minutes, and that was ten ago."

Rune grunted.

"What? Would you rather I call the Uptown Corp. Police?" he asked sarcastically.

"Because for-profit police would show up in the first place?" Rune asked, trying to be funny, but she didn't feel it. All she wanted to do was run away to her apartment on the third floor and hide in her bed 'til the shaking stopped. "Thanks for making the call."

"Sheriff will treat us fair. At least he won't arrest all the patrons just for coming into a Magic Guild establishment," Alf said.

"Why don't you incorporate so we qualify for protection?" Liam asked naively.

"We're not incorporating," Rune answered.

"We are not incorporating," Alf agreed as if he had any say in the decision.

"Well, the business seminar I went to yesterday said that: 'In this corporate world, the small business is almost always doomed to fail or be bought out,'" Liam piped up. "'To be independent, one often has to make a deal with the devil.' Etcetera, etcetera, etcetera."

Rune patted Liam on the knee. "Those classes are a complete waste of your time."

"No, you are a complete waste of time," Alf said pointedly at Rune. "And our time is running out."

As if to punctuate the point, bright swirly red and blue lights appeared in front of the bar. Several figures emerged, creating shadows in the light as they stepped out of their cars and started into the bar to sort out the mess of people. Rune ignored the deputies who moved about the room. They didn't even give her or Alf a nod as they passed. Rune straightened and moved the three steps toward the front to meet the man she dreaded seeing. He sauntered in through the front door with the smugness of a gunslinger taking the street at high noon.

"Oh crap, it's not the Sheriff," she muttered under her breath. Alf's mouth flattened into an unhappy line and he nodded.

Deputy Blakely was in his late forties and wore the tan long-sleeved deputy's uniform, despite the early summer warmth. He even wore a cowboy hat over his thinning sandy blond hair. He considered himself the Sheriff's number two, even though Rune was pretty sure that wasn't true.

Rune tried to smile. "Deputy Blakely, thank you for coming."

He looked down his nose at her, as he always did, his eyes scanning down to her chest before leisurely ascending back up to her face. It didn't feel lecherous, just contemptuous, like he couldn't be bothered to check out the rest of her. Inspection over, he turned to survey the rest of the room.

"Any magic used?" he asked.

"No. It's just a bar fight." Rune took a step back to widen his field of vision and take in the room herself, neatly avoiding his probing gaze in the process. "A couple of injuries, I think, but my detector crystals didn't go off, so no magic." Rune pointed up at the round balls along the wall, each on their own pedestal every five feet in between the lighting sconces. "If they had gone off in the presence of magic, they'd all be glowing pinkish-purple."

Deputy Blakely gave her crystals a look over, again with judgmental silence. A younger officer, dressed in a blue shirt, her hair in multiple braids and bundled into a bun at the back of her head, came up beside him carrying the card reader. Rune shivered at it on sight.

"Your OmniSin, Ms.?" the female officer asked Rune formally, but politely, holding out her hand to receive it.

"One second." Rune went to the bar where Alf already held out her wallet in anticipation of this check. Alf and Rune had their differences, but in the face of outsiders, he was as much her right-hand man as he had been Maddie's.

Rune opened up the wallet and handed the officer her OmniSin card. The officer took it and slid it through the reader while Rune held her breath. Every time she had to do this, Rune waited for the reader to light up red and start beeping like crazy. After a few endless seconds, it beeped green and she let her breath go. The officer handed the card back and moved on to the next person.

"Still claiming non-magic status," Deputy Blakely said as Rune tucked her ID away.

"That's because I'm just a hominal like you, Deputy. Not a drop of magic in me." The lie rolled smoothly off her tongue after six years of practice.

"Uh-huh, sure," he said, making his personal opinion very clear. "The heir of that witch has no magic."

Rune worked her jaw. While witch wasn't inherently derogatory, the use of it when referring to a female wizard was uncouth.

An officer approached, distracting him.

"Sir, should we have the Talent come in to do a sweep?" he asked, ignoring Rune completely.

"No, are you stupid or something? This place is a Magic Guild bar. The whole place will light up. What good is an Aura Reader going to be in here? Oh crap, did you call her in? This is where all of our department money goes, on bull like this," he grumbled. He moved on, supervising as more OmniSins were checked and a couple people were arrested.

"Why won't he just believe that I don't have any magic?" Rune asked Alf, folding her arms again.

"He brought an Aura Reader in here the week after Maddie died, covert-like, as if I wouldn't notice. Had the poor Talent walking all over the place before she threw up from the over-stimulus of magic in the place. Didn't get a ping off of you. Too bad." Alf sniffed at Rune as he passed her to continue supervising the cleanup. "Just stay away now. I'll take care of this. You never ask enough questions anyway."

Rune felt some sympathy for the Aura Readers, even though they were technically a threat to her. Talents as a rule only controlled one kind of magic, be it fire, object be-spelling, or one of the numerous other kinds. A few, like Aunt Maddie, seemed to be able to control several, but such Talents were rare. The extensive list of possible magics was far from clear cut. Whether one called oneself a wizard, sorcerer, witch, etc. was a personal choice, but it was irrelevant to the government. To them, all magic users were Talents. Aura Readers had the power to discern what kind of magic other Talents possessed by reading their auras. Coming into the Lucky Devil with its many be-spelled objects would be like walking into an oven and trying to find another person's heat signature. Rune was glad for the Lucky Devil's protection from such magical intrusion.

More patrons had been checked by the officers. Once cleared, many of them left. Rune sighed at the lost revenue walking out the door, but there was nothing she could do but watch them go.

That's when the damn card reader buzzed harshly. Every head in the room swung to the source as poor Liam's pale face went ashen. He stood next to the stool he had been sitting on, wringing his hands as the device flashed orange, the sign of a convict.

"Hiring convicts now?" Deputy Blakely called across the room to Rune, before he approached Liam and the officer, who looked up for instructions.

"Hey, what are you doing? He's done nothing wrong," Rune said, surging forward just as the deputy nodded to the officer to take out his handcuffs.

"Standard procedure," Deputy Blakely intoned like a mantra, bored and too well-practiced.

"You're arresting him without cause!" Rune said. "You have no right to…"

"We have every right, and you know it," the deputy threw back in her face, a little righteous anger rising in his voice. "He was in an altercation and he's a convicted felon so we get to take him in for questioning."

"Liam is a good kid. He's just graduated college. He's clean," Rune said, ticking off each finger forcefully as she listed his good qualities.

"He's a delinquent teenager," Deputy Blakely retorted tiredly.

"Who got his life straightened out! He just rebelled like hell and made some mistakes. That's not a crime!"

"You're right. Committing crimes is a crime." Blakely nodded to the officer to take Liam away.

"Which he shouldn't have to pay for, for the rest of his life, especially if he didn't do anything wrong this time!" Rune tried to continue, but she was losing momentum, her voice tapering off to barely a squeak. She thought for a moment about standing in their way, to keep them from walking out with Liam, but her insides shook too much, not only from the fight but from the fear of getting caught. And she hated herself for it.

"It's alright, Ms. Leveau," the kid said bravely. "I'm really sorry about this."

"Don't say that, Liam." Rune tried to give him a comforting smile, but the snap of the double set of handcuffs as they went onto his wrists undercut it.

"Oh, I am supposed to open in the morning..." Liam said, his expression concerned.

"Don't worry about that," Rune said, waving it away. "Call me when you get out." She felt sick. "Man, our society is messed up," she muttered under her breath as Deputy Blakely moved off as the officer and Liam went out the door.

"You have no idea," the stranger said.

He came up beside Rune, sticking his hands into his tailored pants pockets. Despite being in a fight, he only looked a little rumpled, which just seemed to make him more charming. The hat was cocked back, showing off a tuft of his dark hair above his forehead and there was a suspicious-looking lipstick kiss on his cheek.

"Please don't move around, until the scanning is done," the officer said to him and held out her hand to receive his OmniSin.

The stranger flashed her a super-charming smile and gave her a wink. Then, with a magician's flourish, he presented his right hand and made a fist, before popping it open. Instantly, the palm of his hand flashed blue, filling with light. Hovering over the surface was a square that looked like a small screen. Raising his left hand, his fingertips glowed the same blue as he manipulated the screen.

The whole room stopped, and everyone turned around to stare with wide eyes at the stranger. To Rune, who was as shocked as everyone else, it was much like the reaction Maddie used to get when she performed magic in front of peoples who hadn't had much exposure to it. A small squeaking gasp escaped the officer he had been winking at and even Deputy Blakely pushed back his hat in a show of amazed disbelief.

"Magic?" the deputy asked, unsure as his thumb scratched at his hairline before resettling the hat.

The stranger laughed as he continued to scroll, truly enjoying everyone's reaction. "No, sir, just the latest augmentation." When he found what he was looking for, he passed it under the officer's scanner and the reader flashed blue. The officer jumped at the sight.

"Oh, I'm so sorry, sir," she said, suddenly very timid as she subconsciously backed away.

Rune had to swallow a gasp. Blue.

"You're a corporate elite?" Rune asked, her eyebrows shooting up further into her hairline. Corporate employees and their families came into her bar all the time, but a corporate elite? In another time, it would be like having a nobleman patronize your bar. It explained his expensive augmentations. They were the newest thing only talked about in tech magazines. Like VCRs, then CD players, then HD before they hit the mass market; they were only limitedly available to those in certain circles of the wealthy and influential. To the magic community, it was just one more inevitable nail in the magical economy's coffin.

"I work for Corinthe Inc, yes. At the moment, at least," he said as if it was nothing, but the whole atmosphere in the room changed.

"Sir, I'm sorry for the inconvenience." Deputy Blakely's manner flipping to become solicitous.

"Not at all, Deputy. You're doing your job." The stranger closed his fist again, making the screen of light disappear. Then, as nonchalant as humanly possible, he tucked his augmented hands into his pant pockets, looking unbelievably cool as he did it. His coat puckered a little with the movement, flashing a glimpse of the inside at Rune. He was wearing suspenders.

Abruptly, the device in the officer's hand buzzed, and the screen blazed orange, pulling Rune's attention from the stranger. After another moment, the device blipped and flashed blue, then shorted out. The officer pushed buttons with increasing panic, trying to revive it, and finished by smacking the thing outright on its side. It remained dead.

"What's wrong?" Deputy Blakely growled, his eyes narrowing at the officer.

"I'm sorry, sir. It seems to have shorted." She continued trying to coax the machine back to life.

"Oh, technology. So fragile," the stranger said, with a smug smile.

"Too bad so many choose it over magic when it lets you down all the time," Rune said, emboldened by this corporate elite who seemed to have taken her side for the moment.

Deputy Blakely shot Rune a harsh glance, which made her want to shrivel up again.

"Technology does have its failings," the stranger piped up, casually as if he was a jazz band personified. "I wonder if the data on that thing will be recoverable. Would hate for any criminal types to get away unpunished. Are we going to have to wait for your department to fetch a new one?"

"No, we'll do it the old-fashioned way," Deputy Blakely said, addressing his officer. "Have everyone take down OmniSin numbers and we'll have to run them back at headquarters. You are free to go anytime, Mr. ... "

"St. Benedict." With the calm, pleasant smile of a pastor on Sunday talking to a sinner, the stranger held out his hand for the deputy to shake.

Deputy Blakely touched the hand briefly.

"If you'll excuse me, Mr. ... St. ..." He grimaced and then nodded sharply instead. When the two protectors of the law moved off and out of hearing range, Rune took a deep breath and blew it out in a gust, as if it was the first one she had taken in a long time.

"Very professional fellow," St. Benedict said, as Deputy Blakely talked to the three officers interviewing the bridal party. "Isn't a bar fight a corporate police matter? Who is your principal company?"

"None. We're an 'at will' establishment," Rune said.

It was St. Benedict's turn to shoot up his eyebrows. "At will? You're a completely independent business? No corporate sponsorship or anything? How do you even have a citizen card then?"

"We're affiliated with the Magic Guild," Rune answered. "Though that's not really any of your business."

"Ha, I suppose not." He watched a couple of officers walk one of the patrons out in handcuffs. "The Magic Guild doesn't have its own police force?"

"The corporate police around this neighborhood are run by the Kodiak Company, and they are mostly trouble for us in the magical community. We tend to trust the sheriff's department a little more since, you know, they still have to have elections," Rune finished.

"*That* was less trouble?" he asked, jutting his thumb toward Deputy Blakely.

Rune held up her finger and thumb with the barest of space between them. "I did say a little bit. He, in particular, hates my guts with a finely honed passion, so, of course, he's the one to intercept the call. That is most likely the only reason he hauled off one of my bartenders."

"You hire convicts?" St. Benedict asked.

"We hire good people," Rune answered defensively. In truth, Maddie was the one who had hired Liam, but Rune approved.

"If they were good people, they wouldn't be criminals," he continued, crossing his arms.

"You don't know what the hell you're talking about," Rune shot back. This guy was really starting to piss her off.

"I know exactly what I'm talking about," he said to her cryptically. Rune shifted back another step and moved to escape. This conversation was closing in on uncomfortable territory, but then St. Benedict added, "Your kid is going to be fine."

Blinking, Rune tried to understand what he was saying. "My kid?"

"The bartender they hauled off. He'll be out in a couple of hours," St. Benedict answered, giving Rune a sly, delighted smile, then wiggled his fingers at her as if that explained everything.

"I wish I could believe it. At least with the sheriff, I can... I don't think they'll torture him."

"Torture him?" St. Benedict scoffed. "That's a little extreme, don't you think?"

"We live in a time where people have been killed in corporate custody for crossing the white line while driving. Privatizing police was the worst thing this country could have done. At least the sheriff is still mostly independent. Or he's supposed to be." Rune folded her arms in front of herself.

St. Benedict asked, quirking an eyebrow. "You speaking from experience?"

She eyed him, then glanced down when she found meeting his eyes too hard. "I had a close friend get caught for embezzling from the corps. Never saw him again," she admitted, the truth lightly dusted with lies.

St. Benedict sucked in a sharp breath between his teeth and nodded twice. "When the corps is the government, stealing from them is tantamount to treason in some philosophies."

Rune forced a weak smile and left it there. "Thank you, by the way, for all of your help with the bridal party from hell over there. I'm terrible at handling things like that. I should really just leave it all to Alf."

"It's not easy to be the one in charge," St. Benedict sympathized.

"You're being gracious," Rune said. "I completely suck at this, and I know it."

"Bridesmaids are easy. Bar fights, on the other hand..." he shrugged.

"You have a real knight-in-shining-armor complex, huh?" Rune asked, flirting just a little.

"I hate seeing a damsel in distress, especially when she's the one putting herself there," he responded.

"Geez, where were you ten years ago?" she answered, blushing again.

"And now?" he asked, shifting his body to face her again, making them uncomfortably close.

"Hey, Leveau!" Deputy Blakely shouted at Rune before she could answer.

"Excuse me, one moment," Rune said and escaped the spine-tingling, dangerous situation before she did something stupid like ask for his number. Corporate Elite were *persona non grata* to someone in her position, even if she couldn't explain it in a million years. It was best to leave that alone.

It took another two hours to sort out the remaining patrons and the sheriff department's paperwork. By then, Alf had all the glass cleared up and had tacked some cardboard over the new hole between the Lounge Bar and the Main Bar. Rune spent that time with the bridesmaids, getting them out of her bar after much back and forth about whether she was going to press charges and whether they were going to sue her or not. Deputy Blakely did his duty well, and stood between Rune and the brunt of it, citing law and consequences as a shield that derailed most of what the women were claiming, especially when he confirmed that he would be reviewing the images from the recording crystals. They got real quiet after that, considering such magical devices were absolutely admissible in a court of law.

Rune hated that she had to release those same crystals to the Sheriff's department for review, though. Crystals were expensive to replace and she never got an answer about when exactly she was going to get them back. Deputy Blakely just grunted at her before he left and that was fine by Rune. She was sick of his face too.

Finally, the room was empty of people. Rune felt tired to her bones. All she wanted, at that moment, was to down a drink, find her shower, and go to bed for a month. Alf was the last man standing, and he was already into his second drink, staring off across the bar with an air of solitude that she didn't dare disturb. To her relief, St. Benedict had disappeared.

"I'm going to my office," she said to Alf, but he didn't even blink in acknowledgment. She decided that was good enough. She headed to the far corner of the Lounge Bar, turning into the long hall that led to the bathrooms. At the far end stood a door with a pebbled-glass window, the Lucky Devil logo stenciled in black on the glass.

Rune beelined to the door, tears trickling from her eyes to trail down her face. She just needed to keep it together for a few more steps. Clearly, the adrenaline rush had been the only thing keeping both her emotions and the bad memories at bay. Now that it was over, everything threatened to come out with a crash.

"Keep it together, keep it together," she repeated to herself as she reached out for the old-world doorknob and turned as hard as she could. It didn't open. Cursing to herself, she remembered that she had left the key by the register. Her Finding ability confirmed that it was there. It might as well have been on the other side of the planet for all the good it would do her now.

Taking a shuddering breath, Rune tried to say the magic keyword to open the door instead, but her pronunciation kept lilting, and the door remained stubbornly closed.

"Maddie," Rune squeaked as she swallowed around the lump in her throat and leaned against the textured glass. "What am I going to do?"

Just then, the tingling sensation of an incoming wish danced across her skin. A weight appeared inside her pocket instead of just the usual slip of paper. Furrowing her eyebrows, Rune dug into the pocket and pulled out a jade coin. Unlike the other souvenir coins, this one wasn't stamped but carved. There were only thirteen of them in existence. It shocked Rune to see it because these were only used for very special wishes, ones that often involved the need for the magic of the talented wizardess who had them carved. The same wizardess who was now dead. Quickly, Rune pulled out the slip of paper and unfolded it. Her heart stopped cold as she read the words written in the neat cursive of the elites.

I wish to find Anna Masterson.

Rune read over the words several times before it occurred to her that she should run. By the time that thought sunk in and she turned to act on it, the hall was already blocked by the silhouette of a man. Rune blinked, then recognized him as the stranger, St. Benedict. His smile hadn't changed, but now the flash of teeth and sparkling eyes looked predatory. Her gaze narrowed in suspicion at the hand he had tucked in his pocket.

"Ah, I found you."

CHAPTER 3

Rune stood frozen outside her office door, a rabbit trembling in a trap. With no way to get through the door at her back, and the chances of bull-rushing past St. Benedict very slim, she felt almost giddy. The years of hiding were over. Someone had finally found her. Even though she was terrified, there was also an insane feeling of relief.

"Did you write this?" she asked, holding out the slip of paper toward him with trembling fingers.

His head cocked to the side again. "I saw that the paper disappeared from his pocket, but I couldn't quite work out where it went. Is that a spell or something?" he asked.

"Yes," Rune responded too quickly.

"So, then, you are the magic-user I'm looking for." He stepped closer, closing the distance between them. Rune eyed the hand he still had in his pocket, trying to guess whether he had a gun or a knife, as if that made any sort of difference at this range. Was he here to kill her? Was he here to take her back?

"What... what do you want with me?" She pressed herself harder against the door.

"I just want my wish fulfilled. I wish to find Anna Masterson," he said, moving closer.

"W-why?" Rune stuttered, shivering with fear.

"I'm not the only one looking for her, and I need to find her first. I was told 'The Lucky Devil' was the place to find help. Has anyone else approached you about this issue?"

Rune blinked. "You... you wish to *find* Anna Masterson?"

"Yes. I understand that if someone needs to be found, this is the place to find that sort of help." He stopped a few feet in front of her. "It took me a great deal of trouble to get ahold of that coin and the instructions on its use. I was led to believe that in exchange for the coin, I would be able to talk to someone who specializes in granting difficult-to-fulfill wishes."

Rune blinked again, trying to force her sluggish brain to work. "You mean, you're here to get me to find Anna Masterson?" She couldn't believe her ears.

He paused, visibly perplexed by her response. "Is that a strange request?"

"Ha. No. No, it isn't. Well, maybe a little," Rune rambled nonsensically.

She was so relieved that she thought she was going to throw up. He wasn't here for her. At least, he didn't know how close he was to finding what he was looking for. The woman once called Anna Masterson started to think quickly again. He said others were looking for her. What did they want? Should she just run now? No.

She had to keep him talking. She needed to know who. And *why*.

"Do you want to come into my office or something, where we can discuss this?" she asked clumsily.

"That would be perfect, yes," he agreed. Still, he had that hand in his pocket. He was hiding something. How much of a bad guy was he? Maybe she should just run now and ask questions later. Why was he looking for her?

"Uh, yes. Yes, well, this is it. But I forgot my keys. One second." She tried to move around him to head back to the bar room, or maybe to run out the door instead. Before she could pass, St. Benedict moved suddenly, blocking her escape. His hand slammed palm-down against the glass surface of the door to one side of Rune's head, causing the door to shudder. She yelped, surprised when it didn't break.

"No, please..." she whimpered.

"Sorry," he said, so close that his breath washed over her face. "I'm... I'm about to pass out here." His head fell forward, leaning against her shoulder. His breathing was labored and warm through the material of her shirt.

"Oh, god! Are you alright?" Rune looked frantically between his hand and his head, uncomfortably close to hers, before doing a double-take back to his hand. Across the glass ran streaks of blood, leaving greasy smears on the pebbled surface and making the palm slide closer to her head.

"Oh god, what happened?" Rune asked.

"Need... to sit down..." He staggered forward. Rune caught him in time, using the door to brace herself under his heavy weight. "I'm sorry," he mumbled. His head lolled as he fought for consciousness. "Blood pressure… loss… body is just reacting… Just gotta sit down."

"But I don't have the key," she said. St. Benedict stopped responding intelligently. "Oh, dammit." Rune took a deep breath and focused on trying to remember the exact pronunciation of the keyword to open Maddie's office door. "*Aprax… Abraxius… Abraxas*. Yes, *Abraxas*…the Latin word for door is…?" Rune gripped the door handle, pressing her thumb on the crystal shard in the middle and called out, "*Abraxas aperio*." With a gratifying click, the doorknob turned and the door swung inward. The desk lamp came on automatically.

She staggered a bit without the door to brace her but managed to lead St. Benedict into the office. His feet moved him forward, but it was like trying to walk a drunk man. She maneuvered him into one of the bucket chairs in front of the desk. Sitting down, he seemed to regain the ability to hold himself up and Rune felt she could leave him for a moment. She went back to shut the door of the office. For a second, she hesitated at the threshold, looking down the long, empty hall.

"I'm really sorry about this… I apologize. Not exactly making the best impression here. But I really do need your help," St. Benedict muttered behind her.

Rune shut the office door behind her.

"*Abraxas*…I don't know. *Abraxas*… lock," Rune ordered, and that idea became a reality. The noise from the bar stopped completely, the clink of glasses, the distant chatter, and even the hum of the air conditioner that you didn't notice until it was gone. Rune looked back at the door in surprise. "Huh. Well, if it was that simple, why did I have to learn all that Latin?" she complained, giving the door a dirty look. She wasn't the only one who noticed the change in the door. Almost immediately, St. Benedict's head snapped up, his eyes locking with Rune's.

"What did you do?" he demanded, his eyes darting to the door.

"Locked the door. Now you're my prisoner," she quipped, lamely, trying not to think about how she threw away her chance to run. Locking the door made her feel a whole lot safer, but that was crazy considering the immediate danger was in the room with her. "We're not at the bar anymore."

"You cast a spell?" he asked, though it sounded more like an accusation.

"Yes, it's a spell."

The clever green-blue eyes calculated. "Yet, you claim you're just a normal human… a hominal. How are you tricking the ID readers, or the Aura Reading Talents for that matter?"

"Maddie set up the spell in the door. I just invoked it. Most anyone can do that," Rune said defensively. It was kind of true.

"But you have magic Talent?" he pushed.

"I'll get the first aid kit. You're bleeding all over the carpet." Rune dodged the question and went to the small bathroom connected to the office, flipping on the light as she entered. She ran a couple cloths under water, then fished out the first aid kit—an old tackle box full of supplies—from the cabinet beneath the sink. Just as she was about to turn back to the office, she caught her reflection in the mirror. Her hair hung in damp waves around her face from the pinot grigio, and across her right cheek was a small cut, with a stream of drying blood marking a line down her cheek.

"Why didn't anybody tell me?" she muttered and picked up one of the dampened cloths to swipe away the blood. The cut was small and barely noticeable afterward. She would deal with it later.

When she came back into the room, she found St. Benedict standing by the window looking through the wood-slatted blinds, which leaked street light into the room.

"You should sit down. I don't think I can catch you twice," she said, and he let the blind clack back into place.

"Where are we?"

"My office," Rune said, dodging the question he was really asking.

"We came into a room on the ground floor, and now we are three stories off the ground. Also, this room should face a back alley and the view is of a main thoroughfare," St. Benedict recounted. "I'll ask you again, *where* are we?"

She nearly backpedaled at the cold, hard expression that still smiled on his face.

"Most people don't notice that," she said lightly as if it was no big deal, and when her attempt to smile back didn't warm it, she sighed. She pointed toward the door. "It's a transfer door. It links two places that are not in the same space to one another. Just like Lucky Devil's pocket links to my pocket. It's just simple magic. Nothing to worry about." St. Benedict's only response was a blank stare. "That's how I got the coin. It went to my pocket using the same method." He continued to stare. Rune shifted from foot to foot. "Could you go back to smiling? It was way less intimidating. You came looking for my help right?"

He wavered again, grabbing the back of the desk chair to steady himself. "Sorry. You're right. I did come looking for magical help. I shouldn't make a scene when I encounter some. I'm not trying to be threatening, I'm uncomfortable not understanding what is happening around me, and it's just taking all my focus to stay upright."

"You need to sit down," Rune repeated. She set down the first-aid kit and rushed to keep him from falling. "Did this happen during the bar fight?"

He collapsed into the desk chair, which rocked dangerously back before balancing forward so that his feet stabilized him on the floor. Somehow in the move, he caught her wrist, using it also to steady himself. Rune waited patiently as he finished leaning over, she assumed to do that breathing-between-your-legs-thing that was supposed to help when a person felt faint. He set his left hand against the desk and she realized too late that he had grabbed her with his bloody right hand. Goosebumps skittered up her skin, but she didn't dare try to pull away. She told herself to suck it up; he was hurt and needed help. He didn't look at her, just hung his head and breathed slowly.

"Maybe I should call emergency services. This doesn't look good at all, and I'm not really trained in this kind of first-aid," Rune started to say, but when she tried to step back to reach for the landline phone, her patient held on with surprising strength.

"First, you are going to tell me where I am," he panted.

"You're just in my office," Rune tried to reassure him, but St. Benedict's grip tightened around her wrist, and she realized that now he was trying to intimidate her. "Ow, that hurts!"

"Where are we?" he asked in a slow, careful voice, his eyes flashing dark again with a deadly warning.

"We're in the former owner's old office, which is in Bucktown. The bar is in the neighborhood of Uptown. They are connected by a door between them. Now let me go," Rune answered too quickly, her voice rising with mounting distress.

"Connected by magic," St. Benedict muttered and released her. Rune backed away, watching as St. Benedict rubbed at his face.

"My apologies again. All this magic has me on edge."

Rune kept her distance.

"Why did you come looking for magical help if you're afraid of magic?"

St. Benedict chuckled to himself. "When you start to run out of options, even the devil's offer looks enticing. If you want to call the authorities again, feel free, but I'm not here to threaten you." The half-smile slipped back onto his face. "So? Do you think you can help me?"

"No. The person you want is Maddie. She was the wizard, and I'm sorry to tell you that she died a month ago." Rune seamlessly mixed a lie with the truth. St. Benedict sat quietly as he took that in, thinking a moment.

"Then may I patch myself up before I leave? I don't need a doctor. I just reopened this, so I can take care of it," he informed her.

"That's...not unreasonable, I guess," Rune agreed.

Inside she let go a sigh of relief. After so many years hiding in plain sight, the last thing she wanted was to be discovered now, and whoever this St. Benedict person was, he didn't seem to suspect her. But how could she ask questions about why he was looking for her when she had just said she couldn't help him? She couldn't afford to raise his suspicions.

St. Benedict started to remove his jacket and grimaced as he pulled the fabric away from his shoulders, revealing the suspenders Rune had glimpsed earlier. There wasn't much blood until he started to peel back the sleeve on his right arm.

"Ahh," he moaned. The material was soaked dark red, a stark contrast against the whiteness of his button-up shirt. "Do you mind turning the light this way for me?" he asked courteously.

The only light, other than the light streaming from the bathroom, was from the desk lamp, which always turned on automatically when someone entered the room.

"Is that magic too?" St. Benedict asked, as he started to unbutton his shirt. She moved the lampshade so that it cast more light on him. "It turned on when we entered."

"It used to run on magic, but after Maddie died, the spell fell apart. I haven't been able to find anyone to recast it," Rune explained, then rolled her eyes a bit. "Well, I couldn't find anybody that's within my price range. So, I got one of those plug things from the hardware store. You know, the ones that turn the light on when it senses motion in the room? Then I just ate instant ramen for a week."

Rune looked about the small room. The office had changed very little since Maddie's passing. Her desk was the most prominent feature of the room, sitting before a double set of windows that looked down from a third-story view. The rest of the room was arranged in typical office fashion; two chairs of wood and dark-green vinyl sat at an angle to each other in front of the desk. A Tiffany lamp of red and white roses framed by green glass sat on the corner of the desk next to a framed picture of Maddie with her arm wrapped around a smiling Rune.

St. Benedict groaned again, drawing Rune's attention back to him as he continued to struggle with getting his shirt off.

"So, not everything is magic then?" he asked through his grunts of pain.

"No, never is. Though, we do still run quite a few things off of Maddie's spells. The whole place was run by magic when Maddie was alive, but now I have to switch things out for the hominal solutions as the spells fade. Thankfully technology has caught up to magic in the last couple hundred years," Rune said as she watched St. Benedict struggle. "Look, I can't take this anymore. Let me help you." She moved back to his side. His sleeve wasn't clearing his elbow on his good arm. Each attempt to free it provoked a groan and then St. Benedict weaved drunkenly in the chair, making it even more difficult to take off the shirt.

"Hold on!" Rune reached down to his waistband to unsnap one of his suspenders which was tangled in the shirt.

"Hey!" St. Benedict protested.

"What? You want to leave the suspenders on, but not the shirt? Because I'm good either way," Rune quipped to cover up the tingles she got from doing, or rather undoing, such a thing. Undressing him was for the greater good after all. She went deprived, however, as he unsnapped the other suspender himself, freeing his shirt completely.

After a little wrangling, he let Rune guide his good arm out of its sleeve. Together they peeled off the sweat- and blood-soaked shirt. He sat there in his undershirt, revealing a long gash along the back of his forearm.

Rune's eyes popped out of her head at the sight of so much blood. "How did a broken bottle do that without shredding your jacket sleeve?"

"It didn't. It reopened an existing wound. The problem is, I didn't get *that* taken care of properly either. Now I'm paying the price for it," St. Benedict answered between gritted teeth. "Do you pass out at the sight of blood?" he asked belatedly.

"I guess not," Rune said, still staring. "We can't do this here; you need stitches."

"It's fine. I've just lost some blood too quickly and it's making me faint. It happens when I give blood too," he said as he opened up the first-aid kit.

"Do you need a cookie?" Rune asked.

He chuckled tiredly. "You keep making me laugh. That's surprising." He fished out one of the sealed, sanitized gauze packets.

"That's good because you're scaring me," Rune said, taking the packet from him to open. "So, what did happen to get you that?"

"You don't know much about the corporate world, do you?" he asked.

"No, should I?" Rune asked as she laid the square of clean cotton against the cut, trying to decide if she should hold it that way or dab at it.

"No, it just explains why you didn't react to my name at all." He winced and held her hand down to stop her from dabbing.

"What about your name?" she asked.

"The saint, it's a designation for my job."

"Oh, like D R for doctor or something?"

"Don't worry about it. It's not common knowledge outside of the upper levels of management. Do you have some surgical thread and a needle?" he asked, peering into the tackle box.

Rune visibly paled. "I can't sew stitches—"

"Don't worry. I can do it if you thread the needle for me," he assured her.

She blinked at him. "That sounds insane."

"Or I can thread it myself."

"To sew up your own arm?" Rune couldn't believe what she was hearing. Then she remembered something.

"Wait. Wait!" Rune started digging through the tackle box. "I think I've got something here." She pulled out a small clasp-closed box. The inside was velvet-lined and held three soft green crystals.

"What are those?" St. Benedict asked, recoiling from the box.

"They're just healing crystals. I'm going to activate this, and it should seal that right up." She selected the smallest one and held it in her palm. She took a deep breath and tried to clear her mind, which wasn't easy, even without the attractive half-undressed man bleeding a foot away. She focused on pushing her energy into the crystal.

"What are you doing?" he asked after nothing happened for a few minutes. Rune blew out a breath of exasperation. The moment she did that, the crystal flared to life, a spark of green crackling inside its faceted depths. Both of them jumped in surprise.

"How are you doing that?" St. Benedict asked, this time with a hint of awe in his voice.

"You don't know how crystals work?"

"All I know is you have to have a Talent to invoke them," he said.

Rune didn't move a muscle as she stared down at the crystal. After six years, how could she make a mistake like that? When she used her Talent on behalf of clients, she was always able to cover it up. Maddie was the proper wizardess, so most people assumed she had been the one to cast the spells. Rune was just the assistant.

"With a lot of training, anyone can do this. It's not my magic, it's Maddie's," Rune said, repeating her answer from before. It was partially true. The spell crystal was created by Maddie, but anyone with a source of magical energy could activate the spell inside.

Clearing her throat, Rune focused on the task in front of her. She moved the reddened cloth to make way for the magic. At last, she coaxed the healing spell stored in the crystal to flood over the bleeding gash on St. Benedict's arm. The green light spilled out like water and slid across his skin to sink into the wound before disappearing.

"It works systemically so you might feel—" Rune started to say, but then St. Benedict flinched back before she could finish, shaking his head and pinching his nose.

"Ugh... feels like an ice-cream headache." He held the bridge of his nose for another few seconds until it passed.

Rune looked down at the crystal in her palm, now completely clear, its spell spent. The crystal itself still had value so she pocketed it for cleaning later. With Maddie gone, she had no idea how she was going to use it, but who knew, maybe she'd come into some money and be able to afford to have it recast with a healing spell.

Maddie's spell worked fast. St. Benedict stared down at his arm in what Rune assumed was wonder. "It doesn't hurt."

"Amazing, huh? I was surprised by it too when I first came to live with Maddie." Rune put away the two remaining crystals.

"I have had little trust or need for magic in my life," St. Benedict affirmed, taking one of the damp cloths and wiping away the blood on his arm. As the blood swiped off, a line of red appeared beneath where the original wound had been.

"Good, it's stopped bleeding. That'll continue to heal over the next hour. You're going to be really hungry and sleep like the dead to compensate for the increased metabolism. Your body will also work overtime to replace the blood you lost, so, like I said, make sure you eat a lot." Rune glanced over the newly healed skin on his arm as she repacked the rest of the first aid kit. "See magic's not so bad."

"Huh," he grunted with a hint of incredulity, "magic cheats, but right now, I need a cheat. I have done everything in my world to try to find her. You are... or were my last hope."

"Why would you want to find her? Is she a criminal or something?" Rune asked, hoping that wasn't too leading of a question.

"Have you ever heard of a man named Justin Masterson?" he asked. Rune didn't respond, but he didn't seem to need one. "Don't concern yourself if you haven't. Almost nobody remembers him, let alone knew him. He was famous only in a few specific circles and most of those circles don't exist anymore. But how much do you know about computer technology?"

"It's the newest big thing and everyone wants one. Computers try to imitate magic, but it's mostly about an exchange of information right?" Rune replied, remembering things Justin told her a lifetime ago.

"Exactly. The world is entering the informational age. It is trying to imitate the effects of magic, like your motion sensor light over there, but unlike your crystals, anyone can use it with little to no training. All computer technology is information-based. We're becoming an information-based world and these data-crunching machines, what if they could read the language of magic?"

Rune blinked at the idea. "But that's not how magic works. It's not just about saying the words to a spell that gives it power, it needs magic force to fuel and shape it."

"But without the magic-user to shape it, to give it the idea of what the magic is to do or become, it's just energy right?" St. Benedict asked, getting excited by the idea.

"I suppose so," Rune conceded.

"Energy can be harnessed. An idea can be translated into numerical code. We are already proving that with the internet. Ideas are flowing faster than ever before between peoples that would never even meet, let alone talk."

"But magic can't be cast by computer. It's impossible," Rune countered.

"We think that now, but ten years ago it was thought that these super machines themselves were impossible. Now, if computers could read and translate spells and then cast them, a whole new world would open up, bridging the gap between magic and unmagicked people in a way we can only imagine. It would put humans on par with the magic races. Then we wouldn't be so dependent on magic for day-to-day living. These machines could do all that work."

"Aren't they doing that now?" Rune asked, arching an eyebrow.

"Debatable, but the problem with people with Talents is that the chance of a particular Talent manifesting is hard to predict, and many people can become underserved if there aren't enough, say, Talented healers."

"Yes, and full-blown magicians and wizards and the like are even rarer. I think I would know this better than you," Rune said, a bit annoyed.

"But irrelevant to my story," St. Benedict countered. "About six years ago, we succeeded, at least theoretically. Justin Masterson, a genius computer programmer, is rumored to be the only person who found a way to translate a magic spell into a computer and for the computer to cast the spell back successfully. His success has never been duplicated and shortly after that, he was arrested on suspicion of embezzlement and a few other corporate crimes, along with his wife Anna. The Kodiak... the corporation that arrested him, lost him, according to their official records. For the last six years, various 'powers that be' have been trying to find him. All have failed."

"So, why are you looking for him now?" she couldn't help but ask.

"Because whoever finds the Masterson files first stands to not only become the wealthiest person in the world, but will be able to..." his smile sharpened. "Well, I think I can find him first, through his wife."

The sick feeling in the pit of Rune's stomach returned. "What about his wife?"

"She disappeared about the same time, but her records show that she was given into a protection program. Now, that turned out to be a lie, but there is no evidence that she was disposed of either. This means she is still out there and free somewhere, which means she may know how to find her husband and all the secrets he has in his head. She may have a few of those secrets herself. Most of the computer technology we all use today is based off of his notes, but the complete secret to cracking the magic/technology barrier was only in his head."

It was strange for Rune to hear all of this from an outside perspective, stated simply as the facts of an event that happened to someone else. Someone who had lived a different life far removed from her own.

"I wish I could help you, Mr. — St. Benedict, but I can't help you find this Anna Masterson."

St. Benedict blinked and shifted a little. "Who I really need is Justin."

"Nor Justin Masterson," she said firmly. Of course, it was about Justin. It had never been about her ever.

St. Benedict eyed her solemnly, and under his gaze, it took everything inside her not to shift nervously like a teenager in the principal's office. *Don't look guilty, don't look guilty, don't look guilty,* she thought to herself. *He doesn't know.*

"You say you can't help me, but you have a first aid kit that any battlefield medic would kill for. My jade coin was supposed to lead me to a powerful magic user, and it led me to you," he said.

"Look, I am sorry about the coin, and if you want I can reimburse you for it—"

"Really? From the way it sounded down there... or over there... in the bar, things have been pretty tight for you money wise since your master passed away," he said smugly as if he knew he had played a trump card.

"We are going through a transition period," Rune said tightly.

"Which is why you should work with me. Do you think that bar fight was something that just happened tonight?"

"You started it?"

"No, but the person I got my information from is the type to think, 'why make one buck when I can make two?' More than likely, I'm not even the first he sold the information to."

"What information exactly?"

"That the old Magdalene had an apprentice with a hidden Talent for finding things, which is exactly what I need, and I'm willing to pay you $50,000 for the service plus expenses."

Rune rolled that tidbit around in her head a moment while this annoyingly charming man smiled, clearly satisfied that he had won some sort of argument. If this was any other job, she would have taken him up on his offer. She had learned enough watching and assisting Maddie that she could...*maybe*...come out of the closet as a Talent. Maybe she could get her wizardess license and take up helping people where Maddie had left off. Rune would have to pay a fine for being unregistered for so long. It was just a misdemeanor, except that would be how they would find her—*Anna*. The moment they checked too closely into her personal history, *Rune's* fabricated life would shred like tissue paper.

She suddenly remembered all the reasons to say no.

If it had been any other job or she was any other person, she would accept his offer to find Anna Masterson and walk the money to the bank whistling. It was to save her precious bar, after all. But that was insane.

"I'm sorry. I have to turn you down. Whoever this woman is, it sounds to me like she is much better off not being found, and I'm not going to be a part of anything that would ruin anybody's life," she said with quiet, final conviction.

St. Benedict's smile didn't fall like she expected. He continued smiling as he picked up his coat and rolled up his blood-covered shirtsleeve to hide the evidence of his nefarious dealings before slipping the coat back on. Once the coat was settled, he slipped his hand into his front pocket and pulled out a business card.

"When you change your mind, feel free to find me," he said confidently, holding the card out between two fingers, oozing dark and sexy confidence. She took the card with a show of reluctance, taking it more out of habit than anything else.

"Thank you for the offer Mr.—St. Benedict," she said, shaking her head when she tripped over the Saint honorific as if it left a bad taste in her mouth. "Sorry."

"Don't be. It was interesting to meet you, Ms. Leveau. I look forward to your call." He doffed his hat, all gentlemanly, before heading toward the door.

"I won't be calling you," she said to his retreating back.

"Yes, you will," he said and tried to turn the door handle for what would have been a graceful exit, except the door was still sealed. He stood there for an awkwardly pregnant moment. "Do you think you could ..."

"Oh, right! The door! Sorry. Let me get that for you." It was another couple of minutes before she remembered the words to unseal it and open it again into the bar proper. Having already said goodbye, St. Benedict nodded once to her in acknowledgment and sauntered down the hallway, knowing he didn't have to look back.

Once he was gone, Rune looked down at the card in her hand. It was black and shiny, written across in matte black print, almost indiscernible until you tipped the card toward the light. His name, St. Benedict, and a phone number graced the front. She tossed it into the garbage.

"Ah, crap," she realized, "he heard my door password. Now I'm going to need to set a new one." She stared at the card sitting on top of the garbage, reconsidering, then shook her head.

"No. No, way. I'm never going to see him again," she decided.

She saw him again the next day.

CHAPTER 4

Rune washed her face in her apartment bathroom, gratefully noting the cut had not resumed bleeding. It was morning, and technically she could have stayed in bed another couple of hours, but she had never really gone to sleep. Her head was still spinning about her encounter with that St. Benedict guy. She thought she would feel differently. It was the closest anyone had ever come to finding Anna Masterson. She should be more shaken up. Instead, she felt eerily calm, maybe even a little confident.

"He didn't find you," she said to the Rune in the mirror, who smiled back. "Maddie was right."

It had been six years since Maddie had taken her away from that awful place. Being so close to where she used to live, she had wondered how she could hide under a new identity and not be discovered and rearrested at some point, but Maddie had sworn that it would never happen. Within the first week of being in Chicago, Maddie presented her with a new ID for one Rune Leveau, giving Anna Maddie's own last name, as well as a birth certificate and new family history.

Her Talent was the only thing she couldn't change about herself and thereby connected her to her old identity as Anna Masterson. Rune opted to deny even having a Talent. Most Talents were tested when they left high school, so no one official would require her to retest without cause. If an Aura Reader should ever make a comparison between Anna's aura records and Rune's though, things would get dicey. Rune never really understood what Maddie did to keep her aura from being read, but so far, it hadn't come up.

Maddie had understood about Rune's choice to hide her abilities, even though it went against everything that Maddie had strived for all her life. Being a magic user activist and leader of various magic-based communities, Maddie had been the pariah in Anna's family. She only remembered meeting her mysterious aunt once as a child at a family reunion. Rune fell in love with her at first sight, much to her mother's horror. After a few weeks of talking about her amazing magical great-aunt, her mother forbade Anna from speaking of Maddie ever again and even swatted her good on the butt when she tried.

Shortly after, the letters appeared. Now Rune knew that her aunt had sent them to her with a modified transfer system, similar to the doors, but then, it was pure wonder when little Anna would wake up in the morning to find a letter tucked under her pillow. Sending and receiving those letters became Anna's first secret. She kept it up until she was a teenager, telling her great aunt all of her plans for the future, sometimes asking for her advice.

It wasn't until Anna graduated that she even knew she had a Talent. When her test came back positive, her mother was quick to make her promise to ignore it, for fear that it would interfere with her upcoming marriage to Justin. Good girls didn't do magic. Her parents wanted that marriage so badly they had been prepared to give her permission to marry the illustrious Justin Masterson before she turned eighteen or even graduated from high school. Anna had been so in love at the time, she listened and obeyed. That was when she stopped returning Aunt Maddie's letters and stopped going to school.

It took a long time for Rune to even build up the courage to use her Talent again. It had resurfaced only when Maddie and a young woman she was trying to help needed it more than anything. The woman's teenage son had disappeared after he had fallen in with a gang of Talented but dangerous kids, with no education and too much power. It was Rune's first true Finding. It had been the proudest moment of her life and a turning point for her in more ways than one. It was the true start of Rune Leveau, the somewhat capable assistant who helped those who could not help themselves.

Anna Masterson, by contrast, had been a young, naive housewife with some minor Talent six years earlier. A subservient thing, she had been a quiet, mousy thing that lived for her rock-star, computer-programming husband, and always did what her parents told her, never causing any trouble. Even when she discovered all the affairs her husband was having, even with women she thought were her friends. Even then, she hadn't caused any sort of fuss about it for fear of it ruining everything.

When the corporate police came in the night, faceless monsters with their guns and nonsensical shouting, it had been a huge shock to that serene, spiritless world she had created for herself.

Rune Leveau closed her eyes and shook her head, trying to shove the memory back into its cold, dark box. Anna Masterson had never come out of that vile place, where her husband abandoned her to save himself, leaving her to pay the price for his sins. Rune Leveau was not some weak and pathetic girl who didn't know what to do or how to take care of herself without her parents or her husband. Rune Leveau had her GED and an AA degree. Rune Leveau had better, more important things to worry about—like saving her bar from being repossessed by the mortgage company—to concern herself with someone else's past. As long as Rune Leveau existed, they would never find Anna Masterson, no matter how long they looked, whoever *they* were.

Clapping her hands together, as if to seal that promise with herself, Rune turned away from the mirror to deal with the problems immediately facing her.

The firm resolve she had in the bathroom melted into a metaphorical puddle as soon as she walked down into the bar. The first thing she saw was the boarded-up ugly of the interior window with chunks of glass glittering at its base.

She had no idea what she was going to do to solve any of it.

Things were quiet, serene. The Main Bar was open for the breakfast crowd, the kitchen already humming as a few regulars came in for their friendly neighborhood breakfast and chat before heading off to work. A half-dozen people were talking and chattering excitedly, mostly about the events from the night before. Liam supplied them with coffee and tea as fast as his four arms could manage.

"Liam! What are you doing here?" Rune asked, squeezing around the bar to grab the kid's arm. He didn't look too bad for having been hauled off to jail, even smelling of soap and shampoo like he had come straight from a shower.

"Hey, Ms. Leveau! They let me go almost right away! Said there was a clerical error or something. I was actually home by my usual time," he said cheerfully, his toothy grin splitting his face from ear to ear.

Rune shook her head in disbelief. "I'm so relieved, but you didn't have to come in this morning, I mean—"

"No, it's fine, I want to be here," Liam said, before being hailed for more coffee from the far end of the bar.

"Well, if you get tired and want to go home early, let me know, okay? No need to be a hero. You already are one," she said seriously.

The kid blushed at the praise. "Aw, thanks, Ms. Leveau." He took off to finish serving the coffee.

Before she could turn back into the Lounge, a rough hand squeezed her arm too hard and yanked her to a stop.

"Where in the seven hells have you been!?" Alf growled.

"What?" she exclaimed, confused. "It's nine o'clock. That's not late—"

"Last night! Went up to your apartment and you weren't there," Alf hissed, holding onto her arm and walking her into the Lounge Bar out of the hearing range of their patrons.

"I was dealing with something," Rune said, shaking off his painful grip.

"What exactly?" Alf put his hands on his hips, looking like a disapproving father as he glared up at her. "You disappeared about the same time as that corporate elite pretty boy."

Rune arched an eyebrow and almost laughed. "What exactly are you accusing me of here?"

"Being stupid," he practically spit.

"He was trying to redeem a jade coin." Rune sat down on one of the Lounge barstools.

Alf's eyes widened a moment, then settled into another ugly mask of contempt. "Of course, he did," he said, "Why else would his kind come in here? So, what does he want you to do?"

"Nothing, I turned down the job," Rune said.

"You what?!"

That surprised her. "What? He wanted the impossible," she started to explain, hoping she could avoid going into detail. In truth, she wasn't sure what Alf knew about her past. He never acted as if he knew anything and she never had felt like sharing with a guy like him anyway.

The short man narrowed his eyes at her. "So, you are giving up Maddie's entire legacy, are you?"

"What? No! Of course not," Rune said, truly offended that he would say such a thing. "You think I should have just said yes?"

"Oh, I don't know. Do we have a severe cash flow problem and a mortgage pending? I think so. How much did he offer you?" Alf asked, pinning her again with his stare. He was doing that so much lately, she began to feel like a bulletin board.

"Fifty thousand," Rune said.

"Dollars?"

"No, kittens," Rune smarted back. "Why are you panicking about this? We're supposed to have a fifteen-day grace period on the mortgage! They can't shut us down like that no matter how much they threaten," Rune argued.

"This is Chicago, sweetheart, things like fair business laws are only for those who can pay for them," Alf chided. "Those bloodhounds aren't showing up here to be friendly."

"Alf, don't worry. I'll get the money before Monday."

"Doing what!?"

"I'll do what Maddie did, maybe?" Rune offered.

"How?! A magic-less, worthless girl who does nothing but sit on her ass?" Alf gestured so boisterously that he knocked over a stack of menus. "If you were going to do that, you should have taken that corporate elite's job."

"It was because he was a corporate elite! That's insanely dangerous for people of our level," she tried to argue once more.

"I don't care if he's the grand pope of my ass crack. You call him right now and tell him you'll take the money. This is serious," Alf growled and slapped down the collected menus onto the bar, destroying the neatness of the stack. "Do you know what will happen when they come for this place?" His face turned bright red, and Rune thought he might pop.

"Yes! Yes, I know. I have a sense of urgency about this, trust me. This is my home. Okay? I get exactly what's at stake." Rune held her hands up in surrender, but it didn't satisfy Alf.

"No, I don't think you do understand. This isn't just about your living, little ms., or your home. This has been my entire existence for twenty-seven years, and I will be dead in my grave before I let a snippet of an idiot girl like you screw it up! God knows what Maddie was thinking when she left everything to you—"

"That's what this is really about, isn't it Alf?" Rune interrupted. "Because Maddie didn't leave this place to you—"

"Don't you dare shout over me you ungrat—"

"...or you'll what exactly? Throw me out of my own—"

"...I swear if you don't shut your face—"

"...go ahead. Give me your best shot!!"

Suddenly they both stopped screaming at each other, breathing heavily as if they had run a marathon. An unsettlingly quiet descended over the bar. As one, their eyes both went wide as they realized what they had done. In the next room, conversations slowly started up again.

They looked away from each other, neither willing nor able to break the silence.

Rune happened to glance across the bar, and that's when she spied the middle-aged woman entering, looking lost and unsure.

She appeared Polish, with delicate bone structure and features, and she was dressed well; too well for someone who would frequent the Lucky Devil Bar. She stood at the door, taking in the room nervously, fidgeting with a piece of tissue in her hand. Lucky Devil sat smiling at her from his booth, but his presence appeared to unnerve her more than set her at ease.

"Huh—" Rune shook her head and stood up all the way, her anger pooling on the floor as fast as it had flared. "I mean, can I help you?" she asked the woman.

Alf said nothing more and left Rune to it, returning to the Main Bar.

"Yes, I am looking—" She looked Rune up and down, and didn't seem to approve of what she saw.

"Are you here for breakfast? We're serving next door. Or are you here to meet somebody?" Rune tried to be helpful, but the woman shook her head.

"Is this the place with the devil?" the woman asked reluctantly.

"Oh. Yes, yeah, sure," Rune said and indicated Lucky Devil in his booth before ducking behind the bar to act busy.

The woman nodded business-like, with an air of determination and went straight to the booth, gripping her purse as if it was a shield, her tissue a lady's, or maybe gentleman's favor. She sat across from Lucky Devil and eyed him with no little amount of apprehension. Then she pulled out a small pair of reading glasses to look at the plastic-covered sheet of paper that had the instructions, finally abandoning the tissue on the table. Rune tried to stay inconspicuous as she watched.

After the woman finished reading the paper, she went with a great deal of purpose to the vending machine, studying it as intently as the instructions. To Rune's surprise, the woman pulled out another slip of paper from her wallet and started pulling the tabs in a specific sequence until the lights in the old cigarette machine powered down with a click. A single green light in the middle of the machine blinked on, revealing a hidden slot. Sitting in the slot on a pedestal covered in dark red velveteen was a jade coin.

A job.

Rune almost whooped out loud, as she marveled at the statistical luck of getting two jade coins in less than twenty-four hours. They weren't cheap and highly coveted since there were only thirteen in existence. The machine itself was only holding less than half of them.

The woman swiped her credit card and pulled the tab. Instead of dumping the coin to be collected below, the jade coin's slot raised the glass in front to allow access. That's when the woman hesitated as if she was committing an act from which she knew there would be no turning back, before picking up the coin gingerly between two fingers. Then the slot went dark, and the glass slid back into place, the cigarette machine powering up to normal. The woman took the coin back to Lucky Devil, performing the ritual of giving her request to Lucky Devil and dropping the green coin into his drink.

Rune's mind raced about what to do. She needed the job, but could she deliver what the woman wanted? If it was a love spell or a luck spell or something magical yet trivial, Rune could use one of Maddie's old pre-filled crystals. Again her concerns about being discovered bubbled to the surface, but this time she shoved them to the side. Caution be damned. Alf had struck a nerve. Whatever this woman wanted, Rune needed to do it. There was no choice. It was that or risk losing the bar.

As the marathon of thoughts and feelings sprinted through her head, she felt the tingling sensation of the coin and the wish being deposited in her front shirt pocket.

"Please want me to find something. Please want me to find something," she whispered to herself over and over as she fished out the slip of paper.

I wish to find my daughter.

Rune almost giggled out loud.

After a few minutes, she emerged from behind the bar and headed for the woman. Somehow she made it all the way to the booth and slid past Lucky Devil to sit down next to him while the potential client's attention was elsewhere. When the woman looked back, she almost leapt out of the booth. Rune may have been too successful at appearing mysterious. She feared for a second that the woman might bolt.

Putting on her best reassuring smile, Rune nodded to her.

"The devil sent me." Rune continued smiling as she said the traditional greeting Maddie had always used when answering a jade coin wish.

The woman looked around the bar. "You are bartender who works here?" she asked, her accent confirming her Polish heritage as Rune had suspected.

Rune decided that not answering the question would be more mysterious.

"I understand you made a wish.," she said as she showed the woman her empty hand, then made the note appear with a bit of clumsy sleight of hand. The trick must have worked. The woman's eyes rounded.

She must be quite worried about her daughter. Rune was sure that was the only reason the woman hadn't picked up her fashionable, expensive purse and run. Instead, the woman held her seat, swallowed, and nodded, reclaiming her tissue from the table. She was dressed well; like a corporate type trying to look casual, but her clothes were too well made and the outfit perfectly coordinated. Her beautifully cut hair and the simple string of pearls made her look magazine-quality motherly.

"Ma'am, you said your daughter was missing?" Rune prompted. Might as well get the standard questions out of the way. "Have you contacted your corporation's police force?"

"They will not help me. I do not have the…" Rune's potential client looked down at her hands and began shredding the tissue in long strips, her cheeks pinking in embarrassment, "the clout in my company to warrant—I am just a low-level account manager. They took my report. They even said she was a high risk, but… it is corporate policy. I never understood what that meant until now. She is eighteen. They say she is just rebelling, but I don't think that is true," she said, quietly, with very crisp diction. Rune was certain that English wasn't her first language. Yet the accent she heard earlier had disappeared, which meant the woman probably practiced to make it go away. The woman collected up the pieces of tissue into her hand to tear into even smaller bits again.

"Not all kids rebel. I certainly didn't," Rune said, offering a smile. That didn't seem to comfort the woman any.

"I was told The Lucky Devil is the place to go to find help."

Rune smiled, "I'm here to listen, Ms. — "

"Janowski."

"Ms. Janowski, please, tell me the story of your daughter. I'll see if I can help," Rune said.

"The long and short of it is we have only our Ally and no other children. Ally is our most precious child. Ally had anything and everything she wanted. People say that produced a very spoiled, self-entitled girl." Ms. Janowski's chin stiffened a little. "She has always been the sweetest girl with the loveliest temperament. She could make you laugh, even when she was small." The older woman's sternness softened into a wistful smile. "She is the light of my life. My husband — he has been so busy lately. He has not had time for her. I think that is where all the trouble started. She started seeing this Southern Chicago boy. Everything about him is bad news," Ms. Janowski said, clearly annoyed.

"Can you be more specific? I mean, what do you mean bad news exactly?" Rune pushed.

"She is a good girl. She volunteered at an endangered youth center, you know, for poor kids. We thought it a good thing, you understand, for her college application, to have some extracurriculars. She wants to change the world. She really has a big heart. But then she met this boy. I never met him, but his father is a maintenance worker of some kind. A laborer," she said with equal parts disgust and distress.

Rune's eyes double blinked before she could school them not to give away too much in the face of this woman's elitist opinions. "So, he doesn't do something like deal drugs, and he isn't part of a gang or something?"

Ms. Janowski seemed to take Rune's reaction as support because she leaned forward, pitched her voice even lower and more urgent, "Of course, he sells drugs. That is all they do."

"Okay." Rune took a deep breath, continuing to focus on channeling the inner serenity Maddie had displayed so easily in the face of similar kinds of economic profiling. "Tell me how long your daughter has been missing."

"She left this morning to go to school, but they called me. She never showed up. After she came home so late last night, I know something is wrong. I feel it in my bones." Tears began to roll down Ms. Janowski's face.

"So, she's been behaving differently lately."

She couldn't speak for her tears, but Ms. Janowski nodded vigorously as she pressed the shredded mass of tissues in her hand to her lips. Thankfully, Liam arrived at the table with two glasses of water. Rune used his approach as the perfect excuse to look away and give Ms. Janowski a moment to collect herself.

"Thank you, Liam. Don't let anybody in here for the next hour," Rune said quietly. Liam nodded and disappeared back into the Main Bar.

As Ms. Janowski gulped down half of her water, Rune spied a yappy little white dog appearing and disappearing from the bottom edge of the bar's front windows. It looked like it was leaping up to look in, whining and barking for attention. The dog noticed Rune noticing and instantly started to bark even more persistently. It attempted to jump higher up the glass while wagging its tail like it was attached to a high-speed motor before the disappearing again below the casement.

"I'm sorry, Ms. Janowski, but your dog seems rather agitated," Rune said, reaching out to tap the woman's hand gently to get her attention. At the mention of the animal, Ms. Janowski's eyes grew round and she turned quickly to look out the window. The dog's jumps were getting weaker and it stopped. Instead, it began to howl.

"That is not my dog," she said harshly. "It is some damn stray that will not leave me alone. My mother would say I've been cursed by a witch, to have a dog following me."

"I thought that was just bad luck," Rune said. If that was a curse, it was definitely one of the dumber ones. Curses took a lot of energy and power to invoke. Simply muttering a curse at someone was not enough; otherwise, every time someone swore on the street, half the city would be damned. "How long has that dog been following you?"

Ms. Janowski waved a dismissive hand. "Since this morning. But I'm not here to talk about the dog. Please, can you help me find my daughter?" she asked, turning back to Rune with pleading eyes.

Rune smiled a toothy Cheshire-cat smile. This would be a piece of pie, since Rune wasn't partial to cake. "Yes. Yes, I can help you Find your daughter. But it's going to depend on a few factors. First, this will cost you about five thousand dollars."

Ms. Janowski's expression, which had brightened with hope, fell.

"Half up front and the other half once your daughter is safely home," Rune pressed on, less sure.

She knew she would only see the initial twenty-five hundred. After the job was done, more often than not, the patron disavowed knowing anything about the magical help they had received. It happened to Maddie all the time, and she was a renowned wizardess. Often, those that came seeking magical services outside of the normal stuff were people with a problem that they couldn't solve any other way, and they were always desperate.

"Twenty-five hundred," Ms. Janowski repeated a little less panicked.

Rune could almost see the scales moving in the other woman's head. The twenty-five hundred dollars plus the thousand-dollar fee the woman had paid for the coin would finish off Rune's mortgage payment with cushion, and that was all that mattered.

"Alright, I can do that," Ms. Janowski said, nodding to herself, then picked up her purse and stood. "Do you need it right now? I can go to an ATM."

Rune was impressed. Not many people, including herself, had the kind of banking power to withdraw an amount like that from any ATM.

"Sure, there's one down on the corner by the coffee shop," Rune said, picking up on the hint that Ms. Janowski did not want Rune to follow her.

Rune moved as far as the door anyway and watched her walk away from the bar, to the ATM. The Finder wondered for a moment if her client was just going to walk right past and never come back, but the woman stopped and conducted her business at the machine.

While she waited, Rune stood in the doorway and took in the Chicago early morning. A few blocks over, she heard the rumble of the Red Line rolling from the northernmost point of Chicago's Northside toward the Loop, the downtown area encircled by the elevated train tracks. A gentle breeze from Lake Michigan brought a sweeter air past the door, and she thought for a moment about whether she should ask more questions. The job seemed straightforward enough. She needed the money, so it wasn't like she could really turn the job down anyway. Right? The apprehension she felt from last night still toyed with her stomach. If anyone were to discover her secret or her Talent... she clenched her teeth and shook her head. No time now to be pussyfooting about this.

A high yip interrupted Rune's thoughts. She looked down. Next to her, sitting quietly on the sidewalk, was the little white dog tail still vigorously wagging. When Rune yawned, it yawned too, which just triggered a second yawn from Rune.

"Oh, stop that," Rune told the perky little thing. "Ugh, I need to go back to bed. It's been a rough couple of days. So, what exactly did you do to get yourself turned into a dog?" The little white shoulders visually hunched and the little white head turned to look at her. Rune flashed the little dog a smile. "Easiest money ever made."

Ms. Janowski returned in a rush, as if she expected to be robbed at any moment, and thrust a white card at Rune.

"Here is your money," Ms. Janowski declared. Rune took the card but wasn't quite sure what to make of it. Everyone Maddie ever dealt with paid in untraceable cash.

"Are you sure?" Rune asked, turning the card over to see the black stripe on the other side.

"Yes, your five thousand dollars is on there," Ms. Janowski declared.

Rune stared down harder at the card. Five thousand dollars all on something so innocuous. It didn't seem real. "The whole thing? Are you sure?" Rune couldn't believe her luck, all the money she needed in one go.

"I will give you the pin when my daughter is home safe," Ms. Janowski said.

"Works for me. Let me present to you your daughter." Rune gestured at the white dog that had edged closer to the two women. "Obviously, your kid here did something to annoy someone and got herself turned into a dog, but you can get it reversed easy enough with—"

A look of panic crossed Ms. Janowski's face. "No, no, that is not my daughter," she insisted, shaking her head.

Rune sighed. Okay, maybe not that easy. There were lots of hominals that insisted magic wasn't real. Or climate change. Never mind that both things were scientifically verified.

"Ma'am. I understand if this is hard to believe, but I can assure you, hominal-to-animal transformations are possible." Rune looked down at the dog, who stared back with pleading eyes.

"If you don't think you can do the job, I will find someone else," Ms. Janowski said. It sounded like the empty threat that it was. If Ms. Janowski could have, she would have already gone to someone else. Plus, Rune really did need this money. She decided the best course of action was to tell her client what she wanted to hear.

"No, no. I can find your daughter. I'm... just... going..." Rune said, trying to think fast. "... I am going to need something intimately connected to your daughter."

Rune shifted uncomfortably under the woman's level stare. For a second, Rune flashed back to memories of another table, where a different well-dressed woman stared at her with haughty disapproval. Rune bit the inside of her cheek and focused on her breathing. She had to ground herself in the here and now.

"Um, it can be something she carries with her," Rune said, refocusing on the task at hand, "Or something that you two share like matching necklaces or bracelets or even a family heirloom or a childhood toy she still keeps. It will help me find her. It doesn't have to be much, but it has to be intimately connected to her."

"Uh, well, we do have something like that, but I would... I would rather not use it," Ms. Janowski said.

"Uh, okay, how about maybe even something she carries all the time, you know that goes on the same paths that she goes on, like a purse or a favorite book."

"She has a purse," Ms. Janowski confirmed. "She didn't take it with her."

The best are earrings or buttons. If someone has left one earring somewhere but is still wearing the other, I can usually find them in five minutes flat. I mean, if they're within five minutes walking distance."

"She—" Ms. Janowski said, looking overwhelmed.

"I think her purse would probably be our best bet," Rune concluded, making her client's mind up for her.

"But... it is back at the house," she said.

"That's fine, I can start there anyway," Rune said and stood up herself.

"I will bring you the purse back here. It should take me an hour." As the older woman turned to leave, the white dog jumped up and started pawing and barking at her leg, desperate to get her attention. "Get off me, you evil creature!" she roared and kicked at the poor thing with the toe of her heels. The dog yelped in pain and backed away toward Rune, before turning around in several circles indecisively.

"Hey! Don't do that!" Rune shouted, sticking the card into her back pocket so she could scoop up the dog.

Again, that look of panic crossed Ms. Janowski's face, this time followed by guilt. Then she left, bolting down the street as fast as her heeled shoes would let her.

"I'm sorry about that, kid," Rune said, sliding a hand over the trembling dog's head and back. "Some people have a hard time dealing with magic. It's not anything you did. Well, outside of whatever you did to get turned into a dog, I mean."

The little dog squirmed and jumped ungracefully out of Rune's arms.

"Okay, okay, sorry. No petting. Got it."

The way the deal went down didn't feel quite right to Rune, but five thousand dollars in one go like that? She pulled out the card and looked at it again. Not giving her the pin was the woman's insurance that Rune got the job done. She shrugged. "Works for me," she said out loud to nobody.

Rune opened the door of her bar. "You might as well come in and get some water. We're going to have to wait for her to come back with that item. Then I can prove you are who you are."

The dog perked up and waggled its tail before looking back at it to snort in annoyance.

CHAPTER 5

Rune's apartment was on the third floor above the bar, the topmost story of the building. The march up the steps was long on most days, but today Rune took them like Olympic hurdles, the little dog hot on her heels. The steps were narrow, in a tunnel of white-painted walls ending in a butter-colored door. Like the two-way door to her office, Rune could use either a key or a magic command to open it. She had to make two attempts at the unlock command before finally pulling out her physical key, but even that didn't deter her excitement.

She was on a job again, even without Maddie, and so what if it had a little hiccup? Nothing she couldn't fix. She turned the handle into her haven and leapt through the door, almost tripping on the door jamb in her haste.

The large windows of her loft apartment looked out over her little neighborhood. If she stood on one of her window sills on a clear day, she could just see over the building across the street all the way to Lake Michigan. It was a long room with an open kitchen in the far corner and bar counter that separated it from what was designated as the living room. Technically, it wasn't a true loft because there was a separate bedroom tucked into the corner opposite of the kitchen. The apartment had a wooden kitchen table that would have comfortably sat a family of six, but right now, it supported piles of papers and mail that Rune stacked up so she could ignore it.

Inside her home, she tugged off her sneakers and almost ate it against the wall when she lost her balance. Her cushy brown couch called to her to lie upon it, but she denied its soft, snuggly advances in favor of the bathroom, her true love in the apartment.

"Make yourself at home," Rune said to the little dog as she trotted in before her host shut the door.

Rune had moved into this apartment after her third year of living with Maddie, once Maddie felt Rune was ready, maybe more than ready, to live on her own, and Rune had finally agreed with her. The previous tenants had been college kids and had destroyed the apartment, so over the course of that year, together, they revamped the place and made it one hundred percent Rune's. This included a waterfall shower head inside a stone-lined shower.

After a soul-changing fifteen minutes in the shower, Rune emerged from a cloud of steam and went into her bedroom, heading straight to her closet.

"I'm going to change into my gear if you don't mind," she called out. The dog who-was-probably-a-teenager jumped up on the couch, her chin on her paws in a perfect picture of dejection. "Maybe your mom will take me more seriously then."

It felt like an age since she had worn any of the gear she had meticulously collected over the years she assisted Maddie. Straight off, Rune plaited her hair into a French braid, then slipped into a pair of running underwear and an industrial-strength sports bra that locked her ample chest into place. Fawn-colored leggings that were soft like yoga pants went on next and then a tank covered by a white pageboy shirt that tied in the back so that it hugged her body, while still looking magical professional. All of these clothes were pretty innocuous on their own, but it was the belt that was something special.

Composed of three sections of leather pouches, linked together by large metal rings sewn at the end of each section to form the body of the belt, it was a custom creation made by a friend of Maddie's in the Faerie Court before it disbanded two years prior. Being Faerie made one think it would also be rife with enchantments of some sort but if it had any spells woven into it, they were passive, keeping it fray-, stain-, and malfunction-free. Each of the sections had two pouches attached with a leather flap that covered the top and were held on with a latch that held snug but was easy to thumb open in a hurry. Each pouch held various useful items: string, a magnet, a hand mirror, chalk, a wax crayon, a lighter, a small notebook with tiny pencils, a little packet of nuts or crackers, just in case she needed a bribe for the fae or a snack for herself. There was a secret pouch sewn into the on the backside of the right section and closed with a tiny zipper. It hid spare money, a credit card, or gems.

Rune buckled the belt and cinched it tight over her hips. Normally, the outfit would include a jacket with mystical shapes patterned over it, but the weather crystal at the top of her wind chime in her kitchen already glowed softly orange, indicating it was going to be another upper-70s to lower-80s day.

Granted, she wasn't actually going anywhere. Once Ms. Janowski came back with the connected object, hopefully, she would leave with her dogified daughter.

Rune padded into her living room, giving a little turn for her visitor.

"Better?" she asked. The little dog sniffed.

She grabbed a cold can of sparkling water from the fridge.

"I wonder if I should do a profile on you. I mean, I'm pretty sure you are Ally."

Ally barked.

"Right. But still, it can't hurt, I guess. Might help convince your mother I did my work. Keep this between you and me. It's really hard to explain how my—" Rune stopped herself. She had almost said, 'my Talent works.' The last thing she needed was to come out of the closet to a client, and then subsequently go to jail.

Intuitive Magic, which Finding seemed to fall under, was easy enough to disguise. But, like most mental magics, it was damned inconsistent. Usually, Rune would simply have a strong, clear feeling about which way to go or where to look. When she didn't get that feeling, profiles helped her focus.

Rune opened her notebook to a fresh page, in the center was a rough generic outline of a person with space around it for notes.

"Okay, let's start with the basic facts. We know your age, gender, nationality, and that your name is Ally."

Rune filled in the appropriate mystical symbols around the diagram at the correct points as if it was a real Finding. She then added the choice words Ms. Janowski had used to describe her daughter around the figure: *sweet girl, loveliest temperament, big heart, save the world.* Altogether everything she had written painted a picture of Ally.

After a few more lines, the writing continued without her guidance, and Rune knew she had it. The page started to fill up with other details, things that she could not know for sure but seemed to have truth to them.

"Loves cookies and cream ice cream. And robins. Would go to the home-made ice cream shops," she mumbled as she wrote. "Wore plaid pants instead of skirts to Catholic school. Hair in a braid to fit under the hair net. Isn't sure if she's pretty enough. Wishes her nose was less pointy." She couldn't explain how she knew all of this was true. It just was. Not once did she look up to confirm with the object of the search herself. In fact, until Rune put the pen down, she forgot anyone else was in the room at all.

Setting the pen down seemed to break the spell. Rune took a deep breath and stretched her back, shaking out her cramping fingers.

"That should do it. Let's go downstairs and wait for your mom to return."

Rune gathered up her things and went to the fridge. She took out a bagel and spread cream cheese generously over both sides. Wrapping it in a napkin to take with her, she went back down to the bar.

The morning crowd in the Main Bar was still around so late in the day, lingering despite the late hour. Rune moved back into the Lounge and slipped into the booth with Lucky Devil so that she faced the door. As she unwrapped her bagel, Ally popped up next to her, looking hopeful.

"I don't think bread is good for your current digestion," Rune said, fighting the urge to share.

It was a nice quiet lull before the lunch storm. Liam had opened up the windows in the Main Bar, and the air blew through into the Lounge Bar, filling it with a sweet summer scent that held only a hint of Chicago's oily smell.

While Rune chewed, Ally suddenly lifted her head, ears perked toward the front window. The shade was drawn over the glass, and it was backlit by the sun, making the window appear like a shadow play. On the far left, the form of a woman appeared. Ally barked eagerly and hopped down from the booth. At the sound, the shadow stopped and hesitated a moment before walking the rest of the way to the bar door.

To Rune's surprise, instead of coming in, Ms. Janowski stopped just before the door. Furtively, she shoved a bulging envelope through the old unused mail slot, before practically running back the way she had come.

Ally barked more desperately as the shadow disappeared. Frantically, Rune rushed to open the door, but it got caught on the envelope Ms. Janowski had dropped inside.

By the time Rune picked up the envelope, got the door open, and stepped out of said door, her client was completely gone.

"Dammit," Rune said out loud to no one in particular. "Why didn't she come in?" The sense that it was a mistake taking a job without Maddie soft-shoed through her mind again. "Your mom must really hate magic."

Having no other option, Rune shut the door again and went back to Lucky Devil's booth.

Ally spun herself in a circle in front of the door, grumbling under her breath. Rune was sure if she could understand, it would be a litany of curses.

Rune turned her attention to the white envelope in her hands. She tore it open at one end. The bottom corner of the envelope held a small pool of crumpled metal. She stuck her finger inside and fished out a silver chain that unfolded as she pulled it out until the charm appeared at the end. She recognized it as the necklace Ms. Janowski had been wearing earlier. It was half of a broken locket embossed with a filigreed heart. It seemed old, like an heirloom passed down for generations. The flip side was empty, no picture or lock of hair or anything; just the spot where one should have been and the tiny twisted metal where the lock hinge had been torn apart.

"Huh. I guess your mom changed her mind about using a necklace instead."

Right away, Rune felt a strong aura associated with the locket. She crawled the chain up into her hand until she held the pendant between her fingers. Almost instantly, Rune's Talent bloomed out. Rune's real eyes closed of their own accord as she savored the little bit of joy she felt whenever she did her magic. She hated how much she loved that joy. In her mind's eyes, she saw the image of a teenage girl. The magical pull was strong, followed by a nice little click inside her being. Without a doubt, the other half of the locket was close and it was with Ally.

Rune's eyes popped open. "Yep, thought so."

A thread of light came off of the locket, curling almost like a smoke tendril to swoop and spin toward its other half. No one else could see this tendril, not even Maddie, when she had been alive. Rune could only see it when the thing she was looking for was close. At that moment, it was the strongest Rune had ever seen as it whirled straight around the neck of the dog.

"Yup, you are definitely Ally Janowski," Rune said. "But judging by your mother's reaction, she's not going to accept that, is she?"

The dog barked once, her head shaking back and forth furiously like she was tearing apart an invisible mouse.

"What did you do, Ally?" Rune asked the little dog. Her tail slowed its wag and drooped a little.

Rune sighed. "This job just got a lot harder, didn't it?"

"What's with the dog, Leveau?" Calvin and his Tigerman partner entered at that exact moment, the door slamming behind them like a thunder knell of doom. They were dressed much like they had been the day before, in matching thuggish business suits, black gloves, and sunglasses that neither took off.

"None of your business. What do you want, Calvin?" Rune asked, setting her hands on her hips with annoyance. "You already harassed me yesterday. Isn't this a little redundant?"

"I go where I want, Leveau," Calvin said.

"Well, then want to go away," she said, impressed that she came up with that zinger on the spot.

Calvin smirked as he sauntered past Rune toward the broken window, now taped over with cardboard in a makeshift repair that only emphasized how busted it was.

"Your problems just keep piling up, don't they?" Calvin said, looking over his black sunglasses at the patchwork repair as if there was something more he could see by examining it that way.

"What? There are no problems here. I've got everything under control. Now, if you're just here to repeat yourselves, then you might as well go or order lunch in the next room." Rune jabbed toward the door with her thumb. She knew she needed to be more polite and professional, but Calvin's smug face made it so difficult.

The sunglasses snapped back over Calvin's eyes as he turned with a cat-eating-the-canary smile. "Heard you had an interesting visitor last night, Leveau."

That took the wind out of Rune's sails.

"St. Benedict," Jasper said, his voice rumbling so close behind Rune that she jumped a little.

"What about him?" Rune asked, not bothering to deny it.

"What'd he want?" Calvin asked.

"Like I'm going to tell you," Rune snapped back.

"You might be better off if you do," Jasper said, his deep voice making it sound like a threat.

"St. Benedict's bad news, kid. He brings the kind of trouble someone like you just can't handle," Calvin added.

"What are you, a gangster?" Rune asked sarcastically. "Who talks like that?"

The smile dropped off Calvin's face. Before she could stop him, he took a couple of steps in and unexpectedly kicked Ally out of the way. She yipped in pain, and Rune rushed over to pick her up, then set her in the booth with Lucky Devil.

"What the hell is wrong with you?! Don't kick her!" Rune admonished for all the good it did. She instinctively petted Ally's head like the teenager was a dog, which only earned Rune a nip for her trouble.

"What did St. Benedict want, Leveau?!" Calvin shouted, almost spitting in Rune's face as he did it.

"I have customers next door," Rune hissed, but suddenly Calvin was too close, grabbing her face with his hand.

"Get your hands off me!" she screeched as she slapped his hand away, too quick for him to hold his grip. Her heart pounded hard. "He offered me a job. I turned him down."

"He offered you a job? To do what exactly?" Calvin asked, taking a step back and sliding his hand back into his pant pocket, annoying Rune with his passive-aggressive attitude.

Rune crossed her arms in front of her in a defensive gesture, and but more to hide to keep her shaking hands hidden. "He wanted me to be Maddie, but I'm not, so I turned him down."

Calvin and Jasper had never manhandled or even touched her before. They had always been intimidating, it was their job, but this was different. Something had changed, but Rune couldn't pinpoint what it was, setting off her anxiety. "He wanted some magic. I can't do that."

Calvin's smile returned.

"That must have sucked. I bet a guy like St. Benedict offered you a nice chunk of money too. What are you going to do now, Leveau?" Calvin asked, infusing her name with mockery.

"Pay my mortgage on time," Rune said with absolute confidence, the shaking already subsiding by sheer will alone.

"Did you hear her, Mr. Locke?" Calvin said to his partner, who still hovered behind her.

"Yes, Mr. Carlton," Jasper said.

"Does it have something to do with this dog?" Calvin asked. Ally whined nervously, and Calvin laughed. "What, you're going to pay the mortgage by dog sitting?"

"None. Of. Your. Business." Rune fought through her fear, trying to hold her ground. Why hadn't anyone come to check on her yet? Didn't they hear her screech? "Now get out of my establishment while it's still mine," Rune said, very quietly and seriously. She stared down Calvin for an eternity while he kept smirking.

"Hey, Jasper, wanna go get a burrito down the street?" Calvin asked, breaking the tension. He looked over Rune as if she wasn't there.

"Sounds good," Jasper answered.

Calvin backed off a step as his partner moved to the side. He returned to looking at her pointedly as if to say, *'we're going to get you, and I'm going to enjoy it.'* Then they left, taking the sun with them as the clouds closed in.

Rune practically collapsed into the booth, nearly sitting on Ally, who yelped again in protest. The little dog scrambled over next to Lucky Devil, sticking both of her paws onto the table and panting.

"What the hell was that about?" Rune asked both the little dog and the inanimate devil. She rubbed her arms, trying to chase away the shakes. "Ugh, I hate this," she said.

Ally leaned forward and licked one of Rune's hands, then comically pawed at her own tongue as if to wipe away the taste.

"I need to get you home as quick as I can and get the rest of my mortgage ASAP. This is getting too serious."

The little dog growled in displeasure.

"Hey, don't growl at me, little Missy. I'm not the one who got herself turned into a dog." Saying that out loud made Rune pause as she thought about the problem. "Okay, I only know of three ways to get turned into an animal, but none of that matters because I can't reverse any of them. It would have been easy for a real wizardess. But I can't take you home like this, can I? Even with the locket, your mother could claim—well, all kinds of things. None of them good. I'll end up in jail, or worse." Rune rubbed her forehead. "You need someone with the right Talent to reverse this."

Ally looked taken aback then furrowed her eyebrows together in a clearly confused look.

"A wizard or a witch—" Rune tried to finish, but Ally barked once then jumped up to press her paw onto Rune's hand. "A voodoo priest, maybe…" Twice more, Ally barked and pressed Rune's hand before settling back. "Ally, I don't have a Talent…"

Ally growled.

"What? What is it? I don't understand you," Rune said, exasperated. "Do you need to potty or something?"

This time the dog nodded her head in a very human yes.

"Look, I'm not a sorcerer or wizard or whatever. I'm just me." Rune sat down and folded her hands on the table. Ally snorted and raised a single eyebrow at Rune.

"Man, that is creepy weird to watch," Rune muttered. The little dog narrowed its eyes. "I'm sorry. It is. I've never seen a dog act so human before." Rune sighed. This was getting off-topic. "Maybe I should pass you on to someone more qualified, and licensed." Ally whined and shook her head no.

"Oh come on, kid. Seriously, I can't help you. Even if I tried poking around in Maddie's old books—" Rune's voice broke suddenly. Shocked at herself, she lifted a hand to cover her mouth as if that would take back the words she just said. "Oh, crap," she mumbled into her hand. The tears began rolling down her face even as she realized what was happening.

Ally cocked her head again then looked around the bar as if checking to see if anybody was listening.

A lump formed at the back of Rune's throat. She swallowed hard and kept talking through the tears. "Anyway, Maddie. Aunt Maddie was *good*. She had several degrees and actually earned the title wizard from three magic schools thrice over. It wasn't just how she self-identified. So, if she was here…" the lump tightened again, and the tears spilled faster down Rune's cheeks. A sob wracked through her, and Rune cried unexpected tears of grief. Some small part of her brain registered a paw touching her.

Rune tried to lift her head to reassure Ally, but another wave crashed over her, pulling her under again. There was nothing she could do to stop it. She had no control over it, no matter how hard she tried to stop. Thoughts of Maddie kept the tears coming.

"I…. I just… miss her… so much," Rune stuttered between sobs, trying to explain the over pouring of emotion she was laying on this relative stranger, even if that stranger was currently a dog.

She was only vaguely aware of someone pressing a handkerchief into her hand. It was cool and smelled of peppermints as she held it to her hot face. Ally whined as Rune tried to wipe her eyes clear, but the tears just wouldn't stop.

Then, just as she feared, she heard someone ask from the direction of the Main Bar, "Hey, is she okay?" She thought it might have been Liam.

Warm arms walled around her, pulling Rune in so that her face pressed up against a finely tailored suit. The suit smelled wonderful and familiar. Instead of pulling away, she burrowed deeper. It felt strange but good. She didn't want Liam to see her.

"Yeah, she's okay. Thanks for asking," a warm voice rumbled from inside the suit. An arm came up to cradle her head, making it easier to feel like she was completely hidden and safe. They stayed that way as Rune cried. He didn't seem to be in a hurry to let her go. The spell broke when Rune pulled away to take a sharp, deep breath, the first in a long while.

"You going to be okay?" he finally asked, releasing his hold to let her sit up.

Rune tried to swallow. "If I can just keep these tears under control, sure."

"Look up at a light," St. Benedict said, turning her so she faced away from him, toward the light hanging over Lucky Devil's booth with its old-world, stained-glass shade. It worked. Like someone flipped off a switch, the tears trailed away, and Rune simply focused on breathing.

"Thank you," she managed to say once she was sure they were going to stay gone and she could dare look down. "Why did that work?"

He shrugged nonchalantly. "Don't know. It's one of those things. Like opening your eyes when you sneeze. We humans just can't do it. We can't cry when looking up at a light. That's why when we cry, we instinctively look down and cover our eyes to make it dark."

Rune nodded as she took in the strange factoid. "Um, well, thank you. I guess. What are you doing here?"

"Here to help you escape, in case you haven't noticed," he said as casually as if he had really said that it looked like rain. "I take it from your blank stare you haven't noticed you're surrounded."

"What are you talking about?"

St. Benedict tilted his head toward the front door in the direction of the thug brothers. "Those guys are just the tip of the iceberg. They asked you about me, didn't they?"

Blinking, Rune shifted uncomfortably in her seat. "Yeah. Did you do something?"

"Yes, I did. I put your name out there as someone who could find Anna Masterson," he said matter-of-factly.

"You did what?!"

He smiled. "I think you're feeling better."

"To whom? Who would care?"

"Well," St. Benedict blew out a breath and crossed his arms as he looked away thinking, then started ticking off his fingers. "I think I spied at least two guys from the Kodiak Corporation sitting at the bar. Maybe two other sets from smaller corps that seem to be aware of each other because they've positioned themselves at opposite ends of the room and keep giving each other the evil eye. Heh, that could be fun..." He trailed off a second as if there was a private joke in that, but Rune didn't get it.

After a pause, he continued, "They'll probably make you a money offer to start, but I expect there's a free agent or two who's thinking of just grabbing you and auctioning you off to the highest bidder."

"Who!?" Rune asked, alarmed.

He shrugged, stuffing his hands back in his pockets. "I didn't pick anybody out per se. Pretty sure the mob is in there too." On the last, he looked at her to see if she was impressed.

"All in the next room, eating breakfast in my bar?" Rune furrowed her eyebrows skeptically. "It's just the summer breakfast crowd."

"Oh, you are right. I could be making all this up. You wouldn't be able to tell if I was, though, would you? Not until it was too late." He looked down at a watch that was hidden by his coat sleeve then held the watch out to her to see. "Interesting breakfast crowd. Do they usually stay through lunch?" The watch read 11:07 am in big white digital lines.

Rune did not like this. "No, not usually."

"Hey Rune," Liam called from the doorway between the Main Bar and the Lounge Bar. "You have a couple people who want to speak to you."

"Oh yup, here they come." St Benedict practically laughed.

Rune sat bolt upright in a panic. "Why would you do something like this?"

"To compel you to help me. I think I've made my position pretty clear."

"Rune?" Liam called, sounding more unsure.

"Uh, just a minute, Liam," Rune called back. "I need to get something from my office."

"Oh, perfect, you sound like you're panicking." St. Benedict unbuttoned the middle button of his jacket as he turned.

"Of course, I'm panicking!" Rune hissed, scrambling to capture Ally. The dog girl realized too late that she was about to be scooped up and got caught by her nape, to which she yelped profusely.

"Rune!" Liam called with increasing panic as someone behind him shoved him out of their way, making him stumble to the side. He tried to catch himself on the window that was no longer there and ripped through cardboard instead.

"Liam!" Rune started forward to rescue her employee, just as the man who shoved him charged toward her. St. Benedict yanked her back and stepped to the side before Rune could be squashed flat. Instead, the man flew past, trying too late to skid to a halt and change direction. As he came back around, St. Benedict stepped back out and arm-barred him in the face, using the attacker's own momentum against him.

"We need to leave now. Head to your office," St. Benedict said with quiet urgency as he pushed Rune ahead of himself to weave between the tables.

More people had gathered at the doorway. Most prominent were a couple in business suits, both on phones making calls. As they streamed past, the woman tried to raise her hand to stop Rune with words, but Rune didn't slow. The rest of the onlookers were mostly patrons, all gaping at the excitement and chattering loudly, trying to figure out what was going on.

"St. Benedict!" their pursuer shouted, picking himself up.

"Ah, I wondered if he would recognize me," St. Benedict said, urging Rune down the hallway toward her office door. "Yes? You roared?" he called back cheekily, just as a second big fellah came at him from the side.

Rune didn't look back, but went straight to the door, fumbling for her keys as she juggled the little freaked-out teenager in her arms. "Aprax...Ab...dammit to hell, will you stop wiggling," she muttered as she managed to get her keys out of her pocket, only to drop them on the floor. She set Ally down, and scooped them up, flipping through them twice to find the one silver key with a circle head in the whole bunch, her panic making the task harder.

"Give me the girl and you can walk away from here," the aggressive man shouted. He was dressed in heavy leather with piercings in his ears.

"Does anybody ever actually take you up on that offer or do you just like saying it?" St. Benedict was asked, clearly unintimidated as the menace knocked aside one of the bar tables, which broke, separating the top from the single metal pole that supported it and rolled to the front of the room. Path cleared, he approached fast to swing a fist that he easily ducked, and sprang to tackle the guy at his midsection.

There were more shoves and bangs, underscored by Ally's yapping. Rune didn't dare look back as she finally pulled out the right key and shoved it into the lock. To her shock, her door opened on its own as someone from the other side pulled it inward. Rune gasped and stepped back out of reach. Beyond the intruder, four others ravaged her office. One man sat at her desk going through the drawers, while the other three threw papers and ripped through her possessions. The moment the door opened, they all stopped what they were doing and looked up in unison, staring at her like statues amongst the cascading papers.

"What the hell?" the man at the desk said.

Rune noticed he had horns sticking up at his hairline, and before she could remember how her mouth worked, St. Benedict appeared next to her and grabbed the door handle.

"Excuse us, wrong room," he shouted just before he pulled the door closed, ripping it out of the guy's hand.

"My office..." Rune said, staring at the pebbled window of her door in absolute shock.

"Okay, not a way out, back the way we came," St. Benedict said. He grabbed her hand to pull her after him, back down the hallway.

"My office!" Rune tried to say again as he dragged her along.

"Yes, yes, I'm sorry about that. Things got out of hand quickly. We're leaving through the front door instead."

Out in the Lounge, the second big man sat in the remains of one of her tables, now smashed to pieces. St. Benedict pulled Rune past the woozy man as he struggled to regain his feet. As she passed him, Rune realized the man was actually a troll, his big-boned, hefty size now clearer to see, as well as the telltale protruding lower canines popping up from his now bloodied lower lip.

St. Benedict tugged her forward before she could take in any more, weaving through the chairs and tables toward the daylight outside and their chance at freedom. Abruptly, Rune tore her hand out of his grasp.

"Wait! Ally!" she shouted and started back into the bar for the stupid, white dog.

"Leave her! We gotta go before someone starts shooting at us," St. Benedict tried to say, but Rune ignored him, going back for the dog that was terrified to run past the semi-prone troll.

"She's just a damn dog! Let's go!" St. Benedict shouted, grabbing the back of Rune's shirt to haul her back.

"She's not a dog! She's a seventeen-year-old girl!" Rune shouted back, trying to wrest herself away.

"What?!" He looked back at the small white dog that shook with fright staring at the troll. St. Benedict growled. "Dammit! I'll get her, get out now!!" He yanked Rune back again, this time propelling her toward the door. He dove for the dog. Ally leapt into his arms willingly, but the maneuver cost him time. The troll found its feet enough to trip St. Benedict as he tried to sprint past again. St. Benedict used his momentum to bounce off a table and land a kick at a chair, tumbling it toward the troll, hitting it hard on the side of its knee. While doing little damage, the troll did yelp and jump before getting his legs tangled with the chair, tripping him up to land hard on his butt. The whole bar shook hard enough to make the glasses rattle from the impact.

Ahead of him, Rune stopped abruptly, faced with another troll waiting at the door. It was as hulking as the one behind him and carried something in his arms, but St. Benedict didn't slow to see what it was. Chucking the damn dog out the door with a yip, St. Benedict bent quickly to pick up the long, wide metal pipe that had once been a part of a table and took a swing. It landed true, cold-cocking the troll across the jaw, dropping him to the ground with a shocked look on his face.

"Oh my god! Christopher!" Rune shouted, shooting St. Benedict an equal look of shock. "You just punched out my florist!"

"Oh," was all he said as he looked down at the troll now lying unconscious amongst broken pottery, dirt and purple flowers spilling out of the box and all over the troll's green apron. "Uh, sorry. Did I hurt it?"

"It!? What is *wrong* with you? He's a person." Rune started to kneel down next to the troll, but St. Benedict yanked her back up.

"We have to go! NOW."

"Liam! Call Christopher an ambulance!" she managed to get out before they were out the door. The street was no better, though. Three more men, two Hispanic and one birdlike person, waited in a loose semi-circle for them to exit.

"Ms. Leveau, you look like you're in need of assistance. Our employer would love to speak to you," said the birdlike creature, its voice as musical as it was menacing.

"Oooh, cartel. You guys running late? Everyone else is here already," St. Benedict joked as he put himself between Rune and the semi-circle to their right.

The birdlike person pursed its beak-like lips, vexed. "You slanderer, St. Benedict," it said, clipping the "t" at the end of his name.

"It is St. Benedict!" cut in another voice, this time to Rune and St. Benedict's left side.

"St. Augustina! You bitch! How are you?" St. Benedict said with honest delight at the sight of the tallest black woman Rune had ever seen, who happened to be pointing a gun at both of them. She was a good half-foot taller than the saint in front of her, and he was a hair taller than six feet. The business-suited gunmen with her fanned out to form an arc on either of her sides.

"Who bought up your contract?" St. Benedict asked, eyeing her backup.

The black woman smiled, her body turned sideways, gripping the gun in both hands as she sighted down it. "The government, ironically enough. Is that her?"

"Her? Her who? Which her are you referring to?" St. Benedict asked, glancing back toward the cartel threesome shifting themselves away, unsure of this new threat. Their leader fiddled its fingers like it was trying to decide something while its bird eyes flickered back and forth between the government cronies and St. Benedict.

"The one standing behind you, St. Ben. I'm not playing games with you here." St. Augustina took steps to the left, filling in the gap the cartel thugs were slowly creating. "Ms. Leveau, listen to me. I am a representative of the United Corporations government. The man you are currently with is very dangerous and a known murderer. I can offer you protection if you come with me now."

The 'dangerous and known murderer' laughed out loud even as he reached behind to grasp Rune's wrist in warning. "If you haven't noticed, you have a Saint in front of your name too, Augustina, and you are the one pointing the gun. But at who, I wonder? You have a clear shot at me, don't you? How come you haven't taken it yet?" Using Rune's wrist to guide her, St. Benedict started taking counter steps to St. Augustina's, toward the lesser threat, the cartel.

"Listen to me, Ms. Leveau, the minute you stop being useful to him, he will dispose of you," St. Augustina continued.

Rune wasn't sure what to do, turning her head back and forth amongst the combatants. None of them looked like good options, but staying with St. Benedict... well, he had been the one to get her into the mess. She just didn't know what to do.

Before she could decide, the biker-looking troll emerged from the bar. He stopped short as the cartel finally pulled their concealed weapons.

"Oh, this is bad," Rune muttered, trying to find a direction to retreat, but they were pretty well surrounded.

"Yes, the tension has ratcheted up nicely," St. Benedict answered her under his breath. "Just trying to see who is going to blow first."

"I don't want to die finding out!" Rune hissed at him.

From where she stood behind St. Benedict, Rune noticed that not only were they surrounded by hostile groups on all sides, but patrons and the corporate suits pressed up against the glass watching. The government lady spoke into her shoulder in a low voice, and the cartel guys sized up the troll with naked hatred. One of the cartel telegraphed his anxiety as he alternated between holding his gun straight up or on its side.

St. Benedict had backpedaled them toward the bar's outer wall, just to the side of the troll.

"I just want to get out of here," Rune said, in a soft, anxious voice.

Then she felt it. Something tugged just at the edge of her awareness. It felt like a Finding, but that made no sense, she wasn't looking for anything. Except a way out. Rune looked to her left and blinked at the gold thread tugging her, almost insistently, toward the alley. This was really wrong. Escape was a concept, not an object, so there was no way to "find" an escape. But the thread kept tugging, as if to say, 'this way, this way, come on.'

Glancing down at her trapped wrist, Rune tried to twist it free. "Let go of me, you're hurting me."

For a heartbeat of a second, the edges of St. Benedict's face hardened. Rune flinched, then he let her go. "Don't you dare leave me," he warned. Shivers ran down Rune's spine. He didn't wait for a reply but turned back toward the confrontation.

"Get out of here!" One of the cartel guys yelled at the troll.

"I got here first," the troll shouted back.

"Everyone put your weapons down now!" St. Augustina ordered.

Just then, Ally started to bark. That was it. The bullets flew. People inside the bar screamed and ducked away from the window. Rune found herself alone against the wall. As soon as the bullets started flying, St. Benedict shoved Rune down onto her knees before he charged straight at St. Augustina. He managed to disarm the woman before she could turn her gun from the troll back to him.

"Really?" he laughed as he got her arm in a lock. "You thought a troll was more dangerous than me?"

"I *thought* you were protecting the woman," she growled back and started exchanging counter moves with him. "You're going to lose your prize." At this point, the troll intervened, and she danced away to let St. Benedict handle it. The cartel crew, before firing any volleys, decided it wasn't really worth it. They turned and ran off. Sirens sounded in the distance, coming closer.

"Rune! Rune, where are you?" the bar manager shouted in a booming voice from the doorway.

Unable to look away to check if his prize had indeed been lost, St. Benedict instead ducked and wove around the troll. He quickly found a nice big opening to land a knee in the guy's lower solar plexus. As his opponent went down, St. Benedict scanned around for any sight of the Finder. Less than twenty feet away, he spied St. Augustina turning down an alley. St. Benedict heard the strange little dog's yap echoing from that direction.

He took off after them, his dress shoes beating the pavement, grateful once again that he had sprung for the ones that were built like a running shoe inside. He focused on catching up with St. Augustina. On a flat surface with no obstacles, he knew he'd never do it. Her legs were way too long. She was simply built for running, even before she'd been augmented. Yet, this was alley chasing and the chances of it being cluttered with boxes, trash, or even a parked truck, made St. Benedict the chasing king.

To his surprise, there wasn't much of a chase. He rounded the corner to find St. Augustina already heading back. The tall woman looked from side to side, peering at the predicted dumpsters, and inside recessed doorways to see if her prey crouched there. She spied St. Benedict and put on a burst of speed to grab him by his coat front, using her augmented acceleration to bull rush him. He tried to dodge, but he had been going at a dead run, and without the joint-enhancing augmentations, he had no chance of dodging her. Despite his added thrust, the other Saint managed to turn just a little to crush him effectively, slamming his head against the alley wall.

"You should have gotten the modifications," St. Augustina gloated.

St. Benedict forced a breath, surprised that his ribs weren't cracked, even while he wondered if his head was. "Oh, you know, I still want to walk if I get to be old. You know, not use it up all at once..." St. Augustina's face fell and she pulled him back to slam him against the wall again, cutting him off.

"Where is she, St. Benedict!?" she shouted in his face.

"I don't..." he made a grab at her hands, which proved difficult to do when stunned. She pulled him away and slammed his head against the wall a third time, and he saw birdies amongst the stars.

"You must have a meeting place... Where are you going to meet up? You always have contingency plans," she continued.

"She's not in this alley?" St. Benedict asked, looking past her with genuine alarm.

St. Augustina blinked twice, then dropped him. He collapsed to the ground like a sack of potatoes, sending a bolt of shock up his spine.

"Now I've really got to visit my chiropractor," he moaned as he shifted onto one buttock, using his thigh against the dirty ground to balance. "Oh, my aching tailbone."

"You lost her," St. Augustina accused as she continued to look up and down the alley. "Who was she, St. Benedict?"

"You chased after her, and you don't even know why?"

"I know that you were going after someone who could find the Masterson files. Was that her?" Then something passed over St. Augustina's face, and her voice dropped an octave. "Or was she..."

"No," he practically shouted. "She wasn't Anna. She was someone who was going to help me find Anna." He rubbed his forehead, surprised to find his fedora still on his head, even if the brim was ruined. "God, I'm tired."

"Stay out of my way," St. Augustina warned him as she walked away.

"Aren't you going to say, 'this isn't over,' while you're at it?" St. Benedict sassed.

The other Saint didn't look around as she continued walking, shoulders stiff with dignity. St. Benedict let the jibes go and focused on breathing. This job had gone sideways too fast.

"Dammit. Where the heck did she go? How am I going to find her now?"

CHAPTER 6

"So, are you just going to sit there, or are we, what, breaking for lunch? You haven't moved for like five minutes and you're sitting in garbage," said a voice in St. Benedict's ear.

He opened his eyes to find he still leaned against the wall in the only patch of afternoon sunshine in the whole alley. Indeed, he sat amongst a few bags of garbage that didn't have the best of smells, yet he still didn't feel inclined to move. It had been a couple of minutes since St. Augustina had disappeared.

"I'm just asking because if you're going to take a nap, then Zita and I are going to have lunch or afternoon tea or something."

"I'm getting up," St. Benedict said. He pushed his achy body and soul up to his feet, needing to lean back against the wall a second to steady his spinning head. St. Augustina must have thrown him harder against the wall than he realized.

"Oh, look! Hey, you're up. Good job," the voice in his ear cheered. "St. Augustina still packs a punch, right?"

"The troll helped," St. Benedict said. As he stretched, he heard his back pop in a few places.

"Which one? The biker troll or that poor florist?"

"Shut up," St. Benedict growled.

"Well, you know, any fight you can walk away from," the voice continued unhelpfully.

"Did you get any footage on where she went?" St. Benedict asked, turning to walk out of the alley, finding his feet as he gained momentum.

"Yes, St. Augustina has left the area…"

"Not her, the Talent," St. Benedict said. At the end of the alley, he hesitated, checking the area with a slow, steady gaze, first toward the

Lucky Devil, then across the street, then down to the right. A crowd had gathered in front of the bar, as well as an ambulance. A couple of corporate police officers from different districts stood there, but they seemed to be arguing more about who had jurisdiction than actually trying to do their jobs. The florist that St. Benedict had punched out sat at the back of the ambulance, awake, and receiving treatment while trying to give his statement to one of the officers. The bar's manager argued with a plainclothes detective who also argued with another plainclothes detective; each wore the emblems of their respective corps on the breast pockets of their suit jackets.

"Where are you parked?" St. Benedict muttered as he backed away from the street just as two more officers started in his direction. St. Benedict turned and headed the other way, ducking into an alcove at the last second as the police officers stopped at the mouth of the alley.

"We're three blocks away, near that frozen yogurt shop. I mean, two klicks to the west—"

"I know where it is," St. Benedict interrupted in a harsh whisper, "and that's not how a klick works."

The officers moved away from the alley without entering it, but St. Benedict didn't think that would be for long. They would canvas the whole area soon. He hurried to the back, where the alley split into a T junction. Unfortunately, to the right took him past the bar, increasing his chances of getting caught; and to the left, a chained metal gate blocked his way. He noted the brick window ledge from the last two centuries, complete with blocked glass that stuck out of the wall about halfway up by the gate.

Blowing out a breath, St. Benedict shook out his arms and rolled his shoulders, then ran toward the gate, a little to the left. Taking a running leap, he pushed off the window ledge. His legs swung to the right as he landed a hand on the bar at the top and propelled himself over the gate with minimal noise. He landed easily on the other side, grateful that nothing waited there to break his legs or eat his face.

Having cleared that hurdle, he turned and headed for a cross-street a block and a half away. He turned the corner and made his way toward a nondescript, black van parked down the street, walking so as not to attract too much attention.

"Nice job on getting your ass kicked by the way. That was top rate. I lost ten bucks off of you."

"That's nice, Malachi. I'll buy you a latte," St. Benedict said.

"Zita got coffee already. Yours is waiting here." Malachi's voice grew distant like it did when he focused on something else.

"Marry that naga right now, Malachi, or I'm going to steal her from you," St. Benedict said as he reached out for the handle of the sliding door of the van.

"Hey, that's my woman you're talking about," Malachi said to his face as St. Benedict opened the van and practically fell inside at the tech's feet, his destroyed hat finally falling off.

"Wow, you look worse than on the cameras." Malachi kicked St. Benedict's legs the rest of the way into the van so he could shut the door. As it closed, the automatic lights lining the top flickered back on, casting a blue-tinged, white light. The inside of the van was decked out with computers and monitors along one side, and the rest of the gear stowed in stacked black, plastic crates on the other. The roof of the van was high enough that if St. Benedict could stand, he'd only need to duck his head a few inches with his hat off.

For now, he just stared up at the lights, feeling the cold metal floor of the van against his back, while Malachi sat back down in front of the monitors and started typing away at the keyboards.

As Malachi typed one-handed, he grabbed up a plastic cup filled with a caramel-colored liquid. It had once been a frozen coffee but was now more slush than anything.

"For milord," Malachi said as he passed it to St. Benedict on the floor, continuing to type with the other hand. St. Benedict took it gratefully and pressed the cold side of the plastic against his forehead, the condensation a blessed relief after the workout he just had.

"Is this your sandwich?" St. Benedict asked, spying it as he sat up to take a sip. There were two sandwich halves, still wrapped in paper, one of them already mostly eaten, the other untouched. Taking up the untainted half, from the plate balanced between two spare monitors sitting on the van's floor, St. Benedict devoured it like a starving man.

"Yes, that's..." Malachi started, but noticed too late that St. Benedict was already halfway through, "was mine. Help yourself, I guess."

"Seriously, ever since yesterday I cannot get enough to eat," St. Benedict said with a full mouth, before slurping half the melting mocha latte after it.

Malachi tapped irritatedly at his keyboard as St. Benedict continued to eat.

"Did you get anything?" St. Benedict asked.

"Well, I do have a lovely view of your troll friend down there on the street. After you got him good in the gonads, he limped off," Malachi said.

"I didn't hit him in the gonads. I hit him in the bladder. You hit him in the gonads, he may drop, or he may just get mad. Hit him in the bladder, fight's over, end of story." St. Benedict pulled up another stool to sit down right behind Malachi, looking at the three monitors that showed different angles of the street below.

"Okay, I didn't ask, but I'll make a note of that," Malachi said dryly and continued tapping away.

"What do we have here?" St. Benedict asked.

"I assume you mean the street cameras, because that question so clearly explains what you're talking about. Such a question, I might note, only a person who has worked with you for as many years as I have could decipher. We are so in sync, you and I, that I can read your thoughts as if they were my own."

"Oh yeah? And what are my thoughts saying right now?"

Malachi looked over his shoulder. "Uh, that I should talk about the task at hand before you pull my brains out through my nostrils," he said.

"Wow, that's amazing!" St. Benedict said with hooded eyes before he took another pull on his latte.

"Right. So, what we have here is the red-light camera from the intersection, a security camera that was Wi-Fi-enabled across the street at the We Buy Gold store, and this last one is some random camera that I can't really figure out where it's coming from, but we have a good shot of the alley so, hey, bonus right?"

St. Benedict didn't answer. He just leaned forward and studied the screen of the last camera. The images from the traffic light camera and the Wi-Fi camera were both low-resolution color, but the images from the mystery camera were high-resolution black-and-white. Everything in the alley was crystal clear.

"Where on earth did she go?"

"Dude, do you have to sit that close? I think you sat in something," Malachi complained, covering his nose with his hand as he talked.

"Where's Zita?"

"She's spending her ill-gotten ten bucks," Malachi answered.

St. Benedict stood up and started shedding his corrupted clothes, pulling fresh ones from one of the bins.

"I think we should just give this one up, Boss. I really don't know what you were thinking, leaking her name to the Dark Web like that."

"Because she was being stubborn and wouldn't take the money, and I don't have the time to seduce her. That means the perception of threat," St. Benedict said. He dropped his slacks, then underwear, which had also been soaked through by whatever he had sat in on the street, before ripping open a fresh pack from the bin.

"Yes, yes. Lovely view by the way," Malachi said, glancing right over his shoulder straight into a full moon.

"Malachi…"

"I'm talking about the street. Geez, not everything revolves around your perfectly god-like gluts," Malachi smarted back. St. Benedict rolled his eyes and tugged a soft, clean black shirt over his head. "Anyway, I think the threat is more than perceived. What exactly did you post out there?" Malachi asked, easily yielding the keyboards so that he could finish off what was left of his half-eaten sandwich.

"That she holds the secret to finding the Masterson Files," St. Benedict said, giving the keyboard a few taps the screen switched windows to the Dark Web message board. A few more taps shut his post down and wiped out anything that would trace to the van. Even if unlikely, best to be thorough.

"Is that true? Does she know?"

The Saint sighed. "It'd better be." He picked up his fedora and gave it a quick reshape. SOnce it was satisfactory, he set it back on his head after raking his fingers back through his hair, tracing the scar hidden underneath his locks.

"So, how are we going to find her, Boss? I don't even really understand how she got away."

"Well, start with this," he said and opened his hand. Instantly, a holographic screen flashed in his palm with data streams running from top to bottom. "I got a chance to clone one of St. Augustina's phones in the scuffle."

"Score, Boss!" Malachi took out his scan wand to pass over St. Benedict's hand. Suddenly, St. Benedict lost his balance, falling onto a stool in the process.

"Hey, you okay?" Malachi asked, concerned.

"Yeah, yeah, fine. That was weird." St. Benedict brushed it off as he righted himself.

The smaller man gave St. Benedict an assessing look. "Is it your augmentations?"

"Probably not."

"Maybe you should lay off using them for a while. You're probably pushing your capability again. If we have another incident like last week, you know I'm going to have to tell Zita."

Just then, the side of the van opened up.

"Hey, Zita, what did you spend your ten bucks on?" Malachi asked, affecting a more cheerful tone as he exchanged a glance with St. Benedict.

Zita didn't seem to notice that they were talking about her. The half-woman, half-snake slid sideways into the van and pulled the door shut behind her with the tip of her tail. Her skin was a warm brown that disappeared beneath a deep maroon, empire-line dress, and reemerged beneath the hemline as a long scaly white body, patched with red and black marks along her backside. She smiled brightly, her sweetheart face set with liquid black eyes that would make a puppy envious, all framed by long, wavy, black hair that shone like a moonlit sky.

St. Benedict watched Malachi's brain scramble at the sight of her. She didn't seem to notice her boyfriend's involuntary stare as she rose up to show him her purchases.

"Mocha yogurt or Blueberry surprise?" she asked, holding out two cups covered in domes, each housing swirls of frozen yogurt inside.

St. Benedict elbowed Malachi, restarting his brain. "Oh! Yeah. Mocha, Please," he managed, one word at a time.

"Oh, sorry, Boss. I didn't get one for you," she said, as she noticed St. Benedict.

"Don't worry about it." He turned back to the monitors to examine them more closely. "Malachi, play back the moment when she disappeared."

"I'll try, but I gotta warn you, Boss, the equipment went pretty wonky at that point." Malachi tapped like lightning at the keyboard. Zita set his yogurt next to him, visibly perturbed that he hadn't taken it.

"Zita, we need to vacate this area soon. Can you get up on the police scanner and keep tabs on what they're doing?" St. Benedict asked her.

She nodded before sliding her way up to the front and into the driver's seat. There she took up a set of headphones and set them on her head.

"For all the good it's going to do us," Malachi grumbled. "Alright, here is right before the fight broke out. You've got the damsel-in-distress pinned behind you against the wall. She looks to her right. I'm not sure what this little white spot is..."

"It's a dog," St. Benedict said.

"Okay, then it's a dog. She sees it, then there you go pushing her down as you rush the troll, I think, and she takes off toward the right.

Now switching to the alley camera, we see her pick up the white thing...the dog, and she goes into the alley and..."

The gray screen showing the footage of the alley warped and went wavy, then disintegrated into static.

"And that's all we got until a minute later the picture just comes back. I have no clue what she did, but she was just gone."

"She used magic," St. Benedict said confidently and pulled the keyboard toward himself. "And it was strong enough to distort the electronics around it."

"Once again, technology is made useless by magic, so why do we even bother? Because of our fallible, hominal nature to give Nature the double deuces in our pursuit of supremacy?!" Malachi declared dramatically.

"All hail the revolution," St. Benedict and Zita said in bored unison.

"I'm serious guys, the ethical and philosophical implications—"

"Can it wait until another day? We need to work this problem."

"Which is? I forget?" Malachi reached for his frozen yogurt. Zita gave Malachi a warning look from across the van. He shrugged at her, mouthing 'What?'

St. Benedict pretended not to see.

"The problem of locating the Talent."

"You know it's ironic isn't it?" Zita called from the front. "She is a Talent who's theoretically known for finding lost things, and we lost her, so we need her to find herself."

"We need her to find Anna Masterson," St. Benedict corrected.

"If she's still alive," Malachi intercut.

"To find Justin Masterson—" St. Benedict tried to continue.

"If he even exists!" Malachi cut him off.

"The research is real. And that is what Maxamillion wants, so we better get it first," St. Benedict warned and took away Malachi's yogurt, eating it himself.

"And like I said, we have all this tech, and even if I started doing internet searches now, we are not going to find her anytime soon, and I'm pretty sure that if we don't find her in the next hour, someone else will, thanks to our fearless leader's miscalculation. Or is it machinations? Would machinations make more sense?"

"Did we get a clear shot of her face?" St. Benedict asked, ignoring him.

"Yes," Malachi groaned, then popped up a low-resolution image on the lowest left screen.

"Alright, good. We can use this to run a search if we can hack into the local camera network for this immediate neighborhood," St. Benedict said.

"Oh, yeah, it's just as easy as that," Malachi smarted.

"Isn't it?" Zita asked from the front. She had one ear out of the headphones so she could listen to both the scanner and the conversation going on a few feet from her.

"Anything on the scanner?" St. Benedict asked, pulling up his stool to Malachi's keyboard set-up.

"Yes, it sounds like the Kodiak Corporation won the right to investigate the case, but Atlantech and Synerpro are still slow to withdraw and turn over evidence," Zita reported.

"I bet Kodiak has more cameras. Malachi, see if you can hack into the municipal camera network."

"What good is that going to do? Magic crashes and messes with cameras. The municipal camera network is a joke," Malachi whined, even as he moved over to the other keyboard to do as he was told.

"We can find her if we run a facial recognition algorithm." St. Benedict fed Rune's picture through several programs at once, sharpening and modifying the image as best he could.

"Okay, fine, I'll play twenty questions. How?"

"Shut up and let me think," St. Benedict said.

"Alright, well, while you think, let me just point out to the room that we don't have a supercomputer to run that kind of search. Not that you're listening," Malachi grumbled as he lapsed into silence.

"Are you in the network yet?"

"Five minutes," Malachi answered, drumming the computer keys in concert with St. Benedict.

St. Benedict cycled back the footage recorded from the camera facing the alley and watched it past the moment after St. Augustina kicked his "god-like gluts."

On-screen, he could see himself doing his dash back and forth between the two ends of the alley before setting himself against the wall. St. Augustina backed up into the alley a few heartbeats later, with a phone pressed to her ear to beat him up in reverse. He stopped the footage and let it play forward.

"She called someone," St. Benedict said softly and looked at a fourth monitor that showed rows of numbers being added inside little boxes. A new one slid up from the bottom at irregular intervals, making the whole tower shift up on the screen as it did.

"Her team's on these cameras too," Malachi said around a mouthful of yogurt.

"You're sure?"

Malachi tapped his screen. "That's government coding, I'd stake my last ten dollars on it."

"I thought you lost that to Zita?"

"Correct," Zita called from the front.

St. Benedict nodded. "And with her access to the government's supercomputers, they'll be running facial recognition software on the Talent if St. Augustina isn't already."

"And we don't have a supercomputer, so we're screwed," Malachi said.

"What are you talking about? I am a supercomputer."

"Dammit, St. Ben, this is why I'm telling you we need to abort this whole mission," Malachi started again, but St. Benedict only leaned back in his seat to see up front clearly.

"Zita, I need assistance."

The naga took off the headset and slid off the seat toward the back of the van. She opened one of the crates and took out a stethoscope and a folded up blood pressure cuff, strapping the latter onto St. Benedict's upper arm before putting the ends of the stethoscope in her ears. With professional detachment, she stared at her watch to count as she pumped.

"I hate this, I hate this so much," Malachi said.

"It'll be fine." St. Benedict stared straight at the screen in front of him before closing his eyes. "We'll piggyback off of the results of the government search. They'll use her ID picture to try to find her... We need to substitute that image with the one I just cooked up." He nodded at the screen in front of him. "Implanting it will throw their software off the chase a bit, while we actually find her."

"This is stupid. You're going to fry your brain," Malachi continued, as Zita began unhooking the blood pressure cuff.

"Your blood pressure is a little on the high side," she reported and then pulled out a small pouch of acupuncture needles from her medical crate.

"It's been a stressful morning. We don't have time for that. Is it acceptable?" St. Benedict said, gesturing a hand for her to put them away.

She shrugged and complied. "Technically."

"If you do this, St. Benedict, I am out, you hear me?" Malachi bluffed.

"Okay, fine. See you later. I'll let you how it turns out," St. Benedict called him on it.

Malachi narrowed his eyes. "Can you at least promise this isn't going to short out your brain?"

St. Benedict turned and grasped Malachi by the chin, looking passionately into his eyes. "I love you, too," he said with intense sincerity.

"Okay, that's enough. Unhand my man before you give him a complex," Zita chided as she disengaged St. Benedict's hand.

Malachi couldn't help himself. He started chuckling. "You're an idiot, and you could be a potato in a minute."

"And I could get a bullet in the head a minute later. Are we into St. Augustina's feed?"

"Yes, and our defenses are holding, so unless they have some amazing new tech I don't know about, we should be undetected in the background noise. What do you want up on the screen in front of you?"

"Everything, just let me control it," St. Benedict said, getting comfortable on his chair.

"Okay, hat off," Zita said, holding out the body pads to stick to his temples, laying the wires with a practiced hand over his shoulders so they were out of his way.

"Is the augconnect enabled?" St. Benedict asked, running final checks as he let Zita do her thing.

"Go ahead and connect your ocular implants now," Malachi confirmed.

St. Benedict drew a deep breath in with his eyes closed. He could hear Malachi's slight wheezing breath and smell Zita's serpentine musk as she stood near, monitoring his EEG patterns, though he had no idea what she saw in the mess of lines. He put them both out of his mind and focused.

He didn't even realize he had opened his eyes. He no longer saw the computer in front of him or even the van for that matter. He saw inside the computer itself, in an impossible world of codes and figures. He had never been able to clearly describe what he felt or even saw when he attempted this. Everyone else he knew who had the ocular implants put in lost the ability to still see the real world, and a couple others had gone mad instantly after their first leap into cyberspace. In fact, this particular augmentation had been shelved indefinitely.

"Malachi, upload the replacement search parameters now," he said, though his voice sounded far, far away to himself. "I'm going in."

Suddenly, his brain flooded with information. Distantly, he heard his body cry out in pain, but it wasn't much of a concern, really, just more information. Important information. If the intake was beyond his tolerance, Zita would have pulled him out already. He had to focus on the task at hand. Images spun past and around him from all directions. Neat lines of code were sifted and interpreted into visual representations that those outside the computer could understand. The stream of data moved at an incredible pace, faster than the human mind could ever hope to. Towering stacks of data sifted through and checked and rechecked, flashing bits of light all around and above, as St. Benedict floated downward amongst them, doing what no computer could ever do.

Take a leap of logic.

While the code cycled through and continued to shuffle its information stacks, St. Benedict waited, watching as it discarded the "not right" data. He let the supercomputer do the work for him, waiting for that feeling to come.

It came and he almost missed it. Way down in the stack pulsed a sensation of "right data" with nothing to prove itself except the feeling of rightness about it. St. Benedict snatched up the data file and tossed it onto the far-right monitor, where he knew Malachi was waiting to catch and process. Three more pieces of data flitted by and St. Benedict caught two. The third went into the whirl, caught by the supercomputer and gone before St. Benedict could do anything about it.

"I think we got it! Holy crap, that is cool! St. Benedict, quit out. Quit out!"

St. Benedict knew he could go now, return his consciousness to his body, but something else beckoned to him. He peered — though that wasn't really the right word — into the data stream. It was like looking into the depths of the ocean. Then the ocean of data stared back.

Before he could react, a shock of pure power hit him, feeding back into his real body. He tried to quit out, but it was too hard. He couldn't drag himself back through the rush of information and hold his mind together. Something was aware of him. Something that was not the supercomputer. Something that searched for him. It had sent out that feeler of electrical code to hold him while it tried to analyze him.

Far away, he could hear the voices of his team.

"Zita, what's happening?"

"We need to unhook him," she said urgently.

"Won't that definitely fry his brain?"

St. Benedict tried to move, to leap back to where he knew his exit was, but he couldn't close his eyes. His body hurt, it was bleeding. He screamed at the pain. Whatever had him seemed to be delighting in his pain and agony.

Then the pain stopped. And St. Benedict couldn't see a thing.

"St. Benedict? Answer me!" Zita ordered, and he tried to fight whatever it was that was covering his face.

"Don't panic, man!" Malachi said from behind. "Zita, unplug everything now! It's frying our sys—"

"Keep his eyes covered!" Zita shouted as she struggled to hold St. Benedict's arms.

"Oh shit! The augconnect. I didn't disengage the augconnect!" Malachi let go of St. Benedict's face, where he had been covering the Saint's eyes with his hands.

St. Benedict's eyes glowed an inhuman bright blue as if lit from within by lightning, the lids pulled all the way back to show the whites dulled by the blue irises.

"Malachi!" Zita struggled as St. Benedict began to convulse, almost throwing himself and her out of the chair.

"I got it! I got it!" Malachi shouted, and the light went out in St. Benedict's eyes.

St. Benedict laid still on the floor of the van, Zita next to him, breathing hard as Malachi rushed back to them to flip St. Benedict onto his back and listen to his breathing.

"Fuck! Fuck," he whispered before going still, his ear to his friend's chest.

"I'm still alive," St. Benedict croaked out, pushing Malachi off of him, "And I can't breathe."

"This was not worth it, man. This was not at all worth it!" Malachi cursed before punching one of the bins with the side of his fist. "Ow!"

"It was completely worth it," St. Benedict said, sitting up a little to point at the far monitor. "Look. We got her." Then the monitor blinked black as everything in the van shorted out.

"Oh, great! Do we? Do we!?" Malachi roared throwing himself onto the ground.

"What was that thing?" Zita asked as she touched St. Benedict's sweaty forehead gently.

"I think a very hostile security program," he lied as he brushed her fingers away and sat up. "Malachi, check the backup for the pirated file, it'll be in there. We've got a Talent to find."

CHAPTER 7

Rune tromped down the street, carrying Ally in her arms as she walked. It had been a rough day so far, and it seemed like it was only going to get worse.

It had been a shock to find the magical door out in the alley. Typically, her Finding magic didn't work to reveal vague concepts like "an escape route." Yet, there was the door, her magic leading her straight to it. It wasn't even locked with a magic password, she just went right through it, and it dumped her out a neighborhood away. Most people would miss it as it looked like a brick wall. Ally had not been willing to go through, fighting her tooth and claw every step through.

Ally was not a very agreeable dog, and Rune was starting to believe not a very agreeable person in general. At the moment, she had Ally locked down in her arms, but she had made several attempts at squirming away. Rune was already pretty scratched up from the dog's very sharp doggie nails penetrating through the thin clothe of her sleeves. Now the damn teenager-turned-dog was whining so pitiably, people on the street were giving them looks.

"Shush! Will you cut it out?! You're the one who refused to wear a leash. The city has dog walking laws, you know," Rune hissed under her breath. She nodded and smiled at an elderly lady who looked down her nose at Rune as Ally made another attempt to escape.

"What is your problem? Why are you trying to run away? Seriously, everyone thinks I stole you or something."

Ally whined again and tried to lean forward so her nose pointed at the ground.

"I would put you down and let you walk, but you keep bolting on me," Rune said, leash laws be damned, Yet, Rune couldn't get a recognizable agreement from the teenager, so she hitched her back up in her arms again. "What am I supposed to do? I have to take you home to your mother and maybe try to explain the situation. Again." Rune could hear how bad that sounded to her own ears. "If I'm lucky, she'll only call the cops on me."

Ally barked that sharp yip that hurt Rune's ears, but she ignored the dog and focused on trying to find her way to the little bitch's house — pun intended. Rune tried to use Ally herself as the catalyst, but it was not going well at all, connecting the kid to her home. She knew that Ally lived somewhere to the north end of Chicago, because she got a clear tug that way a few times, but then her steps would start going southward as the desire of her charge would take over. The change of the intention kept confusing the magic sending her Finding southward. Which essentially sent them in circles.

"Will you cut it out!" Rune said after another hour of walking, "I'm exhausted! You need to go home, you idiot!"

The little dog-girl only growled in response. Rune growled back, which was not helping communication.

"Okay, fine. I know we need to go north. I'm going to get on the CTA," Rune declared when they were in sight of a CTA station.

This one was part of the Red Line and would take them straight north along the Lakeshore. As she imagined how good it was going to feel to sit down, Rune tapped her OmniSin and started to go through the turnstile, when she was stopped by a CTA attendant.

"You can't take your dog in there," said the short, round, annoyed looking woman with artificial strawberry blonde hair and no time for anybody.

"What?" Rune asked, deciding to play dumb. She did not need this right now.

"You can't take your dog. You have to have it in a carrier," she repeated.

"It's not my dog," Rune tried.

"I don't care. You got to have your dog in a carrier. Then you can take it on the train," she repeated firmly.

"But I've already paid my fare," Rune complained, gesturing with her card at the turnstile.

"Well, you should have had the dog in a carrier," she countered, like a customer service ninja.

"But I told you, this isn't my dog. I'm taking it back to its owner. I don't have a carrier." Rune put as much pleading into her voice as she could manage.

"Do we have a problem here?" the attendant asked, her own voice taking on a threatening edge like she was going to physically throw down with Rune right here and now.

Rune wanted to say, 'Obviously, we have a problem here. You won't let me through after I paid my fare, bitch,' but that would get her noticed and still stuck on the wrong side of the turnstile. So instead, Rune kept giving her a dirty look as she backed out from the station with the squirmy dog-girl under her arm.

"All I want is to sit down," she whined, mostly to herself, but she was in a part of Chicago she didn't know very well and had no clue where she would find a free place to sit that allowed dogs.

"Okay, how about we get a cab? I'm sure one of these will take us north. I'm about to make a boatload of money on this job. I can spring for a cab," she said, again mostly to herself and turned to try to hail one.

Not missing a beat, Ally chose that moment to squirm with all of her little might, catching Rune's sleeves, which scraped her claws along Rune's bare arm. The tactic worked. Yelping in pain, Rune dropped her. The minute Ally hit the ground, she took off down the block. Rune shouted her head off after her, but Ally kept running until she disappeared around the corner. People stared at Rune but nobody moved to stop the dog.

Rune was not a runner. About three blocks later, she had to stop. She could see Ally ahead of her, running across the street with barely a glance at the oncoming traffic, but Rune just couldn't keep up.

"Dammit, dammit, dammit!" she heaved out, tucking a finger into a pouch on her belt to pull out a handkerchief, "I really need to take up running." Pushing herself forward, she started up again, going at a light jog. The thought flitted through her head to just let Ally go, and leave Chicagoland forever.

"Without money, legal OmniSin, or even my name, and then the bar gets repossessed, so no home to go home to," Rune reminded herself out loud. "Gods, I'm a failure."

As Rune chased her charge, gripping the necklace so she at least didn't lose what direction she needed to go, she wondered if she was being chased in turn. A strange feeling of being watched washed down her back, one she had never felt before, then was gone as quickly as it came.

She almost didn't see the strange woman approach her. A tattered shirt of sherbet orange draped the woman's thin, bony frame. Over that, she wore a doublet coat of burnt orange, like one might see at a Renaissance Faire, held on with a hodge-podge of 'buttons' made with whatever was at hand; a safety pin, a kazoo tied around the middle with orange yarn, and a scarab that looked like it had been dipped in gold. She had a long skirt made entirely of strips of orange, from burning sun to almost white to pumpkin to the cusp of red. Orange Croc sandals encased each foot. Her hair was tied back with a long sun-orange ribbon across her forehead, with further strips creating a fringe around her face, and a long feather, looking like someone had tried to dip it into orange paint, bounced straight up out of the band. By contrast, her long hair was a bright white and badly in need of washing.

Rune stopped short on the sidewalk at the sight of the woman, surprise painted across her face. Everything about the woman screamed magic, but that didn't mean anything, really. She was probably a magical person of some kind, but she could also be an eccentric old woman. This was Chicago... But she *was* probably a magical person of some kind.

Rune gulped down burning breaths as the woman approached her, bearing a little white dog in her arms.

"I think you lost someone," the woman said with a big smile, showing off fewer teeth than all the ones that were missing.

"Oh my gosh! Thank you so much," Rune said, rushing forward to take Ally from her. The dog gave the orange lady a dirty look. "You scared me, you dumb...dog."

"Ah, yes. My dogs are my kids, too," the orange lady said.

"Uh, yeah. Yeah, she is. My little Ally," Rune said, forcing a smile as she hugged the squirming dog a bit too tight.

"She's so sweet," the orange lady said.

"Yeah, she's having a rough day. She's run away from home, isn't that right, Ally?" Rune said in a baby voice, and the darling dog growled back.

"You've run away from home?" The orange lady's face became very concerned, and then she leaned in a bit conspiratorially. "Is there trouble at home, dear?"

"Oh no, not like that... I'm just... I mean. Well," Rune said flustered, "I guess. I can't exactly go home... right now... But I should be able to soon. I mean, I have a home of my own."

"That's alright, my dear. I know. We all have troubles in our lives." The orange lady wrapped her arms around Rune.

"And we're hugging, okay." Rune tried not to crush Ally.

"It's always darkest before the dawn. Is there any way that I can help you?" the orange lady asked.

"I just really need a place to rest a moment and figure out my next move," Rune assured her.

"Come with me. I have a special place you can go," the orange lady said, linking her arm with Rune.

"Um, thank you. I guess I just need to keep a low profile right now." Rune let the orange lady walk her back down the block.

It was about mid-block when the woman took a sharp turn to the left down a narrow walkway between the two buildings. It was clean and neat with a light sconce halfway down that would light up at night, but now stood dark at mid-afternoon. Rune hesitated at the entrance to the walkway, but the orange lady tightened her grip on her arm and dragged Rune after her.

"Where are we going?" Rune asked, unsure, realizing too late that she was walking compliantly with a strange stranger to an unknown dark place and no one in the world knew where she was.

"It's a surprise, dear," the orange lady said in a mischievously sinister voice.

Ally whined in Rune's arms. Rune was on the verge of turning and running, when the orange lady grabbed her upper arm harder and forced her through a large oaken-colored door, set with glass panes.

"Congratulations! You are our one-millionth customer!"

Streamers and confetti burst from everywhere as Rune and Ally found themselves in the midst of an insane celebration. A large crowd of people stood in an open area cheering and clapping while video cameras reflected back Rune's astonished face on a half dozen monitors all around the room. Above the crowd, in the open space of what seemed like a large parking lot was a banner that said 'The Dog House's 5th annual Pet-tastic Celebration!!!'.

"Welcome to the Dog House's fifth annual Pet-tastic Celebration where this retailer of pet goods and services who dedicates fifty percent of their proceeds to animal-related charities has just welcomed its one-millionth customer!" a woman in a smart business suit and extreme hair said into a microphone she wielded like a baton. "What's your name, Hon?"

"Well, I … I just…"

"Oh my, aren't you sweet? She's shy!" the businesswoman—or wannabe game show host—said to the crowd, and there were echoing aahs and encouraging, pitiable smiles.

"Uh, Rune," she finally spit out.

"And your little dog? What a sweetie," the woman said.

"Ally, but she's…"

The orange lady reappeared and thrust a large basket full of dog products all tied with a huge red bow and covered with little dog bones at Rune.

"Boy, I bet you didn't expect that you'd encounter this on your way to our store today. What did you come in here for anyway?" the woman continued.

"Uh, just looking for a place to hang out for a while," Rune said.

"And you chose our store to come to, just to spend time! That's wonderful. Oh, where are my manners? I am the manager here, you can call me Sheryl. And let me be the first to welcome you!"

"You already did," Rune said, but the manager didn't lose any steam.

"The Dog House is absolutely a great place to come in and peruse because our customers are not just customers. They are part of our family." Ally started barking. "And our furry family, too!"

As people came up and congratulated Rune, the orange lady pulled a harness out of the basket and held it out toward Ally.

"Store policy says that all dogs have to have a leash or collar. Oh my, she likes to wiggle, doesn't she!" the orange lady said and helped Rune get a harness and leash on a distraught Ally, who mourned pitifully despite the jubilation around them.

"Safety is our number one concern," the manager said into her mic, sounding a little strained by Ally's poor showing.

A flood of other people came up to congratulate Rune, and at some point, someone thrust a piece of cake into her hands, followed by several cups of punch, most of which Rune did not drink. Pictures flashed and people chatted, mostly to each other, until the orange lady approached her again.

"Isn't this a nice surprise?" she asked, chumming up to Rune in a way that was too friendly too fast.

"Yes, yes," Rune lied, trying to find a way to take a step back without being rude. What she really wanted to do was flat out run away. How long would it take before those looking for her found her?

That was when she saw him standing across the room, finishing off a piece of cake. He wasn't looking in her direction, just seemed to be casually scanning the room. Rune turned away just before she thought his eyes would spot her.

"What is it, dear?"

"Uh, I just thought I saw someone," Rune said, trying to cover her panic. "Just an old boyfriend that I really don't want to see again. Nothing serious, just… just that." She smiled unconvincing, hearing the lie echo in her own ears.

"Where?" the orange lady asked. Rune dared a peek over her shoulder. He still stood in the same spot, next to the table with the remains of the bone-shaped cake and several more pieces waiting to be claimed on the white tablecloth. With his back to them, he was looking down at the cakes as if he was divining deep meaning from them. Then he selected another plate and started eating again.

"That handsome fellow at the cake table?" the orange lady asked, following Rune's line of sight. "The one with the fedora?"

Rune took another look. The suit was gone, and instead, he wore a charcoal-colored, soft shirt with sleeves that stopped midway up his forearms. He had on dark cargo pants. The only thing he still wore from earlier in the day was his fedora, though it looked more battered. "Would it be alright if I bailed at this point?" Rune asked, bending down to pick up Ally.

"Ms. Leveau? May I have a moment of your time?"

Rune turned in time to come face to face with a serpent woman with large, colorful wings protruding through the back of her very dignified blue pinstriped suit. She was the same height as Rune, except for the feather crest she had on the top of her head instead of hair. It added another four inches, making her seem taller. Before Rune could say anything, she flipped out a card and presented it to Rune between two finely-manicured talons on the tips of her fingers.

"My name is Fernanda Hamilton-Gonzalez, and I represent a party who is interested in your services. May I have a moment of your time?" she asked formally.

"Um, well, as you can see…" Rune tried to take the card and hold Ally at the same time, but Ally won her freedom again.

"Congratulations, by the way, on your win today. I personally have been coming to this store since it opened. I have a Pekinese at home." She smiled down at Ally as she said it. The way she smiled made Rune wonder if she planned on eating the dog.

"Oh. That's nice," Rune said.

"Indeed, yes," she agreed and then cleared her throat. "As you can see, Ms. Leveau, I represent a firm that would like to offer you a special opportunity for a position that is specific to your unique skill set. That is, if you're interested." Rune noted she had said the word interested three times now.

"My unique skills?" Rune asked, alarmed.

"Yes, your Talent." She raised an eyebrow at Rune's reaction.

"You should ask if they cover dental," a voice said from behind her and Rune jumped before turning to see St. Benedict standing there, holding his plate of cake, a fork stuck in his mouth. He didn't look at Rune but had his eyes focused on Ms. Hamilton-Gonzalez as he cut another bite of cake with the side of his fork, then stabbed it with the tines. "Also vacation days," he added, offering the bite of cake to Rune.

"What are you doing here?" she hissed, pulling her head back from the incoming bite of cake as if he had cooties.

"I'm sorry, ma'am, I know this isn't the best of times…" the winged lizard woman said, leaning a bit back, unsure of the newcomer's relationship with Rune.

"No, go ahead, make your pitch. I'm in no rush," St. Benedict said, then finally met Rune's eyes as she stared comically cross-eyed at the bite of cake like it was going to bite her instead. "I'm not putting this down until you take a bite."

Rune narrowed her eyes to slits before opening her mouth and accepting the bite. Chocolate and cherry burst on her tongue. It was delicious, but she wished it tasted like ashes and soot since it came from him.

"You know this is my third piece? I have eaten more between yesterday and today than I usually eat in a week." St. Benedict cut another bite and devoured it. "This is gorgeous cake, by the way."

"What do you expect?" Rune snorted. "You did a week's worth of healing in a day. I told you, you would be hungry."

"Ms. L…"

"No kidding. I keep eating like this, I'm going to have to have my cholesterol checked."

"Ms. Leveau…"

"Sorry, and what company do you represent?" St. Benedict said, not at all sounding interested.

Rune looked back at the bird-snake woman, who shifted her wings uncomfortably. "I am not at liberty to say at this time."

"Oooh, that sounds ominous," St. Benedict teased.

"Will you cut it out?" Rune chided.

"What? I just made a casual observation. It's your life, all twenty minutes of it. I'm just here for the cake and to watch you crash and burn. Oh look over there, another offer incoming. I always wonder how the business-suit types always get to places first before the gun-toting types," he said, indicating his head toward another couple, a man and a woman, also in business attire. One wore severe black and the other light peach and cream. They were making their way through the crowd, beelining toward Rune.

"Ms. Leveau, if you would agree to a non-disclosure agreement, I would be more than happy to discuss my client's very generous offer. I think you would be very pleased with—" Ms. Hamilton-Gonzalez said in a hurry, now that competition had clearly arrived.

"Thank you, but I am not looking for any... offers at this time." Rune held up her hands and tried to give the business card back, which, of course, the bird-snake woman wouldn't take.

"Ms. Leveau..."

"Your five minutes are up, buddy. Don't call us, we'll call you," St. Benedict said, gesturing dismissively with his fork.

"What us?" Rune hissed at him.

"Oh, you want me to leave? No problem. I'll be over at the cake table laughing." St. Benedict immediately started walking back that way with his freshly emptied plate.

"I understand you're busy, but feel free to give me a call at your earliest convenience, Ms. Leveau," Ms. Hamilton-Gonzalez said, and to Rune's great relief, she left.

The orange lady had disappeared, as well. The two business-suit people, seeing their opportunity, picked up the pace. Suddenly feeling highly exposed and vulnerable, Rune followed St. Benedict to the cake table.

"What are you doing here? How did you find me?" she demanded, dragging Ally after her.

"It wasn't hard after your bad luck slapped you in the face," he said, jabbing a thumb at the screens still flashing her surprised face in a loop. "Oh look, Ms. Offer-you-should-probably-refuse is blocking the competition." Rune did look, and he was right, Ms. Hamilton-Gonzalez had moved to intercept the two people in suits.

"Now it's just a question of how long until the real authorities get here. Nice job hiding, by the way. If I hadn't located you ten minutes before you had your five minutes of fame, St. Augustina would have carted you out already. Oh, and there she is." St. Benedict nodded toward the entrance to the parking lot.

The tall black woman flashed her badge, followed by Rune's ID picture. The people standing there blinked in surprise at both items, and the manager who had interviewed Rune came over to talk with St. Augustina. Meanwhile, the three people who had come in with St. Augustina scanned the crowds looking for her.

"I expect you're going to get a bunch more offers in the next half hour. They'll probably be made in dark, little rooms with one of those single lights over your head and a lot of shadowy people standing around." St. Benedict tossed his plate into the garbage can at the end of the table and picked up another plate of cake.

Fear gripped Rune's heart and stomach, locking both in a choke-hold so that she almost couldn't breathe. She stumbled forward and caught herself on the table, her whole body shaking uncontrollably.

Then, St. Benedict was there, putting his arm around her.

"No, she's okay. Too much of the sugar, I think," he laughed, talking to someone standing behind them. "Celebrating too hard, right?"

Rune thought about lifting her head to attempt to smile, but it got washed under the torrent of her fear. "No, I can't. I can't go back to a little room like that."

"It's okay. You don't have to," St. Benedict said soothingly. He pushed a little bit on her shoulder, taking up Ally's leash as it fell from Rune's paralyzed fingers.

"Oh god, why didn't I run away when I had the chance?" Rune moved with him, while unaware she was moving at all.

"It's probably a good thing that you didn't go too far, or I wouldn't have found you so quickly," he said.

"You!" A cord snapped inside Rune's head, bringing her back from the dark place, down the only path she had ever used to pull herself out of it; by getting angry. "You're the one who exposed me like this." She shrugged off his arm and made a grab for Ally's leash. St. Benedict held it out of her way, holding up a hand to stop her.

"Look, here's the deal, straight out. I have no problems leaving you here on your own, because if you aren't going to help me, then you are useless to me. But if you join me, I promise that I will take care of you. You've already seen what you're capable of without me."

"You see, that just seems like the same deal that the rest of them are going to offer me," Rune said, backing away from him, scanning the area for a way out.

"I can't make it any simpler. Either you come with me, or I stand here and let St. Augustina take you."

He waved with a smile at St. Augustina. Her eyes locked on the two of them for a moment across the expanse of parking lot and people, before going wide. Then she drew her gun and fired. Both St. Benedict and Rune flinched, and somewhere in the parking lot, someone screamed. Everyone else stopped moving and stood like sheep staring at St. Augustina. It took Rune a heartbeat as well to look between her and the Saint to see the new bullet hole in the bricks. St. Benedict was already looking at it, his hand still raised in the air.

"Dammit, dammit, dammit!" he said, grabbing Rune by the arm and moving her along the building. In the distance, they heard St. Augustina and her lackeys, yelling at people to get out of the way. "Trigger happy bitch. I was looking so cool, too."

He hissed as another bullet cracked the bricks of the store again. They slipped into the gap between buildings, Rune already completely disoriented as to the location of the main street, which was ironic.

"Why is she shooting at us?!"

"I made a mistake," he shouted over the screams of the crowd. "Okay, someone changed the rules. I always make a mistake when someone changes the rules."

"Who are you talking to?" Rune shouted back as they scurried along the gap, Ally and her leash getting tangled up in Rune's feet.

"My team! They're freaking out right now," he said, looking back. "No, I don't have a gun. Well, it's a little late now!"

The gap dumped out behind the store into a proper alley.

"Find me a way out, now! She's right behind us," St. Benedict shouted as he pulled Rune to the right trying to get her to run, but her feet were just too tangled in Ally's leash. The poor dog was shaking hard, her tail tucked far between her legs.

"She said she worked for the government. Government officials shouldn't shoot at civilians," Rune said, scooping Ally up into her arms while St. Benedict worked to get the leash unwrapped from around her ankles.

"Like I said, the rules have changed. You got the attention of someone more dangerous than I thought. We've got to get out of here now," St. Benedict said.

"*I* got the attention of?! I didn't do anything. *You* got their attention!"

Glaring at her, he snapped open a knife. Rune flinched, but he stuck the knife through the thick leash strap and cut it like it was butter.

"Regardless, we need to run," St. Benedict ordered.

"Why are you doing this? I thought I was on my own," Rune asked.

"You want to argue about it or get out of here alive?"

Not a second later, the backdoor of the building flew open with a bang. St. Benedict whirled, moving Rune and Ally behind him so that he was between them and the threat. Instead, the orange lady popped her head out, her white hair swinging like a flag.

"Cheerio! Do you need to make a graceful exit?" she asked.

"Yes!" Rune said and surged around St. Benedict to move toward the door.

"Follow me," the orange lady sang back and moved back into the doorway.

"Wait, do you trust her?" St. Benedict asked, stopping Rune before she could follow.

"I guess. I don't really know her," Rune said. "I just met her like an hour ago."

"Then why on earth are you following her?!" St. Benedict asked. The answer came in the form of a crash and cursing from the gap they had just vacated.

"Hurry it up, they've gotten away!" St. Augustina's voice echoed, harshly, and way too close.

Together, Rune and St. Benedict rushed through the door, the orange lady pulling it shut behind them.

CHAPTER 8

"Keep going straight along the wall, you can't miss it! Oh, this is exciting," the orange lady said, cheery as sunshine. She secured the door, which rattled and shook a breath later.

"This way," Rune said confidently as if she had been in this place before and knew where she was going. She clutched Ally to her chest, and for once, the dog didn't fight her.

Rune led them along the back of The Dog House's back storage area. On one side was a concrete wall covered in industrial outlets and heating and cooling pipes, and to their right were row after row of shelves and boxes, presumably filled with merchandise. Just before they got to the far wall, Rune spontaneously took a right between two shelves, slowing to step around a ladder.

"Where are you going?" St. Benedict demanded, confused, but still following her despite his hesitation.

"This is the way," was all Rune said and kept going.

"She's right, you better pick up the pace!" the orange lady sing-songed at St. Benedict as if it was a merry chase through the fields instead of a run for their lives.

"There is something off about you, isn't there?" St. Benedict said to the orange lady.

She smiled even brighter, her hair wafting around her face like a white corona. "You've only just noticed, warrior?"

After a few more feet, Rune stopped at the end of the row in front of a blank, brick wall. She reached out with one hand and started to trace around the side of the wall.

"I'm not..." she started, unsure, but the orange lady came up beside her.

"No, you're right," she said and slid through the wall like it was air.

Rune couldn't help smiling, before gripping Ally's harness to pass through the wall into a new realm. The cool rush passed over her as she left the world of Chicago and into the dark, cave-like world of... well, she wasn't sure just yet. The switch from the fluorescent lights in the back of the store to darkness temporarily blinded her, but feelings of urgency drove her forward even before her eyes had adjusted. She didn't have far to go, stopping herself short just before she slammed into a real wall.

She stood in a tunnel made of brick but built in no way that any bricklayer would purposely create. The tunnel itself bent and dipped and rolled like the stones of a natural cave would, but composed instead, of brick and mortar. There were hanging lights every few feet along the tunnel, placed as if the contractor expected them to hang straight down. Instead, the lights hung at odd angles, some swinging from the side of their housings, others high up or so low that the person walking the tunnel would bump their head if they weren't watching. This created strange pockets of light and darkness along the length of the tunnel.

"Rune! Rune!! Where did you go?" the Saint hissed, urgency overwhelming his whisper. He was only five feet away from her, still on the other side of the doorway. His hand trembled as it reached out toward her, but then it stopped and went flat as if pressing against glass, except there was nothing there.

His eyes roved the wall, searching for the doorway. His hand pressed against rough, solid brick. He set his other hand against the wall to check if his right hand was lying. It was not. All he saw was brick, except there did seem to be a straight unbroken line in the shape of a door.

"Rune. Rune!" he called repeatedly at the wall. He was sure he saw her go through it, but no amount of pushing made the same happen for him. It was just a wall. "You can't leave me here like this!"

Suddenly, he punched the wall.

On the other side, Rune flinched a step back. From Rune's perspective, there was nothing but air. She had moved up closer to the invisible wall, watching in fascination until her face was only inches from his hand. Even when he called for her, she didn't dare make a sound, not even after he surprised her when he punched the wall that was very real to him. She watched as blood welled up on his knuckles. It occurred to her that she could turn around and walk away, leave him on the other side. This was the escape she was looking for, and he couldn't follow. So, why was she still rooted to that spot? It was a risk to move forward, a worse risk to reach back. If she just didn't move, she was safe. Isn't that what she always wanted? Simply to be safe?

St. Benedict growled and threw both arms against the wall. Nothing happened. He left himself there, letting the brick bite into his fists. He needed to move. St. Augustina or someone of her ilk would hear him soon, and this time he was pretty sure she would make sure he died. Instead, he stayed there, letting the wall push his fedora back on his forehead as he leaned against it and closed his eyes, breathing heavily.

"Please. Please, don't leave me," he breathed uselessly. The Talent was probably long gone already, taking her chance to escape with some strange magic cheat that he couldn't win against. "Please, you're my only hope now. Please. I beg you."

"Just go away," Rune whispered, barely a breath. It would be so much simpler if he just went on his own. Then she wouldn't have to choose. She could just live with the ache inside, that longed to reach out to him. That ache recognized itself in him. "Just go. Please."

He didn't seem to hear, just stayed there looking dejected as he stared at the wall, his gaze far away.

Her fingers reached through the wall and took one of his hands. His eyes widened as he felt her fingers soften the brick's roughness away and gripped his slack hand. He squeezed them back, and their fingers interwove together comfortably.

"Close your eyes," Rune said to him, and he did, just as shouts echoed off the walls of the storeroom. She pulled him through carefully, not entirely sure how she was doing it. To St. Benedict, even though he flinched when he thought his face should have hit the wall, it felt like nothing, just walking through air.

Rune marveled at this man with his bloody knuckles and the way his face took on a boyish innocence as he let her guide him through. He had scared and threatened her only an hour or so earlier, yet charmed her and fascinated her with his mystery. And now this.

They stood there in the subterranean tunnel holding hands. She studied his face as he kept his eyes closed. He stood absolutely still, vulnerable. Then he suddenly released the breath he was holding. His eyes snapped open and scanned his surroundings. He backpedaled, ripping their hands apart, only to be stopped by the wall that had formed behind him.

"Were you holding your breath the whole time?" Rune asked, amused, tucking her tingling hand away. She hoped the act covered up how unsettled she felt.

"What the hell?!" He stared back at the blank space where he had been standing only a few moments before, and lifted his hand as if to touch it again but retreated from the wall instead. "You pulled me through a wall?"

"Yes."

"Where the hell are we?" he asked.

"I guess I don't really know what it's called. Most cities have things like this. Buildings get built and rebuilt, pushing up against each other over time, and ways of moving through just get formed and warped into being," Rune said looking down the twisted hallway. "This one's pretty cool."

"Where does it go?" he asked.

"I don't know. We'll have to walk to find out."

There was a shift in the atmosphere. Looking back the way they came, to Rune, the space where the doorway had been was gone, replaced by more of the natural-looking brick wall.

"And now what just happened?" St. Benedict asked, eyeing the strange brick wall.

"I don't know. The doorway closed?" Rune shrugged.

"You aren't very informative."

"Couldn't you see it? The doorway from this side, I mean?" she asked, marveling at his outsider perspective.

"Look, all I saw was a brick wall that I somehow just walked through." He readjusted his fedora as he tried to center himself and regain control of the situation. "Can you open it again?"

"No. Not my Talent. I'm not really an Opener. That's a pretty rare talent, but also a pretty cool one. The orange lady opened it for us," Rune said.

"So, she's an Opener?"

"No. She probably had the key, which allowed her to open it," Rune said.

"And why could you pass through it, and I couldn't?" he asked.

"I don't know. Maybe you didn't believe enough." Then in a quieter voice, Rune said, "Or you really did believe I would leave you behind."

St. Benedict didn't seem to hear the last part as he pulled out his phone and looked at it before holding it up to the ceiling of the tunnel, searching for a signal.

Rune turned away from the door and headed down the hallway to where Ally had chosen to sit and wait. The ground of the cave was covered by soft sand and what was left of Ally's leash dragged along the ground.

"Good girl," Rune said, getting a harsh, indignant bark in return.

"No signal. Mal…my team is freaking out right about now," he said, putting the phone back into his pocket and removing the earpiece.

"Passing through gates and other heavily magicked… things, I guess, can interfere with your technologies. I don't even know why you bother with them when magic works so much better," Rune said dismissively.

"Magic works better, you say? Okay, then how about you go open the door that you just told me you don't have the magic ability for, and then tell me how magic is better?"

Rune pursed her lips together since she had nothing she could really say to that in response. "Either way, we need to get moving," she finally said as she started down the tunnel.

"And that odd woman, where did she go?" St. Benedict asked, following.

"I guess she ran ahead." Rune bent down to pick up the remnants of the leash.

"And why didn't you?"

"Oh. Did you want me to leave you behind?"

"No, but I want to know why you didn't. You've been trying to get away from me from the moment we met." St. Benedict looked down at his bloodied knuckles, blinking in surprise that they had already half-healed.

"You asked me not to leave you, so I didn't."

His face blushed a little. "I asked you not to leave me earlier. That didn't stop you."

"You didn't ask, you threatened. I don't like to be threatened, and you were threatening me. It seemed like the thing to do was to get away from you and all of that mess you brought down on me. Violence seems to follow wherever you go," she said as she turned down the tunnel, enjoying the feel of the sand under her booted feet. "When we get out of here, I should find a phone and call to check on the bar."

They reached the end of the hallway. It bent like a natural cave would, to the right.

"This place is amazing," Rune said with delighted awe. She looked down the tunnel to see it continue to curve and bend, its brick walls undulating. "I wish I had a better idea what makes them."

"Because it's so freakish?" St. Benedict asked, eyeing the wall with distrust, tapping at one of the low-hanging lanterns with a foot to make it swing a bit.

Rune didn't respond. She was getting tired of his rhabdophobia, or fear of magic. She stopped at a spot to examine a pipe that twisted up like a silly straw into the ceiling. She reached out and touched it, then giggled. "There's water flowing through it!"

"What does that mean?" St. Benedict asked, his face passing into shadows as he moved past.

"I don't know; that the pipe works somewhere. I can imagine that the building above us doesn't know that it's got a tunnel like this coming through it."

"Then we're still in a building, in the city?"

"I don't know. Maybe," Rune answered dreamily as if she was walking through a museum.

"It's a marvel to me that you can feel comfortable in this strange place," St. Benedict said. Again, he made the magician gesture with his hand. This time, as the blue screen flashed to life in his palm, he slowly rolled his finger across the surface clockwise. The light changed and focused into a white beam that he then turned to look into a cranny.

"It's a marvel to me you can feel so comfortable when people chase and shoot at you," Rune shot back with a smile, the lamp behind her head lighting her hair into a shining halo.

St. Benedict coughed a laugh. "Touché. So, where to?"

"I don't know. I guess we just keep following the tunnel," Rune answered.

St. Benedict turned and placed his hand against the wall, blocking Rune's way as they stood in one of the places between light and dark. "Okay, femme fatale, you need to level with me."

"Excuse me?"

"Look, I get it. You're afraid. You don't trust me. You're playing your cards close to the chest, but I promised you, I'm not going to hurt you," he said.

"Okay. Thank you," Rune said, looking away and backing up a half a step uncomfortably.

"Where are we going?" he repeated, closing the distance she tried to make.

"I told you, I don't know." Rune's eyebrows pinched together.

He sighed. "If you're going to lie, you need to do a better job than that."

"I'm not lying. I don't know where we are. I've never been here before."

"Bullshit, you knew exactly where to go," he challenged, leaning in to use his height over her. "I could accept that you'd blindly followed a stranger who offered help in a dire situation. It's not smart, but it happens. You have to go off your gut, but we didn't follow her. We followed you."

"It's what I do," Rune admitted begrudgingly. It did not feel comfortable to talk about her abilities, but she didn't want him to think she was lying to him.

"It's what you do," he repeated incredulously.

"I don't just find things. I can also find my way sometimes. It's an adaptation of my Talent. I don't really know how I do it. It just seemed like the right way to go."

He didn't say anything, only peered into her eyes. His own went eerily blank and cold, like a dead man's or a man with no soul. Rune was sure at that moment, that if he wanted to kill her right then, not only could he do it, it would mean very little to him.

"Listen, because I am only going to threaten this once," he said carefully, pulling himself up to his full height plus hat. "If you are leading me into a trap or plan to backstab me in any way, it better be to kill me, because if it is anything less than that, I will make sure you suffer when I pay you back in kind. Right now, though, I will work with you here, even protect you, until we get out of this strange place. I swear it. I just want all of this to be very clear before we go any further."

He backed away when he finished speaking, letting light back into Rune's world. She swallowed the dry lump in her throat

"Are you really so afraid of me?" she asked suddenly.

It was the last response he expected, and it made him flinch.

"My power is virtually useless. What exactly do you think I can do to you? I can't make fire or manipulate water. I can't erect barriers or fire kinetic beams or even predict the future. I don't make potions or enchant crystals or even break curses. I barely have magic; just this stupid intuition about where to go that I barely understand and has no formalized, recognizable method to it. I just know, okay! I just know that I should walk to the end of this hall, take a right and then I'll go uphill for about ten minutes, and we'll be there, wherever there is. Sometimes I see light. Sometimes it's like a string that pulls me straight to the thing I'm looking for if it's close. But I can't make it work reliably because I don't know why it works at all…"

Just then, Ally barked a sharp yap, one that made both Rune and St. Benedict look down the tunnel. Nothing moved and there were no sounds, but the absence of anything that would make Ally bark was more ominous.

"We should keep moving," Rune said softly, stepping around St. Benedict.

"Why?"

"Because I'm getting creeped-out standing here."

She readjusted her belt, settling its reassuring weight on her hips. She didn't look behind her to see if her unwelcome companion followed or not.

The brick tunnel ended suddenly, and Rune paused as she passed through a cold wash of air. The warm light was gone, replaced by colder, wetter light that seemed almost slimy. They were still in a tunnel, but the brick had transformed into concrete with pipes in different states of decay, sticking in and out of every inch of the wall and ceiling. The slimy lights were set in grated sconces every ten feet that didn't cast much actual light at all. One even did a flicker dance that made Rune imagine all kinds of horror-movie things happening in this hall. There were wet patches along the seams where the concrete met and a darker, thin puddle of wet lazily drifted across the floor. It smelled awful.

"Oh, this is charming. Is Jack the Ripper going to be joining us?" St. Benedict quipped as he joined Rune and Ally at the end. His voice echoed hollowly in the space.

"We better just keep pushing forward," Rune said without much confidence.

"We're still going the right way?" he asked. Ally whined, echoing his concern and looked up at Rune with her literal puppy dog eyes.

"I...I'm not sure..." Rune wrapped her arms around her middle. There was a distant rumble that grew louder until it roared above them, so loud that the small party clamped their hands, and paws, over their ears.

"What the hell? Are we under a train station?" St. Benedict shouted too loudly as the space became quiet again. The rumble had pushed out another gush of water from the concrete seam, and the cement darkened anew.

"Actually, it could be the Red Line," Rune said automatically. "Or... I mean... this could be anywhere in Chicago or under one of the suburbs. Maybe even the Chicago River, depending on how close to the Loop we are."

He didn't look at her as she tried to explain. She waited for him to accuse her of lying again and leading him into a trap. She supposed she couldn't blame him. He didn't really know her. It was the next logical explanation if he didn't believe her about her Talent. Then again, how did he know anyway? Rune wondered at what point had he figured out she was a Talent for sure? And then she realized she had talked about and confirmed her secret abilities with him and not only that but in front of Ally too.

Instead of pushing her for proof that what she said was true, he stepped forward down the hall as if daring whatever might be lurking there to come out and try to eat him. Rune followed, pulling her hand back before touching the gross wall. The space was narrower than the last passage, and they could only follow him, one at a time. Ally took up the space between them, which was fine with Rune. She really needed to keep an eye on the kid.

"These passageways work on the same principle as the two-way door to my office," Rune said to occupy her mind and the silence. She tried to keep her voice level, tried to sound honest and nonchalant, which only made her sound more like she was trying ineptly to lead him into a trap.

"Is it dangerous?" he finally asked.

"About as dangerous as the CTA. Sure, something could happen, but it rarely does," she said.

"I think I would still prefer the CTA. So, you have been in places like this before?"

"Are you trying to catch me in a lie?" she asked defensively self-conscious.

"Just trying to get a grasp on the situation," he said as he stepped over a puddle gingerly.

Something made Ally perk her ears, and before Rune could ask, the little dog took off, nimbly leaping over the puddle and then around St. Benedict's feet.

"Ally! Get back here!" Rune called, but it was too late. All they could hear of the dog was the clicking of her nails on the stone. Rune almost took off after her, but just as she pushed past, splashing inelegantly through the puddle, St. Benedict grabbed her from behind. He clamped his hand over her mouth. She started to screech and fight, but he hissed hard into her ear.

"Quiet! Something's coming," he said. Rune stopped struggling but shook his hand off her mouth, so she could breathe.

Ahead, several voices echoed a bit into the tunnel. Rune and St. Benedict held their breaths and waited as shadows filled the far hallway.

A strange light appeared at the end of the tunnel they were in, reddish and pulsing. The voices became louder, and two short men holding a leash on either side of a muzzled reptile the size of a pony came into view. Its wings were strapped down and it waddled languidly as if it didn't plan on being anywhere anytime soon. Its captors shouted and cursed at it, trying to get it to go faster but it didn't show any regard for them whatsoever.

"What the hell is that?" St. Benedict whispered breathily.

"A dragon," Rune whispered, her voice excited.

"Really?" he asked as he cocked his head to the side, the brim of his fedora bumping the top of Rune's head.

"If you've never seen a dragon before, it can be underwhelming. I remember seeing a Komodo dragon in a zoo and I was absolutely crushed to see it. It just laid there sleeping, a big oversized lizard, not doing anything fantastic or remotely dragon-like. A real dragon, as we in the magic community define them, are not too much different. Some people think they look really cool, but to me, they're just a larger version of that Komodo dragon, only with wings and longer tails," Rune whispered back, her words cascading as she talked quickly.

"Yes, you sound very underwhelmed," St. Benedict replied dryly.

"Well, it's different when you're face to face with one," she whispered.

The captors were just as amazing as the dragon. They were figures of men, dressed in black business suits, complete with white shirts and black ties. More than that, their hair was long and black, wisping around their heads like they were underwater. Their skin was an inky black except for their faces that glowed white like skulls with black circles around their eye sockets. The eyes themselves also glowed white and blank.

Instinctively, Rune crouched down, and she felt the Saint follow her lead a second later, his hand landing on the middle of her back so he could leverage himself up just a little bit to see over her. She found his hand reassuring.

"Monochromes?" Rune whispered, confused.

"You know these guys?"

"I know *of* them," she said. "What are they doing?"

The first two men were followed by several more people leading other animals. They didn't seem aware of the spies and kept up their slow lumber, past the end of the tunnel, moving into a connecting tunnel that even Rune hadn't seen at first.

Right behind the lumbering dragon followed another creature most people wouldn't recognize on sight.

"What is that?" the Saint whispered behind Rune.

"Unicorn," Rune whispered over her shoulder, even more excited than she was about the dragon.

"Of course, it is."

"Not exactly the fluffy white angelic horses with horns that most people think of when they think of a unicorn. Those don't really exist," she explained.

"Looks like a rhino."

The real unicorn was also being led on a dual tether like the dragon. It had a single horn in the middle of its horse/rhino face; a blade of bone protruded from the top of its skull and stopped halfway down its long face toward its nose. The blade then sharpened toward a strong, wicked point. Its legs were longer than a rhino's, and its body more resembled a horse's. Unlike a horse, it had a buffalo's hump cresting over its front shoulders into a low hung head. This unicorn stood a hand taller than the monochrome man and woman escorting it and its horn was the length of one of them standing. Rune was far more concerned by the unicorn than the dragon. St. Benedict was far more concerned about the four burly guards walking with them.

Gripping the locket still hanging from her neck, Rune focused on the image of Ally, who had disappeared. Just as she got that familiar tug toward the little dog, the canine girl appeared, trotting up from around the corner of the hallway that the party of mystical creatures headed toward.

"Oh, crap."

"What?"

"There's Ally."

Ally trotted casually, and Rune realized she might have just scouted ahead. With a yelp, Ally scrambled backward at the sight of the dragon, her nails making a racket on the stones. A bark leaked out of her throat in half-formed yips. That was enough to catch the unicorn's attention. It was already on the brink of irritation from the way it threw its ponderous head around and with a trumpet of anger, the unicorn reared up on its hind legs, its horn scraping the top of the stone tunnel. It took its captors up with it and the cave filled with deafening shouts. Ally rushed back down the leaking service tunnel and right into Rune's arms, her little doggy body shivering violently.

"You stupid kid," Rune cursed at her even as she petted her head soothingly.

"We need to get out of here," the Saint said, attempting to pull Rune backward and away from the danger.

"We'll be trapped that way," Rune said, not resisting as she almost fell.

"I know!" St. Benedict answered, exasperated.

"Did they see us?"

"They saw something. Now they are looking for it." The shouts down the hall grew louder as four monochromes peeled off from the group.

"And there. They've seen us," St. Benedict acknowledged as if it was funny.

Rune reached out with her senses, extending her Finding Talent as hard as she could, trying to ignore the headache she was developing from using it so much in such a short time. Like before, she focused on a way out.

"Follow me!" she said urgently and pivoted around him, staying low. "Grab my shirt," she ordered as she opened a service hatch she hadn't noticed before. Ally resisted, but Rune shoved her little doggie butt through. Cold, murky water gushed over Rune's hands as she dropped to her knees to crawl after Ally, letting the damp, barred hatch-cover drop wetly onto her back, but when she got to her hips, her forward momentum was arrested by the narrowness of the tunnel. For the briefest of moments, she panicked when she thought she couldn't move forward.

"What's wrong?" her companion asked, urgently hushed.

"I'm stuck..." she called back in a harsh whisper. She scrambled against the sides of the vent, but couldn't move forward. "Give... give me a push," Rune said. Her face burned, red-hot from embarrassment.

"You said you're stuck?" he asked, and she blushed even harder.

"I'm not fat! I'm just very hippy," she said defensively. "Just give me a push and don't laugh."

"I didn't say anything. It's your belt, I think you're caught..."

Rune unbuckled her belt and slid it ahead of herself. It didn't help. She was still stuck.

"Just give me a push! Hurry!"

She felt him lay a warm, wide hand on her derriere and she wiggled back and forth a little. He shoved her sharply. There was a pinch of pain and she was through. She didn't dare look back, knowing she would find him with a smug smile. The inside of the metal service duct was a lot wider than the entrance, thankfully, and she was able to easily crawl through a few feet. The Saint still held onto her foot as she pulled him through.

"Stop, stop," he said abruptly and let go of her altogether. Then he was gone, leaving nothing but the rectangle of sickening light behind.

"St. Benedict?" Rune asked. Lying down on her side, she quickly rebuckled her belt. There were shouts and sounds of a scuffle.

"Crap!" she shouted and tried to back up. Then two hands reached into the duct and caught her ankles, attempting to drag her out. The sudden pulling landed her on her front, soaking her through in dirty water. She tried to scrabble for a grip on the metal walls to keep herself from being pulled out like a rabbit from a hole. Then, of course, she got stuck again.

She could hear the meaty thwacking sounds of fighting. Hopefully, the Saint was alright since she wouldn't be able to help him anytime soon.

The set of hands attacking Rune continued to try to wiggle her free from the hole, leaving her with no other option but to kick to get free. Rune wondered how comical it looked for anyone watching from the outside. Finally, the hands crossed her ankles and managed to flip her over despite her struggles. More water soaked through her once-white shirt. Before she could take a breath, the pair of hands emerged from the darkness above her. Gripping her by the front of her shirt, they pulled her through the shadow. Strangely, Rune could breathe as she was forced through what felt like black gelatin. It smelled like burned garbage bags and old undergrowth. She swore she could hear whispers muttering some vague, indiscernible language inches from her ears, sending shivers down her spine.

Then she was through. The hands that had her were attached to one of the monochromes, his eerie, pearly eyes glinting through pitch-black eyelids. He kept backpedaling, pulling her through the wall and Rune had the disconcerting experience of watching her legs next to her disappear into the service hatch. How the hell was he doing this?

Rune's limbs moved as if through Jell-O as she tried to put her feet under herself.

The Saint was still fighting. It was actually quite impressive. Two men held each of his arms so their third companion could stick a wicked-looking knife in him. Just as the knife-wielder lunged, the Saint placed a foot in his chest. St. Benedict laughed as he swung up his other leg, using all three men as leverage as he clocked his attacker across the face with his foot. It didn't free him entirely, but the fight was far from over.

Rune didn't know what to do to help. Maddie would have always told her to run, or start talking to diffuse the situation. Violence often made these kinds of situations worse.

"Please, st-stop," she stuttered to the one holding her, but the words stuck in her throat. How were any of them going to listen to her at this point? The monochrome men were obviously hell-bent on keeping what they were doing a secret. Maddie's presence alone would have made them hesitate. Most people in the magical community recognized Maddie on sight or "sense" alone, but Rune was barely remembered as Maddie's non-magic apprentice. "I... I'm a Faerie Friend."

The pearly eyes opened a little wider as the monochrome man recognized the term.

The Saint was forced to his knees by his attackers, failing to gain the upper hand as all three had coordinated to entrap him. He managed to get his head up and locked eyes with Rune.

"What are you doing? Run!" he shouted at her, just as a fist came down on him and clipped his head.

"No, stop it! We're not a threat to you, please!" she shouted. "Peace! Faerie Friend!"

She tried to move toward the Saint, but her captor didn't release her shirt. The other three hesitated at her words. St. Benedict slumped sideways, at first looking like he had been knocked out. When one of his captors slackened his grip on the Saint's arm, he suddenly rolled, freeing his hand. The roll allowed him to knock the feet out from under the other captor as his body met the monochrome man's legs.

"I said run, you idiot!" St. Benedict shouted at Rune as he finished the roll on his feet. Then he kicked off the wall to land a knockout punch across the jaw of the one holding her.

"I said 'Faerie Friend,' you idiot! They're not going to believe me now!" Rune shouted back at St. Benedict. The situation had completely spun out of control. All she could think was, *what would Maddie do?* With that purity of thought, she opened up all of her senses, searching for another way out.

This was something Maddie had always pushed her to do; open her magical senses to "see" the world as it really was. It was supposed to be a helpful tool, used to see the natural magic in the world from which to weave spells. All it ever did was give Rune an extremely bad headache

As she opened her senses, her eyes no longer saw the world around them anymore, rather the world deeper than it had been a moment before. Everything around her erupted into a mass of threads made of light and sound and motion, circling and weaving into a chaos that she could barely comprehend. St. Benedict swing—swung—will swing— his arm, the threads echoing forward and back and through. Threads seemed to fly off his arm, but the arch of it followed a single golden thread that connected him to the one monochrome man left standing, exploding into sparks when it met its target. The monochrome on the ground was a black shadow rising up — raised up — will rise — to his feet, blue sparks flying from his form, from his rage, from his fear.

Ally had emerged from the vent that they had tried to escape into; the girl she was and the dog she was, both existing simultaneously in the same space.

Rune's head felt like it was going to split open, but she didn't dare close her senses off to it. As the worlds collided and interacted, the power generated from that interaction, to Rune's mind, was interpreted as sparks flying. The sparks pooled on the ground, instead of burning out like real sparks would. She needed to do something to help. She needed to find a way to...

That's when the mess of threads and sparks coalescing around all of the figures clarified before her. Without hesitation, Rune stuck her literal hands into the mess of light on the ground and tore. The way, her way, opened as the light sparks yielded beneath her fingers. A hyper sense of color wavered in the floor just underneath where the Saint stood. As it tore, his feet passed through, the sudden gravity dragging him down. It ripped him free from his captors as they tried to catch his arms again. St. Benedict scrabbled at the parts of the floor that were still solid while he passed through the hole beneath him but to no avail.

Rune went in after him. It was a strange sensation, passing through the doorway she had made. The energy was raw. It left a taste of pennies in her mouth. As she passed through the hole, her gravity shifted, and she landed on her side, partly onto St. Benedict.

"Ally!" Rune shouted, remembering the dog-girl too late.

To her relief, paws that also looked like hands appeared through the hole, followed by the rest of the little, white dog with its human shadow. The girl's pretty face twisted in fear and panic as she dove blindly. Rune heard shouting on the other side of the hole. Before anyone else decided to come through, she reached back with an open palm toward the portal that was now behind them instead of above.

"*Abraxas aperio!*" The portal closed, the threads weaving themselves together, the sparks finally burning away into nothing. Then there was only the metal wall of the air duct where the portal had been.

"What... what just happened?" St. Benedict asked.

"I cast a real spell," Rune said marveling. "I've never done that before."

CHAPTER 9

"What do you mean you've never done that before? Isn't that how you escaped the alley?" St. Benedict hissed. He had about had it with this whole magic adventure.

The three laid in their escape hole, breathing hard. Rune's body was pressed awkwardly into St. Benedict's chest. The world continued to rise and fall as he gulped in large breaths of air despite the pressure of her weight. His fedora, which had somehow stayed glued on his head, finally fell forward on his face, covering his eyes. He whipped it off and laid his head back against the cold metal of the air duct, his sweat-soaked hair clinging to his forehead.

Rune closed her eyes against the pounding in her head. It was worse than she expected. It was the first time she had opened her Mage senses in ages. She closed them the minute she shut the portal, but the damage was done. All she could do was lie there and count the pulses banging in her head.

The quiet of the air duct surrounded them, only punctuated by their labored breathing. Ally climbed on top of the two awkwardly jumbled bodies, the only one in the entire space who was remotely comfortable.

"Where are we?" the Saint asked.

"I don't know. Safe? Give me a minute. Let me catch my breath," Rune said. Her head was killing her.

"Can they follow us?" he asked in a hushed tone after a long moment of listening.

"I'm not sure, but even if they could, they've got their hands full with trying to escape with their goods. Right? That has to be more important than trying to follow us." Rune kept her voice soft in the close quarters, "I wish I'd had a camera or a scrying crystal."

"Why?"

"Dragons and unicorns are protected creatures. So, what were those monochromes doing?"

"You keep saying monochromes, but other than the obvious coloring, I'm not sure what you mean by that. Are they creatures or just thugs with weird face paint?" St. Benedict asked.

"Both, I guess," Rune answered. "They were Faerie Folk. You shouldn't have tried to fight them like that. We didn't know what was going on."

"They came at us," he argued.

"They're disenfranchised. We could have tried talking first," Rune said, holding her ground.

"Right. I'll remember that," he replied with a cynical smile. After a moment of tense silence, he asked, "What do you mean by disenfranchised?"

"The Faerie Court used to control several Alderman Seats in Chicago. The majority of them were, at one time, on the North and West sides. This all happened about two years ago. Thousands of Faeries just disappeared overnight, and so many more are now just homeless and destitute." Rune swallowed against the lump in her throat.

"Who acquired them?" he asked.

"Kodiak," Rune confirmed as she attempted to slide sideways to get completely off of St. Benedict, but there just wasn't room in the duct, and she was forced to stay put.

"Kodiak, huh? I hate to ask, but what would a monochrome be used for at Kodiak? Muscle?" St. Benedict narrowed his eyes as if trying to recall something he had forgotten.

"How do you not know this? It's pretty common knowledge," Rune asked.

"Haven't been in town long. I know Chicago has gone through a lot of 'restructuring' AKA gerrymandering," St. Benedict said, twitching his fingers into air quotes, "but you make it sound like something else entirely."

"I suppose it depends on your point of view," Rune hedged, turning her neck back and forth to see if she could crack it and relieve her headache a little. "Either way, the Magic Guild is the only non-corporate entity anymore that still holds any Alderman seats, and even then, I don't know about next year's elections."

"You're political?" St. Benedict asked, showing real interest.

Rune shrugged. "I vote. I suppose now that I'm in charge of the bar, I should care a bit more."

"So, what were they doing with the exotic animals?" St. Benedict asked.

"I bet it's an illegal smuggling ring," Rune said. "Most of the Fae went their own way after the Oberon betrayed them all." She looked over at St. Benedict, their faces only a few inches apart. "Maddie and I were a part of trying to save the Faerie Court as an independent legal entity, and when we failed, we tried to help find places for those who were expelled. Then Maddie died…recently…" It was still hard to say those words. "An-and too many of them turned to other enterprises."

"You mean crime?"

"Looks like," Rune said, a pang in her heart. "I haven't followed up on it. After I lost Maddie… it was just too hard."

"Don't worry, I'm not judging you. My life is mostly never following up on where I've been," he said, looking ahead and back again. "Where are we now?" Opening his palm, he turned on the light and shined it up and down the dimly lit air duct. The opposite end was just past St. Benedict's feet. His longer legs were butted up against an enclosed fan. He tapped the casing with the toe of his shoe to test it and it snarled a little against the blades in response.

"What's wrong with your eyes?" he suddenly asked, the light flashing over Rune's face, making her squeeze them tighter in response.

"Nothing," she said as she turned her head away from the light, but it just drove his shoulder deeper into the middle of her back. He shifted, and suddenly she slid to her side onto the metal of the air duct, her back facing St. Benedict. It was far more comfortable to lie like that even if it upset Ally's equilibrium.

"Open your eyes," he ordered softly, still trying to direct the light down onto her face.

Rune complied, snapping them open to look right up into a new expression on his face, concern.

"I'm fine, my head's just pounding," Rune said, instead of snapping, which was what she had been about to do. "When I opened myself up like that to find a way out, I took in everything at once. It's kind of like a sixth sense of everything and everyone. Now, I've got a migraine." That's when Rune felt a smooth tongue licking her hand. She looked up and met Ally's sympathetic eyes still perched on top of her. Rune smiled weakly at the dog, but she couldn't keep her head that way long and she laid it back down.

"So, casting magic does cost you something," St. Benedict said, settling back, at least as much as he could in the cramped space.

"It's like any other sense. If you don't use your eyes for a long time, they hurt when you start using them again," Rune said. "It might also be because I cast a real spell." She chuckled to herself with pride. "I wish Maddie could have seen that."

"What about the spell you cast in the alley to disappear from me?"

"Oh, that wasn't a real spell. That was just a hidden door that I forgot Maddie had put into the alley for quick escapes. I opened the door, like I did the one to my office, but it was her spell. Anyone can trigger a spell if you have the right trigger. I had no clue where it led, though, so I got lost. The door I made just now…" Rune reached a hand to the smooth cold metal of the vent above their heads, touching it as if to try to find some evidence of what she had done. There was nothing but metal now. "That was 100% me."

"Congratulations. Now, how do we get out of here? I don't know about you, but I'm not really partial to coffin-sized spaces."

Rune looked around the small space. There really didn't seem to be a good way out. They were lying in a square metal tube. There was a small vent near her head, the main source of the air they were currently breathing. She rolled over so she faced the vent and looked through the slots.

Below was an office. From what she could see, it had an open floor plan with about a dozen desks grouped in units of four, all empty. Sunlight poured through a row of windows, with slatted shadows from the blinds giving the room some character.

"It's the middle of the day. Where is everyone?" Rune asked herself.

"A really, really late lunch? All at the same time? A company retreat, maybe?" St. Benedict suggested. "Either way, we would need help opening that vent, and I am still not getting a signal here, so we are probably deep in an older building."

"Signal on what?" Rune asked.

"Don't worry about it," St. Benedict dismissed.

Rune narrowed her eyes but chose to ignore it. She hadn't been entirely forthcoming with her badly hidden secrets either.

"I guess theoretically, I should be able to open the portal back up and we can just crawl out. I'm not sure where it'll lead us, though. Magic doors are always tricky," Rune explained.

"I noticed."

Inhaling deeply, Rune prepared to open her magic sight again.

"How does it work exactly? Your seeing magic?" St. Benedict asked, interrupting her concentration.

"Maddie always told me to visualize it as a third eye in the middle of my forehead. Now, please be quiet. This isn't easy for me."

Another deep breath and Rune focused through her pain. The world screamed at her in colors, light, and sound. It was so intense that she couldn't even scream as she clutched her head, her back bowing in a solid arch. She closed her magic sight reflexively, the sense shutting down as abruptly as pulling a plug on a lamp.

Her head felt like she had cracked it open.

"Hey, Talent! Hey, breathe! Hey!" She barely heard the voice as the sounds around her rang hollowly. Breathing? What an extremely absurd concept. Rune would have laughed if she could remember how that was supposed to work. The grip on her head was painful, and it wasn't letting up. Rune didn't register that it was her own fists clenching her temples.

"Rune!" St. Benedict said again as he gripped one of her hands by the wrist, trying to pry it away from her skull before she crushed herself. His other hand still held her shoulder, where he had grabbed her when she had seized. Whether it was because he was stronger or because some part of her heard him, he was able to pry away the stiff fist. Sweeping the strands of her hair that had come loose away from her face, he leaned in as far as he could from behind her and listened for some hint that she was breathing.

"Rune, come on. You need to breathe," he said when he didn't hear anything.

As far as he could tell, she wasn't dead yet. Her other hand still had the strength of the living, unless magic had some means of killing you instantly and setting you into instant rigor mortis. She was definitely going to be dead if she didn't start breathing soon. In desperation, St. Benedict wrapped his arms around Rune's middle. Laying one hand over a fist, he thrust them both hard into her diaphragm. It wasn't a very strong thrust, because he was trying to do it on his side and in a very confined place, but it was enough. Rune expelled a noisy breath and gasped as the vacuum in her lungs forced the air back into her.

"Just breathe. Just breathe," he whispered as she involuntarily complied, her chest heaving up and down.

"I can't feel my face. Oh god. I can't feel my face," she gasped and released the other fist from her temple to slap at her numb face.

"Stop, stop it. Don't hit yourself." He gripped both of her wrists, pinning them under her arms as he wrapped his own arms around her to hold her still. "I've got you. You're safe, just breathe."

Rune blinked, unsure of what was happening. She only knew someone was holding her and she was safe. The world around her came back from the bright depths that had blinded her vision, and the feeling of cotton in her ears melted away. One of her belt pouches was pressing uncomfortably into her side, but she didn't have the will to shift it. She laid her cheek onto the deliciously cool metal of the air duct and closed her eyes again.

"What happened?" he asked.

A wave of nausea flowed over her.

"I tried to open it... my sight... but the feedback was too much."

"Sounds very painful," St. Benedict said.

Rune couldn't help chuckling even though it hurt. "It is a technique used to help see magic, especially magic that is outside your natural Talent. Wait. Did I already explain this?"

"Don't worry about it. Just keep talking," he encouraged.

"You sort of see everything at once, and also forward and backward in time. It can be really overwhelming. A real wizard can filter all of that out and see just what they need to work the spell," she explained, an echo of Maddie's explanation to her years ago.

"And creating magic doors is outside your Talent?"

"Oh yeah. Big time. I shouldn't have been able to do it."

St. Benedict hugged her a little tighter. "I'm sorry, I didn't understand."

Her stomach clenched again, and she turned her head down toward the bottom of the vent. "Oh, let me go. I think I might throw up."

"Where am I going to go?" he asked, amused. "If you're going to throw up, go ahead. Don't worry about me."

"But I don't want to."

"You might not have a choice," he cautioned.

They both waited in anticipation for several moments.

"No go?" he finally asked.

"Nope, I guess not," Rune said and turned back onto her side. He resettled his arm around her. "You... you don't have to hold me anymore."

"Don't really have a choice about that either. My left arm is pinned under you, and my right arm aches trying to hold it off of you."

"Oh," Rune said, hoping he couldn't see her blushing.

He chuckled dryly. "How's your head?" The warm hand that rested on her arm slid up her still-damp sleeve, before dipping below her collar to take a grip at the back of Rune's head. She almost jerked away, but the warm fingers began to knead, melting into the muscles where her skull met the top of her neck. It was both painful and wonderful at the same time. He massaged her neck for a couple minutes, increasing the pressure of the headache before lifting his hand away and taking most of the headache with it.

"Better?" he asked gently.

"Yes, actually. Thank you," Rune said and moved her head side to side, hearing it crack it in two places. "Are you secretly a healing Talent? That feels a lot better."

"No, sorry. Completely magic-less. That was just a little trigger point work. Most headaches live in the neck."

"Comes up a lot in your line of work?"

"You'd be surprised. Long hours doing surveillance, the occasional seduction, interrogation, you know, the basics."

"What is your job exactly? I don't think I've ever asked."

"Yes, I noticed you don't ask a lot of questions, do you? The clue is in the name; Saint."

"What do you mean? You said that before, but isn't that just your last name or something?"

"No, not at all. It's a designation. I am a Saint. It's what I do." He resettled his arm. "Let me try that again. I am a product of the Saint program. A tool of the corporate world."

"How is a person a tool?"

"Espionage. Saints are hired, or bought rather, to fulfill particular contracts that are not exactly legal, but necessary for the corporate elites to function. The best have the designation Saint before their names."

"Isn't that pointless if you can recognize a spy by their name? Very Double-O-Seven of you."

St. Benedict barked a laugh. "Sure, but we are not typical spies. The best secrets are hidden in plain sight. Within the companies I work for, people know to respect my authority when I need to use it. But just like you, most simply think it's my last name."

"What is your first name?"

"Ha!" The sound burst from his throat, "Nice try. You just keep calling me St. Benedict and don't go telling others what that means."

"Or you'll have to kill me," Rune said matter-of-factly. "Remember, you were only going to make that threat once."

He didn't reply, and Rune didn't need him to.

"So, what does a Saint want with me again? I am no use to you. My Talent is to find lost car keys, old tax returns, and sometimes really lost teenagers that don't have a great sense of self-preservation." Ally grumbled in her throat. She was lying right above their heads, her head on her paws.

"And you say no one can do what you do? Use magic to find things?"

"Well, not exactly, no one can do what I do the way I seem to do it. I just get these feelings, right? It's not like tracking Talents. I've heard that when they cast their spells, they see a light that highlights the signs of someone passing. Aura Readers will see a ghost aura imprint and, depending on how clear it is, can determine where someone went. But objects don't have auras and it's things that I seem to be able to find, and people are usually connected to their things. No one else does that. And then the added bonus of this unrelated power is I pretty much never get lost."

"You're able to find an escape route. That sounds useful."

"Except sometimes people can't come with me," Rune said, her voice taking on a haunted quality.

"Someone didn't come with you once?"

"Maddie. It was a couple of months ago. We were out on a job. A shopkeeper had a bogie infestation in his basement. Maddie was taking care of it when she just collapsed. I tried to open a way to the ER, but I couldn't..." Rune said, the tears welling up in her eyes. "Ugh, where's a light when you need one?" She rubbed at her eyes to wipe away the tears. "Look, I could try to open the door again, but there is a good chance I'll also have a brain aneurysm right now," she said to change the subject.

"What do you need to be able to do it?" he asked.

"A full night's sleep," Rune said, "and a crystal with the spell already pre-loaded. I have some chalk in my belt, but inscribing... Yeah, a crystal. That'd be really helpful right now."

"Therefore, in conclusion, we need to get out of here another way," he said. He moved behind her as if he was looking over his shoulder, then said, "Can you exhale completely for me?"

Before Rune could ask what was going on, he squished her against the side of the air duct.

"We don't fit better this way," Rune squeaked out.

"Needs must, sweetheart." St. Benedict pressed his face as close as he could to the vent, trying to see a sliver more.

"I can't breathe."

"I think we can safely guess we are still in Chicago," he said cheerfully as he settled back to let Rune get a breath in.

"What makes you say that?" Rune asked after a nice big inhale.

"To the far right. Avid Blackhawks fan."

Rune pressed her face to the vent and saw what he was talking about; little Blackhawk flags were stuck onto the top of the computer monitor, each showing the Blackhawk mascot with the red, green, and yellow feathers emerging from its crest.

Precipitously, that was the moment when the office staff returned. People in suits flooded into the room, each acquiring a desk with an urgent sense of purpose. A couple of the suits went to a clear board covered with writing and papers. All of them looked a little bedraggled, as if it had been a day or two since they last went home, showered, and changed their clothes.

Rune's eyes went round. "Isn't that the Saint woman who shot at us an hour ago?" Rune whispered.

"St. Augustina, yeah," he agreed, just as softly. "Assuming you aren't leading me into a trap, how did we end up here and a day later than *when* we were an hour ago or so?"

"A day later?" Rune said. "How do you know?"

"Look at the second board above St. Augustina in the corner. The board's dated," he said.

"June twenty-third," Rune read softly.

"Is this one of those weird magic things where you go into the Faerie realm only to come out and it's years later?"

"I guess. I've sometimes wondered if the ways bend more than just space, but this kind of thing…"

"Why hasn't some wizard taken over the world already if they can jump through time like that?" he speculated.

"That's an exaggeration. Time has its own rules, and nobody controls it."

"So, you've done this before?"

"Only once, and I was with Maddie. She was just as surprised as I was. She backed us out of there really fast. She said if we mess with time, it could…be really bad."

"Why?" he asked.

Rune shrugged. "All she said is that time has a way of getting you killed."

"That's cryptic and ominous."

"I always took it to mean that time will do something like cause an accident in order to protect itself or something. Like correcting the paradox, that kind of thing."

"Alright, how do we prevent that from happening?"

Rune thought a moment. "We've jumped forward in time by tearing a new portal out of one of these tunnels. If we go back into the tunnel the same way we came in, then we might go back to the time we left."

"Because that makes so much more sense," he whispered dryly. "And we ended up here because, surprise! Coincidence!" He shook his hands in a show of mock surprise by her face since he couldn't reach his own. Then he shifted behind her. Rune heard the metal sound of him unbuckling his belt. He yanked the belt out and forward. "Here, take this end," he instructed, holding the buckle in front of Rune. She stared at it like it was a snake.

"What are you doing!?" Rune whispered, alarmed.

"Trying to do a bit of my own magic." He wiggled the belt end at her. She took it and drew it out, the leather making a whisper sound as it unwound from around his waist. He laced his hands back through her arms so he could take the belt from her. He drew out a wire, hidden inside with an earbud at the end, and stuck that bud into Rune's ear. A third wire with a pad on it, he stuck into the palm of his hand, the augmentation flashing green as a new screen, and two little radars appeared. Other circles pinged all over the screen, in response to the various sounds in the room. In Rune's ear, sounds came rushing in not helping her now dull headache. St. Benedict pivoted a free finger in the two circles on the holographic surface, making the other ripples decrease along with the sounds until there was only one strong ripple and several smaller ones. The noises calmed into words.

"Where the fuck are you, St. Benedict? You will not screw me again, you hear me?" St. Augustina muttered under her breath, and he smiled to himself. He knew she didn't know he was listening and he would never be able to tell her how funny it was anyway. He was like some kind of omnipotent god, or maybe from her perspective, a demon. But not sharing those kinds of things with his old compatriot; that was the price of the spy business.

A suit approached her desk then, looking only slightly uneasy, and quietly waited to be acknowledged by his superior.

"Can I help you?" St. Augustina asked, with the air of a college professor who just found out one of her students was sleeping with her husband.

"You wanted a status update every hour," he answered.

"I know that. I'm the one who ordered it. What do you have to report?"

"We've run a check on Rune Leveau again, using the President's clearance, but it didn't yield anything new," he reported.

"What?! Nothing?" St. Augustina pressed. "You're saying she just reappeared out of nowhere? In this day and age?"

"She is a part of the magical community. We only have half of those people in the system in any meaningful way—" the subordinate tried to say, but before he could finish St. Augustina waved him into silence.

"What about the rumor that she can lead the way to the Masterson files?" St. Augustina asked, lacing her fingers together in front of her and resting her chin on her thumbs.

"Still unconfirmed as anything more than a rumor at this point."

"It wouldn't surprise me if St. Benedict started that one himself. But then why would he want Leveau anyway? Who the hell is she?"

"Ma'am," another woman said, approaching the table. "I think it has more to do with the previous owner of the bar we found Leveau in."

"Wait, wait," St. Augustina waved at the grunt, "who are you again?"

"Dr. Benita Cruz. I was assigned to your task force for my expertise in the social organization of the magic community. It is my opinion that the person he actually seeks is, or rather was, the Magdalene," the Latina woman said, adjusting her glasses at the end of her nose. "She was Rune Leveau's master and a well-known figure in the magic community. She died a month ago. If anyone could find something like that, the Magdalene would have been the magic person to ask for help. It is my expert opinion that he sought out the apprentice in a desperate attempt to find the files."

"But this Rune Leveau isn't a Talent?" St. Augustina asked as her gaze became distant.

"There are no official records, no," Dr. Cruz confirmed, "but there is also something reportedly off about her. No one who has investigated her has turned up anything."

"She's been under other investigations?"

"A Deputy Blake. She's apparently been his pet project, but nothing official," Dr. Cruz read from a file.

"Any passive tests she's taken have been negative for Magical Abilities," one of the lackeys added. "There has never been a call for an official test since she graduated high school."

"Which is normal," Dr. Cruz added. "You need a judge's order to test someone involuntarily, and there hasn't been enough probable cause."

"Do we have evidence that St. Benedict contacted this Magdalene?" St. Augustina asked as she stood up and started writing on the clear board with a green marker, circling the word "Magdalene," and connected it to Rune Leveau's name already written on the board under "person of interest."

"Oh great," Rune mumbled as she watched.

"I wouldn't worry about it. That's not secret information, right?" St. Benedict whispered, close to her ear.

"I suppose not," Rune conceded.

Another grunt, a tall, burly man with a barrel chest, approached the small group.

"Has interrogation of St. Benedict's known associates yielded anything new about his current whereabouts?" St. Augustina asked the newcomer before he could say anything.

St. Benedict flinched and leaned even closer to the grate. "What?" he whispered.

"Nothing yet. We're letting the snake and the tech nerd cool in separate rooms for now. We'll restart the interrogations soon. The snake gives me the creeps," the deep-voiced grunt reported.

St. Benedict had heard enough. "We've got to get out of here," he whispered urgently.

"Do you know who they're talking about?" Rune asked.

St. Benedict shifted back, a new look on his face, like flowing lava beneath a sheet of frozen ice. He pulled the buds out of their ears and removed the pad on his hand. The screen went blue again and he started tapping along the surface of the rectangle of light. After a moment, he became frustrated.

"Too slow. Too slow. Forget it! I don't care what I promised Malachi," he muttered to himself. He held his hand in front of the grate. Rune's eyes went round as the tips of his fingers started to glow with blue light, the sight of it fascinating to her.

Though Rune couldn't see it, St. Benedict's eyes began to glow as well, the green irises emitting their own blue light. They darted back and forth as if he watched a thousand invisible things fly past him.

"She's got my people," was his delayed answer. His brain worked faster than a rabbit in the wrong hutch. Then a wicked glint touched the corner of his eye and he chuckled softly to himself. "Why bother securing your network at all, St. Augustina, if you're going to leave a backdoor for anyone to just walk into?" he continued, not really talking to Rune as something changed out in the main room. "Oh, hello. A Halon system?" His wicked smile sharpened.

An alarm went off in the office, stopping all activity in the room. From the ceiling smoke erupted, filling the space with the foulest, chemically astringent odor Rune had ever the misfortune to inhale. The room erupted into blind chaos.

"What the hell is going on?!" St. Augustina roared amidst the shouting and scurrying of her cronies.

"She was never savvy with the tech side of things," St. Benedict whispered, delighted at the chaos below them. Rune could only nod as she stared wide-eyed at the panicking office, now lost in a thick white fog.

"Someone open a window already!" St. Augustina barked.

"We can't! These windows don't open like that, we're too high up," Dr. Benita cried, her voice muffled like it was coming from the inside of her jacket.

"What is going on? *Are* we under attack?" St. Augustina called back as she pushed her way through to the far wall.

"We don't know. The computers are down," the grunt answered as if it was obvious. St. Augustina shoved them out of the way and went to the thermostat box on the wall, cranking the fan up as high as it would go.

"Why are the computers down!?" she roared. "What is going on?"

"It's the fire suppression system, ma'am! In case of fire, instead of water, we get... well, this... and the computers automatically back up and power down!" some techie tried to explain.

"Why does it stink?!"

"Well, ma'am, I... I don't really know."

Another voice shouted, "Ma'am, I'm going to have to insist you evacuate as standard fire protocol."

"We aren't going anywhere. Get these computers back on!" St. Augustina ordered.

"That's impossible, until the building turns the main power back on, ma'am."

"I swear, St. Benedict, when I get my hands on you, I am going to make you eat your balls!" she coughed into her shirt sleeve.

St. Benedict chuckled dangerously loud at the comment, especially since St. Augustina was just below them. "I wonder if she blames everything that goes wrong on me?" he quipped.

"I don't understand what you've done..." Rune whispered as she tried to follow their adversary's movements.

"My own little brand of magic. I tapped into the emergency system."

"But what is that? It's not water."

"Water destroys computers. This is a Halon system. Just really smelly smoke that puts out fires but leaves computers intact."

"That's possible?" Rune asked, her head reeling, trying to follow what he was saying.

"I don't know. Is it?" he asked as more smoke roiled into the vent.

"Ma'am, we have to evacuate!" someone shouted in the room.

"Okay, that's it, everyone clear the room!" St. Augustina ordered.

That's when Ally caught Rune's attention. The little dog girl's nails were skittering loudly across the metal of the air duct as she pawed at the sides in panic.

"Ally! Shh," Rune shushed at the dog and tried to sit up to grab her, but only managed to bat her paws away, creating a loud scratching sound instead.

"If we keep moving, we're going to get caught," Rune whispered.

"Doesn't matter. There is nowhere to go. We're stuck here," St. Benedict said, though she could barely hear his whisper as the fan above their heads kicked on full gear, making Ally squeak. The air became smoke as it was pulled through the vent.

"Ugh, it smells like a skunk was getting nasty with an unscented hairspray can," Rune said as she tried to cover her mouth with her hand.

"It's not toxic, so don't worry," St. Benedict replied. The fans blowing replaced the dank air that had been growing in the vent with chilled air that cut right through Rune's damp clothing.

"Oh crap," he said and immediately grabbed his fedora. "I didn't think this through."

"What? Is the vent trying to suck the smoke out or something?" Rune asked.

"Oh, I hate vents," he grumbled. "Every time someone suggests we enter through vents, I want to smack them across the face. They never work out."

"You're more likely to get caught?" Rune asked.

"You're more likely to die. I'll tell you all the ways later," St. Benedict answered, as he slid down and gently tested the other covered fan with his foot.

Ally laid her head down on Rune's shoulder, hiding her face, her wet dog nose making Rune tickle as she whined a tiny whine.

"You sure you can't open the magic portal thing again without stroking out?" St Benedict asked.

"Well…" Rune looked up at the metal surface again.

"Because option one, take our chances calling for help. They would have to cut us out of here, and we will most definitely be arrested and detained for a significant while. Or option two, we see if you can open the way back through, but we may freeze before that."

"You know, I can't make up my mind whether you're reckless or just stupid," Rune admonished.

"There is an argument that can be made for both," St. Benedict agreed.

Rune continued to stare at the metal wall above their heads, thinking hard. She knew if she opened her magic sight again, she would probably seize.

"Do you really think she'll just arrest us?"

"Oh, she'll kill me for sure. She'll probably spare you. She hates unnecessary violence against women," he said.

"She wouldn't really kill you, would she?"

He shrugged a stiff shoulder that became a shiver. "She has her reasons."

"Are you suggesting that you are going to sacrifice yourself to save me?"

"It's an option that's on the table, yes," he answered.

"Well, that's just great," Rune huffed.

"To be honest, not the response I was expecting," St Benedict said wryly. "Look, we better decide soon."

Before Rune could say anything more, a door banged open, and two voices could be clearly heard in the silence of the empty office.

"Look at this mess. We haven't got time to get all this fixed. Come on," whined a young-sounding man, wearing a mask over his face that muffled his voice.

"Just go over and check the thermostat," said a gruff voice, also muffled by a mask.

"These damn paper pushers. Why is this thing on in the first place?" grumbled the first voice as it got louder just beneath the trio in the vent.

"They installed this new system last year. Supposed to vent out this Halon crap, I bet."

"Doesn't seem to be working worth a buck. What are you doing?" questioned the first voice, taking on notes of incredulity.

"If something is wrong, it's probably because someone stuffed something in the vent. It's always something in the vent." The gruff voice was just below them, and Rune felt St. Benedict stiffen next to her.

If only she could think of a way to open the portal again and get them out of there.

"Get off that desk this minute! You can't stand on the desks! That's several code violations, and what if you break something?" the gruff voice scolded.

"Don't get your panties in a twist," the whiny voice answered, and Rune heard the squeak as a screwdriver pulled loose one of the screws on the vent.

Rune glanced over at the Saint in alarm, and her eyes widened as she saw him slide a thin blade from the leather of his belt. He held it in his hand with savage intent. It was clear that the moment the vent grate came off, he intended to attack whoever came through. Urgently, her hand shot out and grasped his forearm. The tense muscles quivered under her touch.

"Let go," he breathed into her ear so only she could hear him. All she could do was shake her head in silent reply.

"Why didn't you bring the ladder?" the gruff voice demanded. It had come closer, right next to the whiny voice.

"Because it is heavy," the whiny voice sniveled. Then the screw came free of the corner. The loss of resistance made the whiny voiced maintenance worker drop his screwdriver, which crashed down onto the desk. There was a sharp sound of glass breaking.

"Now you've done it," said the gruff-voiced maintenance worker.

"Shit!" The whiny one replied.

Rune heard the sound of him jumping down. She felt St. Benedict's muscles relax a little under her hand.

"I've got a repair crystal downstairs. Come on, we'll get the ladder too while we're at it," the gruff one said resignedly.

"Holy crap! Are you a Talent?"

"Yeah, something like that. My grandmother was a hedge witch."

"So, that means you grow flowers or something?"

"None of your beeswax."

The whiny one continued talking as the two voices faded and left.

Rune took a deep breath and immediately began coughing again. The sick smell of the Halon lessened a bit as the fans kicked off. Her head hurt again.

"We have one shot at this. I can get us out, but it is not going to be pretty. I cannot have you getting in my way," the Saint said harshly.

"They're just janitors. You can't kill them for just doing their jobs," Rune shot back.

"I'm not going to argue with you, and I sure as hell am not going to justify this to you."

"Oh, it's us or them, is that what you're saying?" Rune was getting angry.

"It's about options and doing what is necessary," he said coldly, the jovial, charming man disappearing to be replaced with the cold predator that Rune had glimpsed a few different times now.

"I'll find us a way out!" Rune said. She had to do something. As if only waiting for her to say the words, Rune felt a strong tug toward where they had entered the vent in the first place.

"It can't be, I can't open it," she said softly.

"Can't open what?" St. Benedict demanded.

Rune touched the surface one more time.

"What…what is the Latin word for open?"

"What?"

"The Latin word for open? I can't ever remember it."

The coldness retreated from St. Benedict's voice a bit, "What are you thinking?"

"Well, I closed this with Maddie's 'close doors' incantation…what if…what if the door is still there? I just need to open it? I wouldn't need to see it to do that." Rune paused. "Actually, I opened a door yesterday without the incantation. How did I do that?" Rune focused on the metal, trying to picture it opening in her mind.

"Open," she commanded.

Nothing happened.

"Open now," she tried again.

Still, nothing happened.

"Stop it," St. Benedict said. She turned a little in his arms so she could look at him better. His gaze was dark except for the eerie blue glow in his eyes. She knew he would kill, it was written on his face. But why? Just to protect himself? Was he so afraid of her using her magic?

"You're afraid *for* me…" Rune realized out loud. His eyes widened a little in response, confirming the truth better than any words.

The two maintenance workers came back then.

"I can do it," she whispered to him. She had to.

He closed his eyes, his fierce expression relaxing a bit. "Can you figure it out in the next two minutes?" St. Benedict asked, his voice as edged as his blade.

"I…I'm going to have to open my sight," Rune said, biting her lower lip with anxiety.

"No!" he hissed at her.

"I have to. I can't see what's going on," she insisted.

There was the sound of clanking metal from the ladder hitting the side of the vent. Rune opened her magic vision again. Her head immediately felt like it had split in two, just like before. She knew she wasn't breathing again. She could barely sense St. Benedict outside of the pain. But that's when she saw it.

The workers and their world were like a soap bubble of their existence. It rolled toward the too-colorful world around Rune. The bubble stopped outside of the vent.

"The paradox…it's coming." If she wasn't breathing, how did she say that?

"Dammit, Rune," St. Benedict whispered, renewing his grip on the knife.

Rune didn't really hear him. "The sequence of events that will lead to our inevitable deaths. Time is trying to kill us." She said it with perfect knowledge that it was true without really knowing why she knew.

It took every ounce of her will to simply look up at the metal wall. This time she could see it, the crosshatch of threads glittering with their own internal light. There was a seam of light around it, the edge of the portal door she had created.

"Did you hear something?" asked the gruff voice echoing, and the two paused in their work. How could she hear so clearly when she couldn't hear St. Benedict right next to her? Rune focused on the seam. Somehow her arm moved, and she reached out touch the potential in the seam, tearing it open with everything she had. It felt like crinkle paper as she pulled through the fibers of reality. The portal was open.

"Is someone in there?" the voices shouted.

Rune snapped her eyes shut, unable to do anything more. She felt the sensation of being moved, but she didn't care anymore. She just wanted to die and escape the sick pain all around her. Just let it be over and fall into the oblivion encroaching around her. The voices shouted after them, but she drifted away as if in a dream.

Then her body crunched as she landed on rough gravel. The shock of the impact jolted through her body, and she involuntarily inhaled a loud, desperate breath. Somewhere, Ally yelped two angry barks. A pair of hands cupped Rune's face and St. Benedict looked down at her, frantic.

"Rune, breathe!"

"I'm breathing!" she croaked hoarsely, then forced another painful breath into her lungs, curling onto her side. The gravel bit into the palm of her hand, and after a few more easier breaths, Rune tried to look around.

It was a different world than the one she had left hours ago when they had first entered. It was early evening, and the sun was starting to angle away toward the horizon. A warm breeze glided seagulls away from Lake Michigan and ruffling Rune's brown hair, carrying away the cold that clung to her clothes. Her companion's hand was on her back, rubbing slow circles as she worked on breathing.

"Where are we?" Rune finally managed to ask.

"On a rooftop somewhere," St. Benedict answered.

"My, my, that was exciting," said a new voice. Lifting her dizzy head up, Rune blinked at the sight of the orange lady sitting on a crate, her legs crossed as she sipped on a plastic cup of something through a long crazy straw. "About time you two showed up."

CHAPTER 10

"You! Can you help her?" St. Benedict demanded.

Rune wondered if she was hearing things, but she just couldn't find the energy to care. She laid her pounding head back on the gravel, closing her eyes against the brighter light of the outside world. The soft breeze from the lake danced over her, caressing her skin.

"What's wrong with her?" the orange lady asked, unworried as she took another noisy sip from her cup.

"I opened my sight," Rune managed to mumble out.

"Ah, and now you can't open either way of seeing." The orange lady laughed. "And your knight is so very worried about you too. Do not worry, warrior, she will be fine in time. Of course, he isn't looking too good himself."

The way the orange lady took another measured easy sip, working so very hard to seem both unconcerned and non-threatening, was the first thing that tipped St. Benedict off that she was anything but. He had knelt next to Rune after hauling her whole body through that freaky portal she had made. Thankfully, Ally had taken care of herself and leapt out of the hole ahead of them. It had closed the minute his feet had cleared. He couldn't help wondering what would have happened if he had been a second slower. Would his feet still be on the other side of that portal, detached forever?

Hauling Rune out had taken the last bit of his energy. He wasn't sure what was wrong with him, but his limbs trembled, and his vision blurred, going in and out of focus. The hunger inside was sharply painful, as if his very cells were starving, needing, burning. He tried to focus on the strange woman decked in orange, but his eyes kept darting to the cup in her hands. It took everything in him not to rush across the few feet between them and snatch the waxed paper cup, festooned with cold condensation, from her sun-spotted hands.

"Oh yes, you're not doing well at all," the orange lady commented further. Her eyes followed his to her cup and then looked back at him.

Slowly, she set down the cup onto the uneven, gravelly roof. His eyes followed it all the way down, but he didn't go for it. Instead, St. Benedict took a deliberate, dry swallow and forced his eyes back up to her face. In the time it took him to do that, he realized too late that they were surrounded.

There were little more than half a dozen of them. The monochromes, each just as inky black as their coats, white skulls painted across their faces. They emerged seemingly from thin air, each with white, pearly eyes and no irises, unnerving and alien.

Sensing the change in atmosphere, Rune forced herself to open her eyes and they rounded wide as she saw the monochromes staring down at them. Two stood on either side of the orange lady, her color all the brighter for being framed by their darkness.

"Oh, no," Rune whispered, and she tried to push herself up to her hands and knees. A low growl rumbled beside her and she looked quickly for fear that they had brought a dog or something. Or was Ally making a threat? Instead, she realized with a shock that it was St. Benedict growling.

His face had gone strange, not that she had known him long enough to be familiar with all of his common facial expressions. His eyes had lost most of their natural color, turning a pea-soup green instead of their usual emerald. Green tinged the whites, almost jaundice-like. He bared his teeth like an animal, and if he had hackles, she would have sworn they would be up. Instead, his shoulders locked up toward his ears and every muscle in his strong, lithe body seemed to coil as if preparing to spring.

The monochromes shifted with a nervous energy that rippled through them at the sight of the Saint. The orange lady also dropped the grandmotherly, hippie facade and stood up between the two monochrome men who framed her, each moving forward a step as if preparing to shield her.

"St. Benedict?" Rune asked in a small voice. His eyes darted to her, human recognition still present, but faint.

"What is wrong with your knight, child?" the orange lady asked, her voice taking a new commanding tone.

"St. Benedict, what's wrong with you?" Rune asked, unwavering, reaching out to touch him. The skin on his thigh seemed to shudder at her touch under the strain of his pants, and she had to resist the instinctive panic inside to draw her hand away.

"Move away, child, before he harms you," the orange lady said urgently, holding her hand out toward Rune.

"He won't harm me. He's my friend," Rune answered.

"You may be his friend, but is he yours?" the orange lady asked and gestured ever so slightly with her fingers. The circle of monochromes closed in slowly. "Best if you come with us, Faerie Friend."

"Stay back!" St. Benedict growled, his words garbled by his tightly clenched jaw.

"Stay back!" Rune echoed, nervously glancing around the circle.

Then something seized inside of St. Benedict, and he groaned in pain. He started to bend at the waist over his one knee, the crouch looking awkward. The motion seemed to trigger something in the group and as one, they rushed toward the pair in a tide of black.

One second, St. Benedict was collapsed over in pain, but the next, when the first hand grabbed the collar of his shirt, the Saint's hand snapped out to catch the monochrome man's wrist. St. Benedict was on his feet, spinning the man around his body and into two more men coming from the opposite direction. Another, slightly taller man came up from behind St. Benedict, dodging the hurling bodies, to try to grapple the Saint in a bear hug. While he succeeded in his goal, St. Benedict immediately crouched like a football player preparing to receive the ball. He grasped his attacker's leg and levered it up between his own, sending the monochrome man falling onto his backside. Then St. Benedict swung his own long leg, stepping over the leg he had trapped and landing his heel against the skull face's temple. His opponent crumpled, limp, to the ground.

Meanwhile, Rune found herself pulled away by the two monochromes who had stood on either side of the orange lady. Together, they took her arms and hauled her away from the fighting, her feet swinging out as they yanked her back.

"Hey, stop! Let me go!" Rune tried to struggle, but without purchase under her feet she had no choice but to go where they took her. They set her next to the orange lady, releasing her before taking positions in front of both females.

"Do not fear, child, we only wish to help you," the orange lady assured, laying a hand on Rune's shoulder.

"But...but..." Rune stuttered, confused, "then why are you attacking us?"

Before she could get an answer, there was a cry of pain. The two monochromes in front of her, one of which was actually a large woman, moved a few steps forward as one unit. Doing that parted them a bit and Rune could now see what was happening.

The fighting had paused, or it appeared to have, as Rune tried to process what she was seeing. Two of the monochromes backpedaled away from St. Benedict, one trying to pull the other away, but the second was caught somehow on St. Benedict. The Saint grappled with the second one, and a spurt of white liquid shot out of the man's neck as he screamed. Two others grabbed St. Benedict by his arms in an attempt to pull him away and he almost overturned them with inhuman strength, but they won against him and separated him from their companion.

The monochrome man scrambled away with the help of his friend, grabbing at his neck with both hands, white eyes so wide that the black ring around them almost disappeared. The white liquid he was trying to hold at bay sluiced down St. Benedict's chin. To everyone's horror, they realized that the Saint had bitten him.

"He's mad!" the orange lady said in abhorrence.

"St. Benedict!" Rune shouted as she watched a cut across his nose heal before her eyes. His eyes were almost solid green now, the pupils blended away like a black coin lost in the thick pea-soup. He tried to sweep more of the white blood up his chin and into his mouth using his hands. Rune thought she was going to throw up.

"Get him to the ground!" the monochrome woman in front of them shouted. She rushed to help with their wounded companion, who was panicking. At her word, the remaining men rushed St. Benedict at once, managing in concert to bring him down. The orange lady laid a hand on the wounded monochrome man's shoulder and he calmed at her touch. He looked so young as the white blood leaked through his fingers at his neck.

"He's bleeding out!" the monochrome woman said.

"Stay still, stay still," the orange lady murmured and she whipped out a twig decorated with white berries and sharp green leaves. She touched the tip to the injured man's neck. There was a distinct smell of sulfur and something earthy, like wet dirt. His whole body contracted as the wild magic burned at the wound in his neck. Then he sighed with relief and let his hand drop away as he passed out into the monochrome woman's arms.

"That will keep him alive for now, but we must treat it better when we get back to the Circle, or his body will remember and it will reopen."

"What did you do?" Rune asked, curiosity catching her before she could check her question.

"Court secrets," the orange lady answered, unperturbed, but the monochrome woman shot the orange lady a disapproving look as she helped the younger monochrome man to lie on the ground more comfortably.

"He stinks of corporation," the monochrome woman said, her skull-painted face grimacing down at St. Benedict. He was planted face down in the ground and it took four of the monochrome men to keep him from moving, but by the way they all bounced a little, he was still trying.

"Do we kill him?" one of them cried.

"He was trying to eat him! Eat him alive!" another injured one squeaked out in real fear, bordering on panic.

A tremor of fear rolled through the group. St. Benedict fought harder to throw off the monochrome men holding him down, growling and salivating like an animal.

"We should kill him," one of the men holding him down cried.

"He's a demon."

"Possessed!"

"No! Please wait," Rune shouted, throwing her hands up. "You can't!"

"We can't take him back to the Circle like that," the monochrome woman said firmly to the orange lady.

"We don't dare stand up! We release him, and he's going to try to kill us all and anyone else he comes across!" added the men holding him down.

"He's just hungry!" Rune shouted.

Everyone looked at her and blinked.

"What?" the monochrome woman finally asked.

"Two days ago, or something, I cast a healing spell on him with a crystal. It...it has a side effect of speeding up metabolism, I mean, his metabolism. I think he's spell-cursed," Rune struggled to explain.

"You cursed your own knight?" the orange lady asked.

"No, no not..."

The orange lady looked between her and St. Benedict, who had stopped struggling and was breathing heavy under the mound.

"Behold the power of a wizard. Indeed, you are all very lucky this day," the orange lady said, laughing, the silly hippie returning. "That is totally awesome."

"No! No," Rune defended while struggling to process everything. "Well, not on purpose. It…it should have worn off already."

"Two days, you say?" the orange lady repeated. "And he is like this?"

"I just need to give him something to eat!" Rune insisted. She scrabbled into one of the pouches of her belt and pulled out the trail mix she had packed.

St. Benedict was so far gone as the magic drove him mad with hunger that she couldn't get close enough to feed the small pieces to him. Not that they would be sufficient to abate the demands of the spell anyway. "Look at his eyes, it's just a spell."

"Please do not kill us, wizard!" one of the monochrome men shouted at Rune.

"I'm not a wiz…I'm not trying to kill you, but you attacked us! In the tunnel," Rune started to shout back, but the orange lady held up a hand to stop her.

"And for that, we are deeply sorry, Faerie Friend," the orange lady interjected, shooting her companion a regal glance, then sticking out her tongue. The monochrome woman yielded, taking a soldier's stance by crossing her wrists behind her back. "The Fae folk have no wish to anger you, wizard, and to have incurred your wrath was unfortunate. We beg your forgiveness."

Rune blinked at the whole statement. "No, no, it's fine. I mean, not fine, but I get it. Just…help us, please."

"This creature may be too far gone," the orange lady said, her voice full of sympathy. "Your wizard's magic is potent…"

"But it isn't! I'm only a Talent!" Rune interrupted.

The two women and the young man only stared at her, uncomprehending.

"Your reasons for doing this to your knight are your own, wizard, but we can't leave him like this," the monochrome woman said.

"No, there's got to be something we can do," Rune insisted.

The orange lady sighed. "Find a spark of humanity in him, and I will help you."

"What? What do you mean?" Rune asked.

St. Benedict roared and made another attempt to free himself, lifting the group of monochrome men inches off the ground. They called out in fear again.

"You must hurry, child, or we can do nothing to save him," the orange lady urged.

Rune wasted no more time but knelt down beside St. Benedict's head as close as she dared.

"St. Benedict?" she said gently.

He didn't look at her. His pure-green eyes spun in their sockets and focused on nothing around him. White foam bubbled at the corners of his mouth and the small scratches on his cheek were healing rapidly, probably increasing his hunger even more. What was going on? The spell should have receded hours ago, if not yesterday. Instead, it seemed to be consuming him and healing him at the same time, turning him into a raving monster.

Rune was at a loss as to how to help him. Finding his humanity was such a vague notion. She was sure the orange lady didn't mean for her to demonstrate her Talent, or if she did, Rune was pretty sure nothing would happen. But she had to try to reach him. The weight of the eyes, watching all around, was heavy on her even as she tried to ignore them and pretend they didn't matter.

"St. Benedict, hey, it's me. It's your friend, Rune. It's okay, you're safe," she said, the lie feeling leaden on her tongue. She didn't feel remotely safe. The tension around them had ratcheted another notch.

"St. Benedict, please, look at me. You have to show them you're still you in there," she said, taking a risk and reaching out to touch his cold, sweaty cheek with her fingertips. He made to bite those fingers, and she withdrew them quickly, suppressing a squeak.

"He's too far gone. I bet the humanity's been burned right out of him," the monochrome woman said, remorselessly.

"Come on, St. Benedict, show them you're still human," Rune pleaded.

Then St. Benedict closed his eyes, hiding the sickly green behind his lids and seemed to calm.

"Bar," he croaked out.

"What? Bar?" Rune urged, wondering if this would be enough.

He licked his lips and tried again. "Two… women… walk… bar…"

Rune double blinked.

"Two women walk into a bar?" She exchanged a glance with the orange lady. "Are you… are you trying to crack a joke?"

St. Benedict chuckled — or growled — in response. It was hard to tell.

CHAPTER 11

A power bar hit the ground next to Rune. Without any hesitation, she scooped it up and opened the wrap with shaking fingers. Two more hit the ground as well, but she focused on bringing the first bar of peanut-colored, semi-solid goop to St. Benedict's mouth. The smell of the peanut butter snapped his eyes open, and Rune had to be careful he didn't eat her fingers with the bar.

"Slow down, slow down! You're going to choke," Rune worried.

One of the monochromes handed her a second bar, already unwrapped, and she carefully fed St. Benedict.

"Do we get off him now, Lady?" asked one of the men who was holding the Saint down.

Rune didn't look at them but kept her focus on St. Benedict, who was chewing more now as she started to feed him the third bar. She pulled a wet-nap out of her belt to clear off the sticky and spit from her fingers. There must have been some agreement by the monochromes because they all quickly scuttled away from him like they were releasing a crocodile into the wild. Only Rune continued to sit by him, holding out the next bite of the bar.

"St. Benedict?" she asked when he didn't move at first. His eyes finally opened and focused on the bar in her fingers. With wicked speed, he snatched it and stuffed it into his mouth, chewing hard. The move made the group flinch, but he didn't even look at them.

"Is there more?" Rune asked.

"Water," St. Benedict coughed out, sounding more human.

The takeaway cup the orange lady had been sipping from was handed to Rune. She held the crazy straw out toward St. Benedict. He raised his head at it and took the end obediently in his teeth, chewing it up as much as drinking from it. His hands landed on Rune's as they wrestled a little for control of the cup, but she managed to hold on, and he managed to get rid of the straw to pour most of it into his mouth.

"Let me see your eyes," Rune ordered.

St. Benedict blinked several times, focusing on the cup in his hands, before finally glancing up, looking much more human.

There was still green in his eyes, but to Rune's relief, the black pupils had returned and the ghostly outline of his irises. A shudder went through him, and he dropped his gaze again, covering his face with his hands.

"God, those things taste awful," he said, his voice muffled by his fingers.

"Do you feel better?" Rune asked.

"I feel terrible." He looked up from his fingers, then straight at the monochrome lying on the ground. "Did I...Did...?"

"He'll live," the monochrome woman said.

St. Benedict touched his chin where the white blood was starting to dry. "But I bit... I bit his jugular vein..." He shuddered again as the horror of what he had done sank in.

"Don't throw up!" Rune said, placing a hurried hand over his mouth as if that would prevent him from vomiting. "Keep everything inside, or we're going to be right back where we started. He's going to be fine. He's been treated with his people's magic."

"I tried to eat him...alive," St. Benedict said in horror, taking her fingers from his mouth, trapping them in his grip.

"You're cursed. Don't think about it," she soothed.

His eyes went wide as he stared down at his white-covered fingers. Slowly, he turned to Rune while applying pressure to her hand.

"I want to lick it off my fingers," he whispered, sounding sick.

Urgently, and with the smallest gesture possible, Rune shook her head at him before poignantly indicating the monochromes around them with her eyes.

St. Benedict swallowed hard, and something hostile flitted across his face. Then he nodded his understanding, though he still looked sick. He released Rune's fingers, and looked around, assessing the situation. The group of monochromes had not taken their eyes off of them but were now milling around and talking softly to each other. It seemed like St. Benedict wasn't going to renew his rampage.

"I'm assuming that because we are still alive that we are not enemies anymore?" he asked, sounding even more like himself.

"For now," the monochrome woman agreed, still not giving an inch.

"Are you responsible for cursing me?" he asked the monochrome woman.

"I think I did that," Rune interjected. "Probably yesterday or two days ago. I don't know, time's gotten funny on us. Your body... it's continuing to heal you, but the spell I cast on you should have faded already," Rune explained.

"You did this to me?" he asked.

"I'm sorry. I think so." Rune nodded. "I was trying to help you, remember?"

"Am I going to be alright?"

"Well, I guess we have to keep you well fed 'til it wears off. I really don't know what else to do," Rune admitted.

"Needs must when the devil drives," St. Benedict grumbled as he rubbed at his chin, erasing any more traces of what he had done. "It's like I went on a bad trip."

"That's a good way to think of it, actually. But more like you've OD'd on morphine or something."

"Morphine makes me sleep, not go cannibalistic."

"PCP, then?"

St. Benedict cracked a smile. "You don't know your drugs, do you?"

"My mama raised a good girl," Rune answered smartly. Suddenly, she jumped as she remembered something. "Where's Ally?"

Looking around the roof, Rune didn't see the small white dog-girl anywhere. "Ally?!"

"What's wrong, wizard?" the monochrome woman asked.

"Uh, my dog. I've lost my dog. She's a little white thing."

This invoked a bunch of necks to turn left and right, as the monochromes looked around. It made them seem strangely human. Taking Ms. Janowski's locket in her hand, Rune focused again. Almost instantly, she felt a clear tug toward the other side of a mushroom-like vent on the far side of the roof. Ally crouched behind it, lying on her stomach to make herself as small as possible. She whined, and her whole little being shivered as Rune picked her up. "It's okay, Ally, I got you."

She carried the dog back to where St. Benedict remained seated with a loose guard around him. The orange lady was speaking softly and urgently with the monochrome woman, but both of their faces were turned, making it hard to hear.

"They seem to be discussing what to do with us. It's Bahrain all over again," St. Benedict said softly as Rune settled down next to him.

Though they were being watched, everyone kept a healthy distance from them.

"Bahrain? Where is that?"

He looked at her sidelong. "Never mind, boring story anyway."

"I bet, because everything about you has been a snore so far," Rune said half-jokingly.

He snorted in reply, then ran a finger along his collar. Finding something, he held it out between them. "Oh, hey, look at that," he said. "There's a bit of random good luck." He set it into his ear, leaving a finger there to hold it in.

"Mal, are you there? Mal?"

Rune watched him as he focused on the air in front of him, and noticed a new kind of strange flicker in his eyes. She could have sworn they lit up, the green in his whites abating for a moment to flash blue, like a headlight passing quickly over a mirror.

"Where the hell have you been?" came Malachi's tenor voice too loud through the earpiece. St. Benedict felt the grip around his chest loosen for the first time in hours even as his ear started ringing.

"Oh, thank god, you escaped," St. Benedict said.

"Escaped? From what?" Malachi said, sounding confused.

"Wasn't St. Augustina holding you for questioning?"

There was a pause, "Noooooo?" Malachi drawled out the ending into a question that made it sound like he was wondering if St. Benedict had gone crazy. "Should I prepare to be held for questioning? When are you coming back to base?" Malachi asked.

"I don't know, just keep watch. Oh, by the way, what date is it today?"

"June twenty-second? All day and half the night," he said.

"That's what I thought. Good, as soon as I get out of the situation I'm in, I'll come find you two. Stay off the grids. Keep moving every hour. St. Augustina is hunting for you."

"Uh, yeah. I know. When is she not?" Malachi said.

"Uh, *yeah*, I know. I've got pretty good information that she is trying harder than usual and has a good chance of catching you, so take extra precautions—and don't try to contact me."

"Alright, alright. Whatever you say, 'Dad.' We're going dark now."

"Good."

Malachi started to say something more, but St. Benedict didn't wait. Pulling the earbud from his ear, he crushed it.

"I've got to hurry back to them," he said. That was when St. Benedict noticed that the monochromes were gone. Only he, Rune, and

Ally remained on the rooftop amongst the long shadows and the on-coming evening breeze.

"Where…?" he started to ask, his head whipping around to look for them, but there wasn't even a shadow sign of them anywhere. Suddenly, a partially empty box of protein bars hit the ground in front of him, making the three of them jump. One bar bounced out.

The orange lady simply appeared and sat down opposite St. Benedict. He smiled and glared at her with a frightening intensity that Rune couldn't blame him for. The orange lady tucked her legs to the side, under her multi-shade-orange skirts like she was a noblewoman on a grassy hill.

"If you need it, corporate warrior, you should eat it," she said, her voice merry again with laughter, the hippie lady mask making a new appearance.

"Where did your minions go?" St. Benedict demanded instead, his voice edged again with that aggressive growl. Alarmed, Rune scooped up the protein bar and peeled the wrapper off, then broke it in half, offering it to him on her palm.

"Whoever could you mean, I wonder?" the orange lady asked, cocking her head to the side, her old-young face serenely meeting his green-tinged gaze.

"St. Benedict, eat this, now," Rune ordered. With a shaking hand, he took the protein bar and inhaled it like he had before. He finished the other half just as quickly before Rune was able to hand it to him.

"I suggest you mete those out until you can get proper food in him," the orange lady said.

"Thank you for your help." Rune offered a small smile as she pulled the box toward herself. There were seven bars left inside.

"Why are you helping us?" St. Benedict asked through his overfull mouth.

"I am so glad I could help you out after everything you and your master have done for me," the orange lady said to Rune, ignoring St. Benedict.

That made Rune pause, and the orange lady gave her a sneaky, knowing smile.

"I was so sorry to hear about your master's passing. If it hadn't been for her help…" she stopped.

"So, you do know her, Rune," St. Benedict accused.

"No! No, I…" but Rune trailed off, unsure. "At least…"

"No need for such distress." The orange lady raised the edge of her orange hairband to reveal the telltale sign of slightly pointed ears.

"You are of the Court," Rune gasped, surprised.

"I'm sorry, I don't understand," he said, looking between Rune and the orange lady.

"Most Fae don't look a hundred-percent hominal," Rune answered, "But they work with hominal folk all the time, so I thought she was Faerie Friend..."

"That's alright, dear, we have always kept it on the down-low even before the fall," the orange lady said, replacing her band over her ears and letting her white hair fall forward.

"She's not just one of the fae. She's a Noble Faerie. That's why the monochromes obeyed her," Rune hurried to explain, then blinked at the woman. "You must be the Lady Trella."

"Dreamer, helper, friend, quiet keeper of secrets," Lady Trella intoned gravely, then she smiled brightly, "At least, I was once. Now I wear orange and call myself Lady Marmalade—on stage at least."

"It suits you," St. Benedict said, nodding to her.

"Oh, you are charming. You must be a villain when you're not playing the warrior," the Lady chided playfully, but it sent a chill of cold dread through Rune.

"I'm sorry we couldn't stop..." Rune started, but Lady Trella held up a hand.

"It was not your doing that the Fae Court fell, nor your duty to save our peeps, kiddo. You saved what you could. For that, I am awesomely Zen and totally owe you one, not only for my own life but that of my people. If I can aid the Heir of the Magdalene, I will consider my debt totes paid," she said with a nod.

"The Heir of the Magdalene?" Rune repeated.

"Who's the Magdalene?" St Benedict asked, his fingers sneaking into the box of protein bars to snatch another one.

"Maddie. She was known as the Magdalene," Rune said. "Technically, she's right. I'm her heir. She left me everything."

"I am glad to see you have taken up your master's mantel of helping others. Though, I hope the others you help are not as dangerous as this one," she said nodding toward St. Benedict, his cheeks bulging with a protein bar.

"Well, I'm currently trying to help this dog. She's actually a teenage girl who's gotten herself turned into a dog," Rune said, touching the top of Ally's head.

"Oh, you poor thing," Lady Trella said directly to Ally, who wagged her tail with happiness that she was finally being acknowledged.

"I got dragged along for the ride," St. Benedict said.

"You! You have done nothing but make my life harder," Rune started.

Lady Trella looked down at Ally to ask, "How did this happen to you, child? Did you make a deal with a green man or something?"

Rune replied for Ally. "Well, that's the problem. I can't communicate with her, and she's pretty much just barking. I've tried to take her back to her mother, but things have gotten in the way."

"You know, I know of a dog groomer who can speak to dogs. She's a mermaid. What was the name of her shop?" Lady Trella mused.

"Oh, *Taki's*! Yes, I know her, my god, why didn't I think of her?" Rune exclaimed.

"A mermaid?" St. Benedict asked.

"Yes, she's a friend of mine. I just... I haven't really talked to anyone since the funeral... and it's been even longer since I last talked to Taki." Rune swallowed a moment. "We should go see her. I bet she can help." Rune stood up, dusting off her pants as she straightened.

"I'm glad I could help you further," Lady Trella said, before snatching Rune's wrist. "May I ask a favor of you now, little wizardess?"

St. Benedict moved to intercede for her, but Rune held up her hand to stop him.

"You can ask, but I don't know if I can fulfill it. I am not Maddie," she said evenly.

Lady Trella shook her head sadly. "In these dark times when even our havens are gone..."

"...the Lucky Devil is a place where you can find help," Rune said, finishing the little-known quote. "I suppose that is still true," she said, looking down at Ally.

"The help I need is not urgent, but it is important."

"I'll... come when I can. I have to see my current work through first."

"Of course, wizardess," Lady Trella replied. Before Rune could deny being a wizard again, she released Rune's hand and jumped up like a five-year-old child. "I would avoid the monochromes in the future. If I hadn't come back to find you, things would have ended much differently."

"So, they weren't with you?" St. Benedict asked.

"Certainly not, but we were once of the same Court and two years does not wipe away centuries of tradition or obligation. See you soon!" With a wave and the flit of her orange skirt, the Faerie opened a real door, probably the one heading down off the roof, and slipped through it. It clanged shut hard behind her.

"Well, that happened," St. Benedict said.

"And too easily. I may have just committed to something I'll regret later," Rune said, uncertain.

"The monochrome Faeries are just letting us go like that?"

"Looks like. They were Faeries, after all. They can pretty much do what they want. "

"She said earlier that they were of the same Court. What did she mean?" St. Benedict took another bite of a bar. Rune blinked and looked down at the almost empty box.

"Did you eat that whole box?" she exclaimed, snatching it up. Two bars jumped hollowly inside as they flew up with the momentum. He didn't even have the aplomb to look guilty as he put the last bit into his mouth. "Apparently."

"Dammit. We were supposed to mete these out till we can get you more substantial food. I cannot for the life of me figure out why this spell is eating you alive."

"How do my eyes look now?" he asked, not at all apologetic.

"Well… less green. Closer to normal green," Rune admitted reluctantly. "I wish I knew why the spell is reacting this way. It should have petered out by now after it healed your cut."

"What happens when there are other problems in the body?" St. Benedict asked as he pushed himself up to his feet.

She double blinked at the question. "Uh, if you have a cold or something, then yeah, the spell will help cure you of that, too, or at least until the magic put into the spell burns out. How hurt were you?"

He chuckled under his breath as he took up his fedora and slapped dust off of it before setting it onto his head. "Very. Tell me, what does it do for brain damage?"

"It's not a cure-all. I mean, that kind of magic, all it does is empower your body's already existing ability to heal, and I'm pretty sure the body doesn't just heal brain damage. I guess I would have to look it up. Even if it could, the spell shouldn't be acting like this. I'm not that strong in magic. Do… do you *have* brain damage?"

"Probably, I've been hit in the head enough times." His voice dropped, softening, "You make sense of this insanity," he said. He shook his head. "Magic and powers. Those black and white people. They feel like they shouldn't exist to me, but they do."

Rune pointed at the shadows. "The monochromes, they're just people, with wants and needs and desires like anyone else. They're no stronger than you or I, just different."

"I'd say you're a lot stronger than you look, Talent. What do you think, Ally?" he asked, looking down at the little dog-girl. She wagged her tail and barked once. "Yeah, kid, I bet you're getting tired of being a dog, right?"

Ally barked again, her ears drooping.

"One bark for yes, two barks for no. That'll hold us 'til we can get to Rune's friend," St. Benedict said, then looked back to Rune.

"You don't have to come with me," she said, not liking where this was going.

"We've come this far together."

"That was just in the tunnels, 'til we got each other out of there," she hedged.

He smiled that charming, sweet smile that made her insides twist. "You saved my life and didn't stab me in the back. I like that about you." He took a step forward, closing the distance between them until there was only an uncomfortable matter of inches separating them. "Now, let me prove myself to you. I'm a very loyal friend and a good person to know."

"You're a dangerous person to know," she retorted.

"You're in danger anyway, whether I'm around or not. You're in danger of losing your bar, right? You're taking this 'fetch quest' job. No offense, kid," he said down to Ally on the ground. "Just shows how desperate you really are. Now that your name's out there in the dark, shadowy underbelly of our so-called society, how are you going to defend yourself without friends like me?" He moved in even closer, covering half the distance again, and Rune's eyes widened in response. "Help me. Team up with me. Use your powers to help me achieve my goals, and any and all rewards are ours to share, I promise you. Even this." He pitched his voice low and rumbly as he picked up her hand and set it to his lips to kiss the palm.

"To help you find Anna Masterson," Rune said, her voice subconsciously matching his in volume and pitch. The kiss sent tingles up her arm. It had been a long time, and a different life, when she last felt tingles like that...

He smiled, but said nothing more, as hard as that was, letting the request sink in. He had her this time, he could feel it. He just needed to give her enough time to...

"You have no idea... why I can't say yes to your request."

His sexy facade fell like the shattering glass of a storefront. "What?!"

Rune took a wary step back, not daring to look away from his eyes. "The answer is no, Mr. St. Benedict, and it will always be no. I would like you to stop asking me, please," she said coldly.

They held that tension for a long moment, Rune ready to run at his first move to strike her. Instead, he grabbed the top of his hat and swiped it off his head to slap it hard against his thigh, turning away from her as he growled his frustration.

"What? What the hell is wrong with you? Do you have a curse that makes you stupid? Because you definitely need help! I'm offering you a way out of your problems! Why are you not taking it?"

"You're not the kind of person who can solve my problems," she shot back. "You have no idea what my problems are, and I'll solve them myself. Come on, Ally."

The little dog slunk over to Rune, tail and ears both low to the ground, giving St. Benedict surreptitious looks. Rune picked her up, and for once, the teenager didn't fight it. They turned to leave, but Rune hesitated before turning back to hold out the two remaining protein bars.

"Here. You should try not to eat these until you really need to, and try to get more food as soon as you can. Just keep eating until the spell finally wears off," she said, staring at the bars so she didn't have to meet his eyes. After a moment, he took them. Feeling a little better, Rune nodded.

Then he dropped them and grabbed her arm instead. He went to grapple with her, and she yelped. He turned to put her in an arm lock, or maybe to do something much worse.

"No!" she cried. On cue, she was back in the interrogation room, being manhandled, powerless. She felt her knees become water as fear slid into all the old familiar places, making her helpless. Except, this time, something snapped. The fear met something it had never found within her before. Resistance. Rune felt the current roll down her arms and into her attacker. His eyes went wide with shock, and he lost his grip on her instantly. Without him holding her weight, she lost her footing and stumbled backward to catch herself on the wall they had escaped the vent through. Under her hand, she felt it, the thrum of the door she had created once before. She swore she could see it, too, even though her inner sight was closed.

St. Benedict grabbed his arm. It was painful, similar to the harsh numbing feeling of an electric shock.

"Dammit, Rune!" he gasped.

He moved to follow her, to force her to help him if he had to. He raised his hand over his head, intending to bring it down to make her understand who was in charge.

"St. Benedict, stop it!" she shouted.

His whole body jerked back as he complied.

"I've tried everything," St. Benedict growled. "I've offered to pay you. I've protected you. Coerced you. I've offered you everything I have."

"Please don't try to force me..." Rune said, pressing her back against the wall as he moved closer, setting his arms on either side of her, trapping her against the wall.

"I don't have a choice. I need you!" he said desperately. "I don't want to hurt you. I won't hurt you, I promise. Just help me."

"Not like this," Rune said. "Open." Rune stepped back into her door, leaving the enclosure of his arms.

"No. NO! Rune! Don't leave me! Don't, please!" he shouted. He noticed too late as Ally disappeared into the wall, a hand reaching through to guide the dog inside. "Rune, I'm sorry. Please wait. Wait!"

"Goodbye, St. Benedict. Please take care of yourself," came Rune's voice as if she was only a foot in front of him.

She thought that he would say more to stop her.

He thought she would come back through the wall.

He couldn't find a way to take back what he had done.

She couldn't see a way to trust him with her secret.

And as the door sealed shut between them, St. Benedict's legs gave out from beneath him, and he slid to the ground, his head in his hands.

CHAPTER 12

Taki's shop was a fascinating place.

Part aquarium, part dog beauty-shop. The only one of its kind in the world. When Rune pushed open the door, a series of little bells tinkled above her like soft chimes. Three doggie heads sitting at their beautician's stations turned to look at the pair as they entered. Unlike the beautician's chairs common in hominal salons, the dogs were perched on silver tables, strapped into harnesses suspended from the ceiling that held them secure and comfortable while their beauticians washed their coats, trimmed their nails, and styled them glamorous enough to be in a dog show.

The other half of the shop offered quality animal products to the doggie clientele and their "parents." It was a double-wide space with a black-and-white checked tile floor. Taki had taken a huge risk renting out both spaces and knocking out the wall in between, but she needed the room. A chest-high aquarium wound around the perimeter of the room. It was decorated with all manner of underwater topography arranged in different scenes that blended from one to the other. Rune saw everything from a sunken medieval castle — complete with knights and dragons — to pirate ships, and a mermaid beach party. Taki changed the little scenes frequently to match the season, but Christmas was always the most elaborate. Amongst these designer aquarium scenes swam a variety of fish and colorful sea creatures.

Rune smiled, relieved to see the place was still open this late in the evening. Schools of plastic swimming fish took the place of hands on the wall clock, and two schools of them hovered over the seven and the six, indicating it was 7:30 pm.

"Is Taki in today?" Rune asked one of the beauticians when nobody greeted her. The beautician gave her a snotty look, up and down, her eyes slit as she judged what was in front of her and found it lacking. This made Rune look down at her own appearance and blanch a little. The white wrap-around shirt she had been wearing was several shades of brown in places and her jeans were no better. Ally wasn't in the clear either with her once-white paws, each looking like they had been dipped in chocolate. Glancing into one of the nearby mirrors, Rune saw her hair needed to be re-braided badly, and a bruise was forming above her eyebrow. She wasn't sure where she had acquired that. She really did look like a mess.

"She's not taking walk-ins today," the beautician said in a thick, middle-eastern accent. "You have to make an appointment."

"I'm just asking if she's here," Rune snapped back, a bit offended by the hoity-toity attitude. After everything she had been through, she did not have an ounce of patience left.

The hairdresser pursed her lips and heaved an exasperated sigh. "I'll check if she's in, in a minute. Please have a seat."

The other dog groomers eyed both Rune and Ally with varying expressions ranging from concern to hostile. Rune realized she hadn't been in to see Taki in a while, and she didn't recognize any of these faces. They certainly didn't know her. For much of the past four years, since Taki had moved to the mainland, Rune had visited the shop and spent her free time with her friend. For a while, Taki was Rune's closest friend, but when had they stopped seeing each other so much? Rune wanted to believe it had only been a few months and vaguely remembered seeing her at Maddie's memorial, but she was hard-pressed to remember the last time she had talked to Taki before that. Had it really been a year? Two, even?

Ally growled at Rune a little and Rune raised an eyebrow at the dog-girl. Then Rune's stomach growled too, and she realized how hungry she was. Not just hungry, but weary. She wanted more than anything to get out of the public eye, get some food, and finally figure out what she was going to do next.

Ten minutes later, the groomer still hadn't moved from the dog she was working on, paying exaggerated attention to the minute details of how even the opposite sides of the dog's furry face were. Unable to stand it any longer, Rune turned back to the unhelpful groomer. "Will you please let Taki know we're here? It's kinda important. I'm her friend," she said, stressing the urgency with her voice.

"In a few minutes, ma'am," the groomer said, conveying her own disgust and irritation.

They were interrupted by a gaggle of customers bursting through the door. The group was full of merry chatter, drowning out anything else Rune may have said. Each bore a very pretty little dog. The group barely noticed Rune and Ally. It was almost comical to watch the groomer's face battle between continuing to stonewall the intruders and flip to a welcoming warmth for the newer arrivals. The newcomers obviously had appointments and were expecting to be serviced first. They rushed the three groomers, chattering away so fast it was impossible to understand what they were saying.

Rune made a quick hissing sound to catch Ally's attention. The little dog-girl's ear twitched toward her first before the rest of her head followed. Indicating with a little nod toward the back of the store, Rune led the way away from the chaos, hoping she could take the chance to poke her head into the back room on her own.

As they approached the door leading to the back office and storage room, there was a loud splash from the aquarium to their left. A beautiful white-and-orange tail flipped out of the top, and Rune smiled as Taki entered the room. As she swam through her tank, Rune could see she wore a bright yellow tunic that flowed past her hips. It was connected over her shoulders by only a couple of stitches every few inches, creating artful draping around her orange and white scales.

The dainty mermaid popped up at the edge of the tank right beside the grooming tables, to the sounds of awed cheers and fawning from her adoring customers. Ally tilted her head to the side and gave a quick yip that sounded like a question.

"You've never seen a mermaid before?" Rune asked Ally. "Not unusual since the lake here doesn't support them. And Taki is unique even among her people, a mermaid who loves dogs."

Typical of her kind, Taki was just over five feet long. Her pod was actually located off the coast of Japan, so she was a long way from home. Her lower half had the patterning of a Koi, white and orange wrapping around her aquatic body and up her back. Her almond-shaped eyes were orange as well, though, to most people, they simply looked warmly brown. Her hair was black and coiffed on her head in two pompom balls that stayed in place in or out of the water. Her arrival warmed the room and the new clients flowed toward the mermaid with an eagerness akin to a celebrity being swamped by fans. Taki acknowledged all of them with a bright smile, but her love was reserved for the dogs. With eager fingers, she reached out for a little King Charles, who was equally eager to lick her fingers. She gestured for the owner to come to Taki's grooming table. The table was set up with the aquarium wrapping around the three sides of it for ease of access. As the woman approached, Taki noticed Rune. The mermaid's eyes widened as she recognized her.

"Rune! I'm sorry, I didn't see you," she said, her face breaking into an even wider smile. She set the King Charles on the table. "Could you hold her a second," she said to the disgruntled beautician. Taki didn't seem to notice her employee's reaction, but swam up to the edge of her aquarium just before the door to the backroom and held out her arms over the edge toward her friend.

With utter relief and not a second of hesitation, Rune fell into the smaller mermaid's arms as if they had only seen each other yesterday.

"I'm so sorry I haven't been around," Rune tried to say, but Taki shushed her.

"Hush, you. No worries. You've been busy with life stuff. I'm so, so, *so* glad to see you, my friend." Taki's arms tightened a second, and Rune didn't care that she was getting wet through her clothes.

"I'm glad to see you, too. I need your help. Please..." Rune said, "I know, I suck..."

"Of course, I'm here for you, girl." Taki pushed back to look at Rune's face. That was when her eyes fell on Ally. "Oh, my gosh! Oh, come, come, come to me, my pretty."

Ally wagged her tail and tried to jump up the side of the glass. Instead, Rune moved quickly to pick the kid up.

"Taki, may we use your office?" Rune said, trying to pitch her voice down to not alarm the room, but Taki wasn't really picking up on her cue to be discrete.

"What? My office?" she asked loudly. "I have appointments right now, Rune, but maybe we can squeeze you in... though you're the one who looks like she needs the bath."

That was when Rune felt the strange tingling sensation at her right bra strap. Jumping a little, she reached inside her shirt and pulled out the small piece of paper that had appeared there.

"Oh, my," Taki said, leaning on the glass with one arm to peer at the paper. "Did that just appear?"

Rune didn't respond at first as she read Alf's familiar block writing. *"If you're alive out there somewhere, call the bar, damn it!"* it read. Rune swore she could hear his gruff voice reading his own writing.

"Please, Taki, I need to use your phone," Rune said, desperately, trying not to think too hard on the hundred doomsday scenarios that blew through her mind at that moment. When Rune met Taki's eyes, she realized that the mermaid's eyes were roaming over her face like she was reading a book. Then Taki's eyebrows shot up as those beautiful citrine colored irises locked onto something at Rune's brow line. Involuntarily, Rune reached up and touched her forehead. Her fingers came away red.

"Oh. Oh, dear..." Rune said, staring at them uncomprehendingly.

Taki didn't hesitate. She snapped off a stretchy coil of colored plastic from around her wrist that had a pair of keys hanging from it. "Head back. I'll be with you in a moment," she said.

"Um, okay," Rune said. With keys in one hand and holding the other out with bloody fingertips, Rune went into the back. Ally followed with a whine of concern.

The back was just as Rune remembered: a storeroom that was really a glorified hallway. Shelves holding spare merchandise and a cabinet for supplies lined the walls from top to bottom. There was a small janitor's closet to one side, complete with the shop sink and cleaning supplies. The biggest difference between this and a typical janitor's closet came from the fact that half of the space was taken up by a giant aquarium, which made up the wall of Taki's office. Using the office key to get through the door set into the aquarium wall, Rune opened the door into an otherwise normal-looking office.

There was a beautiful white-and-chrome desk that was pushed up to the edge of a little pool, an extension of the larger aquarium that allowed Taki to swim through a short tunnel and pop out at the end. She had often perched on the edge of the lip, which had been crafted into a sort of seat that she could sit on with her tail under the desk. On the desk itself, sat piles of invoices that were kept under glass covers to keep them dry. A stack of hand towels waited on another corner. There was also a landline phone sitting inside a waterproof box with a water-resistant laptop right next to it. Taki had a couple of conventional chairs and even a couch for land-walker guests to sit on fitted into another part of the aquarium.

"Come on, come in," Rune said to Ally, directing her into the room.

As Rune walked through the door, she felt a wave of dizziness and had to sit down on the edge of Taki's aquarium behind the desk. She almost fell back into the water but managed to grab the edge of the desk before she did. She blinked rapidly as her vision cleared.

"What's wrong with me?" Rune asked, her voice sounding tinny in her own ears.

Taki popped up behind Rune, setting her wet palms against her friend's back in comfort.

"Oh my gosh, honey, what happened to you?" she asked as she pulled herself up to sit beside Rune.

"I'm sorry to bring this to you, Taki. I didn't expect things to get so out of hand," Rune said, leaning forward to focus on breathing evenly.

"No worries," Taki said as she yanked open one of her desk drawers to pull out a red vinyl medical kit. "I'm sorry I don't have any crystals. I used the last one your aunt made me a couple of months ago." Taki snatched up a towel to dry her hands and tore open a package of gauze. "Just tell me what happened to you."

"Well, I'm actually not sure why my scalp is bleeding."

Taki gently set the hatched cloth against the wound. Rune closed her eyes, taking relief from the feel of gentle firm hands.

"You look like you've been in a fight. Did something happen at the bar?"

"Yeah, but that was this morning. Or yesterday morning... I'm not entirely sure anymore. I'm losing track of time." She proceeded to tell Taki everything.

The takedown was already in progress by the time St. Benedict caught up with the van. It had been harder to find since he had told Malachi to move randomly, but unfortunately not impossible for either him or St. Augustina. He cursed under his breath. He had wasted too much time trying to chase after the Finder and keep with his mission.

A crowd of onlookers watched as Malachi and Zita were lain on the ground and handcuffed from behind. Malachi, despite his shorter, slighter stature, was putting up a fight, trying to defend Zita, who was subconsciously squirming her lower snake half in terror, making the hominal officers around her very uncomfortable and hostile. Using more force than necessary, three of them tried to tackle her snake half to force it to be still, while another two held down her upper half. One of the officers screamed in her face that they would light her up if she didn't stop resisting.

"Leave her alone!" Malachi shouted, which just earned him a face smashed into the pavement.

"Fucking snake!" drifted a comment through the crowd. "Should just exterminate them all."

The officer pulled out a Taser and jabbed it into Zita's side. Her whole body contracted as small snaps and crackles tickled the air around her. She made a small squeak in place of a scream. Then they stopped as she finally did what they wanted, lying still because she was unconscious.

"Zita!" Malachi cried out again, but no one heeded him.

More disgruntled, hate-filled comments rolled through the shifting bodies of the crowd as they tried to get a better view of the spectacle.

St. Benedict had to grip the side of the building he was standing along to keep himself from running in and spilling blood. It would do nobody any good to get himself captured too, and more than likely would get people killed. Instead, he surveyed the area, pulling his now misshapen fedora down lower over his eyes, his darker clothing helping him blend into the crowd. The sun had almost completely set, and the street lights were clicking on.

He picked out St. Augustina easily enough. She stood imperiously to one side as the grunt he recognized from her office walked about giving orders. That doctor, Dr. Benita Cruz, stood nearby, trying to intercede on Zita's behalf. He took note of that and moved on. If he let his gaze dwell too long, he increased his chances of being seen. Reporters had already shown up, interviewing the crowd and trying to get shots of the scene. The speed of their arrival suggested to St. Benedict that this was staged for someone's benefit, probably his, or at least his *and* whoever else competed with St. Augustina to find Rune.

He grunted and tried to push the Talent out of his thoughts. She was on her own now. Some part of him wondered why he hadn't pushed her sooner, used force or more real threats to compel her to work with him. It wasn't his preference, but it wouldn't have been the first time he had to do what was necessary to accomplish his goal. It would have been fairly easy considering how skittish she was – only she wasn't, really. She had stared down his madness and unflinchingly reached out to him. Even in the fights, she hadn't been a great help, but she hadn't turned all damsel-in-distress either. She was just untrained. If only he had figured out how to get to her... Even his manipulations and lies hadn't worked. She had seen through them.

He shook his head again and tried to focus on the problems in front of him. There was nothing he could do directly, but he noticed right away several people were using their phones to video record the scene. A couple of them were tapped by the reporters for an interview. Taking off his hat and slicking his sweat through his hair to shape it a little, St. Benedict picked his target, a pretty, young, teenage girl talking excitedly to her friends. Her cell phone was housed inside a sparkly peach case, and he could see she had a pretty good view of the scene as he approached.

"Excuse me, miss. I'm with the Chicago Tribune. Could I interview you for a moment?" He flashed his most charming smile. The gaggle of girls turned to him, their eyes going wide with awe.

"Holy crap, Carla! You're going to be famous," one of her friends giggled. Carla mustered up some very grown-up dignity and started preening her hair, which only emphasized how young she actually was.

"Where's your camera?" she asked, and it was everything St. Benedict could do to not grimace.

"I'm a newspaper reporter actually, you know print? I just want to take a couple of statements. Did you see what happened?"

"Print? That's so old-fashioned." one of Carla's friends rolled her eyes and turned back to watch them haul Zita into the van. St. Benedict needed to hurry. He felt St. Augustina's eyes searching for him.

"Actually, I blog. I'm in charge of the news feed on our website. Did you get video of what happened?"

"Yeah, totally!" Carla chirped and unabashedly showed him her phone screen.

"Wow, you've got a really steady hand. You ever think about being a camera operator?" St Benedict crooned. The kid blushed and giggled more.

"See, you can see them take down the snake," she said proudly, and again St. Benedict stiffened his grip on the phone, maintaining his smile.

"Yes, this is amazingly clear," he said as the palm of his hand established a link to the phone. "I'll give you credit in my article for everyone to see, I promise."

Keeping the thought of "dumb teenager" off of his face, St. Benedict evacuated the area, disappearing as the crowd started to shift to make room for the paddy wagon that was driving away. He didn't set his fedora back on his head until he was at least two streets away, and didn't make his piggybacked call until a mile past that.

The phone rang almost to the point of going to voicemail before it was picked up.

"This better be worth my time," came a silky voice on the other end.

"You actually answered a call from an unknown number?" St. Benedict asked incredulously.

"Saint...you," the female voice corrected.

"Yeah, St. Me," St. Benedict confirmed. Someone walked too close to him, and he shifted to tuck his glowing hand against his shoulder so he could talk more covertly.

"That bad, huh?" she asked.

"The kids got picked up by the school principal."

"… I have no clue what that means."

St. Benedict checked his nine, three, and six before sidestepping into an alcove.

"It means I lost my team and I need help, geez, don't they teach you critical thinking in training?"

"Yes, and that's why you're the master criminal, and I'm the first person you called when you royally screwed up," the voice answered calmly. "Unfortunately, it was a waste of a call. I'm hanging up now."

"Well, that was pretty quick," St. Benedict said flippantly before he could be hung up on.

"What is?" the voice asked with a sigh.

"You've already paid a really high price, but you're just throwing away a valuable resource like that...and right when I'm about to hand our boss the means to strike a major blow against a serious competitor. I didn't realize you were the wasteful type, or else I wouldn't have agreed to not backstab you."

"I think I'm going to regret asking you to clarify. Maybe I should just kill you."

St. Benedict smiled. "If I'm wrong, I'm dead anyway."

"Or you'll run again."

⁂

"You think I should?" Rune asked. She had been wondering the same thing after laying out the whole story to Taki.

"That seems kind of drastic to me," Taki said, her tail flipping lazily back and forth as she hung from the side of her pool.

"I don't know. People shooting at me is kind of drastic, too," Rune said.

"Ew, yeah. That's true. But this St. Benedict guy, he said he could protect you?"

"Yeah, but even if he was on the up and up, there are a lot of problems with that."

Taki began ticking off her webbed fingers. "Tall, dark, mysterious, sexy, really into keeping you alive; which one is the problem?"

"Taki, there is…" Rune took a breath, "something about me you don't know. I… I haven't always been the person I've said I am."

Taki smiled. She pulled herself out of the water to sit next to Rune on the bench. "I knew that already."

"What?" Rune asked, surprised.

"You were living at the Lucky Devil. Of course, you've got a story. Everyone who goes there does."

"Well... yes, I suppose."

"And now you're going through all this to save the bar. Wow. That's wonderful and amazing."

"Well, come on. It's my home." Rune paused when a realization came to her. "I suppose it's more than that. It's everything I've got in my life. Certainly the only thing good, for sure. I can't let them take it away from me."

"Them?"

"The mortgage company... and their goons." Rune didn't even try to disguise the distaste in her voice. "And now my stupid secret is going to blow it all up."

"Is your secret really that bad?"

"Yes. Yes, it is."

Taki was quiet for a moment. "Did you kill somebody?"

"What?! No. Never!" Rune regarded her friend. "How could you think that?"

"Hey, calm down. I don't, but I am trying to figure out on what spectrum 'bad' is." Taki flipped a little splash of water with her tail.

"It's the... it's the lying kind of bad. I'm a wanted felon..."

Taki suddenly got excited. "Oh, my gosh! So, Rune is your secret identity? Like a superhero?"

Rune couldn't help it; she guffawed. "No, not in the least."

Taki mocked being crestfallen as Rune had a much-needed laugh.

"Okay, let's back up a bit. I'm still trying to understand something," Taki said when Rune's laughter died down. "Now, if I understand you correctly, this St. Benedict guy came to you to help him find someone."

"Yeah, he wanted me to use my Talent, which I can't because..." Rune's eyes went wide as she realized what she had done again. "I mean... I..."

"Oh, relax. I already know you're a Talent," Taki said, dipping a hand into the water to ladle a dry spot on her tail. Rune almost fell back into the pool.

"You what?"

Taki smiled another impish smile. "Maddie told me a long time ago about your ability to find things. She said you were really strange about wanting to keep it a secret. I figured you'd tell me eventually since we're friends."

Rune felt her cheeks grow hot. "Uh, Taki... I'm sorry..."

"No, no. Don't do that. I get it, okay? I mean, who am I to judge you about what's weird. Come on, I'm a merwoman who chooses to live on land and groom dogs."

Rune took that in. "Now I wish I had just told you on my own."

Taki sat back up and patted her friend's arm. "Needs must when the devil drives."

"Huh, that phrase seems to be following me around. St. Benedict said that too."

"So, right, back to what I was asking about. What or who did he want you to find again?"

Rune took in a big breath. "Me. The person I was before I became Rune Leveau. He heard the rumor about me being a Finding Talent somehow, and he thought I could find her."

Taki's eyes went wide. "So, wait. He wanted you to literally find yourself?"

Rune blinked back at her. "I... I guess, yeah."

Taki lost it. The mermaid's body shook so hard she barely made a sound as she laughed and laughed. It infected Rune again and she joined her, which got even more obnoxious when Taki lost control and slipped back into her pool with a big splash. Rune could still hear the giggles under the water. They were only interrupted when Ally began to bark until the two grown-ups took notice of her. Taki came to the edge of the pool and stretched a hand out to the little dog.

"And how do you factor into all of this, sweetie pie?" Taki asked, suddenly switching to baby talk as she directed her attention to Ally. Ally looked up and cocked her head at the mermaid.

"Taki, please don't. She's not a dog. She's a teenage girl," Rune said, hoping Ally wasn't taking offense to Taki's attention. Taki double blinked. "That's actually why we came to you. I don't know what happened to her, so instead of guesswork, I hoped you could just talk to her. Find out what happened."

"Right. I just can't help it, she is just such a cute little dog," Taki said.

"You can talk to her, right?" Rune asked, hopefully.

"Yes, of course."

Suddenly, Ally became very excited and started leaping and spinning in place as she barked, but the sounds she made sounded like a dog's attempt at words and nothing like the real animal sounds. Her barks moved up and down in pitch and cadence.

"Please, slow down, sweetie. I can't understand you yet, there are a few things we have to do first." Taki reached down to tap a pearly finger on the little dog-girl's head.

Just then there was a knock at the door. "Taki, your appointment is waiting."

Taki blew out a breath of exasperation. "Of course, she would come half an hour late, instead of canceling," she said to Rune under her breath, then to her employee outside, she called, "I'll be out in a minute, thank you." She regarded Ally for a moment. "Can you wait an hour for me to close up shop? It's just that this is the night we stay open later to accommodate a few nocturnal patrons and we are completely booked."

"Look, we're just grateful you can help us at all. Thank you, Taki. I haven't eaten anything since this morning. If you don't mind, I'd like to order something to be delivered," Rune said. "And I should call Alf and check in with him."

"Of course, of course. If you can get this computer to work for you, you can order through Food2U. I have them bookmarked in my browser. There is an excellent Thai place that will deliver here. Order me some pork Pad Thai if you order from there." And with that, Taki pushed herself back into the water. With a few flicks of her tail, she was gone through her system of waterways to the front of the store. Ally barked a bit more and then stopped, her tail drooping straight to the ground.

"Just hold on a little longer, Ally. She's doing this as a favor, so you need to be patient. Now, what I really have to decide is if it's okay to order you Thai or will that upset your doggie stomach?" She reached down to pat Ally's head and got a nip on the fingers for her trouble. The surly teenage dog went back to the couch and lay down. She then proceeded to sulk.

CHAPTER 13

St. Benedict stood quietly in another darkened alley, next to another smelly dumpster, devouring another stick of jerky while he waited. There weren't any souls to be seen or heard, though the eternal sounds of the city were ever-present, muffled and distant. He drank in the stillness, realizing it was the first time he had been still in days. Having always been a dynamic and energetic person, from the cradle on, he would never in a bazillion years have believed that he could come to love stillness so much. He had already lived too much.

He lost the moment of tranquility the minute the woman entered the alley, which only emphasized to St. Benedict how precious those moments were.

"What's with all of the takeout?" St. Rachel asked as she approached, indicating the sea of grocery bags at St. Benedict's feet with a perfectly manicured, clear polished nail.

"It's going to be a long night," he said, reaching out his hand to her to pull her in for a quick kiss. "I'm glad it's you."

St. Rachel allowed herself a half-smile, though she didn't blush at the kiss. She had more dignity than to show how it made her feel. "I thought you were expecting me?" she asked teasingly instead.

"Yeah, well, trolls can be florists."

She pursed her eyebrows together in amused confusion. "If you say so." She looked him up and down with an appraising eye. "You look like hell."

"What? More than usual?" he quipped back, leaning against the wall. His black shirt was untucked from his dark pants. Both were rumpled, with a slight odor of sweat and blood. The signature fedora he wore on his head had lost and found its shape a couple of times and was probably better off in the dumpster he stood next to.

"Yes, and you are still too handsome for your own good," St. Rachel said levelly.

St. Rachel was dressed conservatively, though she made that look equal parts elegant and sexy. Long-legged and shapely, she looked like she had stepped out of a film noir, her blonde hair and red lips the only bits of color on her. She was dressed in an above-the-knee, clinging black dress and a short jacket. Her knee-high black boots left just a thin strip of her skin visible between the two. Almost the same height as St. Benedict, they looked like a matched pair, only she was light where he was dark, and put together where he was a mess.

"Let's just hope this place is equipped with a shower," she said, shaking her head as she pulled out keys, selecting the one that opened the gray metal door. "Though, I guess I should be grateful that you aren't covered in your own blood and carrying your arm in one of those bags."

He chuckled but didn't comment. He gathered up his bags and followed her through, refusing to let her take one as they went in. They entered another backroom full of shelves; nothing much of note except that the shelves were filled with neat boxes of electronic products. St. Benedict picked up an electronics catalog from a messy desk that read 'Microtopia' across the top.

"Oooh, porn," St. Benedict said as he showed St. Rachel before sliding it into one of the bags. She just rolled her eyes at him and led him through to the store's main showroom.

It was a large space with industrial gray-blue carpet and exposed pipes above. It was painted a uniform light tan. Throughout the room were islands and a few chest-high shelves with various electronics and gadgetry. Signs depicting a friendly-looking computer icon with "geek" glasses on it gave a thumbs-up repeatedly throughout the room.

"Don't worry about the security cameras. This place is owned by our employer, so the footage will be kept in-house," St. Rachel said, as she moved toward one of the islands in the back corner, displaying computers of different models and types. She led him past a mock living room with a leather chair and side table in front of a very large, flat-screen HD TV and the latest surround sound experience. A pavilion tent stood above to create a feeling of semi-privacy. Eyeing the temptation of the chair, St. Benedict deposited his bags on the brown Oriental rug that completed the whole setup and joined St. Rachel at the island of computers.

"You can use any of the computer equipment in the store. Our "mysterious" boss will cover the loss. We just have to clean up our mess before five am when the sales staff gets here."

"Not a problem," he said, readjusting his fedora. "Can you boot these up? I'm going to go shopping."

"How many?" she asked.

"All of them, then you can get out of here."

"Dammit, St. Benedict, you need me. You need help."

"You have helped," he said with a wink.

She narrowed her eyes. "Don't wink at me. You are out there without any kind of a field kit, and you lost your support..."

"I'm getting them back," he said, moving between the shelves, comparing two boxes before selecting one.

"You need support on *this*," St. Rachel said, underscored by the chime of the computers as they started up.

"I need seven-fifty Mbps, not two-fifty. What's the point of two-fifty?"

Perturbed, St. Rachel moved to where he crouched between the shelves. "How many years are you going to stonewall me?"

"I feel tired, a little ill, pissed, and determined. There is nothing else to share."

"How are you even going to free Malachi and Zita, anyway?" St. Rachel crossed her arms as she changed tactics.

St. Benedict smiled with delight. "It's exactly like Bolivia." He moved to another shelf and pulled down a couple more things, handing them off to St. Rachel, who took them without pausing as she talked.

"Bolivia? That only worked because we knew exactly when the system update was going to knock everything out. We're talking about a government building here; they don't even know when they're going to have a fire drill."

"Funny you should say that..." St. Benedict said, then didn't finish.

"I can't believe Maxmillion is wasting you on a babysitting mission. We almost have the Masterson files in the palm of our hands, and now we're on hold for—" she continued, but St. Benedict cut her off.

"We will talk more at a later time, St. Rachel. I need to focus now," he said.

"This is a waste of time and resources. I understand you wanting Malachi back, but you have to remember in this war everyone is expendable."

"Including yourself, St. Rachel?" St. Benedict said as he left the shelves for the computer island. He started tapping away at the first keyboard.

"Including all of us in the end," she retorted.

"I know that better than anyone, which is why I would rather spend what is left of my life…" he stopped.

"Spend your life what?"

"Never mind. It was an incomplete thought," he said, reading something on the screen, then turning to go back into the store. "Ah, forgot something."

"What is all of this for?" St. Rachel called after him, staring hard at the boxes of electronics she still held.

"I'm going to try to make a Frankenstein," he called back. "Hey, do me a favor, can you run a soft search on a Dr. Benita Cruz?"

"Who?"

"Benita Cruz."

"I heard what you said. I want you to explain why," St. Rachel rolled her eyes. She deposited her burden onto the center of the island and started typing on a silver laptop.

"She's St. Augustina's magic expert. I want to know more about her," he called back.

"I swear you collect people like girls collect dolls," she muttered and started running the search.

"Are you hungry?"

"At least you can thank me for dinner," Rune replied as she tried to search the web on Taki's computer. It took forever for her to order from the delivery website until she figured out she needed to hit the left button on the mouse instead of the right. Now, she was trying to surf the web. "I don't get why anyone would choose computers over magic. Damn counterintuitive boxes of weird," she concluded, giving up on tech entirely.

The irritated and unhelpful dog beautician from earlier stood at the office door looking unsure, holding two plastic bags with paper bags inside them. "Delivery for you?" she said, holding them out.

Rune got up from the desk and took the food from her with a half-hearted "Thanks," then callously closed the door in her face.

She took the food to the desk and unpacked the paper bags. The takeout came in the typical Styrofoam, which was not biodegradable, and thin cardboard boxes, which were questionably more so. Another thin, clear bag inside contained plastic utensils and thin napkins that were useless after the first swipe.

The food smelled wonderful, though. Rune popped open one of the containers and took a deep whiff.

"You can tell it's the good stuff by the loads of real vegetables in each dish. I hate the stuff that looks like it came from a frozen mix bag of tiny cubed veggies bought in any old grocery store," she said to Ally, who was standing up on her hind legs, pawing at the air toward the containers.

"Do you want to do the bark system St. Benedict talked about before? One bark for yes, two barks for no?" Rune asked as she reached for Ally's share of dinner.

"Yes!" Ally barked.

"Do you want it on the floor?"

"No!"

"But it would be easier for your little self to eat," Rune reasoned.

"Yes," Ally replied and hopped down from the couch a little sulkily. Rune smiled and sat down cross-legged next to her, pulling her pair of real chopsticks from the back pouch of her belt.

"Don't worry, I'll eat with you, too."

The seafood combo was steaming fresh, with bits of crab, scallops, tiny calamari, and shrimp piled on top of white rice with lovely capped mushrooms and bits of broccoli, scallions, and slivers of carrots. Rune vowed to herself, before her first bite, to savor each stickful. After the fifth stickful, she remembered that she had meant to do that, and slowed down. Ally seemed to be enjoying her own plate, lapping up a shrimp before lifting her head and sitting to chew on it comically, smacking her doggy lips.

Taki appeared then, emerging from the tunnel to float a little while in her aquarium. She waved to Rune serenely, then she turned mid-water to enter the tunnel and pop up on her bench.

"At last. Lovely corgi, but so high strung. How are you both doing here?" she asked, surveying the take-out feast on the floor.

"We're better now. Thank you for putting us up," Rune said and moved to the desk to hand her friend her share of the food.

"Oh, no. I'll eat that in a bit. Let's get this little girl some help," she said, leaning out to hold a hand toward Ally. The dog-girl took a small, uncertain step toward Taki, then whined a little.

"It'll be alright, Ally," Rune said and smiled in what she hoped was a reassuring manner. Ally's sudden hesitancy concerned her. "What do you need us to do?"

"Get her in the water with me. It's easiest to understand her if she's in the water," Taki said and pushed herself back a bit from the edge to make room.

"Don't worry, Ally, it's just like a bath," Rune said, slipping off her belt so it wouldn't get wet. Then she picked up the squirming dog-girl. "This is how Taki is going to be able to talk to you. Through the water. All merpeople communicate underwater. You can imagine that verbal communication is tough otherwise. This is just like telepathy, but through the water," Rune assured. "It's really cool, you'll like it."

Ally panicked a little more.

"You won't be going under the water, you just need to be in it, sweetie," Taki said much more helpfully.

"Do you want to be able to say more than yes and no?"

Ally allowed herself to be dipped in and immediately began to fight again to get back out.

"Okay, I better come in with you," Rune said, sliding fully clothed into the water. It was surprisingly warm and soft. "Wow, I forgot how nice this is," Rune remarked as she held the shivering Ally to her chest.

"It's going to be okay, sweetie. Yes, you're a very brave girl," the mermaid said soothingly and brushed back the wet fur from Ally's face. "Now, just think about what you want to say. Don't try to say it out loud. It's less confusing if you think it as calmly as you can."

The room became silent. Ally relaxed in Rune's arms, the ends of her white fur floating in the water. Then Taki's orange-tinged eyebrows shot straight up.

"I see," Taki said softly after a few more moments.

"What?" Rune dared to ask, keeping her voice soft and at the same pitch as Taki's.

"Why about the Lucky Devil?" Taki suddenly asked, crinkling up her nose in confusion.

"The Lucky Devil?!" Rune repeated, alarmed.

"I… I'm having trouble understanding," Taki admitted. "Maybe if I…" She stretched out and laid her hand against Rune's cheek.

The inside of Rune's ears seemed to go hollow, like listening to a seashell. Only instead of the ocean, she heard a young teenage girl's voice talking a mile a minute.

"… and then she told me that we weren't even retainers anymore and I couldn't believe that she would say such a thing. We've been retainers of the Lucky Devil since its founding. Its founding! Do you know how long that is? And Ms. Rune can't understand me, and I don't know what to do because Mama doesn't see me anymore…I mean, she sees me, but as a dog, not as her daughter. And Ms. Rune, I'm so frustrated, she can't hear me and I can't do anything about it..."

"Ally! Ally! I can hear you!" Rune shouted to get the little dog's attention.

"What? Really? You can hear me now?!"

"Yes, loud and clear," Rune confirmed, unable to suppress her smile as she exchanged a glance with Taki.

"Oh, thank god, this has been driving me crazy. Rune. Or my lady? Am I supposed to call you my lady now?" the little dog asked, cocking her head to the side as she wondered.

"I think you can just call me Rune. Now, what is it you wanted to tell me, Ally?" Rune asked. "Something about the Lucky Devil?"

"Yes! That's right! You need to go back, back to the bar. They're going to take it from you!"

"What? Who?" Rune said, the smile dropping from her face.

"My mom! She's tricking you," Ally said, squirming so hard with excitement that Rune nearly dropped her into the water. Taki almost lost the connection, and Ally's voice grew alarmingly soft, like someone had abruptly turned down her volume.

"Ally, sweetie, you must stay still, or I can't maintain this," Taki chided gently.

"Yes, but this is important. Those guys and my mom, they're setting you up so that you default on your mortgage and lose the bar."

"Ally..." Rune felt like her brain was on shuffle. "Look, Ally, even if I miss the payment date, that doesn't mean I'll default instantly. I have a fifteen-day grace period, and there are legal procedures..."

"No... No, you don't understand. It's a conspiracy. My mom... my mom is really good with numbers and she did something to the books and they are going to make sure you lose it. And you can't! You can't because you are the Heir of Magdalene!"

Rune and Taki exchanged another glance; this one worried as Rune tried to swallow, her mouth having gone completely dry.

"Ally, how do you know all this?" Rune asked carefully.

"Because I heard my mom talking on the phone and then those guys came to the house: a tall guy with blonde, spiky hair and a tiger-guy, but the orange kind not the white kind. And I know that's not politically correct, but I can't think of another way to describe him. I only saw them for a moment."

"Is that how you got turned into a dog, sweetie? Did they catch you?" Taki asked for her shocked friend.

"No! No, I did it!" Ally said, wagging her tail proudly.

"You're a Talent?" Rune asked.

The tail slowed its wagging. "Not exactly. I am a Fae! I did this myself. I just... I just don't know how to undo it."

"Wait, wait. You're a Fae?" Taki asked.

"Well, I'm supposed to be," Ally confirmed.

"I see. You're a changeling!" Rune said, putting it together.

Taki wrinkled her nose. "You mean a Faerie? Like the kind that takes your baby and leaves theirs instead?"

Rune shrugged. "Not anymore. The terms evolved since then. You know, like the word gay used to mean happy, and now it means..."

"Gay," they said together.

"Right, exactly." Rune nodded. "Nowadays, it usually means someone who has had their magic taken away. Though it can mean someone who acquires new magic, but that is really, really rare."

"Magic can be taken away?" Taki asked, intrigued.

"Anything can be sealed magically, sure. I mean otherwise, no one would be able to cast magic spells on anything. It's the final step to any magic spell."

Taki and Ally both looked confused.

"Look, it's simple. Someone cast a spell on Ally here to lock her Talent for... I'm guessing shapeshifting, so that she couldn't use it, but over time or if that person has died, the seal on the spell starts to degrade until you get my bathroom and it stops autocleaning." Rune stopped then as a thought hit her. "Maddie... Maddie was the one who cast your seal spell, making you into a changeling. That's why you're stuck!"

"It is?" Ally asked.

"Yes! If you never used your legs before, how would you know how to walk. You've never changed shape before this, right? How would you know how to?"

"Yeah, apparently, that's what we did. My whole family, when I was a little kid. My mom used to shape change into a dog. But I don't remember ever doing it," Ally said.

"Our little Ally here is a Shape Changer Talent?"

"Who Maddie sealed so she couldn't do it!" Rune said triumphantly.

"But that's not fair! I didn't choose to become like a boring hominal person. That was my parents' choice!" she barked for emphasis. "I want to be what my parents were. I want to do magic and serve a wizard and have cool adventures! I wished and wished so hard, and it came true!"

"No, Ally, it didn't," Rune said, her voice getting heavy. "Maddie died..." Ally's tail and ears drooped. "There's no wizardess for you to serve anymore."

"That's okay! Then, I want to serve you!" Ally wagged again.

"Serve me?"

"Yes, serve House Magdalene. My whole family used to serve you and the Lucky Devil. Or actually, served the Lady of House Magdalene, Lady Leveau."

"Rune? Do you know what she's talking about?" Taki asked, confused.

"Well, sort of, yes. The magic community is divided by Houses. She's referring to Aunt...to Maddie, she was the Lady Leveau of House Magdalene, but nobody really follows the old Houses anymore."

"And since Maddie left you everything, that makes you the new Lady Leveau," Taki concluded.

Blinking fast, Rune nodded reluctantly. "I guess, essentially."

"And I want to serve you!" Ally said, trying to bring the discussion back to herself.

"Hey, hold your horses. There is a lot here that isn't adding up. For one, if your mom knows you are a changeling, then why didn't she recognize that you had turned yourself into a dog?"

The little white dog actually rolled its eyes. "She's really good at that whole denial thing. Trust me. She is so deep in her self-focused crap that we can't even speak about having been retainers ever. We have always been a happy little hominal family."

"Wow, Rune, I didn't realize you were so important," Taki said.

"Not really. Maddie was important. I'm... just me."

"That's okay, I can serve you!" Ally said, her cheer unwavering.

"No. No, you can't. We're going to get your transformation reversed, and you are going back to your mother," Rune said firmly.

"No! Why?!" Ally actually barked as the sound of her loud 'no' reverberated in Rune's head. The shock of it stunned Taki, making her lose her grip on Ally, and for a moment, the seashell echo was gone.

"Taki, are you okay?" Rune asked, grabbing her friend's hand before she floated away. Taki shook her head and got a hold on the edge of the tank.

"Yes, of course, that was just loud. Wow," she said.

"I think that's enough," Rune decided, moving to dump Ally over the edge of the tank.

"No! No! No!" Ally barked, but Rune ignored her.

"Rune, are you okay?" Taki asked, moving closer to lay a webbed hand on Rune's shoulder. Rune sighed and leaned forward to set her forehead onto the edge of the tank.

"Oh, Taki," she said, "I should just leave. Just pick it all up and disappear never to be heard from again."

"I wish you had told me you were having trouble with the bar," Taki said, as she set her own arms over the edge of the tank and laid her cheek across her wrists. "If you need money, I can help you out."

"Ha, thanks. Oh, crap," Rune looked up at her friend. "Ally's mom was supposed to pay me the money to meet the rest of the mortgage payment. If this is a setup like she said, I'm not going to get that money now."

"Do you have most of the payment?" Taki asked.

"Back at the bar. Alf has it. Alf! I forgot to call Alf!" Rune jumped out of the water, her clothes hauling water onto the floor with her.

"Towels! Towels, please," Taki called. Rune hastily tossed down a couple of towels under herself as she grabbed Taki's waterproof phone and dialed the bar twice before it went through.

The tone rang for an agonizing age before a gruff voice answered. "What the hell do you want?"

"Alf! It's me," Rune said, relief that he answered washing down her spine.

"Oh, how nice of you to call," he said, drier than the Sahara. "Where the hell are you? When are you going to be back?"

"I've… I'm at Taki's right now," she answered, feeling seventeen again and in trouble with the principal.

"Oh, that's nice. While I've been here fending off reporters and corporate representatives looking for you, you've been getting your hair done," he grumbled meanly.

"Reporters?" Rune asked, ignoring the implication Alf was probably making that she was a female dog if she was getting her hair done at Taki's.

"There was a shootout in front of the bar, and Deputy Blakely is looking for you as a person of interest. What have you done now? Bad enough they shoot up my bar, but then you disappear and don't contact anyone… Are you on the lam?"

"What does that even mean, on the lam?" Rune asked, dodging the question.

"Running away!" Rune heard him click his tongue across the receiver. "Maddie has gotta be rolling in her grave right now."

Rolling her eyes, Rune bit her tongue and forced cordiality into her voice. "Never mind that. Alf, has Calvin and/or Jasper showed up?"

"Showed up? They've practically moved into one corner of the bar."

"Okay, okay," she said, trying not to let the panic take over. "Okay, keep an eye on them."

"Why? What's going on?" Alf asked, a hint of concern finally entering his voice.

"I think they're trying to pull something to take the bar away from us. Can you get the mortgage money together and make sure it's safe?"

"Sure, it's in the office, right?"

"Yes, in the usual spot." Rune hinted at the secret safe hiding in plain sight as a very portly devil that sat next to Maddie's old desk. Alf had a key to everything and knew all the spell words to disarm the magical transport spell that was cast on the devil. Even with the key, its contents would teleport away if it should be opened by anyone who hadn't, literally, said the magic words.

"Does this mean you got the rest of it?" Alf asked, his voice pitching down a bit like he was trying to keep from being heard easily.

"The Janowski gig has fallen through," Rune said, pulling out the inaccessible white card to look at it. She wondered if there was actually any money on it or was Ms. Janowski simply playing her. "I'm working something out."

"What do you mean? I thought the reason you're slacking off at managing your business was because you were out there doing a job. Are you actually just getting your hair done?" Alf asked, sounding disgusted and annoyed.

"Things got more complicated, okay?" Rune snapped, sticking the card back into the secret inner pocket of the belt. "I'll be back later tonight, don't worry. We'll get those creeps their stupid payment."

"Fine," Alf answered and hung up.

"Oh, my god, he is such an ass!" Rune dropped the receiver in its cradle with force and picked up her belt, angrily buckling it on.

"How much did you need again?" Taki asked, drawing Rune's attention back to her mermaid friend. With a wry smile, Taki held up a damp bag that clinked as she shook it, before pulling herself up onto the bench.

"Oh, Taki. I can't let you do this," Rune said, but Taki only smiled sweeter as she started wringing out her black hair into the water, her orange and white tail swishing gently like a little girl kicking her feet.

"That should be about $1,500 after you get it converted to credits," she said.

Rune pushed the small bag away. "That's twice what I need. No, really, I can't take this," she insisted.

"Oh, I'm not giving it to you for free." Taki braced her hands against the bench, bringing her shoulders up to her ears, making herself seem more innocent and sweet.

"I want to know your secret," she said.

"I know your secret, St. Benedict," St. Rachel announced, cutting off the lie he was about to tell, dead on his lips. "I know about your wife."

They had been talking for the last hour while the programs ran. St. Rachel, as usual, kept trying all her tricks to get him to reveal something about himself. He thought it was cute; it had always been a fun game for St. Benedict to evade her, but it hit him at that moment that maybe it wasn't all a game anymore. St. Benedict narrowed his eyes to slits of cold green-blue, a mildly sinister smile painting his lips.

She smiled back proudly. Like she knew she had finally scored a point. "Have I ever told you how much I love that smile? The one you have on right now? Sends shivers down my spine."

"My wife?" he asked.

"Don't be coy," she responded.

"Oh, I'm not," he assured her. "I'm just waiting for you to give me the reason I don't slit your throat right now and leave you in the alley out back."

St. Rachel didn't look away from his steady gaze, two wolves measuring each other carefully.

"Because without me, your rescue mission fails right here, right now," she said evenly.

He looked away, tapping a few more commands into the complicated program he was running.

"If you're wasting your time on rescuing your team, does that mean you're off the assigned mission then?" St. Rachel asked.

"Not in the slightest. I'm just a little bit delayed is all."

"But you still believe that this Rune woman can help you find the Masterson files?" she pressed.

"Something like that."

"But it's our owner who will end up with them," she countered. "I've been getting the impression that isn't what you have planned."

"That's possible."

St. Rachel blew out her breath. She shifted in her seat to undo the zipper of her boots with a long, loud zipping sound.

"Do you know why he agreed to buy my contract for this project?"

"You wanted revenge against the Kodiak Company, and you convinced him to lay down a small country's worth of money for you," St. Benedict interjected.

"Yes," she said coldly. "Yes, my secrets are all bared to you. You would think that you would trust me with yours."

"It was him then, who told you about my wife," St. Benedict concluded. "No other way you would have found out about her yourself."

She reached out a hand and laid it firmly on his arm. "Hey. I am here because I want to be, St. Benedict. Despite our natures, I am your friend here. At least as much a friend as people like us can have. I get it, you had a wife you cared about, but what I don't understand is what this has to do with the Masterson files."

He stared down at her perfect fingers, debating with himself. "It was because of the Masterson files that I lost her and became what I am today."

"That's why you want to find them?"

"That's why I want to destroy them. Everything else is just gravy." He turned back to the computer. "The decryption failed. Damn it."

"Then I only have one question for you. If this quest of yours to avenge your dead wife," St. Benedict's fingers paused mid-type, but St. Rachel pushed on, "if the mission really is the most important thing in your life, and Rune Leveau is the key to it all, why on earth did you let her just walk away?"

"I didn't."

"If you were really serious, you would have eliminated that option for her."

"What do you think I should have done instead?"

"Putting a gun to her head is always an option. And I know it's one that you've used before. So, that makes me wonder."

His fingers stilled on the keyboard in front of him. "Wonder what exactly?" he asked before taking another sip of fancy instant coffee from the appropriated machine he found in aisle eight.

His cohort didn't answer immediately, holding her silence until he sighed and looked at her. She measured his face carefully with her eyes. It always made him feel like she was trying to probe his soul with those dark green, liquid eyes.

"Just ask it already," he finally said, too tired to really want to win this kind of game.

"Did you sleep with her? Are you having feelings…?"

"Oh come on, St. Rachel, what do you think this is, a James Bond movie?"

"Then something did happen," she concluded.

"Based on what?"

"Your mission..."

"I am not off mission. I am doing the mission right now." He gestured to the computers on the island in front of them, each running programs in concert.

"If you were, she'd be here with us right now, tied to a chair with duct tape over her mouth," she said.

"So, you're questioning my integrity to the job because I am not acting like an inhuman monster."

"The Saint Benedict I know wouldn't let any opportunity slip away from him!" she declared at the top of her lungs, the sound of her voice echoing in the empty store. Her words just hung there in the hollow emptiness.

"You're right," he finally said, breaking the tension. "I made a mistake, and now Malachi and Zita are paying the price for it. But no, to answer your question, I didn't seduce her. It wouldn't have worked anyway." He rubbed his forehead, trying to erase the tension that sat behind his aching eyes.

"Go, go lie down. Get some sleep. I can watch this for a few hours," she said, her voice actually taking on a tinge of gentleness. He stood up then, sending the wheeled chair he had been using careening to land on its back. With two steps, he braced himself over St. Rachel in her own chair, their faces mere inches from each other. The tension crackled like lightning.

"What do you want, St. Rachel? What do you really want?"

Her eyes were wide, the eyeliner she carefully applied cracking in places, emphasizing what they meant to hide.

"St. Benedict," she breathed out and leaned forward the tiniest micro-inch, her lips parting in eagerness and desire.

He hesitated on the threshold. It would be so easy to just take those lips and punish them, work out all of his feelings of frustration and let them melt into relief and bliss. It had always been so easy before he became a Saint. There was a time he wouldn't have given a damn about the price, knowing he would never have to pay it. Until that day it had all come due at once.

Taking a deep, shuddering breath, he pulled away. No, he would keep his vow.

"You're right. I need some sleep," he said and turned to go to the leather chair under the tent. He didn't dare look at St. Rachel, didn't dare let her see how close she got that time. He knew he had just embarrassed her, and he wasn't going to make it worse by looking.

"You can't stay celibate forever," she called after him, her voice harsh with hurt anger.

He waved a hand over his shoulder. "Can't be celibate if I still got a hand," he joked and dropped into his seat.

"You're right, St. Benedict. You are an inhuman monster."

"That I am," he said, but softly to himself, as he pulled his hat over his face, a small part of him hoping that St. Rachel would take the opportunity to drive a knife into his chest while he was vulnerable and end the whole debate once and for all. He sighed and relaxed at the thought.

It was like a knife had been plunged into her heart.

"My secret?" Rune asked. She stared at the bag of coins sitting on the desk. A small puddle formed around it as water bled out of the bag.

"Yeah, your secret, about who you really are. And I don't mean just me. I mean everybody. I think you should tell everybody." Taki said, her voice was soothing against the sounds of the lapping water and the semi-darkness of the room. Rune yawned, the weariness weighing her bones down.

"Taki, I can't. I've told you more than I've ever told anybody already."

"But listen. If you did that, told everybody, then this Benedict guy, he would have nothing over you anymore. None of them would, right?"

"Saint Benedict," Rune said, giving a little smile in spite of herself.

"Whatever. He tried to use your secret as leverage against you, right? I'd say his 'sainthood' is in question."

"Yeah," Rune conceded with a nod. She thought for a moment what he told her about the saint honorific. It was one of his secrets, Rune realized. One she couldn't bring herself to share, even though she seemed to be telling her friend everything else.

"Well, he's a bastard," Taki pronounced and picked up her now-cold take-out and a pair of chopsticks.

"Or just desperate. I don't know." Rune traced a finger through the puddle from the coin bag to draw out a line of water across the marble desktop. "It probably seemed reasonable to him. And how am I any different right now? I came to you for help; brought you all my troubles."

"I'm your friend. Take the coins and save your bar," Taki urged. Rune picked them up slowly, setting the bag in her other palm, feeling the wetness seep through her fingers.

"Why the hesitation?" Taki asked after a moment. Rune didn't respond, and Taki splashed at her. "Hey, come on. What is it you're not telling me still?"

"You just now said we were friends. I told St. Benedict I was his, and then I abandoned him." The water of the pool bubbled softly.

"He threatened you, right? That's not okay."

"No, it isn't. It still doesn't change this feeling in my gut," Rune acknowledged.

"So, why can't you help him?" Taki finally asked.

"Well...because...what he wants is impossible."

"Oh, that's right. He's looking for you. Or not you. The old you. The one you can't tell me about. And here, my point comes back again. I think you should come out of the cave already and tell everyone about who you really are!"

"Because I'm not supposed to be me. It's technically illegal to say you are who you are not, and to be an unregistered Talent."

"So, you get a lawyer and you pay a fine," Taki said flippantly. "It's no big deal."

"It is a big deal! It's a very big, big deal," Rune insisted, "There could be jail time, as well."

"Oh, come on, they would never send you to jail. That's a little extreme. That's for people who like, sell children on the black market, or commit serial murders. You know criminal types."

"Taki... you don't understand, okay? It's not going to be as simple as that."

"Because of who you used to be?"

"Yes." Rune's hands were shaking again, and she tucked them under her arms, pressing the wet bag into her still damp side.

"And St. Benedict is one of those people who really want to hurt you?"

"No. He's looking for Justin," Rune said without thinking.

That made Taki pause again, with a shrimp halfway to her mouth. "Who's Justin?"

Rune cursed under her breath and turned away so that Taki could not see her face. She had really done it this time. The pressure in her head and the sickness in her stomach were all getting to her. She knew she had to get out of there. She couldn't let Taki see her like this. "Is it too much of a cliché to say, 'someone I would rather forget'?"

"Yes." Taki took a dainty bite of her shrimp, not noticing Rune's distress. "Who is Justin?"

"He's an asshole I never want to see again!" Rune suddenly shouted. It was too late to stop it now. "And I thought I never would. He's the reason I had to give up my name and why I'm probably going to die alone! What else do you want to know, Taki?! Would you like to know how he embezzled lots of money from his company but was too stupid to cover it up? Or that they dragged both of us to jail in the middle of the night? They tortured me, Taki!" Rune didn't realize she was shouting. Taki stared at Rune with her mouth hanging open. Ally retreated to the door, tail and ears down.

"Anyway, thank you for your help with her," Rune said quickly. She dropped the bag of coins as her fingers went nerveless. She needed to get out of the place. Get away.

"You're leaving?!"

Rune felt her throat closing up. "I told Alf I would be back tonight."

"But what about the mortgage payment?"

"Keep it. I can't take —" Rune started to say, but Taki cut her off.

"Rune, stop!" Taki called.

"Just leave me alone!" Rune shouted again.

"Rune, come on! Stop!"

"No, Taki. I thought I could trust you, but you're trying to trick me! Ally, come on!"

There was a wet thump on the ground, just as Rune reached the door handle. Spinning quickly, she saw her mermaid friend stranded on the tile floor of her office, where she had fallen out of her tank. "Rune! Stop!" she said meekly, wincing as the pain of landing lanced through her scales.

"You want to know why I can't tell anybody?!" Rune was losing control of herself, the shaking inside coming out as pain and rage, all of it directed at her friend. "Huh, Taki? Because if anybody found out that I was Anna Masterson, they would take me back there! Back to that room. Only this time, Maddie wouldn't be coming to save me because I couldn't save her!"

"Rune..." Taki tried, but Rune was already on a roll.

"No... you're just like the rest of them. I can't trust any of you. Only Maddie. I'm never going to be safe." Rune didn't realize how fast Taki could skitter across the tiled floor, but suddenly the smaller person was sliding on the dampness to grapple with Rune's legs, pulling her down onto her back.

"No! NO!" Rune shouted, and somewhere she heard Ally's bark going crazy.

"I'm not letting you run away!" Taki had twisted her fingers into Rune's clothes and was trying to climb up her body. Rune scrambled into a sitting position.

"Get off of me!"

Then the bag of coins slapped hard into her hand.

"I'm not going to let you go!" Taki shouted into Rune's face, stunning the other woman into silence. "You're right, I'm not Maddie, but I am still your friend, Rune." Mermaids didn't cry, they weren't built to, but if Taki had been a land person, tears would have been flowing down her face at that moment. Rune was crying enough for both of them.

Unbidden, Rune's arms wrapped around the mermaid, and they both sat on the ground, while Rune cried and cried. Time stopped having any meaning. At least until a shudder passed through Taki's spine and her tail whipped involuntarily back and forth.

"Taki!" Rune scrambled to her feet and scooped up her smaller friend off the floor. Gently, she set the mermaid back into the water, but Taki didn't let go of Rune's shirt as she winced in pain.

"Carp crap, it burns," Taki hissed through her teeth.

"Should I call an ambulance?" Rune asked, on the edge of panic.

"No, no. I'll be alright. The water burns while my scales rehydrate. I'll be alright in a minute." She let go of Rune's shirt then and sank under the water. Rune sat, watching her friend's form refract under the water. She had known Taki for years. She knew how the mermaid had run away from home and traversed the darker side of Chicago. Her need to be in water gave too much control to some unsavory people, which had put her in deep trouble by the time Maddie had saved her.

When Taki came back up, her black hair coming out of their pom-poms from the struggle, the weight of the water pulling them straight to frame her face. Rune took a deep, shuddering breath.

"That was stupid," Taki said.

"Are you okay?" Rune asked. Ally whined the same question as she jumped up onto the bench.

"Once the spasms stop, it only takes a couple of moments. I'll be fine. The dangers of choosing to live on land," Taki said, wiggling her tail more normally.

"Just take it slow," Rune coached. "I'm sorry for not trusting you." Taki floated for a moment, then blew out an arch of water, the mermaid equivalent of a sigh.

"I'm sorry I pushed. I should have known better. I thought I was helping. Like Maddie helped me. Like you're trying to help her." Taki pointed at Ally. "Maddie would be so proud of you."

Rune shook her head. "What can I do? I'm not Maddie. How can I help others when I need help? I need help, Taki," Rune said. She slumped against the side of the tank, the water rewetting her shirt, warm like blood. A wet hand combed through Rune's hair.

"I know what Maddie would say," Taki said softly.

"What's that?" Rune asked.

"There's always help to be found at the Lucky Devil."

The lost Talent laughed to herself, brushing her tears away and nodded.

"Yeah. Yeah, you're right."

"Despite what you think, I am your friend. I wanted to prove that to you. Take the coins, please. I'm repaying you. When I first left my clan and came here, it was your aunt who funded me with those coins, and I kept what I didn't use, you know, for a rainy day. I'd say for you it's pouring."

Rune had to fight back the tears.

"Thank you," she tried to say, but her throat closed up on her. She could do it. She could save the Lucky Devil.

"You can trust me," Taki said, looking very small and delicate.

"I'm sorry, Taki."

"Maybe when you're ready, you will tell me everything else?" the mermaid asked, lifting her head slowly, hopefully. "All of it."

"Yeah. Yeah. I think I might be getting there, too," Rune said, offering a smile in return. She hugged Taki hard. "Thanks for kicking me in the ass."

"Sure, anytime," Taki laughed. "Hey, Rune, if you want, stay here tonight. You don't have to be alone."

"Okay," Rune smiled and closed her eyes.

St. Benedict opened his eyes.

"Do you still have that thing I asked you to hold for me?"

"Yes, why?" St. Rachel answered.

"Give it back to me," he said, holding out his hand, palm up toward where she was curled up in an office chair. She had kicked off her boots and nylons so she could tuck her painted toes behind her.

"A 'please' would be nice," St. Rachel countered.

St. Benedict remained silent for a long moment. "Please."

From underneath her collar, St. Rachel pulled out two long, linked chains that were looped around her neck. Both chains ended in tiny metal boxes, each etched with different runes. She didn't need to look at the boxes to know which one was his. Pulling the chain up over her head, she held it out to him.

"I can't believe you trusted me with your Saint's box," she said, staring at the bleeding rose carved into the top. He snatched it from her and put it over his own head, sighing with relief as it dropped into its familiar place under his shirt.

"You're right. I was getting off mission."

CHAPTER 14

"Are you sure you're going to be okay?" Taki asked the next morning.

Rune shrugged and gave a wan smile. "I guess, as okay as I've ever been. Maddie left everything to me and that has to mean something, right? It means something to me, and I am going to protect it with everything I got left."

"You sound like a hero in a fairy tale," Taki said. It was around six in the morning, but being the height of summer, the sun was already preparing to burst from behind the buildings.

Sleeping on Taki's rock-hard, office couch had left Rune a bit loopy, but as intense as her anxiety was, she wasn't sure how well she would have slept anyway. Ally was none the worse for wear; whether it was her youth or her smaller doggy stature, was a more well-rested person's guess.

"I wish I could have offered you something better than the office couch. I've never sat on it, I just bought it because of how it looked," Taki apologized.

"It was fine," Rune assured. "What were we supposed to do? Your apartment is underwater. I'm just grateful I had somewhere safe to stay."

"You're welcome back anytime. I'll even get a better couch."

"Meet you out front?" Rune asked, leading Ally out the door.

Out front, the sunlight was streaming through the windows of the quiet shop.

"So, what's the plan?" Taki asked as she pulled herself along her tank to where it ended next to the door. She had a set of keys in her hand and picked out one that was tabbed in red.

"Get back to the bar, take a shower if possible, and probably get a change of clothes," Rune said, tugging on her stiff, dried shirt in demonstration, "then grab the money and bolt for the mortgage office like there is a zombie hoard after me."

"Don't even joke about that," Taki warned, which just made Rune smile harder. "You got the bag of gold I gave you?"

Rune held it up by its string and shook it a little to clank the coins together. "Check."

"Okay, when it's all over, call me because I'm going to be worried until then." Taki held out her arms for a hug, which Rune received gladly, never mind that she was getting damp again. It was just the price one paid to be friends with a mermaid. "And you," Taki added, turning to Ally. "You take care of your mistress, you understand?"

Ally barked, "Yes!"

"I'm not your mistress! And as soon as I figure out how to turn you back into a person, you are going back to your mother," Rune admonished, but neither Ally nor Taki acknowledged it.

"Come back soon," Taki said as she held the door open for Ally, who wagged her little white tail and trotted happily out the door.

"Hey, kid! Don't you ignore me," Rune called after her and hurried behind the dog-girl.

The trip back was quick by taxi. It was a relief to see the dark, wooded front of her bar.

It felt surreal to walk into the Lucky Devil that morning, Ally, still a dog, trotting at her side. Whatever damage had occurred the day — or the lifetime before — had been erased. Rune assumed it was Alf's doing. Even the doorway between the Lounge and the Main Bar had been repaired, the clearly new cubes of glass the only sign that anything had changed.

She didn't run into anyone, which was fine with her. Instead, she let herself up to her apartment to shower and change. The mortgage office wouldn't be open yet, and crashing on Taki's couch had left her feeling stiff and crooked. The warm pulsing water helped to untie her muscles. Ally waited for her on the bed, lounging across it as much as her little body could cover, already asleep again.

Feeling reborn, Rune pulled out fresh clothes from her dresser; a black button-up and jeans seemed to reflect her mood perfectly. A glance out the window told her it was going to rain. Despite it being early summer, it was chilly outside according to her weather crystal, reflecting a misty 61 degrees for all to see. She pulled her knee-high boots on again over clean socks and debated putting on a jacket. She didn't, but at the last second, she fastened on her belt, just in case. It made her feel safer to have it on, and this time she loaded her pouch with homemade nutritional bars from Maggie's secret recipe.

Halfway down the stairs toward the bar, Ally literally on her heels, Rune remembered that she had told Alf to take the mortgage payment from the safe. She decided she should check in with him anyway and knocked hard on his door. Several moments later, he still hadn't answered.

"Maybe he's downstairs? What do you think, Ally?" Rune asked. The little dog-girl actually tried to shrug, which looked completely unnatural.

Downstairs, the bar was starting to come to life. It all looked so normal that it made the last couple days seem like they hadn't even happened.

To her relief, Rune saw Alf and one of the newer servers setting up for the breakfast crowd. She offered up a smile to Alf when he paused at the sight of her coming down the stairs.

"Hey, I'm back," she chirped as she came up to the side of the bar. Alf looked down at the tray of glasses he had brought from the back, still glistening droplets of water from the dishwasher, but didn't say anything. Rune huffed. "Don't be too excited to see me. You might hurt yourself."

"You told me you were coming back last night. I was starting to wonder if I should go looking for a body. You got the payment?" he asked.

"What? No. I thought you would have it. I told you where it was in my office," Rune furrowed her eyebrows with concern. "Alf? Is everything alright?"

"I can't get in there. You changed the keyword or something," Alf groused as he picked up a dry cloth and started drying the glasses.

"Oh. Did I? I didn't think I had, but I'll go see. Sorry about that," Rune said, remembering that she had used a different word the other day. "Wonder how I did that?"

"You better hurry up," Alf said. "Mortgage office opens at nine."

Rune huffed a sigh, and chose not to comment, even though that was her plan anyway. Ally followed after, shooting Alf a speculative look. The little man didn't notice her, but his eyes followed Rune as she moved into the Lounge Bar toward her office. Ally snuffed again dismissively.

Rune stood in front of her office door, and Ally sat next to her, her tail wagging as she watched Rune. At first, the Talent tried a few Latin words while working on opening the door, but nothing happened until Rune ordered it to open in English. Then there was a sharp click, and the knob turned easily to open.

"Huh, I guess I changed the password to literally 'open.' That's not very secure," Rune joked.

"Yes!" Ally barked.

Inside, the office was still a mess, her papers tossed everywhere. Setting her jaw, Rune ignored it for now. She had to deal with bigger priorities first.

Rune bee-lined through the office straight to a dark-red, squat devil sitting on its haunches next to the desk; its round face and round eyes making it look a bit stupid. It also didn't look disturbed at all from the office invasion, much to its owner's relief. She stroked the top of its head and said another Latin-esque sounding word. The statue moved as if alive, and Ally jumped up to all fours to bark at it.

"It's okay, Ally, it's just an enchanted object," Rune said as the statue opened its fat arms to reveal a black box inside. With a glum expression, the fat devil held out the box and opened the lid, going still as a statue again once it had. Inside the box sat a large white envelope with the word "Mortgage" written across the front in blue pen. Rune removed the envelope and opened it. She flipped a thumb through the papers inside as she did a quick count of the bills and a couple of checks. She only needed to recount once.

"Okay, this plus what Taki gave us, takes care of the mortgage this month. Now, we just need to get to the office when they open at nine." Rune and Ally glanced at the devil clock on the wall together. "And it's almost eight, so perfect. We take another quick taxi there and be waiting for them when they open. Then we win."

"Yes!" Ally barked.

"Oh, I want so badly to pet your head, you make such a cute dog," Rune said, her face joyful as she closed the devil back up.

"No!" Ally barked, and Rune genuinely laughed.

"Don't worry, I won't. Let's get going." Together they headed to the door, and both jumped when Rune opened it to find Alf standing on the other side.

"Before you go, there's someone you need to talk to," he gruffed.

"What? But I have to get going," Rune said perplexed. At the end of the hall stood a short man, a little taller than Alf, of some Asian descent. He stood holding his hands, rubbing them, worried.

"His name is Mr. Chen. His mother was a friend of Maddie's. He says he needs help," Alf said.

"Um," Rune bit her lower lip, unsure of what to do. "I guess I can hear him out for a quick couple of minutes, but then I've really got to go."

"You have all day, remember," Alf growled.

Rune forced a smile and led Mr. Chen to Lucky Devil's booth to listen to his story. Ally sat next to her on the bench seat.

After what felt like an eternity later, Rune narrowed her eyes at the man sitting across from her. "Let me get this straight, you want me to find your keys?" she asked. Rune glanced up at the clock over the Lounge Bar and had to resist grinding her teeth. It was already nine-thirty, and she had thought she would have been to the mortgage company to drop off the payment and be back by now.

"It's not just my keys, it's my entire life," Mr. Chen said in abject despair.

Sighing, Rune leaned back in the booth next to Lucky Devil and tried to nod politely as he launched into his story again. It had something to do with his office. He had been placed in charge of the storage keys after his supervisor, Gary, left and nobody else wanted the responsibility. Then he went on about his mother and how he had her keys on the same ring because she was getting old and her sight wasn't too good anymore. Then he went on about how his girlfriend left him again, apparently for the fourth time, but they share a storage locker and if he didn't get his stuff out soon, she was going to steal everything, and that's when he noticed his keys were gone…

Rune blinked and nodded in the right places, then glanced over at the clock. Another hour had passed. This had to end. She had something she needed to do. Just as he was starting the part of his story about his mother again, she cut the conversation short, "How did you get my contact information again?"

"My mother. She had one of your coins and said to ask you to help me," he said.

"You mean she said to get help from my aunt?" Rune knew that wasn't right, but was having a hard time remembering why. Where was Maddie, anyway? That clock was ticking insistently loud. Ally began rubbing at her ears with a paw like they hurt.

"Oh, no, no, she said to ask for the apprentice. You are good at finding things, right? You can find my keys?" he asked, pushing the small, neat glasses back up the bridge of his nose. He had to be well into his thirties, but he had such a baby face, it was hard to tell. He wore a red polo-shirt and slacks, but he twiddled his smartphone in his hands nervously. Corporate type, but a corporate type coming in on a Monday morning; it had to be a serious emergency, which was why she had agreed to hear him out. Probably, and where did she need to head to? Or was it something to do with Alf? Rune's head was really starting to hurt.

"Look, sir, I can definitely help you, but it's going to have to wait a couple of hours. I have a really important... thing I have to do before the end of the day, and I really need to get going..."

"No, you can't leave! This is a matter of life or death," he said and glanced at the door like the boogieman was going to come in at any moment and haul him off to some nasty purgatory. If only it would.

"They are just keys," Rune said. She couldn't keep the derision out of her voice anymore. This was just such a waste of her time. Where was Alf? "If you want a faster solution, hire a locksmith." She stood up and picked up her mortgage envelope. The bag of coins Taki had given her, still in one of the pouches of her work belt, jangled. Why had she put her work belt on? And why was she wearing a different shirt? Wasn't she wearing white?

"No, wait, please!" Mr. Chen gripped her forearm with a strength that almost hurt.

"Hey," said a familiar voice, and a hand appeared on the guy's shoulder. "I think the lady said she was done talking to you." A feline hand appeared on the other shoulder and instantly, the man turned white as a sheet. He turned back to look up at the twin grinning faces of Jasper and Calvin.

Suddenly, things came more into focus. Rune realized the little man had been casting something on her. Shaking her head sharply, she blinked several times. "What the hell?"

"Why don't you run off now?" Calvin suggested to the shivering little man who Rune was now staring daggers at. Jasper added a little growl to encourage him along.

"Thanks. I'm not sure what that was about, but... thanks," she said, as she watched the little man hightail it out of there.

"You're welcome," Jasper said and sat down on one of the barstools across from Lucky Devil's booth.

"Got your mortgage payment, Rune? It's Monday," Calvin said, sticking his hands into his pockets and leaning against the back of the booth. He was dressed in a slate-gray suit with a light-blue dress shirt, his hair spiked in front again with too much gel.

"Why do you wear your sunglasses indoors? Seriously," Rune said. Jasper chuckled, unmoved by Calvin's dirty look, which lost some of its potency behind the aforementioned sunglasses.

Smugly, Rune pushed past Calvin and waved the envelope near his face. "Got the payment right here, in full, big guy. Now, if you'll excuse me, I'm off to walk it in personally." She was feeling pretty cocky, and it felt good, like how she felt when she was drunk, but before she realized what happened, Calvin snatched the envelope out of her hand.

"Hey!"

Stepping just out of her range, Calvin flipped open the flap of the envelope. With a thumb, he flicked through the bills, apparently counting to himself.

"My, my, Mr. Locke, it looks like our little magician's apprentice almost managed to pull it off," Calvin said. "Only a thousand short or so. Oh, so close." He hissed the last part through his teeth.

"Give that back," Rune said, and attempted to reach around him to grab the envelope, but he effectively, too effectively, shrugged her hand away. Ally started barking up a ruckus, but something sounded wrong about her bark; it sounded more hollow than it should have.

"My gosh, that's a lot of dollar bills. So untraceable and everything," he said, folding them back into the envelope.

"Give that back to me, Calvin," Rune said, putting as much warning in her voice as she could.

"Not to worry, not to worry. You've done it, you've made your payment on time and in full," he said as he turned around to face her so that she could watch him tuck her envelope into his inner suit pocket. "Come on, Mr. Locke, let's give her a round of applause," he said as he started a condescending, slow, staccato clap. Jasper mimicked him. Rune felt her face get hotter and hotter.

"This is stealing. You can't do this," Rune said.

"We're not stealing." Calvin put his hands back into the pockets of his pants. "We're a delivery service. We'll take it over for you, so you don't have to go across town to deposit it yourself. We're saving you a trip, right, Mr. Locke?"

"No, we're not," the Tigerman said truthfully.

"You're no fun," Calvin said.

"You can't do this. I won't let you." Rune rushed Calvin, clawing at his coat, ultimately unsuccessful in getting her envelope back.

Calvin caught her left wrist, but her right one tried ineffectively to score across his chest. Unused to fighting, Rune was distracted by the pain lancing through her left wrist as his larger hand crunched and ground the bones. Before she knew it was happening, Jasper grabbed her around the shoulders and yanked her back from his partner. Still not giving up, Rune tried to kick her feet off the ground to buck free, but Jasper hiked her up until her feet no longer touched the ground.

Ally made attempts at ankle-biting, but she was easily ignored. Between Ally's barks and Rune's shouting, it was shocking that nobody came to investigate. Where was everyone? Her bar had never been this empty before.

That's when she realized they were alone. Alf and two other bartenders should have been moving around, getting things ready for the lunch crowd, with at least a half-dozen patrons trickling in the minute the bar opened. Where were they? What was going on? She had only a few moments to internalize these questions while she struggled against Jasper.

Calvin straightened his clothes with an irritated brusqueness. He slicked back his hair again, trying to regain his 'cool guy' composure and promptly got knocked sideways by Rune's kick.

"Damn bitch," he muttered.

"Screw you!" Rune barked.

He backhanded her across the face, and the world spun, then got bright, then dark, then bright again, before settling on just dim. Tears rolled down her face, and she reflexively tried to cover her hurt, but her arms were still uselessly pinned.

A yelp drew her attention back as Calvin kicked at Ally, who had turned her vicious little attack onto his ankle and actually scored a hit.

"No! Don't kick her, she's just a kid!" Rune shouted. "Ally, don't!" But Ally didn't quit as she picked herself up off the floor. She growled as viciously as any wolf. Calvin looked genuinely afraid. He swung another kick at Ally, but her nimbler feet took her out of the way that time.

"Calvin! You coward!" Rune shouted at him. He directed his angry gaze back at her like she wanted him to.

"I said, shut up!" he roared and moved to backhand her again, but this time Jasper released one arm from holding Rune to grab his partner's arm in mid-swing.

"No. No hitting. She cannot fight back," he said, calmly, almost sagely.

There was some sort of silent exchange between the two of them that Rune couldn't see. Jasper released Calvin's arm to renew his double grip on Rune, just as she started to struggle free again.

"Don't do that again," Jasper said, his voice rumbling like thunder through Rune's back.

At first, she thought he was talking to her, but then Calvin answered him with a childish sneer. "Geez, Jasper, you're so chivalrous."

"We have what we came for," Jasper answered him. Calvin looked put out but straightened his perfectly straight shirt collar again to cover it.

"Let's get out of here," he said.

"What about the money card?" Jasper asked.

"This is robbery," Rune said.

"Oh, right. You better set her down," Calvin said, ignoring Rune's comment. He waited while his partner set her down so her feet touched again. The dark button-down shirt Rune wore was pulling at the buttons, gaping so much that Calvin's eyes were immediately drawn to it. At that moment, Rune wished she had worn a tank underneath and then immediately chastised herself for victim-blaming herself since she was, in fact, the one being assaulted and robbed.

"Why the hell are you doing this to me?"

Calvin looked her straight in the eye with all the intensity of a lover and the smirk of a teenage bully as he slowly lifted the edge of her shirt to search her jeans pockets. Rune tried to squirm again, but the arms behind her held her fast.

"Isn't it obvious?" Calvin asked. "For the money."

"Get on with it," Jasper rumbled.

Her frisker only smirked more as he reached around her waist like he was going to embrace her and slid his fingers into Rune's back pockets, taking a very hard squeeze of her posterior.

Rune squawked angrily, and Jasper gave another warning growl that Calvin heeded, putting both hands up in a gesture of surrender.

"Check her belt," Jasper said.

A few more snaps later, Calvin ran a finger along the inside of her belt and found her secret compartment. He stepped back abruptly, holding the white cash card in between two fingers like he held an ace. With furrowed brows, Rune stared at the card, trying to understand its significance to Calvin.

"That's useless to you guys without the pin code, and that's if there really is anything on it," Rune growled, her desire to fight surprising even herself. When did she become so bold? "Maybe you want to hit up the cash register while you're at it?"

Calvin just chuckled. Rune was wary that she didn't get the joke.

"Oh, don't worry, we'll be back for the cash register later, when they kick your fat ass out onto the street, Ms. Rune Leveau," he said, mockingly dwelling on the honorific.

"Not yet, if you please."

They all turned as one, or rather the Tigerman turned, and Rune *ipso facto* went with him, to regard a woman sitting at the bar. For the briefest moment, Rune felt relief that someone was going to help her. Relief boiled into horror as she recognized the face she could never forget. The face of the woman who still haunted her nightmares.

"Don't tell her our plan yet. I want to see if she figures it out," the woman said, sitting at the bar in her crisp white suit, her hair styled exactly as it had been six years ago.

"We got everything in hand, boss, what are you doing here?" Calvin asked. Rune barely heard his question.

"Oh, Anna, you don't look happy to see me. I'm hurt," the well-dressed woman said, feigning a pout Rune hadn't seen in six years, except in her nightmares.

CHAPTER 15

The well-dressed woman stood up and polished off the contents of a strange teacup. She licked her lips delicately, looking deep into the cup like she was reading the tea leaves. Whatever she saw pleased her because she set the cup down on the bar with a smirk on her face. Then she sashayed over to Rune, who stood petrified as a stone statue. The woman, whose name Rune realized she never knew, faced Rune squarely. She looked Rune down and up, then right back down again.

"You've gained weight," she said with the disapproval of a beauty-schoolmarm.

Rune didn't know what to say to that. A wave of shame washed over her, and she ducked her head as her cheeks blushed crimson. She may as well have been back in that room, chained to the table. All the will drained out of her. She had failed Maddie. Failed herself. Failed everything.

"Where is she? Where is my daughter?" Ms. Janowski cried, who Rune realized had been standing by the well-dressed woman, worrying her hands as she looked around. "You said if I did as you asked, you would restore my daughter to me. Where is she?"

Ally perked up, jumping onto a chair near her mother to bark and bark. Ms. Janowski looked down at the little dog, unsure, before looking anywhere else, at anyone else, waiting for someone to direct her to her daughter.

"In a moment, Janowski. All accounts are about to be settled, I assure you." The well-dressed woman set her hands behind her back, looking delighted with herself. She regarded Rune carefully for a moment as if assessing a prized deer she had caught and was planning to mount her head on a wall somewhere.

"Oh, I can't stand it! Please ask the question, we know you're dying to ask," the well-dressed woman said, giddily, like it was Christmas morning, and Rune was about to unwrap her present.

"Where did you come from?" Rune asked, trying to swallow the dry lump in her throat.

"No! No, no, no, no, no! That is the wrong question! Try again!" The well-dressed woman screamed in her face, gripping Rune hard with one hand.

Rune whimpered.

"Ask me, now," the woman repeated, quieter.

"Uh, how?" Rune tried.

"NO! No, no, still not it!" Her face flushed red and warm spittle bathed Rune's face. Jasper hugged Rune a little tighter and leaned back, yet she found it more reassuring than constricting and realized it was a similar feeling to how her manacles had made her feel when she had been locked to the interrogation table

When the well-dressed woman had calmed down, the enraged expression wiped away and replaced with calm placidness. "It has always been like this with you," she said, shaking her head in disappointment. "Never asking enough questions, always complacent to just accept things as they are, and never looking any deeper. It's what got you into this situation in the first place. Why is that? Afraid to look at yourself? Afraid to let yourself see what you really are? Yes, that's it. You are so ashamed of your dirty magic. Your husband knew, didn't he? But that's okay, he'd accept you anyway if you stayed the perfect weight, never argued with him, and let him do whatever he wanted to whomever he wanted. Then you would be okay. Just never ask any questions, right? God, you are so pathetic," she finished with another of her delighted and measured looks that raked Rune's soul. "Guess again."

Staring at her, wide-eyed, Rune's mind slipped away like sand—becoming completely blank. A small part of her screamed to stop as the old coping mechanisms fell into place, shutting her will down to make her compliant. Being compliant was how to stay safe. *No, it isn't,* a small part of her tried to argue.

Rune glanced over at Calvin. He looked as freaked out as she was, which was not reassuring. Anna had always taken her cues from how the guards were reacting that day. Meeting her gaze, he widened his eyes at her to silently push her to answer the well-dressed woman. He still held up the white cash card like he had forgotten about it, its blankness holding no answers. Were they working with her the whole time? Rune double blinked. Why were they doing this, if the woman knew where 'Anna' was this whole time?

"Why are you doing this, after all this time?" she asked, practically shouting.

Like someone dropped a window shade on a particularly violent storm, the well-dressed woman's face went completely calm, almost serene. The lackeys both exhaled their held breath, and Rune felt the tension ease a bit in the Tigerman's arms. Apparently, that was the right answer — or question.

"Why? Indeed, why? First though... what's your name?" Rune's hated torturer murmured airily. She sounded high. Had she always been like this?

"M-my name?" Rune stuttered.

"Please do not stutter. Tell me your name clearly, so we can all hear."

"Rune Leve..."

The well-dressed woman slapped her hand on the table. "Your name!"

"Ru..." She couldn't say it. It was a lie. Everything that Rune had ever been... was a lie.

As if sensing the impending kill, the well-dressed woman whispered softly one last time. "What is your name?"

"Anna Masterson," Anna said clearly, and everything that had ever been Rune crumpled away.

Satisfied, the woman took the card from Calvin, who practically jerked his hand away as if she was a viper about to bite him. Turning the card over in her hands, they all watched as the white, thin plastic peeled away, revealing something that shimmered with rainbow colors underneath. With a squeal of delight, she held up the card, flashing it around like a winning lottery ticket.

"Oh my, my, this is delightful. No wonder your aunt was so protective of you. Do you know what this is?"

"A ma-gic trick?" Anna answered obediently.

The well-dressed woman giggled, her voice sharp and piercing like shattering glass. She tapped the glittering card against her teeth. It emitted an impossibly clear tone as it struck that made Rune's toes curl and the hairs on the back of her neck stand straight up.

"It's a crystal?" Anna tried again, hating herself for answering.

"Good, good. You're stumbling into the answers you seek more or less," she said and slipped the card into the inner pocket of her pristine white jacket.

"What answers? You're just asking questions!" Rune snapped back. Everyone looked at her, and Anna's face reflected her own surprise. What had just happened? Rune was a lie.

"I would have thought the sight of the crystal would answer everything for you, Apprentice," the woman said, cocking her head to the side as she studied Rune, calculating.

"I'm...I'm not an apprentice... My aunt..." Anna stuttered, trying to walk it back.

"No, you aren't, are you, Anna? You've been lying to everyone. And all those lies are sand under your house, and now the house is collapsing in on itself." The well-dressed woman sighed and shook her head disapprovingly before she waved the money card in front of Rune again. "Do you know what this is, then?"

"A...an aura-reading crystal," Anna answered. "When I used magic, it imprinted in the crystal."

"Silly mortals. Wave a bauble in front of your face and you snatch it up with greedy fingers. But it was just fool's gold. Well, I suppose fool's gold is the wrong analogy. I suppose the crystal itself was worth about $5,000." She shook her head at Anna with pity. "There is nothing about you that isn't a waste, is there?"

That was a lie. The voice that had been Rune knew it. This well-dressed woman didn't know anything about Rune Leveau and what she was worth. Anna trembled, struggling to keep Rune back. She couldn't say that, not to her.

"It's the eternal curse of you creatures, always revealing your greatest secrets so easily. I am privileged to have been the first to find out what was so clear to see. You're like a child trying to hide its shadow from the light of truth."

Everything this woman said sounded wrong. Mortals? Creatures?

"What is she talking about, Leveau?" Calvin asked under his breath, sharing a glance with his partner.

"An exact match. I've memorized every nuance of your aura pattern, Anna. You can change your name, change your ID card, your social-security-number, even your hair color, but an aura, never. I suppose that's why you told everyone you couldn't do magic at all. Auras are tricky things. Everyone's looks like everyone else's, but if anyone actually caught sight of your aura while you were doing magic, you'd be found out, right?"

"What? Wait, what is she talking about? I thought we were here about the bar?" Calvin asked, still not quite catching up.

"Of course, it is, but this place isn't *just* a bar, right, Mr. Locke?"

"No," Jasper answered, his voice rumbling.

"What the hell?" Calvin asked, shooting a glare at his partner. "You hiding things from me, Jasper?"

"We don't need to explain anything to you, Mr. Calvin, whatever your last name is."

"This is about Maddie's House, not Justin?" Anna asked.

The well-dressed woman smiled brightly. "Yes and no. Parts and pieces. I don't know the whole picture myself," she purred. "Like this place, right? This place is more than a bar. Not just this building, but what it stands for, too: The House of Magdalene. The title. Access to the Archivist. Such an unworthy heir your aunt left behind." The well-dressed woman tsk-tsk-tsked. "Oh, I just realized. You never called her your aunt, did you? You denied even that relationship to protect yourself. Imagine, she risked the sanctity of her House to save such an ungrateful piece of shit like you."

"I'm not an ungrateful piece of shit," Anna said softly.

"If you say so," the well-dressed woman answered, tucking away the card with her eerie, serene smile.

Anna blinked again. What was going on? Why hadn't she been slapped or punished in some way for her insolence? Why was she asking such ridiculous questions, provoking her tormentor?

"You're going to kill me then?" Anna asked.

"Oh, maybe. I don't know yet. I have been searching for you for so very long. Ever since I lost track of you. I think you have a lot to atone for." The woman began to pace and talk as if she was alone in the room. "You put me through so much, trying to find you again, and now I have it all: your wizard house, you, and soon we'll find that loser husband of yours."

"Justin?" Anna asked. "I don't know where he is."

"Yes, but that doesn't matter, does it? You can find him anytime you want, can't you?" she asked. "That's what you kept from me all those years ago. The secret I was working so hard to pry out of you. You're a fucking Talent. Then you became the apprentice at the Lucky Devil. You can find anything, right? No matter how hard you tried, that rumor still persisted, didn't it? If you really wanted to find him, you would."

"No," Anna lied, shaking her head.

'Yes, that's true,' the Rune inside whispered, pushing to break free.

"What the hell?!" Calvin cut in, loosening his tie like he couldn't breathe. "I don't do jobs without knowing what's going on. Now explain to me what the hell you are talking about or this deal is over." Calvin pointed a threatening finger in the well-dressed woman's face.

He tried to lord his height over her shorter frame, but it was like a tree trying to intimidate a landmine. She smiled a cold, feral smile.

"Silence, minion," she snapped. The storm she suppressed flashed across her face before fading to calm once more. Calvin's face morphed into a black rage, and he raised his hand to strike her, but at the last minute hesitated. Instead, he pivoted and swung his hand across Anna's face, the more vulnerable target. It felt like her face exploded a second time and she cried out as her head snapped to the side. Anna blinked hard and started to cry while Jasper started to growl behind her.

"You fucking—" Calvin began but unexpectedly went flying sideways. He slammed hard against the back wall, knocking a ceramic devil off a decorative shelf. It crashed loudly to the floor. Both Anna and Jasper stood there gaping at the well-dressed woman who had punched Calvin like a handball.

"You idiot. Do not lay a hand on the Heir of Magdalene," the well-dressed woman roared, her face contorting into an inhuman mask.

Anna couldn't focus on what was happening as she tried to get herself under control. Remembering something a kind man once told her, she lifted her head to look directly at one of the lights above the bar. Like before, her tears immediately stopped. She focused on her breathing. She had to do something. She couldn't let any of this happen to her again. She had to fight back.

"What the hell hit me?" Calvin croaked.

"I will do it again if you remain insolent. The Magdalene: most powerful force in a generation, the last light in the dark of this world consumed by cruel technology that masticates and defecates the soul, and you dare lay a hand on her chosen heir?" The well-dressed woman encroached on Calvin, who had been knocked silly and wasn't standing up very quickly. He tried to scramble away from her as she threatened him.

Rune watched horrified. She needed to run. She needed to fight.

"I'm tearing myself in two," the woman, who was compelled by both Anna's and Rune's instincts, realized softly to herself. "I'm still the prisoner..."

A great pressure bore down on her, one she hadn't truly noticed until then. It was the House. It was calling out to her. She could almost hear it.

"*Choose*," it seemed to say.

Choose? Choose what? Between Anna and Rune?

"No! Please!" Calvin begged.

Jasper dropped his prisoner, who went to the ground like her legs were made of jelly. The Tigerman rushed between the woman and Calvin, ears back and teeth exposed, growling with a thunderous rumble.

"Choose!"

"Stop it! Not in my house!" Alf shouted, striding in from the Main Bar, where he had been standing and listening.

"Not in *your* house?" the well-dressed woman purred her question.

Alf turned to the well-dressed woman. "Yes. You will not shed any more blood in the House of the Magdalene."

"State your name," she ordered, her twinkling eyes not leaving the prisoner as she spoke.

"Alfonso FitzMagdalene, steward of the House of the Magdalene," Alf repeated quietly but firmly.

"And whom do you serve?"

"The Magdalene and her appointed Heir," he confirmed.

"Oh, but isn't your Heir right here?" the well-dressed woman asked, with mock exaggeration.

"I do not acknowledge Anna Masterson or Rune Leveau, as she called herself, as the proper heir," he stated even more quietly. "Such things are not for the likes of such a Talentless con artist."

The prisoner could only stare at Alf. What could she say to him? She wished she could feel shocked, but she simply didn't. Alf met the prisoner's eyes with a defiant challenge, daring her to say something about his betrayal.

The silent exchange added more delight to the well-dressed woman's face. "Oh, she isn't Talentless."

"What?" Alf asked, turning to look at the well-dressed woman.

She held up the crystal card again, flashing its rainbow colors at Alf, whose eyes went wide. "This crystal technology of your kind is quite fascinating. What our modern technology can't detect, these shaped rocks can." The well-dressed woman laughed again, maniacally. No one joined her, and she abruptly stopped.

She blew out an exasperated breath and rolled her eyes. "Fine. I digress." She flicked her hand, dismissively. "You better scurry along, boys. Let's end this." She smiled with too many teeth. "You got what you came for, and so did I. Mr. FitzMagdalene, will you please open the way for them?"

The prisoner tried to get up, tried to stop them, reaching for the strength in Rune's will to fight. Yet, Anna's instinct to keep small and compliant held such strength at bay.

Jasper grabbed a handful of his partner's coat to haul him to his feet, barely waiting for Calvin to get said feet under him. Alf immediately moved toward the double doors that led to the Back Bar, both Tigerman and hominal man following him. Instead of pushing through the doors like the prisoner expected, Alf stopped in front of them and held both his palms out.

"*Aperiant viam ad Archive,*" he said in clear, perfect Latin. Two devils, set in little alcoves on either side of the door, moved of their own accord. Their arms expanded impossibly long, each reaching for two knockers, one above the other that the prisoner had always assumed were decorative. Once they grasped the handles, light began to emit from the edges of the doors. Then, in perfect unison, the devils opened the doors into a room that the prisoner couldn't really see from where she lay on the floor. It seemed impossibly large, larger than it should have been.

In fact, the whole bar had changed in the time since Alf had spoken last. The bar itself and Lucky Devil's booth remained, but the ceiling now extended twice as high, disappearing into thick darkness. There were many more doorways within the room, interspersed with darkness. The tables and chairs had multiplied in styles that the prisoner didn't even recognize.

On the walls were devils: different sizes and shapes, from different cultures. Some, the prisoner had seen every day, decorating the walls of the bar. Others spread out next to them, all new to her, and yet…they also seemed like they had always been there. They were all inanimate but unnerving nonetheless.

Calvin and Jasper also gaped in awe, as the bar they had become familiar with warped around them.

"What are you waiting for? Go!" the well-dressed woman ordered. A crease furrowed her brow when she immediately seemed to reconsider. "No, you, Tigerman, you stay with me."

"What?!" Calvin exclaimed, looking at his partner.

"Just go, finish the job," Jasper said, calmly pushing his partner through the door. Calvin hesitated for a moment, to his credit, then was gone.

"No, stop!" the prisoner tried to get up again, but her legs wouldn't work. "Stop, please." Tears rolled down her cheeks.

"Oh lord, you are so pathetic," the well-dressed woman gloated. "Well, Tigerman will just have to carry you, I guess."

"First, give me what you promised, ma'am," Jasper ordered.

"In due time. My master will see that you get your compensation," the well-dressed woman nodded.

"Alf..." the prisoner pleaded.

The little man raised his hanging head to pop out his chest indignantly. "You are not a Leveau, no matter what Maddie said. I do not acknowledge you as Heir of the Magdalene house."

"But Alf, they're going to take the bar—"

"No, I made a necessary deal to save the bar... House." he looked at the well-dressed woman.

She sighed. "Well, I suppose that's technically true. The Kodiak Company will take your bar. It's all very neat, really; I get you, and he gets his wizard house, or something..." She waved a dismissive hand toward Alf.

"No, this is not for me. I do this to preserve the dignity of the House of Magdalene. I shall hold it in trust for the true Heir of the Magdalene according to my duty and privilege," Alf informed her.

"Yes, but I don't really give a damn about that," the well-dressed woman said, condescendingly.

The true Heir of the Magdalene?

"*Choose!*" Rune, who struggled not to feel weak as Anna, almost screamed under the pressure of that word in her skull. "*Choose!*"

How? Alf was right. She had so little magic. How could she be this Heir of the Magdalene?

The prisoner blinked as she realized that was a bald-faced lie... that Anna had always told herself. She had magic. Both when she had been Anna and when she had called herself Rune, she had always had magic within herself; she could feel it now that she couldn't 'unsee' it. Anna had hidden it, to keep herself safe. Anna suppressed it. Anna lied to everyone about it. It had been a choice Anna had made, that Rune continued, to do whatever it took to stay safe.

"*Choose,*" the House pleaded.

Choose? Choose. Between being Anna or being Rune? The choice was obvious.

Rune's eyes widened as the voice that had been Anna faded, but with her... something else was going... something Rune didn't want to lose.

"*Choose!*" The House repeated again, urgently.

Like electricity, Rune felt a jolt pass through her. Magic. Raw, true magic was set free at last within her being. It was hers, all hers, coming naturally and easily. A sense of relief washed through her as the torn parts of herself healed the prolonged separation from her internal source of magic. Her second sight opened cleanly with no pain.

Rune saw Anna through the second sight. She knelt—was kneeling—will kneel across from Rune.

"They will hurt us. No one will save us," Anna said, had always said. She pulled away—was pulling away, from Rune. Rune felt the magic going with her again. No. She needed—will always need this part of herself, no matter how much it hurt.

Rune grasped Anna, holding her close.

"I found me, Anna." A laugh, a merry, light-hearted laugh, pealed through the magic, making it sparkle as Anna and Rune became one. "I finally found myself."

CHAPTER 16

Easily, Rune Anna Leveau stood up to face the well-dressed woman, who seemed to sense that something had changed.

"Maddie left this place to me," Rune said, closing her second sight again so she could focus on the present world. Her heart still beat with fear — that would never fade — but she knew with iron certainty, nothing would ever push her down to her knees again. They were going to take her bar, her House, her last connection to Maddie. Stopping them was far more important than her fear.

Alf squared up to face her. "You cannot claim it if your retainers do not acknowledge your claim," he said coldly.

Rune realized he was right. The House had its own magic, and the pressure of it was still calling to her. That was the key that was keeping her from reaching out to it and fully claiming it as hers. Though Rune had chosen, she now needed to be chosen in return.

A small whine caught Rune's attention, and she slid her gaze sideways to see Ally hiding under the table.

"Since I am the only retainer left of this House and do not acknowledge you…"

"Oh, that's enough. We all get the point," the well-dressed woman snapped.

"Ally," Rune whispered. She had an idea. Turning her gaze back to the well-dressed nightmare in front of her, Rune focused all of her will on staring her down.

"I…am… the Mistress of this House. And you are not welcome here," Rune stated carefully.

"What did you say to me?" the woman asked, her voice turning deadly, "A last- ditch effort to be brave. It's so obvious that you are still so very afraid."

Rune swallowed but did not give up. "I am Rune Anna Leveau, Heir to the Magdalene."

"You are not—" Alf started to say, but Rune didn't let him.

"I only need one retainer to acknowledge me as Mistress and Heir. I call forth Ally Janowski, retainer of this house. Changeling child." Rune turned to Ally, who popped her head out from under the table, her tail wagging so hard it was making her whole body shake. "Ally, you declared yourself a retainer of this House, correct?"

"Yes!" Ally barked.

"What is the meaning of this?" Alf shouted, but Rune pushed on.

"Ally, do you acknowledge me as your Lady and Mistress?!"

"Yes!" Ally barked.

Something changed in the room then. There was a sort of listening, as if there existed an audience, silently surrounding the room, waiting to see what happened next. And then Rune realized…all of the devils were looking at her.

"Ally, no!" came the piteous cry of Ally's mother, whom everyone had forgotten. Tears streamed down the mature woman's face as she wrung her hands around a shredded pile of tissues in her hand, blood seeping into it from rubbing too long and hard. "Ally, please," she pleaded.

The little dog girl's tail slowed at the sight of her mother, but she did not go to her. Instead, she walked forward and sat herself beside Rune.

"No," Ally barked twice.

"She says no," Rune translated gently. "I'm sorry. I tried to bring her back to you."

"You…" Ms. Janowski turned to Rune, her grief morphing into rage. "You stole my daughter from me!"

"No, I…" But what could she say? In a way, it was true.

"Enough. Let's go. Tigerman, take her," the well-dressed woman ordered, straightening up on her high-heels, tugging her white jacket straight, but she seemed more agitated as her eyes darted toward the devils on the wall. Ally started barking and growling, positioning herself to defend her mistress. Rune knelt down and wrapped her arm around the little dog, ignoring the oncoming Jasper, and looked toward the devils scattered around the room. They all looked down on her, their flat eyes waiting. She needed to do something, but nothing came to her.

"I am the Mistress of this House," Rune tried again. Her voice echoed in the new space, getting louder as it drifted away. Then she looked straight at Jasper. "You will not touch me."

"Shut up. I've had enough," the well-dressed woman snapped. "No one's going to help you!"

"There is always help to be found at the Lucky Devil!" Rune shouted, her voice booming like thunder.

As one, every devil turned its head to look at the well-dressed woman, and for once, she was struck dumb. The devils were no longer statues, but pseudo-living creatures.

"Christ on a cracker," Alf muttered under his breath as he stared wide-eyed around him before his gaze landed on Rune. "It can't be possible. Only a true mage can be the mistress of a House. Even if you have a Talent, that's not enough—"

"What is this?" The well-dressed woman shrieked.

"She has called the devils," Ms. Janowski said, her mouth and eyes wide as she looked around the room.

"What does that mean?"

"The House has accepted her as its Mistress!" Alf shouted, his voice near panic.

"What are you talking about? It's just a house, not even that! It's a bar," the well-dressed woman said with disgust, which was strange since she had explained this, just moments before.

"A wizard's House is not just a house, or a castle or a place. It's so, so much more," the well-dressed woman said, her voice harsh again.

Both Alf and Ms. Janowski jumped as the well-dressed woman answered herself.

"You're not her, from six years ago. You're just a nightmare with her face," Rune proclaimed, calmly taking in the creature before her. The strength in Rune's voice had an inverse effect on the well-dressed woman, who flinched and retreated a few steps.

"I am her. I am!" the thing screeched, shrilly.

"Then what is your name?" Rune asked, stepping closer. The eyes of the devils followed, the small moves amplified by their large number.

"I asked you a question! Who are you?" Rune demanded.

"I... I... you know my name," the woman laughed as if she was being teased at a cocktail party. She stumbled against one of the table chairs, knocking it over, revealing the well-dressed woman's growing panic.

"No. I don't. You never told me. I was only allowed to call you ma'am," Rune said, shaking her head.

The well-dressed woman's face fell, becoming small, the fragile confidence and arrogance she radiated moments before now dissolving as she struggled to remember such a simple fact.

"Are you even human?" Rune asked, with a serene laugh, like she was already laughing at the punchline before she could even finish the setup. Her nightmare became even smaller before her.

"Yes, Rune, she is human, but she may not be all human anymore," Alf said, moving a few steps away from the well-dressed woman, literally and figuratively abandoning her.

"She's demon-possessed, isn't she?" Rune asked, finally putting it all together.

"No. No." The well-dressed woman struggled, then she refocused on Rune, her features twisted again. "Yes, yes. Once the Master has taken your home and taken your friends and taken your name, then he will come for you. You and I are going to be great friends again. I will present you to him to redeem this worthless woman, and keep my side of our bargain when he comes to claim you."

"That's not going to happen today," Alf said as he made it to the wall and grabbed something down from it.

The well-dressed woman turned on him then, spit flying from her lips as she screeched, "Tigerman, don't stand there! Take her."

"This is all against protocol—" Jasper said, but the well-dressed woman slashed her hand in the air to cut him off.

"Don't lecture me on protocol, you Animal." Rune winced at the sound of the racial slur. Jasper said nothing, but his ears flattened. "Take her now, or you will get nothing!"

Jasper didn't hesitate any longer, surging forward, his clawed hands outstretched toward Rune.

Rune felt strangely calm as she stood watching him come for her. With ease, she opened her sight. She saw Jasper's fear and his determination as he charged her. She felt some compassion for him then. Even though she didn't know what it was, she could see he had something truly desperate on the line. Refocusing, Jasper seemed to slow so that she could see all of him. A black shadow covered his future, present, and past selves.

"He is caught in a situation that contradicts how he sees himself," she heard herself say out loud, her voice echoing strangely. Or maybe it was in her head. "It is, he fears, how others see him. He is trying to find the right answer, to remain who he thought he was supposed to be. I can relate."

Rune closed her sight, and time resumed at normal speed, but it moved even faster than she could react. Jasper was almost on top of her. Instinctively, Rune raised her too-slow limbs to block him. Suddenly, a body blocked Jasper's movement forward, grappling with the large Tigerman with equal strength. Rune stumbled back, landing in Lucky Devil's booth, now vacant.

"Holy Cannoli!" Rune called out as she realized it was the Lucky Devil, moving as if alive.

The other devils cheered, making a ruckus like fans in a stadium. Finally, Lucky Devil got the upper hand, his wicked grin still plastered to his face as he forced Jasper several steps back toward the bar. Ms. Janowski squealed as they crashed near her, knocking stools in her direction.

"Ms. Janowski, this way!" Rune called, waving her hands to catch the woman's attention.

"My... my lady, please forgive...my betrayal—" she started to say as she scuttled over, but Rune waved her off and pulled her into the booth.

"Never mind that, we're all having a bad day," Rune said quickly. She picked up Ally, who continued to bark, and handed her to her mother. Rune asked, "You used to be a changeling too, right? Can you explain to your daughter how to change back into a person?"

"No, I cannot remember..." Ms. Janowski stuttered, more tears threatening as she stared down into her daughter's doggie face before pulling her into a hard hug. "Oh, my baby girl. My baby girl. I am so sorry! I am sorry I denied you."

Ally moaned, licking her mother's tears just as desperately. Letting the mother and daughter reunion unfold, Rune turned her attention back to the fight. Jasper had managed to throw off Lucky Devil, clawing at the figure, sending pieces of paint and wood flying. Rune groaned inside, wondering how much it was going to cost her to repair Lucky Devil, provided he was in mostly one piece when this was all over.

She didn't see the well-dressed woman until it was almost too late. She was on Rune like a wild creature, gripping her hair and pulling her out of the booth in the most painful way possible. The woman was a disheveled mess, her cool, collected persona destroyed as her hair flew every which way. Her pristine, white clothes were now marred with dirt and something wet that had landed on her from the bar brawl. On a hunch, Rune opened her second sight and almost gagged. Instead of a being, moving forward and backward through time and space, a corpse stood rotting even as it moved. Black tendrils of smoke ate away what was left of her flesh before drifting to the dark places in the expanded bar.

"You fucking bitch! You monstrous bitch!" the corpse screamed as she pulled out a gun and pointed the barrel at Rune. As the gun came toward her, she snapped out of the second sight. The idea that she was about to die passed through her mind. Time slowed, and Rune knew she could not move away in time. The nightmare, that this woman would someday kill her, was coming true. Yet, Rune simply didn't feel as afraid as she thought she would.

"You can't control me anymore."

The well-dressed woman's hand shook with rage. "I can still make you die!" she screamed, spit frothing from her mouth. Her finger tightened on the trigger.

The shot never came.

"Protect your mistress!" a man's voice called as he moved to stand between Rune and the gun, his shorter form seeming larger than ever before. It took several blinks for Rune to realize who protected her.

Alf stood between her and the gun.

In one hand, held aloft, was the 18th-century mining lantern that usually hung as a decoration in the Main Bar. In his other hand was one of the long, tapered lighters used to light the tea lights inside the glass votives on the tables. He clicked it on and directed the flame toward the wick inside the lantern. There was a spark, and a sickly, yellow-green light washed across the room, drowning out the pale light coming from the overhead lamps. Two winged devils alighted on either side of the well-dressed woman. Her face twisted in terror as their clawed hands sank into her shoulders.

"Hold her still!" Alf shouted at the devils, then shot back at Rune, "Don't just stand there, do something! Gods, girl, you're just useless in a fight."

Rune shivered when the green light touched her, like insects marching all over her skin. The well-dressed woman screamed and recoiled from the light before it could touch her, her force so strong the devils lost their grip. There was a ripping sound as her coat tore away, and smoke wafted up, darker from the tears. She shot a black look at Alf. "You... you..."

"You're not welcome here, creature! Be gone. I banish you from this House!" Alf shouted over the woman.

She opened her mouth and emitted a strange, strangled scream and then turned as if to go. Instead, she simply disappeared into one of the dark patches in the wall, like she had wiped herself from existence. In her wake lingered a crackling sound, similar to eggshells being ground underfoot; it persisted, infusing the entire room. Then the green light flashed and dissipated.

People suddenly appeared all around Rune, looking at her, as if they had been there the whole time. A wash of dread at all the concerned, staring faces overcame her, turning her legs to jelly. Then they buckled.

"Liam, pick her up, get her out of here," Alf's voice came, and two pairs of hands stopped her backward descent. Rune immediately calmed herself as she reached back and gripped her young bartender's arm for reassurance. Alf went to the bar where the new server now stood, gingerly setting the ancient lamp down on the bar surface.

"Shouldn't we call the sheriff, or an ambulance, or something?" Liam asked, his voice coming from right over Rune's head as he tried to help her stand. Her legs still wobbled, but she managed to get them under her.

"What good are they going to do for her?" Alf scoffed.

"We should call an ambulance!" one regular patron said.

"Is anyone here a doctor?" another called.

"What was that? What just happened?" someone asked as they came in through the door.

"Did you see all of the devils?"

"I was frozen in place!"

"We were frozen in place. That was real magic."

"Why couldn't I see you?"

"Perception magic? Maybe?"

"The real Magdalene House! That was amazing!"

"Someone should inform the Sheriff's department."

People continued chattering around Rune, but she ignored them and smiled weakly at Liam.

"I think… I think I might throw up," she said, as the rising tide in the back of her throat piled on the pressure.

"Out of the way, octopus," Alf ordered, appearing before her with one of the rag buckets that usually lived behind the bar. "If you're going to hurl, do it in this," he added callously.

Rune refused to take it, looking down on Alf even as he offered it. Liam took it instead, holding it awkwardly at their side. Assessing the room, Rune recognized the other patrons as a few regulars from the breakfast crowd and a few others from the lunch group. Even good old Franklin was there, awkwardly helping the waitress pass out water and coffee to everyone.

The bar hadn't changed back, though. The room was still larger with the many doors, the many black spaces, and the many, many devils watching. The devils themselves had returned to a state of inertia, yet no one else in the bar seemed aware of them. Ms. Janowski and Ally were still seated in Lucky Devil's booth, and the Devil himself was back in his rightful spot, though definitely looking worse for wear, his lowball glass partway up to his mouth as if he was parched after the fight. An unconscious Jasper laid at his feet, with a couple of more people checking him out.

"Where's his partner? The blonde one who's always with him?" one of them asked.

"Gone through that magic door," Alf answered.

"Oh, man, I couldn't see that."

"Liam, herd everyone into the Main Bar," Rune ordered, her voice taking on new authority.

Liam blinked before saying, "Yes, ma'am," and proceeded to do as he was ordered.

Rune took a seat on one of the stools at the bar, nodding with a smile to the few patrons who asked her if she was alright and waving to reassure Franklin, who looked worried. Once the Lounge had been cleared, there was a clamoring behind the bar, and Alf came up with a bottle of the pure-ginger beer they had imported from some Scandinavian country. He popped the top using the edge of the bar. In true bartender fashion, he automatically laid down one of the thin black cardboard coasters they used, each stamped with a red winking devil, and set the ginger beer on it.

"Drink that. It's room temperature, so it shouldn't make you gag. What are you still doing here?" he asked, directing the question to Liam, who hovered at the doorway.

"Well, sir... I thought..." the kid stuttered.

"No, you weren't thinking. Otherwise, you'd be out there during the height of lunch rush, calming people down and getting them all drinks. Now move, kid!"

Liam jumped at the order, but looked to Rune instead of moving.

"Thank you, Liam. I appreciate this," Rune said, smoothing over Alf's orders like silk over gravel.

The kid gave Rune a sweet half-smile and disappeared into the Main Bar, pulling the divider door shut behind him.

"You better drink this," Alf said again, and Rune nailed him with a glare. There was a silent contest between them, but for the first time in their entire relationship, Alf looked away first. "I'm not justifying anything to you," he said and hopped down from his bar box.

Rune said nothing, and didn't touch the ginger beer, but looked around the room again. The devils were all looking at her, yet they didn't scare her. Each of their expressions reflected the same concern and care for her that her patrons had shown. They were hers to protect, and they, in turn, would protect her; she knew that with every fiber of her being, though she couldn't explain how. The sense of protection was like having Maddie back again.

When Alf came into view again, she mustered her courage for what she intended to do next, which was to fire his ass. Before she could get a word out, he hit the floor, kneeling on one knee, his opposing fist on the ground before her. With his eyes fixed on her ankles, he took a deep breath.

"I, Alfonso FitzMagdalene, Steward of the House of the Magdalene, do acknowledge Rune Leveau as my Lady and Mistress, the true heir to the House of the Magdalene," he declared loudly and clearly.

The same thrum went through the room again, and Rune felt another connection, her bond to the House becoming stronger. It hit her so hard, she had to grab the edge of the bar to stay seated on the stool. Once the room settled again, Rune looked down at Alf. She didn't know much about how Mage Houses worked, or what the devils in the walls really had to do with it. She sighed as she looked down on the only person who could probably teach her and who had just sworn fealty to her.

"I guess this means I can't really fire you," she said.

CHAPTER 17

"No, you can't fire me," Alf agreed dryly, still kneeling before Rune as he said it, "but you can kill me. As my liege and Lady, my life is yours to do with as you wish."

"What? That's absurd!" Rune exclaimed.

"I betrayed you, the designated Heir, to our enemies and have put our House in danger. It would be well within your rights to do away with me, your humble retainer. All retainers, when they have declared themselves to a master or mistress of a Mage House, are bound, mind, body, and soul to their service unless released. My life and future are yours to deal with as you choose."

Rune then shot a glance at Ally in her mother's arms, now understanding her mother's fears better. To give over one's entire life like that, almost like a slave; who would want that for their child? "Ally, too?" Ms. Janowski clung to her daughter even tighter.

"Yes," Alf answered, unwavering. "She has the honor of being the first to accept you as her Lady and Mistress to the day of her death. So is the duty of all retainers, even if that day is today."

"Well, it's not going to happen today, so get off of the floor," Rune exclaimed.

"It is the law of the Magi," Alf defended as he did as he was told and stood up, groaning when his knees creaked.

"Last I checked, the law of the Magi doesn't hold up in a real court. I mean, okay, I kill you; it's not like I wouldn't go to jail for murder," Rune said.

"Oh please, I'd take my own life before I let you go to jail," Alf said derisively.

"Really? Because I think a few minutes ago you set me up so Calvin could steal the mortgage payment for the bar and get away, so don't give me that!" Rune snapped, her stomach twisting.

"I won't be able to do that again, now that I've sworn to you," Alf said simply as if that solved everything. "Now stop your whining and drink your ginger beer, girl. You've got to get yourself under control so we can solve this problem, not have a hissy fit about it. You've been hit with a double shot of magic and your stomach is going to hate you for a while." He turned to Ms. Janowski and Ally, leveling his gaze right at the girl dog. "As for you, you need to turn back to your human form if you are going to be any good to us."

"She can't," Rune said at the same time as Ally barked no.

Alf held up a hand over his shoulder toward Rune, keeping his focus on Ally.

"Helena, you should have let Maddie train her, then we wouldn't be in this mess," he said, not unkindly to Ms. Janowski.

"We both made the decisions we thought best," Ms. Janowski replied unapologetically.

Alf pursed his lips together but said nothing more as their unspoken history passed silently between them. Instead, he just set his hands on his hips and looked down at Ally, who meekly wagged her tail.

"Just focus on what you want to be, kid; best advice I can give you," he said. Everyone waited expectantly, while Ally looked back and forth amongst the adults as if expecting more instructions.

"Come on, Alf. It can't be that simple," Rune said, pushing herself up from her seat to come over to the group. She had the bottle of ginger beer in her hand but still hadn't drunk any yet.

"Why not?" Alf challenged.

Rune didn't know what to say to that.

"If she's your retainer, then she needs to prove it by controlling her own magic. This should be as natural to her as breathing," Alf declared. "Are you your Mistress's retainer or not?"

The teenage girl dog snorted once and then nodded at Rune. She wiggled to be let down on the ground and shook herself once. She spun in place a few steps, like a dog worrying a spot, trying to make herself revert. At first, not much happened, then something shifted, and she started to expand. The minute she started growing, she jumped and stopped, reverting back to her small dog shape.

"No, that's it, kid, you're doing it," Alf assured her while Ms. Janowski put her sore fingers to her mouth in a mix of emotions.

Ally wagged her tail in delight and started growing again. Her bones shifted and stretched into arms and human legs, while her head rounded into a human skull. Where there was once a little white dog, now crouched a young, long-limbed teenage girl, completely naked.

"Oh, geez!" Ally exclaimed, her voice sweet, and almost began to revert into a dog again when she realized her nudity. Her mother laughed and grabbed her daughter anyway, hugging her close.

"Okay, the girl might be of some use after all," Alf declared and turned back to see that Rune still hadn't drunk the bottle of ginger beer. "Oh, for pity's sake, do I have to feed you like a little bird, too? Drink it. You need the sugars."

"You first," Rune challenged, narrowing her eyes at him as she held out the bottle to him.

He swallowed a mouthful without hesitation, then offered it back. At that point, she really had no choice but to take the bottle and shoot it back.

"I will never betray you again, my lady, and I will prove that as many times as it takes," he said in a low rumbling voice.

The bite of the ginger felt good on her tongue. Her throat came alive as the wet chased away the dryness. She hadn't realized she was so thirsty.

"Okay," she said after she had swallowed. "I guess I forgive you. Not that it's going to matter, anyway. They took most of the mortgage payment, and without that, it sounds like they are going to take the bar soon no matter what. And I couldn't do anything." Rune sat back down on one of the stools at the bar, exhausted.

"It's not all your fault, my lady," Alf tried, but Rune waved him off.

"Doesn't matter who's fault it is, it's my responsibility," she said. "I'd be on my way back right now if it hadn't been for that guy…"

"Chen has a Talent to hypnotize and hold people's attention, especially when he's droning on about one of his stories. If he casts it too hard, people will be so bored they even forget to blink," Alf explained as he headed back behind the bar to fetch a second ginger beer. "I was actually impressed that you managed to shake it off that last time."

Rune blinked at that. "So, he was part of the plan, too?" Ms. Janowski looked down ashamedly instead of meeting Rune's eyes.

"Right. I guess this is the time to exchange stories," Rune said, finishing the contents of the first bottle and accepting a second, before looking around the room at everyone still conscious. "And figure out what to do with him," she added, nodding ahead at Jasper's unconscious form on the floor.

Alf sighed. "This started after Maddie died; Calvin and Jasper approached me about pulling some shenanigans to yank this place out from underneath you. Of course, what they didn't understand was that it wasn't that simple."

"Obviously," Rune agreed dryly.

"I knew that you hadn't taken charge of the Mage House since the spells were starting to fall apart, and it didn't seem like you had any intention or even any clue about it. You were even ignoring the summons by the Magic Guild."

"And now you know why!" Rune declared as she hopped up to grab an abandoned coat from last winter that still hung on the coat rack. She passed it to the still naked Ally. "I'm a fugitive! If I had claimed the Mage House and used my magic, then it would have only been a matter of time before…" Unable to finish, Rune gestured in the direction the well-dressed woman had exited.

"I knew you had some sort of secret that was between you and Maddie. She kept going on about your potential, but I hadn't seen a drop of magic come out of you. You just seemed good at finding things, and I never heard of a more passive piece of crap power than that. I just knew you were lying about who you were and using Maddie as a shield. Maddie even gave you her name, and you weren't even blood."

"That's not true!" Ally piped up, looking silly in the oversized man's trench coat, all buttoned up. "Rune… tell him. You're her niece. You said!"

"Great-niece," Rune answered, the truth coming out easier this time. "Maddie was my great-aunt. When my parents abandoned me after my arrest, she came for me. To hide me. That's why there's a mortgage on this place, to pay for my release from the corporate prison I was trapped in, and to pay for changing my identity."

Alf covered his eyes to hide his own shock. "I see. I never… I never understood why she put the House in such a dangerous position, but the money needed to do such a thing… It must have been astronomical."

"We thought—well, she thought that just changing my name entirely wouldn't be enough. She had my whole data profile modified on a government level, so she put in the Magic Guild archives that I was taking her name as an apprentice. I didn't want anyone to know I had magic, so I was listed as a non-Talent."

"A wizardess' apprentice with no magic?" Ally asked, arching a beautiful eyebrow.

"It's not unheard of, just stupid," Alf explained.

"I never wanted anything to do with my power again at the time."

"But you were her apprentice. You did jobs with her?" Ally asked.

Rune nodded. "Yes, I used my Talent when we needed it the most, and when Maddie could make it look like she did it. She gave me a new ID card, and my history was altered…"

"That was me," Ms. Janowski said. She had taken a seat at one of the tables near Rune's stool, looking exhausted as she slumped there. "It was the price for being released as retainers."

Everyone turned to look at her. "I wanted a corporate job, and she allowed me to take one. I got one at a subsidiary of Kodiak and when I was offered a promotion, I begged her to release us from the retainer-ship. She agreed only after I modified your records. I was never so scared in my life. Every second I was doing it, my heart was pounding, pah-pah, pah-pah." Ms. Janowski brought the tissue to her face again and looked very much like she was going to faint. Alf placed a bottle of ginger beer before her with a glass of ice.

"Can I have one?" Ally asked, sitting down across from her mother.

"Are you 21?" Alf asked.

"Uh, yes?" Ally tried.

"Okay, kid, let's see some ID."

"Oh, come on, I've been a dog for three days! I don't have my ID on me," Ally argued.

"Well, this stuff is five percent, so tough luck, kid," Alf said as he shook his head and went back around the bar to get her a can of juice.

"It's hard to believe she found me after all of these years," Rune said, as she stared at one of the dark shadowy places in the wall. "Why would she even still be looking for me, though? I have no idea where Justin is and…"

"Yeah, what was with that woman? Was she even real?" Ally asked, crossing her arms and one bare leg over the other.

"Ally…" her mother chided.

"Oh, come on, you had to see it, right? She was all… Wrong. Right? What was she?" The teenager looked to the other adults for an answer.

"She was a nightmare, nothing more," Rune said.

"No, she was a person. A real person," Alf said and cracked open a ginger beer for himself.

"But Ally was right. She looked wrong. Very, very wrong," Rune said, "but she looked exactly how I remember her six years ago."

"Best guess? Demon-possessed. Probably sold her soul for power," Alf said.

Rune took a long pull of her second ginger beer, her stomach finally settling.

Ally made a face. "Ew, people actually do that?"

"It is a way for Talentless people to get power," Rune agreed. "It's also insanely illegal and dangerous, obviously."

A fresh look of guilt crossed Ms. Janowski's features. "I never wished you harm, my lady. I just wanted to keep my Ally safe."

"I could release her from her retainer-ship," Rune started to say, but Ally jumped to her feet.

"No! Don't! This is what I want! Mama, please, I want this," Ally insisted.

"But your school, your friends..."

"Mama, this is more important than..."

"I would still send her to school," Rune cut in. Mother and daughter both looked at Rune, like mirrors of each other.

"What?!" Ally blurted in shock.

"I'm your lady and mistress, right? You have to obey me, and I say you have to go to school and listen to your mother. After you graduate, then we'll discuss what you can do with your future."

Ms. Janowski looked between her daughter and Rune, going back and forth a few passes before finally asking, "So, she can come home?"

"N—" Ally started.

"Yes, of course," Rune spoke over Ally. "She'll come to her part-time job as a waitress here at the bar after school and on the weekends when she doesn't have school activities."

"What?! On Saturdays?!" The teenager was absolutely shocked.

"Yes. If you want to be a retainer, Alf here is going to have to train you. The rest of the time it's school and home. I think I'm being very clear," Rune said, trying to keep a serious face, amused as she was by the look of shock on Ally's face.

"I think I can agree to that," Ms. Janowski said, nodding.

"But what about the bar and the woman? You're going to lose everything. I can help!" Ally almost sounded like her yippy dog self, her voice was pitched so high.

"She's got a point, Rune," Alf said.

"We have to get the money back. If we still make the payment, then we can buy some time to figure out how to deal with the rest of it. Either way, I'm not taking you back into danger, Ally," Rune said, firmly. "For now, Alf is going to take you and your mother home."

"But, Ru-une," Ally whined at the same time Alf *harrumph*ed.

"You're really going to saddle me with such an uppity kid?" he groused.

"Yes, I am. And what happened to my lady?"

Alf narrowed his eyes. "My lady," he muttered in the smallest, growliest of voices.

Rune's expression bloomed into a radiant smile. Oh, she was going to love making him say that every day, morning, noon, and night.

"I'll figure out what to do with the Mage House," Rune said, casting an eye at the walls filled with silent, still devils.

"Okay, I don't get this. If the bar is really a Mage's House, which is a mystical, metaphysical thing, how can they have a mortgage on the physical building? I mean, if they bulldozed this place down, wouldn't you still own the Mage's House?" Ally asked.

Rune stared blankly then looked over at Alf, whose face was just a big scowl.

"You seriously don't know this either?" he huffed.

Rune smiled a grimace.

Alf ran a hand over his face. "Okay, this is going to be a quick, dirty version, but essentially..." he paused for a moment as he groped for words. "There are two realms. Well, actually, there are many, but for what concerns us right now, there are two. This realm and the Dreaming, right? That's where all the magic comes from. The Mage House is in the Dreaming."

"What... but—?" Ally furrowed her brows as she tried to process that. "Then, if the Mage House is in this Dreaming place, how can you mortgage it?"

"Because they're connected," Rune said, looking to Alf for confirmation.

He nodded. "Yeah, through the Mistress or Master, I guess. Which is you now, Ru...my lady,'" he corrected, making a sour face. Then he turned back to Ally. "The building is still a physical building, and the mortgage company still gave us money for it. The Mage House doesn't just exist in the hearts of children, kid. This is its physical location. They claim the building, boot us out onto the street, and we're still screwed."

Ally thought for a moment. "Couldn't we just move it then? The magicky part in the Dream-whatever?"

Alf blinked a bit surprised. "Yes, it's possible, theoretically, if we had a wizard who knew how to do the spell, and about a hundred other magic users to supply the power on this side of things."

"Right," Rune said, "That's a little outside our resources. Looks like I've got to get the mortgage payment back."

"Oh, and we have the resources to do that?" Alf asked, sarcastically glancing up at the clock.

"Um, well, my Talent is in finding people. I was literally made for this," Rune said.

"Okay, then do it already!" Alf responded.

"Okay, slow down," Rune hedged.

"You can't do it, can you?" Alf accused.

"Look, it's not as easy as that. I can't just snap my fingers and, boom, I know exactly where to go," she said with a demonstrative snap — and just like that, she knew where to go. "Alf, do we have a business card for Calvin?"

"A business card?" the little man repeated back to her.

"No, wait, I have one right here." Rune reached into a pouch on her belt that held the small brick of business cards she had collected over the years. Calvin's was a third of the way through from the top.

"Okay, so now you can find him using that?" Ally asked.

"If I'm already close enough to him, it can work. These things are designed because people have the intention of being found. I can use it to find the person who gave it to me," Rune explained.

"And how are you going to get the money from Calvin once you find him?" Alf asked. "Punch his lights out and rob him?"

"Rob him? He robbed us," Rune argued.

"Not my point, and you know it. You can't look to me to help you. I'm too weak, the girl is no good to you, and that's the sum of your retainers. Congratulations," Alf said. "If you are really serious about being the Lady of the Magdalene House, you are going to need to acquire some more diverse retainers."

"I'll figure it out." Rune stared down at the top business card on the stack.

"What we really need to get is a warrior type," Alf continued, but Rune was only half-listening.

"What about the devils? Can't they help you?" Ally asked, and everyone looked around the room. The devils remained in their statuesque state, yet Rune knew they were listening.

"No good. They are bound to the House, collected over generations of Wizards of this House. They can't leave here as long as the House stands."

"What? Like they're in jail?" Ally asked.

"This place is a nexus point for a lot of things. You see those doorways? Things come through them all the time. What you're seeing is the inner workings of the bar, exposed," Alf said.

"They're not locked up," Rune said, cutting Alf's next growl off. "They're here to protect, hold back the darkness of the.... out there."

"Really?" Ally said.

"Yes," Ms. Janowski agreed. "The House is always expanding, and they cannot cover it all anymore. So, the Lady protects the rest. It is work that can never be completed."

"Oh!" Rune's eyebrows shot up as she realized something. "That's what it means; the saying that is. There is always help at the Lucky Devil."

"They're weird-looking," Ally said softly under her breath. Her mother chided her with a hiss.

"It's not just the devils. It's the doors as well, and the black places," Rune said.

"The House is not finished. It may never be, like she said," Alf continued to explain. "That's another reason why we can't lose this place."

"We won't," Rune assured. "And I know how I'm gonna do it!" Quickly, the new Lady of the Magdalene House wove through the tables toward the back office.

"Where are you going?" Alf called.

"To get something out of my trash!" Rune reached for the handle of the office, and it opened easily to its new mistress.

"What?" Ally asked, cutting Alf off.

Rune bee-lined for the trashcan. "A business card."

CHAPTER 18

She found him in a coffee shop.

It had taken some doing, but surprisingly, when she left the bar to go in search of him, the tendril of magic generated by his business card directed her to the New Wave coffee shop only a mile away. She had spent only a little time walking aimlessly toward the vague pull of the card, but it grew stronger as she went, and she was able to pinpoint exactly where he was.

Standing outside the shop's windows, Rune saw St. Benedict sitting at one of the tables that bordered the glass on the opposite side of the shop. There was no one else sitting there, just him, his back facing a bit of wall that jutted out, painted rust-red, that framed his dark clothes nicely. A computer sat open in front of him, and he typed furiously at it, with a line of prepared coffee cups set up before him. Another coffee cup sat to his left, his current cup, a ring of pink cardboard hugging its Styrofoam middle. A stack of empties took up the last little bit of space on the table. It was near one in the afternoon and the cups with the plates gave Rune the impression he had been sitting there for quite a while.

He was dressed differently than the night before. Like Rune, he looked like he had showered. Today, he wore gray suit pants with no jacket, the sleeves of his light-blue dress shirt rolled up to his elbows. The same fedora sat on top of his head looking slightly less crushed, and Rune would actually have said it was pushed up too high on his forehead to be flattering. He looked like a young businessman working at the local coffee shop instead of the office. The view made Rune's heart pound, and she tried to tell herself she was just nervous about what she was about to do. *It has nothing to do with seeing him again,* she lied to herself.

As if he heard her thoughts, he stopped typing and adjusted the hat, running his other hand through his dark hair before setting it back. He picked up his coffee and raised it to drink. That's when his eyes met hers across the room, through the glass. The cup stopped at his lips and he simply stared. They stayed frozen like that for an eternal second, then she raised her hand and waved.

Rune couldn't stall any longer. She went inside, rehearsing her greeting in her head a dozen times until it didn't resemble anything by the time she wove her way through the jumble of tables, chairs, and the people occupying them. The whole time, she felt his eyes on her, so she tried to act casual. She hoped her smile didn't look sickly or weird.

"Who hit you?" he asked before she could get two words out.

She blinked in surprise and involuntarily reached up to touch the tender spot on her cheek where Calvin had smacked her. It had swollen up a bit and was still a bit hot. Her eye would be purple and dark tomorrow.

"Ha, is it that obvious? I thought I was getting away with it," Rune said, trying to lighten the atmosphere a bit, but it just made her feel more awkward. "Would it be alright... if I sat? I need to ask you something. Uh, it's a business something. Not a... not a personal something, I promise." Yeah, real smooth, Rune.

He slid his computer back and closed the lid, which Rune took as an invitation. She sat in the chair opposite him. The row of empty cups made a wall between them, and she started to shift them to the side, more out of nervousness, before he quickly jumped in to help. Wondering why she was so nervous, she collected her courage and turned to speak to him again.

"Rune, who hit you?" he repeated, pitching his voice lower so anyone nearby wouldn't hear. The look on his face was so intense that Rune felt compelled to tell him the truth.

"Calvin and Jasper. Or rather, Calvin. He backhanded me."

"Who are Calvin and Jasper?" he asked.

Rune stared at the new row of coffee cups. "The two corporate thugs who work for my mortgage company. They came by this morning and took all of my mortgage money. I tried to stop them, and that's when," she gestured with her own hand across her face, "I'm apparently not very good at taking a hit. I went down like a sack of potatoes—or I would have if Jasper hadn't been holding me. Either way, I got relieved of my mortgage and the office closes in four hours."

St. Benedict didn't say anything to that, just opened his computer and started typing.

"You were right," Rune continued. "Turns out, I do need your help and I am way in over my head. So, that's why I'm here."

He nodded, then flipped the computer around so she could see the screen. "I wondered what happened after this point," he said. On-screen was a little window, playing grayscale footage of the inside of Rune's bar. She leaned forward, shocked as she watched herself sitting at Lucky Devil's booth, listening to the now infamously boring Mr. Chen talk. Almost immediately, a dozen lines appeared across the screen, warbling so hard it almost entirely erased the picture.

"You were spying on me?!" Rune asked aghast as she focused on the ghost image of herself before the playback faded entirely into static, and there was nothing more to see. "Where is this camera angle? There aren't any cameras in my bar!"

"Apparently there are now," St. Benedict said nonchalantly, before reaching forward and tapping a few keys to make the static play forward faster, the mischievous smile returning to his face. "Probably our mutual friend St. Augustina, though I would think she'd be able to spring for more HQR cameras. They're a little more magic-resistant. These were most likely installed after you and I made our dramatic escape, watching and waiting for your return."

Rune blinked as she thought about that. "Then why didn't she take me this morning after I came home?"

"Probably because she was busy with my team. They got taken last night. Shows us the extent of her resources, I think," he said like it was a joke that Rune just didn't get.

Rune sat back, thinking over the events of that morning. "Could someone else have installed the cameras? She wasn't the only person interested in me."

"Like who?" St. Benedict asked, hitting the stop command on his keyboard.

"Kodiak Corporation."

His fingers paused over the keys as he took that in. "What makes you say that?"

"My sources told me they are the ones using my mortgage company as a front to acquire my House," she said.

"You have sources?"

"Apparently," she smiled. Ms. Janowski had explained everything, and despite the long, technical explanation, Rune had gotten the gist. "My source tells me that my mortgage had been a part of a package that my mortgage company was politely forced to sell to them. I mean, sell to the Kodiak Company. Why do they want my bar specifically? I mean, it seems like they want it specifically…maybe to pressure me into doing what you wanted? Finding Anna Master —"

"And you were informed of this change?" he asked, cutting her off. She could see the gears turning in his head.

"Not yet," she said, glad her embroidery of the truth had worked on the corporate spy.

"Yeah, that sounds suspicious. If they are trying to pull any shenanigans, those would be the right circumstances to do it. By the time you got a lawyer and did what was needed to fight it, they would already have your bar."

"And probably me, which is why I am here." Rune steeled her resolve. "I want you to help me get my mortgage payment back."

"From this Calvin guy?"

"Yes."

"And why didn't you ask this guy where he was?" St. Benedict tapped on his keyboard again and the playback started back up. The static had resolvedinto a clear picture. It was still the Lounge Bar, but she saw herself, more roughed up, sitting on a stool at the bar. Alf was behind the bar and pushing a third ginger beer on her, but that time she had declined. Ally and Ms. Janowski sat at the nearby table talking to her. While Ms. Janowski was explaining more of the details of the attempted coup, Jasper regained consciousness. On the screen, the Tigerman sat up holding his head. Lucky Devil had knocked him out cold. It was surreal watching it again from that angle on the screen. "I remember those two were together the night I introduced myself," St. Benedict mused quietly.

"It didn't occur to any of us to tie him up." Rune watched as the image of Jasper dashed out of the bar through the front door.

"That much was obvious, but I thought there would have been a chance to ask him prior to the feed coming back," St. Benedict said and spun the computer back toward himself again.

Rune squirmed in her chair and wished she had gotten a cup of coffee so she had something in her hands. Then, as if deciding something, St. Benedict threw back his head and emptied the contents of his cup down his throat, his Adam's apple bobbing as he did.

"So, you want to hire me to get your money back for you?" he asked, taking charge of the conversation.

"Essentially, yes, and in exchange, I'll give you what you want. I'll take you to Anna Masterson," she said.

His eyes flipped instantly from cavalier mirth to cold iron seriousness. "You'll take me… to Anna…" he said very carefully, picking at her choice of words for their hidden meaning. "What do you mean by you will *take* me to Anna Masterson?"

Rune swallowed and reminded herself to inhale then exhale. "I meant what I said before. I can't find her for you using my magic, but that doesn't matter, because... because I already know where she is."

"You could have taken me to her before," he said even quieter. It wasn't a question, but Rune answered it as if it was.

"I can take you to her now," she said just as softly, matching his intensity. "But first you have to help me save my House. My bar," she corrected swiftly.

St. Benedict studied her for what seemed like a long time. His fingers drifted up and grasped at something under his shirt, the skin of his fingers going white as he clutched it hard. From under the shirt, it looked like a tiny square box about half the length and width of one of Rune's fingers hung on a chain around his neck, the chain peeking out of his neckline as he clutched at it.

"And what is going to stop me from just taking you now and torturing you until you tell me where she is?" he asked, drawing her eyes back up to his face and away from the box he covered with his hand.

"You would do that?" she asked, her eyes going wide.

"I have done so before when the situation called for it," he said, quiet and deadly.

"Because...because you won't do it," she said, thinking fast, trying to resist her panic. "I don't know your reasons, but you had several chances to do far worse to me over the last couple of days." Her eyes widened as she realized that was true. "Look, the honest truth is, I'm small and I'm weak. I hid my entire life, behind someone else, and there is very little I can do against someone like you. But I'm asking you, please, help me protect what's most important to me and then I'll do whatever you want, willingly. You won't have to force me, I promise." Rune knew it was true even as she said it and her words seemed to have an effect on St. Benedict. He blinked and sat back, holding the box under his shirt with the desperation of a sinner clutching at his holy relic. Maybe he was.

"What's going on here?" a woman's cold voice came from behind her. Rune turned to look up at a beautiful, statuesque woman standing so close to the table, Rune was shocked she hadn't noticed her sooner. Everything about her was perfect; even the way she crossed her arms as she peered down at Rune, assessing her much less favorably than Rune was assessing her. Her pert, ruby mouth pouted just a bit, both looking sensual and emphasizing her annoyance. When Rune didn't answer right away, she put a hand onto St. Benedict's shoulder in a very familiar gesture, a gesture that told Rune, 'I claim this man as mine, back off, bitch,' more simply than words ever could.

"This is Rune Leveau. We've just finalized an agreement to our mutual benefit," St. Benedict said, cracking his mirthful, wicked smile again.

"You mean you'll help me?!" Rune asked excitedly.

"In exchange for my helping you solve your problem, you will do the following. Condition in the first," and he held up his thumb, "You will help me get my team back, right now, from our mutual acquaintance, trigger-happy St. Augustina—"

"But the deal was only for Anna—" Rune started, but he didn't let her finish, popping out his pointer finger.

"Condition in the second, you *will* take me to the location of Anna Masterson. And condition in the third, because you know everything comes in threes, so why not, you will do me one more service at an unspecified later date. In exchange for that, I will save your ass and your house—"

"Bar," Rune interjected.

"Bar, whatever, out of this fire it is currently smoldering in, and leave you alone forevermore. That is the deal." He set his fingertips on the table lightly. "Do you accept these conditions?"

Rune bit her lower lip and looked at him, but he said nothing more. He and the woman just stared her down, waiting.

"The… the problem with the first condition is that if I don't have that payment in by five today, I'm screwed," Rune said. The clock over the coffee bar showed that it was already 1:34 pm.

"Oh, I'm sorry, I didn't realize you had another alternative. By all means, if you have another offer like this at your disposal, go right ahead. Don't let me stop you," St. Benedict quipped, leaning back in the chair. The woman on his shoulder smirked.

Hesitating a moment, Rune knew if she had any real alternative, she would be doing that instead of sitting at this table. Any delusions she had that he was her friend had disappeared when the other woman had appeared. Maybe this was who he really was, and Rune was finally getting to see it.

Rune smiled softly, a wave of quiet passing over her. "There was never any real hope for me, was there? Against the corporations and people like you?" she asked, letting the realization be said out loud so she could hear it too. "I spent so much time and energy being afraid."

She shook her head at herself. "Now I feel...I guess this is what serenity feels like; when you know you've already lost."

She looked away, out the window. It was too hard to meet his eyes for this next part. She felt so peaceful inside, why were their tears pricking at her eyes? "You win, St. Benedict. You get everything you want."

The woman smirked harder, but something else passed over St. Benedict's face.

"Hey, hey, Rune," he said gently to get her to look at him, trying to ignore the pang that stabbed through him when she did. "I'll help you."

Her resigned smile didn't change.

"Perfect," the other woman declared brightly, "Now that that's sorted, would you get the hell out of my seat."

The callousness was a little shocking, but Rune nodded, clearly understanding this woman was attempting to make the pecking order clear.

"I'll go get a coff—" she started to say, to cover her getting up.

"Don't you think you should be going?" St. Benedict said to the other woman, cutting Rune off to the other woman's dismay. She huffed out of her nose in annoyance.

"Oh, by the way, this is my associate, St. Rachel," St. Benedict said, naming the woman finally. The two Saints had a momentary staring contest, exchanging silent words. St. Rachel looked away first.

"I think I'll get going," St. Rachel said as if it was her idea.

"Do you have the updated itinerary?" St. Benedict asked.

"Send it to me later," she answered.

"Or now," he said and held out his palm to her as if requesting a high five. St. Rachel paused a moment, before huffing again and laying her hand against his palm, her elegant long fingers and immaculate fingernail polish looking dainty against his larger, longer hand. It struck Rune then, how good they looked. If she had been a casual observer, she would have thought they were together, holding their hands like that. Even the size of their hands was well-matched.

There was a zapping sound, like static electricity, and then St. Rachel pulled her palm away. Rune caught, at the last second, the sight of a glow on St. Rachel's fingertips before it faded. Without another word, she turned on her high-heeled boot and left. Rune dropped her shoulders in relief.

"This is Calvin, right?" St. Benedict asked, bringing Rune's attention back to him. He turned the laptop around again to show a lightly colored and grainy video of the outside of a building downtown.

Calvin, in the suit he was wearing earlier, walked out of the building, looking slick and confident as he mockingly saluted the doorman.

"Yes, that's him," Rune said, leaning forward to get a better look.

"Well, your friend Calvin left here at seven a.m. today, as you can see by this timestamp."

"What building is that?" Rune asked.

"The Kodiak building, downtown," St. Benedict said, "And this exact same building is where my team is being held."

"So, there is a good chance that Calvin might be headed to this place?!" Rune asked.

St. Benedict gave her a half-smile and nodded. "You see, I got it all figured out, and we can make this work if you help me with your Talent. Find my team, get your money back."

"One last question," Rune asked. "With all this tech and your corporation, wouldn't it just be easier to give me the money?"

"Ha. Yes. Yes, that would be easier. Except I've lost my access to resources right now. I could probably get it, but not today. Not in time, and you said that was a factor."

"Yes. It is," Rune nodded. "Which leaves us with getting it back from Calvin."

"How long ago did Calvin leave?" he asked.

"I'm not sure," Rune glanced over at the clock again "I suppose an hour ago?"

He grunted and closed his computer. "Alright, we had better double-time it to the Kodiak building," he said, taking a last swig from his coffee.

"Wait, what?"

"My car's outside, come on." He dug into his pocket for some keys and took off toward the nearest door. Rune scrambled after him, collecting up the coffee cups in a big swipe of her arm, dropping two in a panicked hurry. "Just leave them," he said.

"I can't do that, it's rude," Rune argued and managed to higgledy-piggledy drop them into the trash bin. Gentlemanlike, St. Benedict waited for her at the door, holding it open so she could pass through and move in front of him.

"To the right," he said with urgency and pushed her toward a non-descript, gray sedan sitting in the shade just down the street. Events were moving too fast.

"Get in," he ordered as he pulled up on the passenger side handle to crack the door open before coming around to the driver's side. It chirped in greeting.

"You don't lock your car?"

"No, I did. The handles have sensors that are coded to my hands. Faster than trying to find your key," he said as he slid in next to Rune. "Give me a couple of minutes, and we'll get going."

"This is happening too fast, I don't even know what your plan is," Rune said.

"We're going to walk into the Kodiak building, you're going to lead me to my team, and we get them out, simple," he said, then depressed a button on the dashboard. The car buzzed to life.

"What, just like that? If they're being held, it's not going to be that simple," Rune argued. "And what about my mortgage payment?"

Instead of answering her, he reached behind her into the back seat and grabbed a metal suitcase. "Move your elbow, please," he said politely and set it on the armrest in between them. He tipped it up and set his thumbs on two sensor pads next to the latches holding it together. One popped up instantly, but the other made a funny click and then did nothing else. St. Benedict growled and rubbed his thumb a bit more against the sensor, but it still didn't pop open.

"And I can't just find people, just like that. I keep telling you..." Rune said, "I don't look into a crystal ball or something and poof, I know where they are." She made the universal circle gesture in front of herself for crystal ball.

"It's all negative thinking with you, isn't it?" St. Benedict said, then licked his thumb and rubbed the sensor again, cleaning off whatever blocked the scan. This time it popped open immediately. Rune's eyes grew round as saucers as he pulled out a long black-and-silver gun.

"Oh, this is not good," Rune said, eyeing the shiny weapon as he pulled off the stiff metal bracelet attached to the handle and snapped it over his wrist.

"Can you use a gun?" he asked as he checked his over with quick snaps and clicks.

"No. I can't," Rune said firmly.

"That's alright, just more opportunities to be badass for me," he said, giving her wink that was not at all reassuring.

"I do not like this plan at all," Rune said seriously, not giving him an inch.

"This is going to be simple, don't worry. Walk in and walk out," he said.

"We're not killing anybody," Rune said, firmly.

"What?"

"I'm not going to be a part of murdering anybody," Rune said. "It was never Maddie's way. We always tried to find alternatives to killing people."

"And if things are going to plan, you won't be violating your policy," he assured soothingly. "Come on, trust me. Everyone is going to be too distracted to pay any attention to us, anyway. Do you remember the air duct we landed into through your magical, mystery tunnel?"

Rune blinked at him a moment. "Yes, it literally just happened yesterday."

"Right, except you told me we moved forward in time a day, correct? So, it's actually happening..."

"Right now!" Rune said, her eyes going wide as she put it together.

"Which means that in about forty-five minutes... right?" He looked at Rune for confirmation.

She was already nodding. "We know that there is going to be an emergency in that building." she finished. "Wait. You mean the building that St. Augustina was using as her headquarters is the Kodiak building?"

"Yes, interesting, isn't it?" He shifted the car into gear and drove. "The same company that is trying to get its hands on your bar is also hosting the offices for the governmental task force that is trying to find the Masterson files."

"What does that mean, exactly?" she asked, buckling herself hurriedly.

"No idea. It's just interesting," he said. "Maybe when we're in there, we'll get some idea of what else connects all that together."

Rune only nodded, since she wasn't about to share the reason she thought there was a connection. Namely, that she was Anna Masterson, and the appearance of the well-dressed woman confirmed to her that Kodiak knew it too. The hostile takeover tactic on her bar, could it all be because they were trying to get to her, and through her, Justin? But then why... She shook her head. None of this was really making sense as far as she could see. She was so lost in thought that she missed St. Benedict's next question.

"Sorry, what?"

"You need an object, right? To find people?" he repeated.

"Yes, typically. If they have a strong enough connection to the object, something seen as an extension of themselves. Like a sheriff's badge or a child's favorite toy, or whatever you got under your shirt there."

At her mention of it, St. Benedict reflexively grabbed the small box on the necklace under his shirt.

"What do you know about it?" he asked.

"Only that it's important to you, so if I had that, I would probably be able to find you easily if you were close enough to me. Oh, I forgot!" Rune pulled out Ally's mother's locket from around her neck. "I meant to give this back to Ms. Janowski. Because Ally had one that was a matched pair with this one, I was able to find Ally with it."

"Oh. That's how you kept track of —"

" — of Ally, right," Rune nodded.

"Right, the dog-girl," he said.

"Well, she's not a dog-girl anymore. Got that reversed."

"Ah, good job, I guess," he said. "Then that's how you got the rest of your payment."

"Not exactly. Occupational hazard of this kind of work, that part of the job sort of fell through."

"The getting paid part?"

"But I had a friend loan…well, not really loan, I guess she owed it to me, but I didn't know… I got the rest of the money from her."

"Your friend Taki who can talk to animals?"

"Yeah, right." Then Rune added, "She's a mermaid."

St. Benedict blinked. "You're kidding." They drove quietly for another block before he added, "Well, if not getting paid is an occupational hazard, I think I understand why you are in the situation you're in."

"And I bet you make all of your clients pay upfront and through the nose," Rune shot back.

"You better believe it."

Rune smiled at him, but they both lapsed into silence again as the car pulled onto the 90/94 highway that cut through the city of Chicago, taking the drivers toward the Loop or the Southside beyond. The four-lane highway was a river of flowing cars and was actually moving at a decent pace that afternoon.

Both were lost in their own thoughts as the view of the Loop rose up in Rune's sight. Silver and black buildings stabbed toward the sky, framed by gray-blue clouds ghosting at the very tops of the Sears and Hancock buildings at either end of the skyline. The Loop was where the elites and their corporate dynasties played and ruled, their business-class world high above the ground, supported by the restaurants, drugstores, and shops.

Having mentioned Taki, Rune's thoughts drifted away from the oncoming Loop and back to her friend. As she thought about calling Taki after all of this was over, a powerful pull went out from her heart and up north. Rune touched her chest, surprised at the sudden pull — and then Rune saw her in her mind's eye. Taki was in her tank talking with a customer, smiling but also checking the clock with a hint of worry in her eyes. Worry for Rune. Taki's love for her pulsed down the line before the image faded.

"Huh. That was new," Rune muttered out loud.

"What?" St. Benedict asked.

"Nothing," Rune answered dismissively. "Do you love your friends?"

"What?" St. Benedict asked, blinking at the sudden change of subject. "No, of course not. They're my team. Not my friends."

Rune's eyebrows rose at that. "You're not the type to have friends, is that what you're saying?"

"I'm not the type... yes, that is probably the best way to put it. Having more than myself to rely on is a liability."

"But you rely on your team," she argued.

"It's on a per-project basis. St. Augustina and I have been on several projects together, and you see how well that working relationship is when we are on opposing sides."

"Oh, I see," Rune said glumly.

"Why do you ask? I can't imagine you were hoping we were going to be friends?" he asked, glancing at her a couple times when she didn't react to his comment.

"No, of course not. You're going to be the end of me," she said, dreamily unworried like she was lost in thought as she worked the problem in her head. "It's just that... I thought of something, but if you don't love them, then it wouldn't work. Probably wouldn't work anyway, it may only work for me. I don't know, I've never tested it."

"What? Tested what?"

"Well, sometimes, I'm able to find people who are really important to me. Like my best friend, Taki, just now. I know exactly where she is. I'm pretty sure if I followed the pull to her, I'd go right to her. I wonder..." And she focused on Ally. A similar pull transpired again, not as strong, the line to her very new and fragile. Then Rune put her hand on the locket. Ally's line became even sharper along with a flicker of an image of the teenage girl asleep on a couch in pajamas and wrapped in an afghan. She smiled at the image.

Rune glanced over at St. Benedict, who was frowning at the road. She rolled over what he had said in her mind. "I don't believe it for a second."

"What?" he asked, the polite smile returning.

"If your team were that unimportant to you, you wouldn't be working so hard to get them back, even bargaining for my services to get them back, when before it had all been about finding Anna Masterson."

His smile went sickly sweet. "More things are going on than you can possibly fathom."

At that, Rune burst out laughing, bright peals of it filling the whole space inside the car. St. Benedict just stared at her, but it made the laughter come harder.

"I'm sorry. I'm sorry, oh gods," she cackled, and it just sent her off on another peal. "I must seem like I'm cracking up."

"Right. Okay. Was it something that I said?" St. Benedict asked.

"Maddie, my master. She used to say that all the time." Rune wiped a tear from her eyes. "Oh, that is just funny."

"Glad I could lighten the mood," St. Benedict said.

"Okay, okay," Rune repeated and cleared her throat. "That way is probably not going to work, then. I'll have to find your friends another way."

"How did you find me?" St. Benedict asked, as he turned off on an exit toward the heart of the Loop.

"Oh, easy. Your business card." She held up the tiny black card with just a phone number on it. "These things are designed for the express purpose of allowing people to find you. It doesn't work the same way as an entrusted object, but if the person wants me to find them, it's good enough."

"How is it different?" He took the card from her and turned it over in his hands as they waited for the light at the end of the exit to change.

"This sort of pulled me toward you, guiding me to where you were. I think of it like a thread that connects us, but more like a feeling than an actual thread. You placed the intention to be found in it, I just activated that intention and followed where it led."

"So, the same theory could be applied to phone numbers? Like if someone gave you their phone number on a napkin or something?" he asked after a few seconds of thought. "Because I don't have anything in this car that would connect to Malachi or Zita; that was all in the van. But if a phone number would work… Except no, I bet their phones have been confiscated."

"I...I'm not sure. I guess if we could test it..." Rune hedged.

"No time for that." He pulled into a parking spot and killed the engine.

"Are we here?" Rune asked, confused as he opened his door and quickly got out.

"No, we're several blocks away, but it's as close as we're going to get by car." He opened the door for Rune and half-helped, half-hauled her out. Rune didn't need to ask why. In the distance, she heard the faint echoing of sirens and brief flashes of red, white, and blue reflected off a building five or so blocks away. Cars on the street were already backed up past the block they had parked on as traffic was ground to a halt to make way for the emergency vehicles.

"Here, put this on." St. Benedict handed her a dark-blue, nylon jacket from the back seat of his car. It was monogrammed on the back with a symbol of a backward C and a dot in the middle.

"Aura reader?" Rune commented as she pulled the jacket on over her darker clothes.

Suddenly, St. Benedict's business clothes made more sense as he tossed his fedora in the back of the car and buckled on the shoulder holster before layering on the missing gray blazer. He reached into one of its pockets and pulled out a leather wallet that had a government ID badge inside; he flipped it closed so fast, Rune barely had time to see it.

"How do I look?" he asked as he tore through his mussed-up hat hair with a comb. Instead of having the taming effect he was going for, it forced his hair into a strange faux hawk. Rune tried to suppress her smile as she took the comb from him.

"Bend forward," she ordered. He hesitated a moment, then complied, bringing his face closer to her. She ignored the nearness, the image of St. Rachel fresh in her mind. She ran the comb through in easy, gentle sweeps, going with the wave of his dark hair instead of against it to shape it into something more like a pompadour. "There, that's better," she said when she finished. "Now you look like the new hotshot detective."

He took the comb from her and stuck it back into his coat pocket. "Just stick close to me, rookie, and we should be fine."

"Yup, let's go save your not-friends!" Rune slapped him on the shoulder with determination, before turning to march toward the flashing lights. She moved off with such conviction that she missed St. Benedict's face as he furrowed his eyebrows and stared after her. She also ignored the tingles in her fingers from running them through his hair.

CHAPTER 19

As they took off down the street, a trill of excitement went through Rune's spine. This was happening. They were taking on the shadows that had come after her and everything she held dear, and they were going to strike back. Her new partner in anti-crime walked beside her without comment, just a predatory look in his eye. While he looked like an elegant corporate hunting dog, she knew truthfully he was a wild wolf that would turn vicious without warning. Instead of intimidating, Rune found that idea comforting.

They proceeded in high-tension silence, their hurrying feet eating up the sidewalk, punctuated as Rune tripped over every other sidewalk crack. After she ran into a little old lady with an oversized dog out for an afternoon walk, St. Benedict grabbed her shoulder.

"Slow down. Walk with purpose, but don't run. You'll attract too much attention," he said calmly. He eyed her face for a second. "We probably should have done something about that eye."

Rune touched her black eye. "Don't worry. It was just a work-related accident," she said, continuing forward.

"Rune, wait!" St. Benedict called urgently.

"I'm fine, hurry up," she said just as she was about to walk out in front of a CTA bus. Suddenly, the monogrammed jacket was yanked back, and her foot flew out, missing the bus by a breath of inches as it squealed to a stop in front of her.

"Are you okay?" a woman next to them asked. Rune stared wide-eyed at the side of the bus, her shadowy reflection staring back at her from the blackened windows.

"She's fine," St. Benedict said for her, his arm across the front of her shoulders as he hugged her hard against him. "Rookie. First day on the job, just getting a little too excited," he said jovially and shook Rune a bit in a friendly gesture, but the tips of his fingers dug into her flesh, telling her otherwise.

"Oh my, what is going on down there?" the woman asked, looking past Rune and St. Benedict toward the sirens. She was an older lady with over-permed hair and glasses with transition lenses in them.

"Building on fire. Excuse us, ma'am. We need to get to the scene," St. Benedict answered, sounding polite but official. The lady laid a hand on her cheek and breathed an, "Oh my," as he pulled Rune after him across the street.

"Okay, maybe you're right. I need to slow down," Rune said when they were out of earshot. She pawed at his arm, which still hung heavy over her upper chest, and he let her go. "Thanks for that."

"Next time, you can stop me before I run out in front of a bus," he said, giving her the small version of his smile, one meant to reassure. "Now, stay a step behind me and go where I go."

"Right. Walk with purpose," she said and followed his lead across the street.

They were only half a block away from the dramatic scene. Several ambulances and fire trucks pulled up like a real-life game of "traffic jam," blocking the street while emergency workers walked amidst them. Many were aiding drenched office workers. A few of the workers were being given respirators for smoke inhalation, which was odd since there was no actual smoke or fire in the building. Uniformed police officers set up barriers and tried to keep the bravest onlookers from crossing into the paths of those trying to help.

"How are we going to get in?" Rune asked, eyeing the chaos that was the glass front of the building.

"Each building is defined by one simple principle, though those within often don't realize it. The idea of who belongs and who does not. The old eternal battle of all peoples. Emergencies violate that principle," St. Benedict said. "Okay, if you spot anything, don't say anything, just give me a tap. Try to keep it casual," St. Benedict continued quietly as they approached one of the officers at the line. In a practiced motion, he took out the wallet and flashed the badge at the officer. The officer didn't even glance at it, just waved them through, keeping his focus on the gaping crowd, a mix of tourists and business workers.

The smell of the Halon was everywhere, emanating from the clothes of the people. The memory of it penetrated Rune's nose putting her right back in the air duct, her body pressed against St. Benedict's. She remembered wanting so badly to get away from him and that whole situation. Yet here she was, by his side again, working with him by her own choice, and something felt so right about it. Instead of running from the problem or waiting for someone else to solve it for her, she was tackling it head-on, or mostly head-on. Her path was kind of zig-zaggy, but she couldn't shake the feeling that she was going the right way.

More people passed them as the duo moved amongst the emergency crews. It felt like they were a pair of ghosts; nobody even acknowledged them. St. Benedict led Rune around the side of the building to an alley. More people poured out from the back doors, but they were far fewer than at the front. Other emergency crews escorted and herded them toward the front or other ambulances parked at the end of the alley.

St. Benedict didn't acknowledge any of the people escaping. He simply came to the edge of the door, and when there was a gap, went inside with Rune close on his heels.

"Hey, buddy, no going back in once you've evacuated," a firewoman shouted, her voice muffled inside her helmet. St. Benedict ignored her, letting the stream of people block the firewoman's ability to stop them. Rune kept close, focusing on the faces around them. They were moving through the back of the building, amongst the general feeling of dirtiness that even the most immaculate buildings had in their rears.

"It's like some kind of metaphor or something," Rune said to herself, smirking at the idea.

"What is?" St. Benedict asked, his voice a low-pitched half-whisper, as he looked up and down a crooked junction, holding her back with a hand on her arm so they lined up along the wall.

"It just seems over the last couple of days, I've spent a lot of time in the backs of buildings," Rune whispered at the same level, as another panicked group went past them toward the exit.

He chuckled. "There's an elevator over there, we're heading to that."

"You're supposed to avoid elevators in case of fire," she said as she followed him around the corner.

"There's no fire, remember?" He pushed the up button.

"They'd still be disabled in an emergency," Rune countered.

"Which is why it's strange that this one is still working, isn't it?" he asked, cocking a charming eyebrow at her.

She pursed her lips together. He had a point. It wasn't the only thing that was unusual about their building invasion. "Huh, it's weird to think that right now, we're upstairs in the air duct."

He looked back at her, blinking as the implications of that hit him too. "I suppose that's normal for you." He turned away.

"Not really."

St. Benedict didn't say anything more, and they lapsed into silence again, waiting for the elevator.

"How many people are we looking for?" Rune asked, to break the tension.

"Two: Malachi and Zita. He's a human, and she's a naga." St. Benedict hit the elevator button again. When nothing more happened, he looked around the elevator doors.

"Ah. Okay, *is* it working?" she asked, watching him.

"My intel said that this would continue to work, even in an emergency situation..." he muttered.

He focused on a black box to the right of the elevator button. He flicked a finger at it. Then he did the magician roll with his fingers. Instantly, the holographic screen appeared in the palm of his hand. Even though she had seen it a couple of times now, Rune's eyes still went wide as he did it.

It took a moment for her to remember what they were talking about before. "Can you tell me anything more about them?"

"About the elevator?" St. Benedict asked, half-listening.

"No, the people you dragged me in here to Find."

"What do you want to know?" he asked.

"I don't know, just some details about them, something that might help me find them, you know with my eyeballs, if not magic," she said.

"Malachi is about this tall." He slashed the air at his shoulder height with his not-glowing hand. "Brown hair, too long because it's been three months since he got it cut again, and last time it was because Zita told me to take him. She was going to introduce him to her clan, and he was being stubborn about it."

He went back to manipulating the hologram on the surface of his hand. When he found what he was looking for, he stopped talking and turned his palm back toward the black box. A small red light in one corner flipped to green and pinged a cheerful note. Hitting the elevator button opened the doors this time.

"Zita and Malachi are dating?" Rune asked as she got in, still marveling at St. Benedict's hand. It was bad manners in magic circles to inquire when someone was enacting magic, so she held her tongue about it, but her brain burned with curiosity.

"Yes, she's about this tall." He slashed at chest height. "Though I've seen her rear up higher. It's hard to tell with nagas." He bent forward a bit to look at the elevator panel. Another of the black boxes was positioned at the bottom. He waved his palm in front of it again, and the red light went green, but then his hand hovered over the buttons.

"What's wrong?" Rune asked.

"I'm not sure what floor," he said.

"What? I thought you were a super-secret corporate spy with a plan," Rune teased.

"I have a badge and everything. St. Augustina's office is a temporary one, and I was able to narrow down the floor they were on to seven, nine, or thirteen. I was counting on you being able to lead us to them," he said.

"That was your plan?"

He looked at her askance. "Well, can you do it or not? Otherwise, I'm going to guess here." He gestured at the elevator buttons.

She inhaled deeply. "Um, okay. Give me your hand, I can at least try my idea." She held her hand out to him.

He extended his left hand, and he held it out to her palm down, like she was going to kiss it or something. "No, give me your right hand, the glowing one," she said, reaching out for it.

Instead, he withdrew it. "Why?"

"I don't know. I'm improvising here. I just think I'll have better luck with that hand," she insisted.

"That doesn't make any sense."

"It's magic, it's not about sense. Think of it as a leap of logic and give me your right hand," she repeated.

He gave it to her, and Rune took another deep breath, placing his large hand between both of hers. It was warm and rough, calloused on the palm just under his index finger, probably from endless hours of trigger practice. He had several small scars along the back and his nails were clipped short and even. The fingers themselves were long and tapered and strong, like a piano player's.

"Okay, Malachi, he's your friend, shorter than you, brown hair. What else, kind of nerdy looking?" she asked. She closed her eyes so she could focus on the image of Malachi.

"Not really," St. Benedict shifted uncomfortably. "More like a slacker, slovenly clothes and questionable bathing habits — before Zita. He's my computer tech guy. My back-up."

Rune closed her eyes. "You've known him for a long time?"

"Yes."

She snapped her eyes open. "Look, I can play twenty questions, or you can tell me the story of Malachi. I thought we were in a hurry."

"What do you mean?" he asked, getting defensive.

"The story of Malachi. Who is he? Not just the general stuff, the little details, the things that you love about him."

"I don't love him. He's just a…a guy."

"I can't make this work if you don't try. You want to find him, right? So, start talking about him," Rune said and closed her eyes again, reaching for her magic to fuel the image of Malachi and focus on the connection of St. Benedict.

"Bit sarcastic and cynical. An acquired taste, like coffee. Zita softened him up quite a bit, but you kind of have to like the bitterness. I'm like that too, for that matter."

"Friends can often be reflections of ourselves, and he's who you are risking your life and your original mission to save… even though you don't have orders to do so." Rune's voice took on the edge of an echo. Her eyes snapped open wide as her magic suddenly thrummed through her.

Rune saw threads flowing wildly around St. Benedict as she opened her second sight. His expression was now enhanced, the edges of his face sharp and full of secrets, his gaze intense as he stared at her, but there was also mirth dancing around the surface. The smile he wore was always a mask to cover the darkness underneath. She drifted her gaze up and down his body. To her, it seemed like he had two bodies, one from a long time ago that she could barely make out, as it was covered by his current one. At his hand and in his brain, she clearly saw the glowing places, pulsing with a cold blue light. There was also one over his heart, but it pulsed much fainter with only the slightest hint of power. Around the blue glowing parts was another source of light, tiny, fine threads of green that were working to fix, to mend, but unable to push away the blue light.

St. Benedict watched Rune's white glowing eyes drift up and down his body. It was like she could see through him. Her eyes reminded him of his own when his tech augmentations were working. He resisted the urge to shift away, letting her see whatever she was going to see and think whatever she would of it. He would endure this and more to help his team.

"My healing spell's still inside you!" Rune said, staring at the faint-blue light over his heart; her spell was wrapping around it. Her echoed voice sent a shiver up and down St. Benedict's spine.

She reached out a hand and laid her palm over the blue light. She felt the tug of the spell's green threads as she placed a part of herself closer to him. "They should have resolved by now... the energy spent..." The threads flashed and pulled more power from Rune.

"What are you doing?" St. Benedict asked, alarmed, capturing her hand to pull it away. His words startled Rune, and she withdrew both her hands, retracting her sight at the same time; the world returned to normal.

"I... I..." she stuttered and took a step back from him. She didn't know what to say, but her heart was beating a thousand times a minute. It was like that blue light was a piece of his secrets, something very important about him, but how to ask him about it when she couldn't even form the question? What had she seen exactly? She would have to sort it out later.

"I'm sorry. I was trying to do what you asked. I thought if you had a strong enough connection to Malachi, I would be able to trace it like I do people connected to me. It just wasn't working that way."

"And you needed to feel me up to do that?" St. Benedict covered his discomfort with his wicked smile, trying to make a joke out of it. Rune just couldn't find it funny.

"I'm sorry. I don't think it's going to work this way. Something else started to happen." She looked at the elevator door, so she didn't have to look at him.

"Okay, fine. I'll figure something else out," he said and brought his fist to his mouth. "St. Rachel," he said to it.

"My healing spell is still in you. I think the reason it hasn't dissipated yet is somehow I'm still feeding it energy."

He glanced over at her but didn't get a chance to respond as he reacted to something Rune couldn't hear. "Yes, we're inside, but the Finder is no good. Don't have enough to lead us to them. Have they exited the building yet?"

He listened to the answer, completely ignoring Rune.

"The Finder?" she muttered.

Frustrated, she slipped a finger into the pocket that held her stack of business cards. Calvin's sat on the top. The second she touched it, a pulse came to life.

"Oh!" she exclaimed, surprised.

"What is it?" St. Benedict asked at her loud utterance.

"Calvin is nearby." She pulled the card off the top of the stack, rubbing it like a good luck charm. "He's straight up and over a little bit. The ninth floor. I know it!"

"Okay, St. Rachel, we got a lead on something. Stand by." He opened his palm again toward the little black box, but before he could touch a button, the elevator started to move.

"Get to the side!" He pushed Rune to the opposite side of the elevator so that she was partly hidden by the lip. He did the same, creating an open space between them. The Saint took out his gun, holding it in both hands, the barrel pointed at the ceiling as he braced himself to fight. Rune wished she had anything to help him, wondering way too late what she did with that shield crystal that her Aunt Maddie had made her.

The door slid open a long minute later, on the ninth floor.

"I don't care what you dumbasses think; I'm not going back there," came Calvin's whining voice through the opening doors. He was talking to someone behind him, his body twisted around so he couldn't see inside the elevator. Just beyond him, an assembly of black-suited people glared at him with varying degrees of contempt. Front most was St. Augustina, looking like an exasperated social studies teacher, her eyes wide as her focus shifted from Calvin to St. Benedict, then Rune, barely covered on either side of the door. Her Saint instincts kicked on as she reached for her gun at her waist slightly faster than the lackeys behind her.

St. Benedict didn't even hesitate but stepped forward and grabbed Calvin's vulnerable back, putting the gun against his head. The Saint gripped Calvin's shoulder and hissed, "Don't move."

"What the hell!" Calvin exclaimed, but his body obeyed St. Benedict's order and went still.

"There you are, St. Benedict! You ass," St. Augustina said measuredly, her eyes calculating the new situation.

"Hey, St. Augustina," St. Benedict shouted back, only a single eye appearing over Calvin's shoulder. He strong-armed his human shield forward, moving his own body sideways in careful, shuffling steps. "Came to pick up a few things. You don't mind, I hope."

"How the hell did you do all this?" St. Augustina snapped her question like a whip. "How did you get into my system?"

"I'm a Saint, sweetheart. We trade in miracles, right?" he answered back.

"You're a fucking devil!" she roared back.

"Rune, step up behind me, quickly," St. Benedict said under his breath before shouting back at St. Augustina, "Yup, suppose so. I got a witch and everything on my side."

"You like to repeat history, don't you?"

"Did I just blow up your entire working budget? Or did I take all your resources away in handcuffs, along with the van that had my favorite hat in it?" he said, taking several more steps forward.

Rune followed right behind him, wishing again she remembered where her shield crystal had gone. She didn't relish the idea of using Calvin as a body shield, no matter how much he deserved it.

As St. Benedict and St. Augustina continued to exchange insults and banter, the threesome covered half the distance to the little group at the opposite end. That was when something caught Rune's eyes as she swayed a bit out of time with Calvin's shielding steps. Scales. Naga scales to be exact, being led down the hallway by another small, black-suited group.

"St. Benedict," she whispered and reached out a hand to grab the waistband of his pants, which stopped his sliding forward and pulled Calvin up short. "Your team is over there!"

"Malachi, you still alive?" St. Benedict immediately called out.

"You owe me a vacation," came the weaker call, followed by a grunt of pain as one of the lackeys encouraged him to shut up.

"Get those two out of here now! Everyone is getting out alive, do you understand? Today's the day to bring your best," St. Augustina instructed. The rear of the group detached and moved down the hall, and Rune just barely saw the back of a man, around her age, and the diamond pattern of the naga as they disappeared out of sight at the end of the hall to the left.

"They're getting away," Rune said, urgently.

"Fuck, Leveau, is that you?" Calvin asked and attempted to twist around to look at her, but St. Benedict shook him back into place.

"Obviously, you're not too worried about your brains if you think you can try to turn around when someone has a gun pressed to your head." He jabbed a little with the barrel of the gun to reinforce the point.

"Ow! Fucking hell! Did that bitch hire you to strong-arm me, man?" Calvin asked disgustedly. "Wow, that girl's got more balls than I thought."

"Harris. Anyone you want me to pass a message to?" St. Augustina asked Calvin.

"What?! You're leaving me?"

"You served your government well," St. Augustina said, but Calvin took little comfort in that.

"Okay, I've had enough of the banter. I think we need to just make a deal here so we can all move on with our lives," St. Benedict said.

"There's nothing to trade for. I have a mission, and I'm carrying it out. What you are going to do is lay down your weapon, and we'll take you into custody," St. Augustina said, making a discrete gesture to her lackeys behind her. At her silent command, they fanned out evenly behind her, becoming a wall of ammo.

"You really think I just walked in here without several aces up my sleeve, sweetheart? You know that's not how I roll and you know it's going to be too expensive to call my bluff."

"Everyone, prepare to fire on my count," St. Augustina said instead.

"Oh, fuck me," Calvin said, in rising panic. "You... you can't kill me!"

"Yes, she can. She can do it very easily," St. Benedict said. "Isn't that right, St. Augustina? You're very good at killing people!"

"Three....two..." she counted, but before she could fire, one of her lackeys grabbed her shoulder.

"Code Black!" he shouted, indicating his earpiece. "We've been called to initiate a Code Black right now, ma'am."

"Are you... Dammit. I'm sick to death of this bureaucracy shit!" St. Augustina spat the words. "Pull out now!" As one, the group backed away quickly.

"What, you're doing your command codes in colors now?" St. Benedict tried to jibe. St. Augustina didn't slow in her retreat, though she stared murder at him the whole time. St. Benedict moved forward, but Calvin was reluctant to comply at the speed he wanted and a gap formed in the hall.

"Where ya goin', St. Augustina?" St. Benedict taunted, desperate to bait her into hesitating.

"One of these days, I am going to put a happy little bullet in that brain of yours. Will be righting a lot of wrongs on that day," St. Augustina promised before she backed around the corner.

"St. Augustina!" St. Benedict roared, but it did no good.

"You can't leave me here!" Calvin shouted as well for good measure.

Behind them, Rune knelt to the ground focusing on a few splatters of blood that the two men had ignored and stepped over in their slow shuffle pursuit.

When the men reached the corner, St. Benedict lined himself up with the wall so he was covered and pushed Calvin out for the potential shot. The blonde idiot even flinched in anticipation of a hail of bullets.

"Where are they? Augustina!" Calvin shouted down the hall instead. St. Benedict pushed him out another inch and peeked around the corner to confirm that the hallway, ending in an alcove, was indeed empty.

"On your knees, hands on your head," St. Benedict ordered, kicking at the backs of his knees, keeping the point of his gun pressed against the back of his head. "Rune, get over here, I need you," he shouted.

"Yeah, boss?" she asked as she came around the corner.

He did a double-take, then decided to ignore her cheek and nodded at the walls.

"Ah I see," she said and went to investigate. The three walls of the empty alcove were indeed solid and wall-like, covered with bland white stucco texture.

"They must have gone through a doorway or something," Rune said, laying her right hand against each wall but sensing very little.

"Like another one of your magic doors?" St. Benedict asked, adjusting Calvin's legs with his foot so they were farther apart.

"I don't know. Maybe? It's really outside the purview of my magic," she said before adding, "I think," under her breath. "But I can figure out which way they went with this." She opened the palm of her left hand, showing it to her partner.

"What is that? Blood?"

"Yes, your friend Malachi's blood from when they hit him. You don't get a more personal connection than that." She closed her hand over it protectively. "I can find him with this for about an hour-ish."

"You freaky witch," Calvin growled.

St. Benedict slapped him upside the head with an open palm. "Shut it 'til I tell you otherwise." Then he hit him again. Calvin grabbed his head.

"Geez, what was that for?"

"The feminist movement," St. Benedict said.

"What?" Calvin asked, which earned him another smack.

"For hitting Rune, idiot."

"Actually, he hit me twice," Rune piped up, not looking at either of them.

There was a fourth smack.

Rune took a deep breath and focused on the memory of Malachi from the glimpse she had gotten of him a few minutes before. Immediately, there was a tug straight ahead.

"They went straight ahead," Rune reported, smiling confidently then waved her blood-covered hand in front of the still blank wall.

"Apertus." Immediately, an outline of a door appeared and hollowed out, like it was being burned away with light.

"Wow," St. Benedict said at the spectacle.

"Okay, I think I'm figuring out how to do this finally," Rune said, unable to suppress her proud smile. "They didn't lock it so it was just a matter of turning the knob, magically speaking."

That was when Calvin dropped the pepper-bomb from his hand. Immediately, Rune's eyes slammed shut, and she felt like she was choking.

"Goddammit!" St. Benedict shouted as he tried to cover his mouth. Too late—he started coughing. It took two tries to kick the little bomb back down the hall, but the damage was already done.

"Shit, he ran," St. Benedict cursed and pushed Rune toward the new opening she had made.

"That-skinny-assed-something-really-insulting!" Rune shouted in burning agony.

"No, don't rub it! That will make it worse. Just keep blinking," St. Benedict instructed, pulling her hands away from her face. "We need to flush this out of your eyes." He looked up and down the hallway for some source of water, but there wasn't even a fountain.

"No time! We need to catch him!" Rune blinked hard to get her eyes to water even as her nose began running like a waterfall. Through the haze that was her vision, she saw St. Benedict slam his elbow into the window of a locked office door. It cascaded in a shower of safety glass, designed to pebble up when broken, onto the beautiful cedar floor of the hallway.

"Jackpot!" He swiped a bottle of water that sat on a tray near the door.

"They're getting away! Chase after them!" Rune shouted.

"Shut up," he said as he brushed the strands of her hair back and tipped her face up. "Hold your breath." He dumped half the bottle over her eyes as Rune struggled to hold them open. The cold ate through the painful burn-itch and when the water had done its work she could see significantly better. "Drink the rest," her partner ordered, thrusting the bottle at her before wiping the remaining water away from her face with the inside of his jacket.

"What about you?" she said, trying to give the water back.

"I'm fine. Implants in my eyes are already clearing that crap out."

She looked up at his aforementioned eyes and saw them glow that unearthly blue again.

"Oh, well, that's handy."

"Come on, hurry, drink," he said as he ran a check on his gun again. "We can't chase them if you're half-blind and choking."

Rune wanted to argue more, but the sting in her throat made it impossible. Instead, she downed most of the bottle.

"Take the jacket off, too. It's all over it," he added, ditching his and helping her to remove hers.

"I can't believe you're spending time helping me. I thought you'd take off after them and leave me behind," she said as he took the dregs of water and downed them to wash out his own throat.

"No need. This is a hunt now, not a chase, and we've got an edge. We can find them now, right?"

Rune glanced down at her hand, still holding Malachi's drying blood. "Yeah, you're right. We can find your people." She slipped the business card out of her pouch and held it up, "and Calvin."

He nodded. "Alright, the hunt is on. Sniff them out."

She started toward the newly opened magic door before she caught fully what he said.

"Did you just call me a dog?" she asked, taking his hand as she walked through the solid-looking wall like it was nothing.

"No," St. Benedict said, feigning innocence.

CHAPTER 20

"If anything, we're a pair of dogs. One that tracks and one that brings down the kill," St. Benedict said. The conversation about dogs continued for a few minutes while Rune tried to navigate the strange world they now found themselves in.

It was another warp in the city architecture that created a tunnel, this one concrete and industrial on one side, with dirty light-blue siding from the outer wall of a house on the other side. No sounds could be heard, and it was lit well enough to show that it was empty. Another door waited at the other end, but St. Benedict still moved them down at a walking pace, despite the urgency Rune felt. She still sensed Malachi and Calvin, both pulling, calling to her, to head straight forward.

At the end of the hall, St. Benedict stopped them and indicated she should go behind the door and open it while he lined up on the other side. As she opened, he seamlessly stepped around the corner, checking for enemies.

"Holy hell," he exclaimed.

On the other side of the door stood a forest.

"A Faerie Court door, connected to a corporate building," Rune mused as she looked through the door herself, following him in. They stepped through the trees, daylight streaming through leaves and vines and panes of tempered glass. It *looked* like a forest.

"No, it's not a forest," St. Benedict said to himself, obviously having the same thought.

"An atrium?" Rune offered, looking around. They were surrounded by innumerable plants of different sizes and colors, some with flowers, some with curious-shaped leaves. There was a faint echoing sound of birds and water bouncing off the glass walls.

As the pair stepped from the foliage onto a graveled path, their eyes went wide at the better view of the room. It seemed to be the size of a football field encased in glass. Set into those glass walls, every three feet, were doorways, standing open, showing room upon room. It was a cacophony of color against the clarity of the glass, each room decorated in a different scheme. The plants and trees only obstructed the views a little. Some rooms seemed large beyond their doors, while others were narrow, like the hallway they had just exited.

"Look, there are people!" Rune pointed at a door to the left of them. Instantly, St. Benedict snapped his gun back up, pointing it at the possible threat. "No, don't!" She pushed down on the barrel of his gun so that it pointed at the floor. "In the room. I mean, that room. There," she tried indicating again.

Indeed, inside a room that looked like someone's dining room, they could see a young woman sitting at an oval, wooden table typing at her laptop, a small child sitting next to her tapping away at a tablet that was encased in a big, red case with friendly arms and legs sticking out of its sides. They didn't seem to see Rune or St. Benedict, or even to be aware of the atrium only a few feet away from them.

"It's a hub," St. Benedict said, spinning on the spot to look at the other doorways.

"No, not exactly. It's the literal Faerie Court," Rune said as she spun the other way, looking closer at each of the entryways. "These doors all lead to somewhere else, different places in Chicago. When the Faerie Court was a governmental body, they had government buildings, or rooms rather, across their districts, connected here."

"That seems very strange," St. Benedict said. A monument a few feet down the path caught his eye.

"Or very secure. Their alderman's offices were accessible from every district they controlled. It was a great work of magic, nearly impossible to duplicate today. The cost would be astronomical."

"The founding of Chicago," St. Benedict read aloud as he stared down at a plaque at the base of the strange statue, an abstract shape that closely resembled a large flame curling around itself.

"That's mostly symbolic. So little remained after the Great Fire, it was one of the last times magic and non-magic communities really came together," Rune said, coming up next to him to look at the statue as well.

"Yes, thank you, I know that," St. Benedict said, and started looking around them again.

"Yeah, well, you haven't had to live with the fallout from the Court falling two years ago. It changed everything. Having to carry those ID cards now and there was all new licensing for magical establishments. It's been a real mess. There are so many in the Magic Guild who have lost their businesses because of corporate machines taking over the remnants of the Faerie Court. They've bought up and fought over everything that remained of the Faeries. Took what they wanted or needed to run things and tossed the rest."

"I can see how a network like this would be pretty useful," St. Benedict said, nodding at the doors.

"Yeah, never mind the number of Faeries that have been thrown out to live on the street," Rune grumbled as she touched the statue with a fingertip. At her touch, it lit up from the inside, the flame glowing a gentle rose-pink and yellow. Inside the heart of the statue was a small image of the cityscape. She smiled sadly. "It still works. It only lights up for Faeries and Faerie Friends. Maddie and I were both granted status as Faerie Friends. We did what we could to stop what was happening, but no one could have predicted the Oberon selling everybody out."

"And then promptly dying," St. Benedict added. It was common knowledge.

"It was only two years ago, but it seems more like a decade," Rune said, nodding sadly. "We need to get moving." Holding up her hands again, she felt the duel tug pulling her further into the atrium. "This way," she said and headed down a gravel path.

"So, you were there?" St. Benedict asked, as he pulled Rune back from progressing and took point again, his gun aimed down, ready to snap up the second it would take to respond to a threat. He didn't want to risk shooting some innocent person inside one of the numerous rooms.

"Yes," Rune replied tersely and fell silent. Up ahead, sounds echoed and bounced off the trees, voices that were hard to make out, but clearly people talking just the same.

St. Benedict slowed and crouched down by a tree to peer around.

"This is bullshit!" Calvin crowed, louder than before.

"Shut up!" a woman's voice growled, one that made Rune's blood run cold.

"We have to move now. This idiot led St. Benedict right to us. I know it," St. Augustina stated.

"Then go, you fool," the well-dressed woman, said. "I care not for the vigilante spy, nor your little quarrel with him."

"Quarrel!"

"He's going to kick your lopsided ass, lady," Malachi said, giving a dry laugh that ended in a gurgle of pain.

"Mal!" a softer, sweet voice called before she cried out in pain as well.

"Shut it, you worm bitch!" one of St. Augustina's lackeys shouted, the ugly slur making Rune flinch.

"Johnson, curb your anger right now," St. Augustina ordered.

St. Benedict gripped the handle of his gun harder, narrowing his eyes to sharp green points, a deadly smile creeping across his face. It sent another, different chill down Rune's spine.

"Take this," the well-dressed woman said.

"What the hell is it?" Calvin asked.

"The means to summon power."

"What? Magic like what Rune can do?" Calvin asked, sounding excited and contemptuous simultaneously.

"Nothing like what she can do. With that, you can summon..."

"What was that?" St. Augustina hissed, and all fell silent.

St. Benedict and Rune exchanged glances. Neither of them had moved. They looked around themselves, straining an ear for some sound out of place. Gently, Rune felt a tap on her hand and looked up at St. Benedict. He pointed at his eye, then wiggled his fingers in the universal gesture for magic, and lifted an inquisitive eyebrow. She knew what he was asking, and after a second of hesitation, she nodded.

Carefully, Rune took a risk and opened her magic sight. She muffled a small cry, it hurt, but nothing like the splintering pain she had known before nor the pain-free bliss she had experienced in the elevator.

When she looked around, she had to muffle another cry, this one of amazement. In sharp relief, the shadows of the trees jumped to life. She could see them all around, tiny sprites of light, all different colors dancing around the plants. Pixies, brownies, and other various types of the smaller, more vulnerable Fae were clustered about, staring apprehensively at the group of invaders below, and for that matter, at Rune and St. Benedict as well.

Holding out her hand, Rune tried to coax a little brownie near to her. Its hat looked like it had a brown mushroom cap slapped on its head. Twiggy brown hair stuck out from under the hat and the pale off-cream of its clothes made it look even more mushroom-like, if it weren't for the overly large brown eyes that were both eerie and cute at the same time.

The little brownie eyed Rune along with its fellows, a toad woman, squat and green, and an elegant pixie male, covered in purple and white colors like he was wearing an iris.

"Faerie Friend," Rune mouthed silently at them and held her hand out more insistently. The toad woman nudged the brownie in the shoulder and gestured enigmatically at Rune. The little brownie heaved a big sigh, but the pixie, who had been looking down his tiny, perfect nose at Rune, suddenly perked up. His long ears twitched forward as his white eyebrows shot into his shock of purple hair. He leaned forward and whispered something to the other two. All three exchanged looks before the toad woman hopped off. The pixie and brownie exchanged a few more hurried words, and then the pixie flitted off on gossamer wings to the leaves, a purple light quickly lost in the rainbow of other little lights. Soon, the whole canopy buzzed and it seemed to Rune that the colors were drifting closer. If felt like hundreds of pairs of eyes were now looking at her.

As for the little brownie, it seemed to screw up its courage, because it marched over to where Rune crouched. It planted its little feet into the ground before her and set its fists on its hips in an authoritative pose despite its small stature.

"Are you the Heir to the Magdalene?" the tiny voice of the brownie demanded with the force of a mosquito.

Rune didn't dare speak, but she nodded.

"Have you come to free us?" it demanded, a note of hope coming into its little voice.

Rune double blinked. She opened her mouth to say something but stopped herself at the last second. She looked over her shoulder in the direction of Calvin and the others. The brownie followed Rune's gaze.

"Are you friends of them, the suited people?" the brownie asked, a little more suspicious.

Rune shook her head a definitive no.

The brownie cocked its head to the side. "What's wrong with you? You can't speak?"

Rune tried to mime being quiet and then tiptoeing with her fingers, before gesturing hopelessly at St. Benedict. She stopped miming when he saw her, her cheeks blushing deeply. She had forgotten that her status as a Faerie Friend allowed her to see through invisibility magic these little Faeries naturally possessed.

"Oh, he's the warrior, and you're the wizard! You're on a mission!" the little brownie exclaimed.

Rune nodded. It was as good an explanation as any.

"I want them out of here!" St. Augustina's voice cut through again. The group in the distance had started talking.

St. Benedict pulled his focus back toward Augustina's voice and away from Rune and her gesturing to the air. Making a choice, St. Benedict angled up his gun and shot.

The blast was a cacophony in the relative peace of the atrium. The dancing lights above scattered and screamed at the sound. To Rune, with her activated second sight, it was an overwhelming show of power and light. She saw the waves of energy flow off of the gun, as well as the intention, like fractured light, coming from St. Benedict himself. Once he had fired the gun, he grabbed Rune's shoulder and dragged her back up the path they had just come, jarring her out of her sight. Even as he rushed her, she was able to scoop up the protesting brownie before it got trampled.

Behind them, more chaos erupted. Rune heard St. Benedict chuckle as St. Augustina roared and fired in the direction where they had been.

"Would you believe that woman makes the world's greatest tiramisu?"

"What are you doing?!" Rune hissed at him.

"Scaring the rabbits out of the brush," he said.

"But the pixies!" Rune cried in horror, far too loudly. She watched as the little people screamed in terror, their organized flight of lights deteriorating into scattered chaos. Two little lights completely halted in their trajectories and plummeted to the ground. They burst into zaps of color like tiny fireworks before burning out into nothingness. Wails of grief ripped through the discordant cries of the little Fae. In her hands, the little brownie's scream joined the others.

"Noooooo!!" it wailed.

There was another round of volleys, and two more lights failed.

"No, stop! Stop! You're killing them!" Rune screamed. She stood up and rushed toward the lights, waving her empty hand while she continued to cup the brownie against her in the other hand. "This way! Faerie Friend! Get away from there!"

"What are you doing!?" More shots fired around her, but Rune didn't even register it before St. Benedict tackled her to the ground. The shots continued overhead, and Rune tried to stand up in her panic.

"Keep down!" St. Benedict shouted as he slapped his hand against the back of her head and tucked her head under his arm. He kept her that way for several heartbeats after the roaring of the guns had stopped. "We need to move now!" St. Benedict ordered in a harsh whisper, but Rune ignored him and rolled onto her back.

"Are you alright?" she asked, talking to the brownie in her hands.

"Where are you, St. Benedict?!" St. Augustina shouted.

Rune looked at him then, tears burning in her eyes.

"They're killing them," she whispered so sorrowfully that St. Benedict thought his cold heart was going to break.

"Who are you talking about?" He couldn't see anyone else.

"The Faeries. They're just children," she said and looked straight up into the air, but there was nothing there.

"St. Benedict!" St. Augustina shouted again. "You're not doing this to me again. Not this time."

"Oh, this is not the time to go off your rocker," he muttered to Rune and dragged at her arm to get her to crawl after him through the exotic foliage. After a few feet, they stopped against the exterior glass wall. "Oh, I hope whatever we just crawled through wasn't poisonous."

"Why won't the rest come?" Rune asked her hand desperately. She paused as if listening to something, then looked at her right hand. "Blood? Oh, gods, Malachi's blood."

"What?" St. Benedict asked, incredulously.

"We smell of blood. The other Fae are avoiding us," Rune explained, missing his confusion entirely. Without thinking, she started wiping the blood on the dirt they sat on.

"Well, that might be the right idea since it's us they're going to be shooting at," he said back, then noticed what she was doing. "What are you doing? Don't we need that to find Malachi?"

"Oh, crap! I'm sorry," Rune said as she stopped but the damage was already done. "I... I can't feel him anymore..."

"Don't worry about it. St. Augustina is making enough noise..." St. Benedict assured her as he handed her his gun. "Hold this."

"What are you doing?!"

He yanked at the knot of his tie and opened the top of his shirt quickly to pull out the tiny box at the end of his thick chain. With quick, sure fingers, he spun the chain about his neck and unclasped it.

"In case we get separated," he said as he quickly looped it over Rune's neck and reclasped it, "you can find me with that, correct?"

"Yes, probably, but—"

He took the gun back from her and checked it again.

"Okay, I'm going back in, you stay here—"

"We have to get out of here. They're just little folk, and without someone to protect them, they'll get slaughtered." Rune jumped and looked down at her hand, the one holding the business card. "Calvin has moved. He's heading that way," she said, gesturing down the wall from where they squatted.

Almost on cue, the well-dressed woman roared, "Get back here, you cowardly piece of filth!"

St. Benedict moved, darting up along the wall in the direction Rune felt Calvin go. She scurried after the Saint, not nearly as smoothly.

"No, slow down. This way," she said when she felt a pull just outside one of the doors that St. Benedict had already sailed past. Instead of waiting for him, she turned in through the door herself. The tingle of energy as she passed through slid down her skin and the little brownie giggled because of it.

"You are a great one if you can take a small one like me through a door," it said as they left the warm air of the atrium for a cooler room lined with wooden boxes on either side, like a large, dark cargo hold. "Lady Wizard, you do not need to hold me like this. If you put me in your hair, Acorn can hold on."

"Is that your name? Acorn?" she asked, just in time to get her face slammed in with a board.

CHAPTER 21

"Shit, you're not the other guy," Calvin said as he looked down at Rune, who had been flung backward when he hit her with the board. She didn't hit the ground but bounced off St. Benedict who had followed her in. He didn't catch her either, just seamlessly turned her to the side so he could rush Calvin. She landed on her elbows and knees, one hand clutching her mouth. It actually took a second for the pain to register.

"Mmm, hmmm," she moaned through her hand. She definitely tasted blood, and her eyes were watering again. St. Benedict didn't slow, grabbing the board that Calvin still clung to in his hands. He used it to drive Calvin back. The poor blonde idiot tried to throw a punch, but St. Benedict sidestepped it and attempted to put the arm in a lock instead. The board clattered to the ground. Calvin tried to throw another punch with the other hand but that too was countered. St. Benedict slapped the blonde's ears, and Calvin cawed in pain, grabbing at his head instead of fighting. His legs would have collapsed underneath him if St. Benedict hadn't grabbed the front of his jacket. Taking both lapels in his fists, St. Benedict walked him back and slammed him hard against one of the crates. It took a few more seconds of rough handling before he could get into Calvin's front jacket pocket. Again, Calvin made a feeble attempt to throw a punch, but he was rewarded with another slam against the crate.

Rune managed to look up at that point, still grasping at her face. She wondered if it was blood or saliva trickling from between her fingers.

"Are you alright?" St. Benedict asked, glancing quickly over his shoulder, but all it did was encourage more squirming from Calvin. "Stop right now, or I will choke you into unconsciousness, do you understand me?" There was a moment of more resistance, and St. Benedict applied a bit more pressure.

"Okay! Okay," Calvin relented.

"Hey Rune, tell me you're okay," St. Benedict ordered, not taking his eyes from Calvin this time.

"I don't know," Rune said. She was crying at this point, her mouth hurt so badly. She inspected her palm; there was a little blood but not nearly as much as she thought there would be. "I'm alive. The money, does he have it?"

"Fuck you, Leveau!" Calvin spat, and suddenly, his world went sparkly. Just as he was about to lose to the oncoming darkness, St. Benedict let him go. He crumpled to the ground and St. Benedict started pawing through his front jacket pocket again.

"Yes, got it. Come on, we've got to get out of here," the Saint moved back to squat down next to Rune

"Let me see," he said, and carefully pulled Rune's fingers away from her face. Just as gently, he opened her mouth. She mewed a little, and he cooed at her as he turned her face toward the overhead light. "You might have a few loose teeth, but you didn't bite your tongue. Amazing that he didn't hit your nose either. You definitely need some ice in your future though, for that cheek," he advised.

Rune nodded but couldn't stop the tears no matter how much she tried to swallow them down.

"Hey, hey, you're okay," St. Benedict said, brushing his thumb against her unhurt cheek to push away the streams of tears.

"I'm looking at the light, but it's not stopping," she said, panic mounting.

"It's okay. It's the pepper spray from earlier. You're okay," he assured her. She forced her breathing to slow, and the panic subsided. The world, which had been growing darker, brightened again. "There you go, you see," he continued to soothe her, smiling a warm, genuine smile as he brushed back a rebel lock of hair from her face.

"The witch. The witch. That bitch, the witch. The witch did this. Damn you!" Calvin said, his voice rising in intensity as he rose up. "You bitch! You think you can do this to me?! I'm going to make you pay!" he screeched, his blue eyes rolling madly.

Rune looked up, the retort she was about to snap back dying on her lips as she saw him up on his knees. In his left hand, raised over his head, was a pendant. It was a simple thing, wrought of gold bleeding into silver; two circles, one large and one smaller, connected by a line between them.

"The symbol of Oberon," Rune breathed.

"Father!" piped the little brownie clinging to her hair. Rune jumped and touched Acorn, who had saved itself by climbing on top of her head. She realized she had completely forgotten about it in the confusion and was relieved that it hadn't resulted in a squished Fae.

Calvin's eyes were wild and fiercely angry. He smirked triumphantly as fear skittered down Rune's spine. Before she could shout, "Stop, you fool! You'll kill us all!", he had already moved, slamming the pendant, the symbol of the Faerie king, into the cement of the warehouse floor.

Immediately, smoke billowed from the ground in large black and gray tendrils, wrapping themselves around Calvin's form. For a moment, it looked like the living smoke was consuming him, but the idiot scrabbled out of it, crab-walking backward comically, his triumph now genuine terror. The smoke continued to billow and grow. Calvin's retreating form became obscured, and Rune completely lost sight of him as the shape of a Clydesdale emerged from the smoke.

"We need to run! We need to run now!" Rune shouted, turning away from the forming nightmare. St. Benedict stayed crouched, staring with wide eyes as gray smoke gave way to inky, glistening black skin. He didn't move even as Rune tugged on his shirt.

"St. Benedict! Move!" Rune screamed in his ear, startling him into motion as the thing behind them stamped its feet into corporeality, paws instead of hooves hitting the ground. It whinnied, the sound echoing strangely as if it came from some great abysmal cavern where souls were lost and never recovered.

Despite their stuttering start, they were halfway down the row of crates before Rune heard the thing coming for them. She dared a glance back over her shoulder and almost lost her mind to terror. The creature had fully formed into its body, and it was nothing made by nature. This thing had the body and head akin to a horse with a twisted horn of a unicorn bursting like a black spear from its forehead. Its paws were each tipped with wicked, long claws. With another warped whinny, the thing reared up on its hind legs and tossed its head, the horn scraping against the wooden crates, tearing gouges out of their sides.

"What the hell is that?" St. Benedict asked aghast, slowing as he watched it hew out great chunks of wood.

"Don't stop! Don't stop! Keep moving! What you're doing is the exact opposite of what we should be doing!" Rune shouted and grabbed his sleeve again, this time so hard it tore. St. Benedict's brain snapped back on. He seized Rune's hand, and together they fled from the danger.

Unfortunately, the row ended in a concrete wall.

"Who stacks boxes this way?!" she screeched in panic. The crates had been stacked so that they butted up against the wall, effectively blocking them into a dead end.

"We have to try to go up!" St. Benedict called.

"I can fit here," Rune insisted, but she was only able to squeeze her shoulder into the crack between the boxes and the wall. "Okay, maybe I can't."

"Come on, I'll boost you up," he said, interlacing his fingers to make a stirrup for her to step up into. "That thing's advancing, hurry!" He was right. It had started to prowl down the space, not charging like a unicorn or a rhino would, but predatorily stalking them, studying them as they scrambled for escape.

"It's a nightmare. Um, looks like a creature from Chinese or maybe Korean culture. I don't know, for sure, but it could be a Poh," Rune said as she looked.

"A what?!"

"It's like half-unicorn, half-lion, and completely bloodthirsty."

"Wonderful, study it later," St. Benedict said. "Come on!" Rune stepped up into his hands, bracing herself on his shoulders.

The Poh must have sensed what they were trying to do. It roared again and bounded into a charge.

"Here we go!" St. Benedict said, just as Rune started to say, "What about you?" But she barely got it out before he launched her into the air with a cheerleader lift. Rune caught the edge of the box, scrabbling her feet against the side. For half a second, it felt like she was going to fall back to the ground, but then she gained enough purchase to pull herself up over the edge of the crate.

Below, she heard the terrible scraping of the Poh's horn on wood as it roared again. It was attempting to skewer St. Benedict, but missed, piercing the sides of the boxes instead. St. Benedict's gun fired several times, and Rune rolled over to throw her arm down in an attempt to pull him up. It quickly became obvious that he was too far away for her reach from the ground, even if he jumped.

St. Benedict had backed up and away to the other side of the aisle, dodging the horn before it lanced him. Twice more, he fired into the cloud surrounding the nightmare, but the bullets just seemed to sink and disappear into the inky cloud instead of real flesh. The horn was very real, however, as it rained down pieces of wood all over its prey.

"St. Benedict!" Rune screamed uselessly from above, her voice echoing in the space above the crates.

The Saint tucked and rolled, then found himself again against the concrete wall. The Poh twisted as it reared up on its horse legs to angle its horn toward him before falling back to earth, using momentum to add force to its thrust.

Instead of letting his soft, pierceable flesh be run through, the Saint pushed off the wall into a roll past the Poh. With a loud crunchy crash, the horn penetrated the concrete wall, burying it all the way to the thing's skull, sticking it fast.

"Run, Run!" Rune shouted at St. Benedict as she pushed herself to her feet.

St. Benedict took off back down the aisle. Rune tried to keep up, but the crates stacked on top were of different sizes and shapes, creating a maze for her to navigate, slowing her down. She lost sight of her partner after the first pile. As she scurried, she dared to glance back over her shoulder. The nightmare roared as it whipped its body back and forth, trying to dislodge its horn from the wall. If it had been a living creature, it would have killed itself instantly upon impact.

"Oh, Calvin, what have you done?" Rune asked herself out loud.

"He summoned the wrath of Oberon!" a little voice piped from her hair.

"Acorn! Are you alright?" Rune asked, having completely forgotten about the brownie in her hair.

"I got squished once, but I'm tough," the little person said proudly. "Can you take me back to grandmother tree?"

"In the atrium? I'll try if I can find the door again. We have to rescue St. Benedict's friends, too," Rune said, touching the brownie's little body. Instantly, she knew where the door was in the mess of crates.

"What about my kin, wizardess?"

"We need to rescue them, too," Rune agreed. She moved around another box and almost tripped in a hole made by the layout.

"Little ones hurt all the time," Acorn said solemnly, making Rune's heart ache as she remembered the bursts of colored light as the little Fae died. "That's why the black kin are coming."

"What? What do you mean?" Rune asked.

"To save us. They promised. The black kin, our father's honor guard, they promised," the brownie declared resolutely. Rune's mind drifted back to a day ago.

"You mean the monochromes," Rune said, remembering when Lady Trella, the orange lady, had asked Rune for help. Rune reached up and touched the little body of the brownie, as light as a feather in her hair.

"I can't wait to tell them a new father has been chosen. Maybe this one will live longer," Acorn said hopefully.

Before Rune could ask what Acorn meant by that odd statement, she heard a roar and crash, the sound of concrete bricks being flung.

"The guardian is free," the brownie declared. Rune didn't like the sound of that.

"St. Benedict! Where are you?" Rune shouted as she clambered up and over a small pyramid of mismatched boxes.

He appeared instantly against the edge of a box a few feet from her, having taken a running leap to get that high.

"Here!" he grunted at her as he tried to muscle his way up. Rune closed the distance between them to grab him under his arms, throwing all her weight back to help pull him up. She wasn't entirely sure if it helped or not, but he clambered up onto the box.

"That thing...that..." he panted, sweat dripping down the sides of his face.

"I know, I know. It's not real," Rune said, panting herself. "It's a creature made of magic, and it won't stop 'til we're dead. I just don't get how a guy like Calvin could summon such a thing," she said,

"Bullets won't work, so what do you got?" he asked, rolling onto his belly to look over the edge for the monstrosity.

"I *got* running away and finding the exit. At least if we make it back to the atrium, we could shut the door and maybe trap it," Rune said.

"Will it work?" he asked.

"I don't know, it's the only plan that keeps us alive," Rune said, a little snappy.

"Right, got it," St. Benedict said cheekily. He rolled over to look up, eyeing the expansive space around them. "I wonder where we really are."

"A warehouse somewhere, once controlled by the Faerie Court. Best I can guess," Rune offered.

"We need to get higher," St. Benedict decided and went over to the next stack of boxes that would take them up another ten feet, halfway to the ceiling. He scaled them easily and surveyed their surroundings. "There's a rope up there." He pointed over her head. The rope hung from the catwalk another twenty feet above, one end tied securely around a strut. The end pooled on top of another small hill of boxes about five feet away.

Somewhere in the warehouse, the Poh whinnied again, the teeth-grating echo coming from everywhere.

"I don't think it can find us yet, so that's encouraging," Rune mused.

"You're the expert," St. Benedict replied. "Now head over to that pile."

"Not really the expert. I'm mostly just hoping more than actually knowing," Rune said.

"Never tell me that. Stop undermining yourself. No one's an expert in anything. We're all just making it up as we go along." He climbed down.

"That's not true," Rune said, shaking her head.

"It is for me." St. Benedict jumped down from the last box.

"No, no, there is a big difference between you and me," Rune insisted, her stomach feeling sick as she continued to shake her head. "You are..."

"Yeah, there is," he interrupted, "conviction." He grabbed her hand to lead her over to their escape.

They goated over the uneven terrain toward the rope. St. Benedict got to the rope first. He perched upon the box where it was pooled and pulled a knife from what seemed like nowhere. With a quick sawing motion, he cut away the excess rope at the bottom and stabbed the knife into the box to free up his hands.

"What are you doing?" she asked.

"I assume you can't free climb a rope?" he asked.

She shook her head 'no' with a derisive laugh. "I prefer stairs."

"Not a problem. I'm making you a stirrup. You're going to put your foot in this and hold the rope steady while I climb to the top. Once I'm up there, I can haul you up with your foot in the stirrup. You just have to hang on," he explained.

"I never expected gym class to come back and haunt me," Rune said. That actually earned her a small smirk from the Saint.

"Could be worse. I could make you do a hundred sit-ups," he quipped as he finished tying a secure looking knot at the top of a small noose.

Rune looked up the long rope to the top, marveling. "Really? You're going to haul up two hundred pounds of dead weight?" she asked, incredulously. That made him pause, and he eyed her up and down.

"You weigh two hundred pounds?" he asked. "You don't look it."

"What?" she challenged, looking at him deadpan, pinning with a stare.

"Nothing. I have absolutely nothing to say," he said, turning his focus to the rope. "Don't worry about it. It's fine. I can haul a guy of two-fifty if I do it quickly, just come over here and hold this down." He held open the stirrup he had tied for her to put her foot into. Rune obediently stepped into it and grasped the rope with both hands, the fibers biting roughly into her soft hands. "Okay, I'll have you up in a jiff, don't be afraid," he said.

"Don't worry, I'll distract myself by watching your ass as you climb," she said in an attempt to be light-heartedly flirtatious and then immediately wished she could die on the spot when her ears burned.

He double blinked at her.

"Sorry, that came out... I mean..."

His smile deepened as he turned to the rope to start climbing. Rune tried to look anywhere but where she had said she meant to. He climbed with ease, pulling his lithe body hand over hand in a way Rune could never imagine doing even if she was fifty pounds lighter.

"Hold it steady," he said partway up, and she jumped, realizing she had let it go slack. This naturally turned her gaze upward.

Unfortunately, his backside wasn't nearly distracting enough to make her forget the looming threat when it roared just a few feet below where she stood. The Poh prowled loudly.

"Stay calm, just focus on the rope," Rune told herself, as the rope jumped in her hands as St. Benedict climbed it.

Then the Poh roared as it leapt up the side of the box, its claws digging into the wood with painful sounding squeals. The length of its horn swooped by Rune so fast, she felt the air blow against her cheek. With involuntary, animalistic panic, she screamed and tried to dodge away, but her foot was caught in the stirrup, and she immediately fell sideways. Then the Poh was on top of her, its paws planted on either side of her head. Its long horse-shaped face leaning over her, waving side to side as it turned first one eye then the other to peer down on her, very unhorse-like.

Rune screamed so hard she wasn't making any sound, only an airy whistle. Suddenly, the Poh stuck its nose down at her, the cold, slimy feeling dabbing away at her face while its foul-smelling breath blew up her nose. Then a warm and cold sensation rolled through her, raising goosebumps all along her flesh. A single thought poked through Rune's terror, like a light in the middle of a storm.

"Are you reading my aura?" she squeaked out loud, sounding croaky. The Poh lifted its head abruptly and snuffed once like it was disappointed.

"Faerie Friend! Faerie Friend!" piped the little voice of brave Acorn, and the Poh leaned forward once again as if trying to suss out the little person in her hair.

Then it screamed, whipping its head up as something dropped on it from above. The momentum sent both it and the Poh over the side of the elevated crates, crashing to the cement below. Along with the whinnying, roaring screams of the Poh, Rune heard St. Benedict cry out as well.

"Oh god, oh no," Rune said, as she rolled up to crawl on all fours to look over the edge of the crates at the ground below, fearing she would see the bloody end of her partner. The Poh was just below her, pushing itself to its feet, St. Benedict's knife sticking out of its back, basted in black-red blood. The Saint was also on his back a few feet beside it, stunned and grabbing his opposite shoulder in pain.

"St. Benedict," she called out, and their eyes locked. He gave her a half-smile and took a deep breath, trying to roll onto his hands and knees, but it looked awkward and wrong as he did it.

"Just wait! I'll come down to you!" Rune called, as she desperately scanned up and down the crate she was looking over, trying to figure out how exactly she was going to do that.

"No, stay up there!" he answered.

The sounds of their voices seemed to rouse the stunned creature, and it yowled like an enraged cat. With uncanny agility, it sprang to its paws.

Both the Poh and the Saint crouched like mirror images of the other, staring each other down. St. Benedict flashed it a feral smile. "Here kitty, kitty, horse thing. You son of a bitch."

The Poh answered with another yowl.

Before the Poh could make a move, St. Benedict lunged at it, leaping for its back, and the knife still stuck there, but then he feinted at the last second. While the Poh tried to slash right, he rolled left, tumbling on to his feet, this time behind the nightmare creature.

"St. Benedict, here!" Rune shouted, trying to reach a hand down to haul him up, but he ignored her.

He rolled again to the left as the Poh took a swipe at him. Blood spurted from St. Benedict's body as the claws connected, spraying red across the boards of the crates. The Saint took advantage of the hit to spin with the slash. In a tumbling feat, his momentum vaulted him onto the creature's horse-like back, grasping at the knife to keep himself seated. His dress shirt hung open, shredded across the front, and the Poh went utterly mad, bucking back onto its horse hoofed hind legs, twisting and spinning to dislodge its attacker.

Rune watched helplessly from above. She had no spells to throw at the thing, no weapons, and no skills to take out a creature of nightmare. Even her knowledge of the manifestations of nightmare magic was pretty useless except to understand exactly how dead they both were.

But then, I'm not dead, am I? Rune thought. *I should have been a disemboweled corpse. Sure, I am a Faerie Friend, yet what would a nightmare care for that?* She did not have a scratch on her. Was it pure dumb luck? Her companion, on the other hand, was another story; his wounds attesting to how hard the Poh was trying to kill him.

"I have to get us out of here," she said to herself. Again she reached out to find the door that they had come through. It was there at the end of this aisle of crates, suddenly only ten feet away. It didn't seem like a door. All she could see was the concrete wall and a poster that said '45 days since a work-related accident', the number '45' written in blue marker. As she looked at it, the blue number faded away, and a new number was drawn in its place by an invisible hand, creating a large zero and then slashing diagonally through it. "What the hell?!" she muttered to herself.

"Rune, you can make it!" came a shout from below. "You see the door, right? Get out of here!"

"I'm not leaving you behind!" Rune shouted back.

That's when she saw it, just below her on the ground, amongst shattered pieces of amulet where Calvin had originally cast his spell; the envelope with her mortgage money. The immediate future of her bar and employees sat on the ground in the middle of the aisle a few feet from where they came in, its white face staring up. It even had the handwritten scrawl across its middle.

"We must have dropped it when we were attacked by the Poh," she said out loud.

"Rune, go!"

All hesitation gone, Rune slid over the side and dropped to the ground below. Her motion caught the Poh's attention, and it swung toward her. Rune stood up and faced down the Poh. It reared up, clawed forepaws grasping at the air as it trumpeted its challenge to her. The move solved its other problem as the knife in its back lost purchase in the smoky flesh and came free. St. Benedict fell back, the air knocked out of him again as he slammed against the crates and crumpled to the ground at the Poh's rear feet.

The Poh pranced onto all fours, dancing in triumph, kicking its back legs into the boxes just above St. Benedict's head.

"Stop it! Stop!" Rune screamed and rushed over to St. Benedict, placing herself between him and the Poh.

The Poh stopped its bucking and trotted about in a circle, its wicked horn swishing like a sword. It licked at the blood on one of its paws as it studied the new situation.

"Rune, what are you doing?" St. Benedict croaked behind her.

Without turning, she replied, "Get up. I don't think it will hurt me for some reason."

"You idiot. You should have stayed up there," he told her, groaning as he used the side of the crate to gain his feet again.

"You're the idiot. You're single-handedly fighting a bloodthirsty nightmare monster," she shot back. Rune reached back without moving her eyes from the Poh, which stopped in mid-lick of its paw to emit a low, menacing growl.

She took St. Benedict's arm and placed it around her own middle. "I'm your shield now. It can't get to you through me. We're getting out of here together," she said. "The door is ten feet behind us. We can make it. You look and pull me after you."

St. Benedict looked over his shoulder and saw the wall with its poster. "Where? Where is the door?"

"Just aim for the wall, I promise you it's there."

"How do you know?" he asked.

"Conviction," she said.

After a breath, she heard himself say softly, "I trust you." His hands on her waist guided them toward the door. As they moved, Rune kept her own arms outstretched toward the Poh. Its eyes narrowed intelligently, and it set its paw down. After two more steps, the Poh countered their movement, its head down as it alternated between sinister yowling and its grating whinnying.

"Don't stop," Rune said when it began to follow them, and St. Benedict hesitated. She didn't dare break eye contact with the nightmare's blood-red eyes. "It's keeping pace with us. It won't harm me, just keep moving." After several more steps along the edge of the crates, Rune stepped on something.

"Oh!" she said softly. She rolled her foot over it and it made a crinkly sound.

"What's wrong?"

Very slowly, she pointed with one of her fingers, turning it under but not daring to lower it. "The money. My mortgage money, it's just down at my feet."

"We're going to have to leave it."

"But it's right there," she said, resisting St. Benedict's pull to go backward. The Poh stopped its own advance and waited silently for the first time, like it was waiting to see what she would do.

"Why won't you attack me, huh, big guy?" Rune asked it. It did not respond, only stared its bloody gaze with unnerving stillness like a stone statue. "I wonder why? I've been wondering that for a little bit now." Slowly, Rune bent her knees while she spoke, forcing her companion behind her to go down with her.

"Rune," St. Benedict said in warning, "We're almost to the door."

Her fingers brushed across the rough concrete, feeling the ground for the envelope. "Don't worry, I won't let it stop us, I swear. I just..." She found it, her pointer finger brushing across the corner of the paper envelope.

The Poh's eyes narrowed further to red slits when she touched it. She could swear the billowing blackness began to grow from its back. That's when it sprang.

Rune cried out an incoherent sound as the world slowed for a moment, and she saw the horn aim for her middle. She knew it would pierce through her and then St. Benedict behind her. For some reason, she had time to think about whether it would hurt or not. How fast would she die like that? Would it be instantaneous, or would she linger? She had been so sure it wouldn't hurt her. It was such a dumb gamble.

The seconds boomed past as the horn came closer and closer. Then it slowed — or rather, the distance between her body and its horn remained constant as she was pulled backward. Sight and sound rushed back in a hurry as St. Benedict hauled her bodily through the door. Then they were through and back into the atrium.

"Close the door!" Rune shouted. Involuntarily, her Sight opened. Tendrils of light, reacting to her command, snaked across the door, filling it closed.

The Poh realized too late what was happening and roared, powerless to stop its prey from escaping. It slammed both paws into the wall. On the atrium's side, Rune panted heavily, unable to gulp down enough air as she stared wide-eyed with her normal sight. The doorway still seemed open on her side, but the magic seal within kept the Poh raging on the other side.

"That was... so stupid..." St. Benedict said, also panting, his breath rising and falling quickly against her back. They had landed backward onto the ground, Rune sitting squarely between his legs, her back to his front. He still had an arm around her waist and clung to her tightly, the adrenaline pumping in his body, not ready to let her go.

"It can't get through," Rune said, patting his arm reassuringly. "It can't get through."

"Did you get it?" he asked.

It took a minute for Rune to process the question, then she lifted her right hand with her envelope clasped in it. For some reason, she found this unbelievably funny, and she laughed. St. Benedict stared up at her hand too, and the laugh began to infect him as well.

CHAPTER 22

"That was quite a brush with death," said a musical voice, just as their laughter began to die down.

Rune was unsurprised to see Lady Trella, leaning by a tree just over their shoulder. The afternoon light created a corona around her. She was as orange as ever, a bright flower in the exotic green of the garden.

"What are you doing here?" Rune asked because she didn't know what else to say.

"The little ones cried. There is not a Faerie whose life passes from this world, that its people do not know of it. And so we came. Especially now that you opened the way for us. So, thanks, man."

"We," Rune repeated, picking up on the deliberate pronoun change.

From the shadows amongst the trees and foliage, figures appeared all around with skeletal painted faces.

"What did you call these guys again? The monochromes?" St. Benedict asked, as he assessed their situation with a casual air. The monochromes' black stares didn't seem to shake him.

"I see you still retain your warrior. Have you solved his problem yet?" Lady Trella asked.

Rune double blinked and then looked back at St. Benedict. He was roughed up, with a cut on his lip that trickled a little blood. The slashes of his shirt were glued down to his chest and edged with red. She knew he had been knocked around, not only dislocating his shoulder but possibly breaking other bones as well — and he just sat there flashing her a nonchalant smile.

"What? Is there something on my face?" he asked her.

"Are you healing?" she asked and in a blink, she opened her Sight. It was becoming second nature to her. Her eyes widened as she saw what she had seen in the elevator, the green traces of her healing spell dancing around his body. There was a concentration of the glistening threads going to work on his lip and at the back of his skull where he had impacted, fixing and healing.

"My spell... how can it still be healing you without you going mad?" she asked, mostly to herself, as she scooted back from him and opened the rents in his shirt. There were a few jagged gouges near his top left shoulder and at the right lower section of his ribs. The rest of the blood seemed to just be long smears originating from those two deeper points. Otherwise, there was only unbroken skin underneath.

"See, not so bad," he said, taking the remnants of his shirt from her fingers and covering his bare chest.

"But you're not going mad with hunger? Your metabolism..."

"I took care of it, don't worry," he said, as he tried to layer his torn shirt over itself and tucked it in to make himself decent again. He grunted in pain when he tried to push off the ground with his left arm. Though he managed not to grab the shoulder, a spasm went down to his fingers. It was more than enough to tell the threat around him that he was compromised.

The monochromes didn't move a muscle, just kept watching as Lady Trella approached.

"Clever man, using your artificial magic to control a true spell. While it is said that magic and technology don't mix, you seem to be living proof that that's a load of crap," she said delightedly. She crouched down next to him, her skirt covering her legs to make her look like an orange frog as she peered at him, fascinated.

"Clever. I suppose so," he said with bravado, leaning back a little as if her close proximity and curious gaze were invading his personal space.

She blinked and seemed to come to a decision.

"You said I let you in, how... how did I do that?" Rune asked.

"You showed us the way into the building, the way to enter without an invitation. Our hearts have greatly desired to return to this place, to bring our children home." She held out her hand, and sitting in the middle was Acorn, holding, to Rune's shock, her mortgage money envelope.

"What?!" Rune exclaimed, looking down uselessly into her now empty hand.

"Be careful what you set on the ground. Children don't know when to leave what's not theirs alone," the larger Fae said as little Acorn gave a cheerful little wave.

"Please, give that back to me. My life depends on it," Rune said, grimacing at the cliché statement, but it was the truth.

"And these little lives depend on your help. Will you please give it now? In exchange, we will hold on to this for you until you need it," the orange lady offered.

"Depend on me how?"

"Where did that little person come from?" St. Benedict asked, but no one heard him.

"Little kin are not property!" Acorn shouted, raising a fist like a tiny revolutionary.

"Property? What do you mean?" Rune asked.

"According to heartless corporate law, little people are not recognized as anything better than pets. These children were snatched when the Hall of Cold Numbers stole our court," Lady Trella said sadly.

"I don't want to carry packages anymore!" Acorn lamented.

"Hall of Cold Numbers?" St. Benedict asked.

"Corporations?" Rune offered, trying to decipher the riddle. She liked it better when Lady Trella was the orange hippie versus the cryptic Fae Lady.

"Oh. I get it. The new thing in the upper echelons," St. Benedict agreed. "Have your own personal pixie pet."

"You knew about this?" Rune asked, shocked.

"No. I'm just trying to follow the logic here. I didn't know little Faeries were a thing 'til two minutes ago," St. Benedict nodded at Acorn.

"We ask only one thing, Heir of the Magdalene. Please, for the sake of the alliance and love between our Court and your House, help us save our people," Lady Trella asked, bowing her head in obeisance. As one, the monochromes, in their shadowed places, knelt as well. It felt like the ancient times to Rune. The monochromes were knights of old beseeching with honor from the powerful wise wizard. Unfortunately for them, they were asking her.

"I'll do what I can."

Abruptly, St. Benedict grabbed Rune's arm, pulling her up from the ground where she still sat on the same level as Lady Trella's crouch. "Rune, can I speak to you a moment? I need your help with something."

"Uh, sure," she said, the metaphorical spell broken. She followed him, not that she really had a choice, as he was already dragging her over to a tree a few feet away. A monochrome man rose as they approached.

"Hey, kid, glad to see I didn't kill you. You want to skedaddle over there for a moment?" St. Benedict said, jerking a thumb over to where Lady Trella also had popped up to her feet. Rune was surprised to realize that the younger monochrome man, with his hair particularly swoopy, was indeed the kid who St. Benedict had attacked the day before. His expression was a little hard to read, but the kid's too-quick movements as he passed them conveyed his anxiety about being too close to St. Benedict.

"St. Benedict, I..." Rune started.

"Don't talk, just listen, and grab my arm a sec. I need a hand here," he said, pitching his voice to a whisper as he glanced over her shoulder to count again how many hostiles he saw. "Fifteen accounted for unless they got more I can't see."

"What are you doing?" she whispered back.

"Calculating odds, now... Okay, hold onto my upper arm here at the elbow with both your hands and don't let go. Come stand in front of me." Unsure, Rune complied, encircling her smaller fingers around his firmly muscled upper arm. "Brace your feet too." She stepped a foot back, glancing over at the others, who watched curiously.

"Alright, I will do most of the work. Just do what I say, and I think I can get this back in," he said as he grabbed onto Rune's shoulder with the hand connected to the elbow she was holding.

When he winced, Rune became even more uncomfortable. "St. Benedict, what are you about to do?" she asked as he started to take several fast, deep breaths.

Suddenly, he jerked his shoulders back, and there was a loud popping sound. Rune yelped and lost her grip. "Oh, god! What did you...? Are you okay?"

He sighed in relief. "Yes, calibrations done," he said.

"That's not an answer," Rune said.

He chuckled a little. "I suppose not to you. It's a Saint joke. Don't worry about it."

Rune glanced down at the ground, biting her lip. "Look, St. Benedict, I know what I said over there but...about your team. We'll find them. I'll figure it out—" Rune started, but he cut her off.

"No, you're going with them," he said, nodding toward the Fae. "We've probably lost our shot of getting my team back. I'm going to have to regroup with St. Rachel and figure something else out. We'll part ways here."

"No, I can't do that. I have to help you find Malachi—"

"Yes, you can, Rune. You made another deal. Don't worry about me. I'm not worth it. I'm just a tool. Treat me like a tool."

"You're not—"

"Rune, listen to me, they have your payment. I can't get it back from them, not right now, with these cards that I have left to play. You go with them, get out of here. Get your money and don't even think twice about it," he said sincerely, which just made Rune's heart ache more.

"Exactly what kind of person do you think I am?" Rune asked.

"A good one. A very good one," he said, which made her pause her follow-up argument. "And I am a very bad person. Someone like you shouldn't worry about a piece of garbage like me. My only worth is in the service I can render to you. The right move for you here is to dump me for the better offer. There is nothing wrong with that."

Rune didn't know what to say at first, so she said nothing.

"With all those guys there, you have a much better chance of getting out of here alive and unharmed," he continued.

"I don't care about that," she heard herself say finally. "I mean, I do care about being alive, but I don't care... I mean I won't leave you... like this."

His smile took on a frustrated turn and he huffed at her. "Fine then. Look at it this way. Their cause is far nobler than mine. They're trying to save their children, right?"

"Well, yes... sort of..." Rune hedged. "That's not quite right—"

"Look, I get it, cultural context and all, doesn't make sense but I don't have time for you to explain it all to me."

He took her hand in both of his and kissed the back gallantly. Then he turned to the orange lady and nodded toward her. "Ma'am, it was a pleasure to see you. Hope I never do again."

Lady Trella looked genuinely surprised. "The Heir of the Magdalene is turning me down?"

"No, not at all, she is completely on board with your search-and-rescue project. I, however, am not," he said, then turned on his heel and started walking away, his feet crunching against the small gravel on the path. All of the eyes of the monochromes followed as he went silently.

"St. Benedict, wait. I can do both, we can all get out of here together," Rune tried, but he didn't look back. "St. Benedict!" Rune called, half-admonishing, half-pleading.

He turned then, and his smile softened a little. "Good luck," he said just to her, then looked over at the small group of black men and one single orange lady. "Don't suppose any of you happened to see which way those I'm looking for went?" They stared stoically back at him and he shrugged. "Worth a shot."

Just before he turned away, one monochrome man on the edge pointed toward the back of the atrium. "Second from the back," he said and received a smack on the arm from the one standing next to him. St. Benedict saluted a 'thanks' and turned away for the final time.

Rune didn't like any of this, but she was torn in the middle. How could she abandon the little Faeries? But St. Benedict...

"He is noble in his own way, isn't he?" Lady Trella said, appearing beside Rune as they watched him go.

"I don't think so," Rune said, more bitter than she intended.

"Can we go now?" a high-pitched whine came from the orange lady's shoulder, Acorn having had enough with waiting.

"Yes, we may. Play the call!" Lady Trella declared as if commencing a party. One of the monochrome men pulled out a flute from some mysterious pocket and started to play a lively tune. The notes danced through the air, tripping and trilling up and down the scales. After the first stanza, the garden, in the full light of the afternoon, became even more aglow with Faerie light.

Colors of every hue of the rainbow poured out of the trees and leaves, swarming around the larger black men, their colors popping even more than before. With shrieks of joy and laughter, the pixies landed all over the monochromes, finding perches on their shoulders and inside the pockets of their coats. Several of the men opened up black satchels that they carried across their chests and lowered them to the ground for the brownies and other ground Faeries to climb into. When all of the shoulders had been taken, the remaining pixies chained together like long whips of flowers so that every one of them was somehow connected to one of the larger members of the Fae. Even the orange lady had her share, though somehow it was only the orange- to yellow-colored pixies that had chosen to alight with her.

"Should I take some?" Rune asked, wondering why none of them came to her.

"No, wizardess. That is not necessary. You will need to be free, so you can lead us out of here," Lady Trella said.

A thread of anxiety wound through Rune as she met the expectant eyes looking at her to lead them out. What was she going to do?

A tiny tickle feeling drew Rune's attention from her thoughts to her shoulder. Acorn, without her noticing, had appeared there, holding onto her hair as it sat on her shoulder. It gave her a toothy smile.

"What are you doing there, traitor?" Rune asked.

"We go home now?" Acorn asked.

Rune furrowed her eyebrows a moment. "Isn't this place your home?" She looked around at the Faeries gathered around her.

"Our home is where we are," Lady Trella said cryptically, the hippie vibe warming her voice as she smiled. Rune nodded understanding.

"Home is family, sure," she agreed, watching the way the small Faeries laughed and petted the monochromes, who were very gentle with each of them.

"Lead the way, wizardess. Lead us away from this graveyard," the orange lady declared dramatically with a flourish of her hand.

Rune double blinked. "Graveyard?"

Around the small band, mist began creeping out from between the trees and bushes. The air became crisper and colder with a taint of bog in it. The afternoon light had grayed into the harshness of an oncoming storm. The swift shift in the atmosphere had a sobering effect on the pixies, who stopped their singing and laughing to pull closer to the now wary dark shadows that protected them. Their bright lights dimmed and Rune's thoughts replayed the fierce flashes of light when their kindred had died to stray bullets.

Not again. Not on my watch, Rune thought, resolutely, the strength for what she must do burning from deep inside her. She was not going to let herself be intimidated into inaction anymore.

"What's happening?" One of the younger monochromes, more like a teenager, asked.

"It's the Faerie Court, kiddo. It is not like the world outside, where it stays still until affected upon. The Faerie Court is ever-changing, ever-shifting. Our door to leave is closing," Lady Trella said serenely yet ominously, swaying as if there was music playing that only she could hear.

"We've gotta move now," Rune said, though it was mostly to herself.

A familiar howl and whinny cut through the grating air as the mist began blotting out patches of things around them. Rune wondered if the nightmare Poh had found its way through a doorway. Was it still hunting them?

"Stay together," Rune said and began walking on the gravel path that St. Benedict had disappeared down earlier.

The atrium walls were simply gone. Rune thought at first they were obscured by the mist, but as she broke from the path to head in a direction she knew she had seen a door set in the glass wall, all she found was a door standing in the middle of nothing.

"What the hell?" she muttered to herself and approached it. Instead of an open entryway, there was an actual wood-paneled door with a brass knocker and a brass bar instead of a doorknob.

"The doors are already closing," Lady Trella said, to a chorus of anxious pixie screams. The piper had stopped playing a while ago, and the lack of his song wasn't helping.

"Hey, piper guy, play something," Rune said, pointing to the monochrome man, who still held the pipe in his hands.

"What should I play?" he asked, his blank, white eyes moving in a way that Rune would call darting if he had pupils.

"Something 'feel good'," Rune said, her own mind blanking on any song names. "Something that you like that makes you happy."

The piper stood there a moment, his fingers lightly tapping over the holes as if he was already playing.

"Play "Honey, I'm Good!" one of the pixies in his wreath shouted.

"No! "I Can't Get No Satisfaction!" another shouted.

"No, Beatles! Play "Help!" said a third, which set off a chorus of giggles.

Then the piper thought of something and brought the pipe to his lips. He played three bars of music, and then as one all the Faeries sang out, "Jeremiah was a bullfrog! Was a good friend of mine!"

Rune's face broke into a huge grin and returned her focus to the problem of the door. Walking around it confirmed that the atrium wall was gone. Trying the door handle and knocking the knocker also did nothing. It neither opened nor budged.

"Apertus," Rune said to the door. It still didn't budge.

"Didn't really want to go through that way anyway," Rune said with a sniff and peered at their surroundings through the ever-thickening mist. The garden they had been in was completely swallowed and replaced by ominous trees and tombstones. Thankfully, Rune saw another door barely outlined in the mist. It was further away than it had been in the atrium, but she didn't know if that was because the doors were disappearing or if the space itself was changing.

Another whinny-roar, this one echoing from everywhere, abruptly cut off the silly singing and piping.

"Come on, this way, hurry," Rune said softly, touching Acorn, who clung harder to her hair.

The band of Fae followed quietly now, trekking through the forest toward the next door.

"Okay, what are the chances this one is still open?" Rune asked out loud as they approached. This one was metal with a handle, very institutional looking.

"Only the king or queen can unlock the doors," Lady Trella answered her, her usual twinkle dampened.

Rune nodded. "And you are not exactly here with the queen's permission."

"The queen... has lost her senses entirely. The king, as you know..." the orange Fae said softly as Rune started looking around the door.

"Betrayed you all," Rune finished, nodding.

"He's dead. The king is dead."

Rune went still as she took that in. "He's dead?"

The heavy silence of the Fae confirmed it more than a yes would.

"But I thought... that isn't possible. The Oberon and the Titania always die and are reborn together," Rune said. What Rune knew of the Faerie social structure was limited, and the Fae, even when they held power, kept their inner workings fairly private. But two years ago, when the Oberon, King of the Faeries, had betrayed his people, selling the Faerie Court to the corporate world, she had learned that particular secret.

The wind howled again, a strange wind that seemed to have a mind of its own.

"What is that?!" one of the monochromes called out, pointing into the void of the misty air. A black tendril of smoke whipped around with the wind like it was blindly seeking something.

"What the hell is that?!" a brownie shouted in even more alarm.

"Our cue to leave. Come on, everyone, let's keep moving." Rune reached out a hand to one of the monochromes. "Everyone link up, don't lose each other. We can make it to the next door, I promise," she lied.

"Have faith, kiddos. This has happened before. The Wizard led our people to the wood door, then the door of metal, lastly the door of dreams, and through that to the realm of devils," the orange lady declared like she was uttering theatrical prophecy in her own personal production of Shakespeare in the park.

"Right, realm of devils," Rune said, nodding, figuring it would be better to give the group some confidence and hope.

They walked through the mist for endless minutes, the haze so thick that Rune only saw anything when they passed a tree. It was unexpectedly sudden when she came nose to wall with a mausoleum. If she hadn't had her hand out in front of her, she would have smashed right into it. As it was, the palm of her hand stung against the rough side of the cold concrete instead of her nose.

"It's not a door," she said dumbly to the wall, then glanced back at the fae, the end of the train almost swallowed up by the mist. "Can you guys do anything, like create light or erect a barrier?"

"We are men of shadows," the nearest said, a tall one with hawkish features, as if that was obvious.

"I can change my color!" piped one pixie.

"I can burp the entire alphabet in Spanish," said a brownie proudly, and started to demonstrate.

"Right," Rune said, smiling indulgently as she moved around the mausoleum. The building was the size of a shed and to her surprise, the front had a lit lantern above it. Rune's eyes almost popped out when she saw the miniature version of the front of the Lucky Devil, her bar. It was cast in concrete, down to the minutest detail. "Wow. What... what is this?" Rune asked, taking a few steps back to look at it fully. The only thing that wasn't miniature about the concrete replica was the door. It looked exactly like the front door of the bar.

That's when it all made sense; why Lady Trella was so sure that Rune could lead them out of there. While the other doors could only be opened by the queen or the king, there was one door, only one, that Maddie alone could open. And now, presumably, so could Rune, as it was a shared part of her Wizard's House.

To test the theory, Rune went up to the door. "Apertus," she breathed. There was a clicking sound, and the door swung open of its own accord, easily and soundlessly. Through the door, Rune saw the warm, familiar interior. She saw the bar, and the tables spread out in the room and even the edge of Lucky Devil's booth. A cheer came up from the little people at the sight of the bar beyond.

The wind blew around again, drawing in more of the darker smoke, instead of blowing away the fog. It had not only a chill to it, but a sulfurous smell as well.

"Oh, so close," a mirthful voice said from over Rune's right shoulder. She spun around and standing clearly, untainted by the mist, was the well-dressed woman.

"What the hell are you doing here?" Rune called into the wind, her voice almost carried away by it. The well-dressed woman's voice came out loud and clear.

"What do you think you are doing, Anna?" she asked like a mother who had caught her daughter breaking curfew. Rune squared her shoulders and swallowed past the unbidden lump in her throat.

"I'm sorry, have we met? You keep calling me this Anna woman, and I have no idea who you are talking about. My name is Rune Leveau and I'm pretty sure what we are doing is none of your business," Rune answered and tried to gesture subtly for Lady Trella and her crew to go through the door.

"I think it is very much my business. Anything you do is my business. You are my responsibility," she said, the same ice in her voice. The black mist rolled back more, billowing like a backdrop behind her.

"The door is open, go through," Rune said to the Faeries, keeping her eyes fixed on the woman turned demon. Not one of them moved. "What's going on? Go! Go."

Abruptly, light burst forth, boiling away the fog. Rune looked away from the well-dressed woman toward the Faeries and the source of the light. They all stood still, staring at the well-dressed woman in shock. Lady Trella stood next to them, her hand alight with flame. A roiling ball of energy akin to a miniature sun floated over her palm. It burned away the mist, casting real, long shadows onto the ground. As the white mist rolled back though, the black smoke remained, its tendrils more real and familiar now that they were clearer. They crisscrossed above the well-dressed woman, leading into a twelve-foot shadowy mass hovering behind her.

The well-dressed woman looked smug.

"You have already lost, Anna. If you come quietly now, I'll forgive you for everything. We'll start fresh. A clean slate—"

"A new day," Rune Anna Leveau finished the familiar epitaph.

"Rune, please," Lady Trella said desperately, her voice straining like it was difficult. "Get the children out."

"I don't understand. Let's go," Rune encouraged. The monochromes stared at the black smoke as if hypnotized.

"Go with her, children, go," Lady Trella said, her flame trembling around her hand.

The pixies detached from the monochromes, and each of the larger Fae dropped the bags they were carrying.

"You still don't seem to understand how screwed you are, Ru... Anna. I know you're stupid, but even this is ridiculous," the well-dressed lady cawed. Rune turned to shoot a dirty look at her, but that's when she saw the shape of the dark tendrils complete its manifestation behind her. It was the Poh, or at least a bigger, darker, angrier version of the Poh. Its horn flashed wickedly as it bucked its head and trumpeted a roar. A shiver rolled through the monochromes as one and Rune's eyes went wide.

"What...?" she started to say, but then the well-dressed woman started to cackle.

"Oh, I just have to tell you what's going on. I can't stand it anymore," she declared, then pointed a finger over her head at the great swinging head of the Poh. "The Kodiak Corp not only acquired the Faerie Court but the spirit of the Oberon as well, and he is our slave. Every one of your little friends is now subject to his will. Have I explained how screwed you are thoroughly enough for you?"

"Excuse me, a moment," the orange Faerie declared, the sun in her hand burning a moment brighter against the oncoming shadows. "I am Trella of the First, and I am still in full control of my faculties, good sir."

"Ma'am," Rune muttered.

"Madame," Lady Trella doubled down.

Lady Trella's declaration made the well-dressed woman check herself. "But you are a subject of the Faerie Court?" she asked.

"Yes, I must obey my liege, but I still have enough will before he commands to order all the little ones through the door now!" she shouted. In a squee of delight, the pixies rushed through the Lucky Devil door. The brownies and other smaller unspecific Fae bailed from their bags and rushed the door as well.

"No! Wait!" the well-dressed woman shouted, but none of the little folk heeded her, and in a trice, they were through the door. "No, grab her! Grab Rune Lev...dammit! Anna Masterson!"

Lady Trella did just that, grabbing Rune's arm.

"No!" Rune tried to shout, but the frail, elderly-looking orange Faerie was stronger than she had seemed.

"I must obey. I have grabbed you," she said. "And now I'm gonna throw you through the door because nothing else has been said about that." Rune could barely protest before she was thrown backward through the door, her eyes wide in surprise as it slammed shut solidly.

For several breaths, Rune waited, lying on her back on her bar's floor, staring at her closed front door.

Nothing happened.

"It's alright, child, you can leave the door now. They can't come through," Maddie said, a note of amusement in her voice.

CHAPTER 23

Rune turned in a hurry. Something that looked exactly like her Aunt Maddie smiled at her. She looked Rune up and down from where she stood next to Lucky Devil's booth.

"You look mostly the same, so I'm guessing I've only died recently," she said, setting a bottle of whiskey on the table.

Rune tried to work her mouth, but it just wouldn't function. Maddie looked back at Rune with furrowed eyebrows, concerned. Rune didn't need to say anything as those same eyebrows shot up in understanding.

"Oh, gods, child. I've just died," Maddie said, understanding softening her voice.

That opened the gate inside, and the tears flooded down Rune's face, and then those same warm, safe arms were around her cooing at her, holding her. Rune clawed at the smaller body of the older woman like she was the only anchor left in the sea of her grief. Rune cried and cried for ages until there were no tears left in all of the world.

"Okay. Okay, girl. That's it, you're fine now. It's alright," Maddie said.

"No, it's not. It's not. It can't be," Rune struggled to say.

"Alright, you are alright. You are alright."

"You're not real," Rune tried to argue, her voice coming back with a bit of warble.

"Of course, I'm not, sweetie. I'm dead," she said as if it was a joke. She gestured a finger around the room. "This isn't real either, in case you were wondering." Looking around the room, it seemed real enough, from the bar to the back of the booth where Lucky Devil sat drinking his whiskey. Rune double blinked. Lucky Devil was literally sitting there drinking whiskey in his booth, his wicked smile flashing at Rune. He noticed her observing him and raised a shot glass to her that he then downed before turning the glass over and setting it on the table.

"You leave it hanging open, flies are going to fly in, kiddo," Lucky Devil said to Rune as he picked up the whiskey bottle and unscrewed the cap. She closed her mouth in response, and Maddie laughed her merry laugh, turning to join Lucky Devil in the booth. Then he did something Rune had never ever seen before; he scooted to the right to let the older wizardess sit down.

"Let me down! Let me down! I want to play," Acorn called, and Rune moved as if mechanical, picking up the little brownie from her shoulder and letting it down to the ground. The pixies and other little Fae were dancing around the room, tearing it up as they played. Acorn cheered as it ran off to join its friends.

"Come, dear, it's alright. If we meant you harm, you'd already be doomed at this point. That or you'll miraculously escape out of our little trap. Either way, you might as well have a seat," Maddie said, gesturing to the booth bench opposite them.

"Harm? Why would you do me harm?" Rune spoke, her brain chugging out the question.

"No clue. We just thought you thought we were some sort of evil illusion or something. We're not," Lucky Devil said, cutting Maddie off to answer for her.

"No, she knows that. She can tell the difference between illusions and not," Maddie admonished.

Rune looked at the door behind her, wondering if she opened it and left, would she be on the street in front of her bar, or would she be back in the Faerie Court? Where was St. Benedict? Was he alright?

"Rock and a hard place, right? Well, this hard place has the hard stuff!" Lucky Devil said as he poured out three shots before sliding one across the table and in the same move he made to take a shot for himself. "Sit down, girl, I'm tired of drinking alone, and now I got the two best-looking girls in the bar."

"This is a dream," Rune said, staring again at her aunt.

"See, I told you, she would figure it out. Though for clarification, this is one of many dreams imprinted on the bar. Dreams with the stuff of magic in them, so they have the potential to be made real. There are several dreamtimes in the bar. At some point, you're going to have to explore all of them."

"This is magical?" Rune asked, looking around again.

"Yes. One of my better spells, really. This is one I set up for the first time you crossed over into the dreamscape." Dream Maddie smiled brighter. "It looks like you have become head of the House. I knew you could do it." Maddie took up her shot and clinked it with Lucky Devil's.

"But, Maddie, I... I'm not really a wizard — " Rune started, but Maddie waved her hand as Lucky Devil held out Rune's shot for her to take.

"No, no. I don't need to hear more. This is your journey. I'm just here to help answer any questions. Think of me as a mystical clone from a sci-fi novel. I'm just an imprinted copy of all of my knowledge at the moment I made this dreamscape for you. You'll be able to ask me questions about things I knew at the time, if I can remember them," Maddie said.

"You make that sound so reasonable," Rune stated.

Dream Maddie double blinked. "Isn't it?"

"No. No. Most people don't leave magical clones of themselves for their relatives to find in dreamscapes," Rune said, her voice registering higher as she started to freak out.

"Well, I was one of the most powerful wizardesses in the world, sweetie. It's reasonable to assume I didn't do a lot of things like most people." Maddie's smile never wavered, only her eyes crinkled even more with bright mirth.

Rune couldn't argue with that. Somehow, that helped calm her down a bit, and her shoulders dropped in response. "When did you make this dream?" Rune asked.

"I have no idea, really. That part is kind of blurry. Oh! I also wrote you several books that you should look through. Left you lots of notes. I was created to help you understand them all. But don't worry, I won't be asking you any questions about your life now, I won't remember them anyway. I'll forget everything again once you leave here," she said.

"Crap on that, I have a question. What's with all the little fireflies and walking mushrooms?" Luck Devil asked.

"We came from the Faerie Court," Rune said, finally sitting down across from them in the booth. She wasn't sure if she was ready to accept all of this yet, but she decided she might as well sit. After everything that had just happened over the course of the day, Lucky Devil actually talking to her made as much sense as sitting across from her dead aunt's magical illusion ghost — and her backside was feeling stiff from being shoved by Lady Trella anyway.

"Oh, how is Titania? I haven't talked to her in ages!" Maddie declared, clasping her hands together in pleasure.

Lucky Devil paused with his glass partway to his lips. "I thought you weren't going to ask any questions."

"Oh, right, I forgot."

"Well, actually," Rune started, "could I tell you what is happening, and then you can give me advice as if you were Maddie? I know you won't remember it but you would still be able to tell me what you would do, right?"

"I suppose so," Maddie nodded. "You have a problem in the Faerie Court?"

"Sort of. There is someone I left behind. We parted ways after I promised to help him to help save these little ones," Rune said, gesturing with a finger at the swarm of twinkling lights dancing around the hanging stained-glass lighting fixtures. "I think I should go back and help him, but I don't know what I could do."

"Oh, Rune, don't you think you're underestimating yourself?" Maddie asked. Lucky Devil took another shot.

"No. I think I have a very clear estimate of myself, and it's not just that, there's the other Fae there. They're being used by a malevolent force, and I'm afraid more innocent beings are going to be hurt for no good reason. But if I do go back, well…" Rune looked around the bar. It looked exactly like the real one.

"What is it, dear?" Lucky Devil took a shot. "Just say it all."

"It's just so selfish," Rune chided herself.

"It's okay to be selfish," Maddie answered.

"If that clock there is correct, I have an hour before the mortgage payment is due, and if I don't get it in, I'll for sure lose this place. Lose everything you left me."

"But, we have a grace period…" Then Maddie checked herself. "Oh, no wait. I see what you're saying. They have started to make moves against you now that I'm gone. Yes, I was afraid of that."

"But that doesn't even matter, I guess, because I lost the payment," Rune said, taking down the shot waiting for her on the table.

"Ms. Leveau!" a little voice shouted from the ground. Everyone looked over the side of the table down at Acorn, who stood there holding an envelope the size of the Publishers Clearing House Check relative to its little body. "Lady Trella said to give this to you."

"There, you see," Maddie said with a pleased smile. "Now you don't have to go back."

"You are already two shots down," Lucky Devil said, refilling Maddie's shot glass.

"I shouldn't," Rune said.

"What's wrong?" Lucky Devil asked, his horns waving at Rune as he turned his head drunkenly; the hat kept in place only by the horns themselves.

"I don't think I should really be drinking when I'm in the middle of a life-or-death situation," Rune said, before adding, "sorry."

"Well, if this is just a dream, does it really matter?" he asked before downing his and Rune's refill in quick succession. He opened up both red hands, still holding the shot glasses, and gave the gesture for 'give me applause.' Maddie complied, with Rune offering a token clap a few seconds later. A pang stabbed through her heart afresh at her aunt's smiling face.

"Maddie," Rune said softly. Maddie sobered, but never stopped smiling. Instead, she reached across the table and took Rune's hand.

"I know, child, I know. It's been hard on you, hasn't it?"

"I'm so sorry, Maddie."

"For heaven's sake, why?"

"I'm a failure! I can't do it. I'm losing the bar. Everything I do, it falls apart. I don't know what to do, and everyone is looking at me to fix it, I'm so...so sorry," Rune hiccupped out.

"But why is the bar so important to you?" she asked. Rune stared at her incredulously.

"It's the bar! It's my home. It's... it's..."

"It's just a place, Rune," she said very seriously.

"It's more than just a place!" Rune shouted, standing up like her legs had a will of their own. "Why did you leave it to me, anyway? It was your legacy! All your magic, your home. You left me everything! And I don't know what to do with it all! I can't handle it! I'm not like you. I'm barely a magic user, and this thing with being your heir? How am I qualified to be the Heir of the Magdalene?"

"Your future—" Maddie tried, but Rune wouldn't let her finish.

"What future? You mean the one with the house and the kids? My marriage... I failed my marriage! God, the hottest looking guy I've seen in months...not only is he out of my league and a bad bet anyway...I just left him to die. Exactly what kind of future do I even have?!"

"...is up to you," Maddie finished as if Rune hadn't interrupted her. She sat as if she was the calm center of a storm. It was another thing that Rune dearly, dearly missed as much as she always hated it, and like always, it made her stop the ranting.

Maddie looked Rune squarely in the eyes, and for a moment, Rune wanted to push past her influence and keep screaming until there were no more words, no more tears, and no more will left to fight. Instead, she took a shuddering breath and sat down. Lucky Devil was already holding out his bright-white pocket handkerchief to Rune to blow her nose. Then Rune finally took the shot of whiskey he offered her. The burn was good, the smoky hot taste familiar and comforting, and the heat settled into the center of her chest to stay there.

"Now, I would like to make one thing clear, my girl. There is only one reason I left you all my worldly possessions, and it is not because I expected you to take up my mantle. But you can take up my mantle *if* you want it. I gave you everything because I love you." Her eyes were shining when she said that, taking Rune's hands back in hers, squeezing them firmly. "I love you fiercely, since the moment you were born, long before I discovered your Talent. I took one look at you, my dear, and my heart was gone, firmly fixed to you. And that is all there is to everything I have ever done. There is no way you could deserve it, deserving never factored in, but it was because I loved you."

"But I've brought so much grief to your life. If it wasn't for me, your bar would be safe," Rune said, but Maddie shook her head and renewed her grip.

"I would sell that place a thousand times if it meant you were safe and happy, and if being the Heir of the Magdalene is what you would like, I have left you everything you need to be that. If you don't, that's fine. That's fine, sweetie. You do not have to go back there. Those people are not your responsibility. You can walk away. That is a legitimate choice. Go out there into the wider world and live. Find what will make you happy. Find love. Have an adventure or two or twelve. All I wanted was to support you in whatever choice you made." She paused a moment and seemed to consider something, "And as for love. You will find it because it is always there. Justin…" she paused again. "I will leave you this: You will see him again, and when you do, you will have to decide for yourself what you will do about him, but when you do, I hope you find a way to let it all go, so that love can come back to you in a way that will be for your greatest good."

"You mean he and I will get back together?" Rune asked appalled, even as a small lost voice that she had buried long ago in that cold white room, still hoped he would come for her. Tell her he loved her. Tell her that it was all a mistake.

"I'm not saying that. Maybe you'll find a new love, but only after you have made room for it by letting go of what—" she stopped then at a touch of Lucky Devil's hand.

"You're saying too much, Maddie," he warned gently, and she nodded in agreement.

"It will be so hard not to give you all the answers," Maddie laughed and sat back, leaving one hand with Rune so she could use the other to wipe her own eyes. "I get now why prophecies are always given so cryptically. Otherwise, you'll spoil the endings when it's the journey you should be focusing on."

"But what about the bar?"

"Don't worry so much about the bar, kiddo," Lucky Devil said, giving Rune his signature wink. "It has a funny way of taking care of itself. How was that? Vague and mysterious enough for you?" He winked at Maddie as well, who playfully batted his arm.

Rune stared down at the envelope as the other two fell silent. Neither choice seemed great, but something was calling to her, drawing her to it. She bit her lower lip as she realized what it was she really wanted to do and it scared her to her marrow.

Delicately, with great reverence, Rune laid the envelope on the table and flattened it with her hands to push out all of the air. Then, she stood and straightened her shirt.

"So, what are you going to do?" Maddie asked.

Lucky Devil took another shot. "Gods, I'm going to go blind if I keep this up."

"I think I can help," Rune reached out her fingertips and touched the mortgage payment one last time. "I know I am probably screwing this up, but people might die, and I could try to help them. I think that's really your legacy, Aunt Maddie." Then Rune furrowed her eyebrows. "No, wait. That's not what you said. I am your legacy, and I'm going to represent you well."

Resolutely, Rune turned and went back toward her front door, grasping the necklace St. Benedict had given her, with its tiny metal box that seemed to have something clinking inside.

Just as she reached the door, Rune turned back and was struck afresh by the sight of Maddie sitting there. For a moment, the lump was back in her throat, and her eyes misted. She didn't try to suppress it this time because maybe it was just a little bit okay now. Just a little bit. "Can I see you again?"

"Yes, but we are only here for sage advice. You want answers, you better just Google it," Lucky Devil chimed in. Rune furrowed her brows and then nodded with a crooked smile on her face. "And come have a drink with me when it's done," Lucky Devil added, "I'll be here." Then he stopped, frozen in place like he always was. The bar shifted, not in any discernible way, just something was different about it, more awake. The little Fae still wandered around like children, but Maddie was gone ... or not gone.

Rune smiled to herself as she turned to go back through the door.

CHAPTER 24

St. Augustina's day was going from bad to worse.

"This place is insane!" she whispered as the fog wrapped around a tree that had appeared out of nowhere.

Their leader's fear did not inspire confidence in the rest of the group, who were already freaked out and trigger tense. It didn't help things that the two men assigned to bring Zita with them didn't know the first thing about how fast a naga could move.

"Move it, Rattler," one of them cussed at Zita. They both dragged her and her long heavy tail across the ground. She tried to move like they ordered, but she could never get enough coil under her at any given time to properly push off the ground.

"Leave her alone! She's trying," Malachi said for the hundredth time.

"I said shut up!" one of his own guards growled and promptly backhanded him across the face again.

"For god's sake!" St. Augustina cursed herself as Malachi's fresh blood sprayed across her. "Cut that out, Peterson! I really don't have time to manage your stupid."

"There's something moving in the trees!" one of the other guards half-whispered in panic. All focus turned outward as the group circled up, their prisoners dropped into the center.

It was the first time the suited lackeys had been hands-off in a while, and Malachi shuffled on his knees closer to Zita, who practically curled into a coil around herself, mewing softly.

"Hey, hey. Are you okay?" he whispered breathily to her as he laid his cheek against hers in comfort and to get his lips closer to her ear so they couldn't be overheard.

"Stop," Zita breathed, then swallowed and tried again, "Stop running your mouth so they'll focus on you and leave me be. You're going to have a brain embolism or choke on your own blood at this rate."

"Yes, doctor," Malachi said, then split apart from her suddenly as Dr. Benita knelt down next to Zita.

"Are you alright?" she asked, eyeing an oozing gash on the side of Zita's tail where it met her hip.

"Sympathy for the prisoners?" Malachi asked acidly, hooding his eyes at her.

Dr. Benita ignored him, but touched around the edges of the gash, making Zita hiss sharply. "We need to treat this," Dr. Benita said louder to her compatriots.

"Fuck the snake! It's her fault for not complying," said one of the men who hurt her, before spitting in Zita's direction. It hit Dr. Benita instead.

"It's not her fault. She tried," Malachi said. "You fucking gorillas wouldn't let her get her tail down so she could slide. Nagas need to coil up to move forward. You were practically dragging her."

"Form up, we need to keep moving. I swear to whatever god is listening, we are all getting out of here." St. Augustina held up a glowing crystal.

"What the hell is that?" the gorilla-like man asked, just as shaken by the crystal as whatever was in the mist.

"Stay quiet," St. Augustina ordered and held the crystal out in the palm of her hand. Nothing happened for several endless minutes.

"Maybe it's broke," someone said before getting shoved.

"Madam, are you a Talent?" Dr. Benita asked, adjusting her glasses.

"What? No, I'm not a filthy magic user," St. Augustina said, closing her hand around the crystal.

"Then that isn't going to work for you. It's crystal technology. You have to be at least a low-level magic user or Talent to operate those," Dr. Benita lectured.

"That damn woman gave it to me. She said it would lead us out of here," St. Augustina said, staring down at the plum-colored crystal.

"What about the snake?" one of the men suggested.

"What? No, I can't..." Zita started to protest, but it didn't stop St. Augustina from thrusting the crystal into her hand as two of the men lifted Zita up by her arms.

"No, that's a common misconception that all non-hominal peoples can inherently do magic, but—" Dr. Benita tried to relay, but no one was paying any attention to her.

Malachi, again, tried to intercede but had his legs kicked out from underneath him to land hard on his side.

"Make it work," St. Augustina ordered, thrusting the end of her gun into Zita's forehead. "This mission will not fail."

"I... I can't!" Zita tried to explain, tears running down her face.

St. Augustina shot a round into the air and replaced the gun close to Zita's forehead so she could feel the heat coming from the barrel.

"I said, make it work," St. Augustina repeated herself, enunciating each word.

A distinct tang of piss came from below Zita, hanging from her captor's arms. Her face twisted up as she started balling her serpentine eyes out.

"I'm a doctor. A doctor!" she continued to cry out.

"Leave her alone! NO!" Malachi screamed as he struggled to stand, but he was held down by his two captors, unable to do more than buck off the ground.

"You can't!" Dr. Benita tried to say, holding her hands out like she wanted to push the gun away, but too afraid to actually do it.

The gun exploded to a cacophony of screams.

St. Augustina stared at the blown-up computer component of her gun, a wisp of smoke came out of the top, an echo of the smoke explosion from her office only a couple of hours before. A tiny feedback shock shot through her hand as the gun sparked one last time before it died.

"St. Benedict," she said with deadly softness.

"Really, St. Augustina? I hacked your system hours ago," St. Benedict said from behind her, coming out of the mist like he had just teleported there. He had his own gun out, held in one hand as the glow of his other hand softly died, having finished its task of blowing up her gun's onboard computer.

"It's still a gun, St. Ben. Even with the accuracy targeting gone, I'm still good enough to fight you," she said, maintaining her deadly softness as she slowly turned to cast her eyes on him.

"I put the safety on too before I blew it. Good luck with firing a gun that doesn't recognize your ID anymore," St. Benedict answered, taking his gun in both hands to steady his shot. "Now, like I said before. I'm taking my people and leaving."

"Leaving! There's no leaving here. We're all going to die," one of the men said, in total hysteria. The mist was so thick at that point that even seeing each other was becoming difficult.

"None of us are getting out of here, St. Benedict, unless your snake bitch can make that crystal work," St. Augustina said, turning fully to face St. Benedict, who had become more of a ghost in the mist.

"Why would she be able to do that? She's not a Talent, you idiot!" Malachi growled again. Zita was still weeping but had calmed considerably after having not been killed by St. Augustina.

"How about this then, St. Auggie. Since you have your hands full trying to get yourself and your people out, you give me my people, and we abandon each other to our fates?"

"Your people are wounded. What good are they going to be to you getting out of here?" St. Augustina asked, looking for the con.

"Then more reasons to dump them. Who knows, you might get lucky and I get killed in the process, trying to protect them."

"Ha, you'd abandon your own people if it meant your survival, and we both know it. Nice bluff. It's all about risk versus reward, right?" St. Augustina said.

She didn't see Malachi until he had kicked the legs out from underneath her. Like a felled tree, she toppled straight back, throwing her now useless gun into the air.

Perfectly coordinated, St. Benedict stepped forward. His eyes flashed blue as his enhanced sight triggered on, and targets appeared around each of the six remaining enemies — even though they were nearly obscured by the mist. As if they moved in slow motion, he saw them all raise their own weapons to fire. With quick precision, St. Benedict fired six times in rapid succession. They weren't all kill shots, going instead for disarming shots with speed. Two men took shots to their shoulders and immediately fell back, dropping their guns. A third probably died from a shot in the ten zone. The fourth guy was shot through his hand, which grazed his cheek and took off his ear. The fifth and sixth, the ones holding Zita, were headshots and dropped. The fourth recovered enough to actually get a shot off first, but not being a Saint, missed St. Benedict's head by inches, and received a bullet to the chest for his trouble. Luckily for the fourth, he was wearing Kevlar and only had the wind knocked out of him.

The fourth hadn't even hit the ground before St. Benedict started moving, stepping quickly over St. Augustina, who was knocked dizzy on the ground. He lifted Malachi up onto his feet first.

"You gotta run for yourself. You got this?" he asked as he slapped the smaller man on the shoulder.

"Yeah, yeah, I got this," Malachi said and shifted his feet a bit to prove he was steady even with his hands handcuffed behind him.

St. Benedict moved on to Zita but remembered to keep his gun pointed in the face of the last remaining enemy combatant, Dr. Benita, who was still kneeling on the ground.

"Zita, Zita. Are you alright?" St. Benedict asked, while he kept his eyes on Dr. Benita, who kept her own eyes on the end of his gun.

Zita was still crying but trying to shake it off. St. Benedict laid a reassuring hand on her without looking, "Okay, okay. It's alright. We're getting out of here." He turned his back to Zita and squatted, switching his gun hand smoothly from right to left. "Loop your arms around my neck, I'll carry you out."

"No. No," Zita sniffed, forcing herself to get under control. "I can move. It hurts, but nothing is broken. You need to keep your gun up."

"Son of a bitch," St. Augustina cursed and rolled onto her side to push herself back up. St. Benedict took a step forward and kicked her back down.

"Don't get up, sweetheart. Not if you want to keep breathing."

"You backstabbing, cunt sucker," St. Augustina continued, but she stayed down.

"You didn't take my offer, so don't bitch about it now," St. Benedict said.

"The last time I took one of your offers, everyone died. Everyone I promised to protect," St. Augustina said, her eyes glowing orange. Her own augmentations were firing, and St. Benedict knew he couldn't take her in a hand-to-hand fight, even on his best days.

St. Benedict hesitated a moment. "Come with us," he offered softly.

St. Augustina laughed breathlessly. "Not a chance in hell," she answered back just as softly, every inch an Amazon warrior goddess. "I have to get my people out of here. The ones you haven't murdered." She rolled to her hands and knees before checking the vitals of the man beside her, completely ignoring St. Benedict as if he was inconsequential now, practically daring him to shoot.

St. Benedict thought about it.

Malachi came up beside Zita and attempted to hold her. Instead, she offered him a weak smile and pushed off to slither beside him. As they moved past, St. Benedict retreated back over the bodies of the dead at his feet, keeping himself between his people and St. Augustina.

"I hope you make it out of this, St. Augustina," St. Benedict said.

She shot him a look, both sad and determined, as she helped up one of her men. It was a look that made a man regret everything he had ever done in his life. In other circumstances, he would be on her side in a conflict like this. The rest of her people got back to their own feet, gravitating to her like the beacon of hope she was. Then she led those that remained off into the mist.

He nodded his understanding as he continued to step back into the mist.

"Wait, take me with you!"

He double blinked as Dr. Benita came forward.

"Excuse me? This is not a general rescue here," St. Benedict answered, readjusting the aim of his gun to train it on her, stopping her in her tracks.

"Please. I just want to get out of here. I'm a doctor too, I can..."

"Dr. Benita, I know. Your degree is in xenosocial studies, not medicine. Nice try." He was already far enough into the mist that he was obscured and ended the conversation at that moment by rushing off to disappear completely.

"Wait!" Dr. Benita called, but he didn't turn or respond. He only hoped that she wouldn't follow. He didn't need things to get any more complicated.

Within a few feet, he caught up with Malachi and Zita. Without breaking pace, he came up beside Zita and looped her still-shackled arms over his neck and wrapped an arm around her waist.

"Come on, sweetheart, we need to make double-time," he said and with a burst of speed pushed on through the mostly white world.

"St. Benedict, where are we?" Zita asked.

"Don't worry, I got this completely handled," St. Benedict lied as he looked around them, trying to find something that looked familiar. That's when he noticed Malachi was missing. "Hey, we've got to keep together... Malachi." They slowed down and looked backward and forward but there was nothing around them except mist and the few shades of trees.

"Malachi!" Zita called, but her voice didn't travel far, swallowed in the dense mist around them.

"Dammit, Malachi!" St. Benedict called again.

"Over here, guys. I found a door!" Malachi's answer came, sounding incredibly far away to St. Benedict's left. Together, he and Zita moved toward the voice and, sure enough, found a door made of cheap plywood standing in the middle of nowhere.

Malachi stood beside it, staring at it.

"We have to stay together," St. Benedict chided as he set Zita down.

"Sorry, man. I stopped to tuck my feet through, you know, so my hands were in front instead of behind me, and I just saw this... I mean, look at it! It's a door in the middle nowhere. It's like something out of a Stephen King book." He reached out to grasp the handle and tried to turn it. It didn't budge.

"I'd like to say this is the weirdest thing I've seen this week, but that still belongs to the troll florist," St. Benedict said as Zita unlooped her arms from around his neck so he could take a closer look. "There were doors like this earlier, leading out to different places entirely."

"So, this could be our way out?" Zita asked, looking exhausted as she leaned against a tree.

"Except that, I can see what's on the other side of the door, which is nothing," Malachi said, demonstrating by stretching his locked hands around the edge of the door and moving them up and down.

Just then, a scream cut through the air. It sounded like a woman's scream but ended strangely.

"Oh, that's disconcerting," St. Benedict said.

"Disconcerting, he says. Thanks for that, Admiral Understatement," Malachi snapped.

"Maybe... maybe the door will open with this?" Zita offered, holding open her hands to show the plum-colored crystal inside.

The small group stared down at the crystal, which did nothing under scrutiny.

There was another scream in the distance, though this one had more of a whinny to it that reminded St. Benedict of the shadowy Poh. It was too close and another sound, another scream, this time a man's followed close on its heels.

"Oh, this is bad."

Not for the first time since they parted ways again, St. Benedict regretted letting Rune go. Her magic acumen was exactly why he had wanted her to come with him on this mission. Instead, he had let her go, and easily at that. Not wanting to dwell on his reasoning, he took a few steps back from the door and attempted to kick at it, aiming for just below the doorknob. It was like kicking a stone wall.

"Okay, it was worth a try," St. Benedict said as he hopped around on one foot, feeling the impact all the way to his knee. He tested his foot by slowly giving it weight again. He felt the magic inside him, still burning hot as it rushed to repair what was probably a couple of sprained tendons. His metabolism was becoming ravenous again, the monster it spawned demanding to be fed. He needed to eat something soon. The augmentations were only forestalling the inevitable.

"It's magically sealed. This whole place is magic. You can't just open that door with force," Dr. Benita said as she appeared out of the mist.

"What the hell do you want?" Malachi demanded, placing himself between Dr. Benita and Zita.

Instead of replying right away, Dr. Benita held up a pair of silver keys. "These are the keys to your cuffs. I'll give them to you if you take me with you. Get me out of here."

"That's very mercenary of you, leaving your friends to save yourself," St. Benedict said, taking steps forward on his now-repaired leg, sauntering over to her, stopping only when he was within grabbing distance of the keys. Sensing that, Dr. Benita flipped them back into her palm and took a counter step back.

"They're all dead," she said, tucking her hand under her arms and sniffing hard, looking terrified.

"Dead?" Malachi asked. He exchanged glances with the other two.

"Something... came out of the mist... grabbed them one by one. St. Augustina..." Dr. Benita swallowed, "she charged off and just left me. I didn't... I didn't know... what to do..." She tried to continue but simply degenerated into tears.

With an impassive face, St. Benedict held open his hand to her and waited. She looked down at it as if she couldn't believe what she was seeing, then gingerly reached out to take it. Before she could touch him, he simply stated, "Keys."

She arrested her reach and double blinked.

"You... you promise, right? You'll get me out of here," she asked hesitating.

He didn't say anything, simply waited with enigmatic eyes.

She handed him the keys. Without a second glance, he went over to Malachi and quickly unlocked the smaller man's cuffs, then passed the keys to him, so he could unlock Zita's.

"Don't suppose you're a Talent?" the Saint asked Dr. Benita, who could only keep hugging herself while he checked the bullets in his gun.

"You're not going to kill me, right? I'm helping you," she insisted, eyeing his inspection of the gun.

"We should just kill you," Malachi groused.

"Shut it, Mal," St. Benedict said, turning his focus out into the mist. He blinked three times to initiate his augmented sight and tried to see if there were any heat signatures in the mist. No one said much of anything. Zita rubbed her sore wrists once they were freed from the cuffs, and Malachi embraced her hard for the first time in over a day. Dr. Benita stood awkwardly, shivering in the cold.

"No," she finally said. "I'm not a Talent, I'm just interested in the subject. My thesis was about..."

"Okay, that's enough. You help Zita and stay close," St. Benedict said. He lifted his gun to point at something out in the mist.

"You see something, St. Ben?" Malachi asked, pitching his voice down to a whisper as he also peered out into the white unknown.

"No. That's what scares me," St. Benedict answered, scanning slowly.

"Where is your companion? The woman who everyone was calling the Finder?" Dr. Benita asked as she moved to stand beside Zita.

"I lost her," St. Benedict said.

"What do you mean, lost her?" Malachi asked.

"She left, is what I mean. She got to safety," St. Benedict said.

That's when the door opened.

They didn't notice it at first, not until the hinges squeaked in mid-swing. Then as one, they all turned to stare at it.

"Did that door just open on its own?" Malachi asked, freaked out.

"Looks like," St. Benedict said and approached the door to look through it. "Okay, long hall. We can handle long halls."

"We're seriously going through?" Malachi asked.

"We can handle long halls, Mal. Better than we can handle dark, foggy, magical forests," Zita said with conviction and slithered her way over to the door to look down it herself.

"Zita, wait," Malachi started.

Ignoring him, she nodded once, then made her way through, using the door frame and wall to steady herself. St. Benedict grabbed Dr. Benita by the shirt and pushed her through.

"You stick close to her and make sure she gets out, you understand," he said coldly to the smaller Latina woman. She nodded.

"I have a bad feeling about this," Malachi said, tugging on his hair in a familiar nervous gesture.

"All my feelings are bad right now, so we just have to keep moving," St. Benedict said and then spoke to his gun handle. "Unlock for general use."

There was a high-pitched beep followed by a click. Then St. Benedict held the grip out toward Malachi to take.

"You keep them safe. If something comes, I'm going to lead them off."

"What? No, I can't take your gun," Malachi said.

"It's not a bouquet of flowers," St. Benedict said, a smile cracking his face.

"Oh, shut up. It was the one time," Malachi retorted.

The Saint chuckled and put the gun in Malachi's hand.

"Just take it and go. Protect your ladylove. I'm right behind you."

Malachi hesitated for another moment, and then went through the door, gun in hand.

St. Benedict watched them go, bracing himself in the frame of the door.

"Thanks for that," he said to the creature behind him. "Thanks for letting them go."

It didn't reply, only stabbed the point of its horn through him. St. Benedict stumbled a step, then looked down at his blood staining the black horn, trying to process what was happening. Then it hurled him back into the darkening mist, slamming the door shut behind without a cry of protest from him.

CHAPTER 25

Rune marched her way through the weird gray light. The ground was soft and spongy like football field turf under her feet. Creaks and squeaks, a few cries of small animals communicating in the gloom. Rune sensed, rather than saw, the trees surrounding her. They stood like dark, silent sentinels, punctuating the smoky world with black slashes. All of it made Rune's skin crawl, but she kept walking, letting the strange, silver box marked with runes on each side lead her forward.

She had tried to examine the box more closely when she had first come back through the door, which gratefully opened back into the Faerie Court instead of the bar's front street. What surprised her the most about the box was that it looked magic-made. The markings had been carved into the silver and looked like magic letters from one of the thirteen magic languages. She didn't recognize which one, and the diffused light didn't really help things. She hoped she would get a chance to look it over later. Someone would need to be a serious magic user, like a full wizard, to make something like this little box. What was St. Benedict doing with a magic item, and a silver one at that?

Rune's mind kept drifting over the question as she walked until she almost tripped over a stone block in her path. She was not in the least bit surprised to discover upon standing that it was, in fact, a gravestone.

"Hello, vaguely ominous symbology," Rune said and patted the top of the stone like it was a puppy. The stone was cold, the rough top biting into her palms. She dismissed it and looked around.

"St. Benedict!" she boldly shouted, getting more worried as time passed. She hadn't run into anybody. She did not see a single dark shadow of the monochromes or Lady Trella, or anyone else for that matter. With only the necklace to go by, Rune stepped around the gravestone and continued following her lead, hoping that it was taking her to St. Benedict and not his dead body.

When she came upon the Poh, she was almost as relieved as she was terrified. It stood in her path, glaring at her with its left blood-red eye, its whole body slightly darker than its surrounding smoke cloud. It pawed the ground once, claws tearing up a chunk of turf beneath it. It didn't attack, which was even more disturbing.

"Where is he, disgusting Pure One?" the Poh said with a sneer, though its mouth didn't move. The voice was in the smoke itself. "Where is the male?" Earth crumbled through its claws, adding to its threat, like it intended to crumble her up in much the same manner.

Rune licked her suddenly dry lips. The Poh was talking to her instead of attacking. *Okay, something has changed,* she thought to herself and decided to answer truthfully, as if the Poh was a friend.

"No clue. I was going to ask you the same thing," Rune said, trying to not sound as scared as she felt.

The Poh huffed at her. "Bitchy witchy," it whispered menacingly. Rune took the warning for what it was and backed up a step. "You should leave. You are not wanted here, bitch witch."

Apparently done with her, the Poh swung its horned head away from Rune and disappeared into its own smoke again.

"Hey, wait. Uh, you, you are a servant of the Oberon, right?" Rune called after it, desperately trying to think of what to say to keep it from leaving. It didn't answer her question, but continued on, becoming almost invisible in its own darkness.

"Why won't you attack me?" Rune practically shouted as she started to follow it.

It turned its head toward her once more and eyed her again.

"Is it because I am a Faerie Friend?" Rune pressed. "You want to attack me, but even back in the warehouse, you avoided me." She realized too late that she had moved closer than she had meant to get. The Poh responded to her closeness by rearing up and screaming its whinny roar, the clawed front paws tearing at the air. Rune froze in place. Then the Poh crashed back to earth, knocking Rune onto her back. It planted its paws firmly on either side of her body, its nose only inches above hers. She could smell the foul decay of its breath as it panted over her, flecks of stinking spit drizzling down on her from above.

"I hate you!" the Poh said, "I desperately want to hurt you. You have ruined everything. You are so small-minded, so stupid that I just want to smash your face in!" The Poh tore up the turf on either side of

Rune's head viciously as it shouted, its voice coming from all around her. It was all Rune could do to cover her face with her hands. Dirt flew everywhere, but then the Poh stopped, panting hard. Rune remained untouched.

"I can't! I can't touch you!! You're a fucking... virgin!" The Poh shoved off the ground and bounded away, leaving a stunned Rune where she lay, not yet sure if it was safe to sit up. Virgin? Where the hell did it get that idea?

"I hate you," the Poh growled a few feet away, sounding pitiful as he said it.

"But why?"

"Stay away from me, bitch witch! I can't hurt you, but I can tear your male to pieces. I will shower you with his blood," the Poh screamed at her.

Though they were not getting anywhere with this conversation, Rune kept working on keeping the Poh talking. As long as it was here talking, or screaming rather, at her, it was not doing what it promised to do to St. Benedict. Rune peeled herself off the ground and brushed the dirt from her caked clothes.

"You ask stupid questions to distract me," the Poh said, realizing what she was doing. "I will have my revenge!"

"I haven't asked you any... okay, I asked one question, but you don't have to get so upset," Rune said. It was like talking to someone who had gone crazy.

"A virgin, a virgin. I can't touch you because you're a virgin. So much better than the rest of us, right?"

"I can assure you, I'm really not," Rune said, more under her own breath, but the Poh answered as if she was talking to it.

"Oh, but you are," he said, swinging his horn dangerously close to her middle. Rune backed up again. This time the horn kept pace with her as the Poh talked. "Blood and bone. Guts and brains. You've never snuffed them out. Never had true power. Never sullied your soul or opened the unclosable door. But he has..." The Poh stopped short just as Rune bumped into the gravestone again.

"But him," the Poh continued, a shiver running through its whole body. "Oh, he's a murderer! He stinks of death and blood! How does it not enrage you to your very soul?!" The Poh thrashed again, but it seemed to be more ecstasy-driven from its bloodlust. "The holes made in his soul from the lives he's taken. I shall thrust my horn inside and tear and rend the dark creature from this plane and consume it in glory!"

"Okay, you need some therapy," Rune said, again under her breath.

There was a call then, some strange sound cutting through the black-and-white mist. Rune thought it sounded like a hunting horn. The Poh raised its head, its horse-like ears perked and swiveling around toward the bellow.

"At last," it said in absolute pleasure, then he was gone. He simply vanished, the black smoke merging away with the white fog.

Rune stood up, once more alone.

"St. Benedict," she said. She had to hurry. Time was running out. Rune grasped the Saint's necklace once more and got moving again. Almost immediately, she was turned around in the shapeless void of the mist. "St. Benedict!" she shouted, and nothing replied. She ran quicker than was safe, which was when she ran straight into a person's back.

Her careless momentum knocked him forward, and he took two stumbling steps before flipping around in panic, his arms covering his face in a defensive gesture.

"St. Benedict?" Rune asked again, more carefully than hopefully.

"Rune?" asked a lighter, more tenor voice. One distinctly not St. Benedict, but familiar just the same.

"Calvin?" Rune declared in surprise.

The blonde man covered his face with his arms, his jacket torn and hiked up around his narrow torso. A couple of buttons had been torn off his shirt, making it gape wide, showing off the once white t-shirt underneath. He looked awful, but Rune wasn't too terribly surprised. Calvin was only a hominal after all, and she highly doubted he had much real exposure to the magical realms or their strange, alien rules. The poor guy—well, maybe not the poor guy—was obviously terrified.

"Calvin," Rune repeated when he didn't respond. He just kept his hands up.

"No, don't touch me, go away!" he shouted at Rune like a frightened little pony, his voice a little muffled by his arms.

"Calvin, I'm not going to hurt you," Rune said truthfully. Carefully, she stretched out her own hand and took one of his fingers in the smallest of touches, to encourage him to lower his hands. "Have you been here the whole time?"

Calvin openly wept, looking more like a lost five-year-old boy than the badass man he tried to convince everyone he was. His legs buckled underneath him and he collapsed into a heap on the ground

For a half-moment, Rune thought about just leaving him there; just walking away into the mist, not saying anything. Would he even notice if she left? This guy did summon the Poh, so it would have been poetic justice if the Poh got him.

"Hey, come on, you can't stay here, you idiot," Rune said instead and kicked at one of his large fancy dress-shoed feet. That got his attention and he looked at Rune, his face blotchy and dazed from crying.

"Leveau?" he asked in a small voice. This time he seemed to take real stock of where he was. "What happened?"

"You tell me. You're the one who summoned a monster to devour us all," she said.

With the lethargy of an old man, Calvin pulled himself up and stood. Rune did not help him.

"Where are we? Why is it so smoky?"

"Oh!" Rune declared as there was a ping in her brain. "It's not smoke, it's miasma. That's not good. Take shallow breaths."

"Is it poison?" Calvin asked fearfully.

"Most likely. Side effects may include vomiting, diarrhea, semi-real hallucinations supported by magic that pin you to the ground and tell you they hate you. Consult with a doctor if symptoms persist."

"What?"

"The miasma is probably feeding off our fears and anxieties. All the things we're worried about. I expect I'm going to see a well-dressed woman around here somewhere and you'll see… whatever scares you."

Then she pinched him hard on the arm.

"Ow! Bitch!"

"And now we both know neither of us is an illusion," Rune said, and she flashed a cheeky smile.

"How you figure?"

"You felt me pinch you, right?" Rune asked. "Illusions can't actually hurt you."

"But you said it pinned you down and yelled at you, whatever 'it' is."

Rune's face fell. "Aw, crap. I did. So, was the Poh real or not?" She looked around some more but saw nothing horse-like. Lifting up St. Benedict's necklace again, Rune refocused on her mission. Instantly, she felt the connection to the Saint but something was different. It wasn't leading her anywhere.

"We need to keep moving," Rune said, getting more worried.

Before Calvin could exchange any more words, another figure started to form in the miasma. At the same time, they locked their eyes on it, and Calvin gripped Rune's arm painfully in fear. As the figure approached, Calvin pulled her closer. She couldn't decide if it was a protective gesture or he was prepping to use her as a shield, but knowing another human being was next to her in the face of a shadowy unknown was more reassuring than not.

"God, what is that?" Calvin whispered in squeaky fear.

"Just stay calm, it might not be real," Rune hoped. She was surprised at her own calmness in the face of this unknown. Maybe because she had faced her own worst fear earlier that day.

Rune and Calvin backed up slowly, shuffling their steps in the smoky mist as the thing walked toward them at a normal pace.

"Oh, god. It's... it's..." Calvin whispered, even more panicked.

"A woman?" Rune asked and squinted harder to see her better. "No she's a doe, I mean a fawn."

The fawn looked like a harmless sort of person, her hair up in a bun and her deer-like feet popping out of the bottom of cropped pant legs. She wore a sun-colored apron and her dainty hooves made soft clicks on the turf. That made Rune pause. Her own footsteps barely made a sound on the turf and it was more thunk-like than click-like. The fawn woman seemed to be moving around as if she was in a room far, far away. As she moved, Rune got the impression of a yarn shop, with woven baskets full of differently colored coils. The woman seemed to be arranging things neatly, her deer-ish face smiling contentedly as she finished laying out a rainbow fan of fine, silky string on a table.

Then Calvin, another Calvin, entered the scene. He was dressed in a much cleaner suit, his hair slicked back and looking cocky as hell. The fawn was immediately apprehensive, eyeing him like he would attack her at any moment. He gesticulated at her, speaking words that Rune couldn't hear. The fawn looked down at her hands, clutched in her apron. Noticing her submissive posture, Calvin leaned against the counter, a sadistic smile on his face. He was obviously enjoying his cruelty as he had enjoyed torturing Rune. It made her ears burn. Why was she helping this ass at all?

Rune tried to pull away from him at that point, but he grasped her harder, not tearing his eyes away from the scene.

"No, don't," Calvin, the real Calvin, whispered.

"Let me go," Rune hissed and tugged away harder, freeing herself.

"No, don't do that," he continued unheeding and she realized he was talking about the scene playing out in front of them. "Say you're sorry. Just say it. Don't... no..."

Without warning, the Calvin in the scene stood up and raised his hand to strike the fawn. She screamed silently in response and cowered. He didn't land his blow, but there was another exchange of words, then she scrambled behind the counter where her cash register sat. She fumbled as she opened it up, withdrawing an envelope inside that she offered with a shaking hand.

"Oh, no, please. Please don't be afraid of me. I'm sorry..." the real Calvin continued to mutter.

"Is she a friend of yours?" Rune asked, looking back and forth between the opposite faces of the fake and real Calvin.

"No, no. She's just a client," he said softly.

Rune scoffed, "Client? That's not what it looks like to me."

"Of Heartland Mortgage," he said.

"Oh. Okay, sure, 'Client'," Rune said, making air quotes.

"I don't have to see her, though. She always sends her payment in on time. I just want to see her. I should just leave her alone." He half-whispered, as if the little voice in his head, the one that everyone often ignores, was actually given a chance to control his voice.

"She's not real, Calvin. It's just an illusion." Rune tried to back up, but he stayed transfixed, staring at her.

"What are you doing here?" he asked the apparition.

Then the fawn woman looked up and stared straight at them, or rather straight at Calvin. Their eyes met for a long, long beat of a heart. She smiled at him, a serene, loving smile.

"No. No, you have to get away! Get away from me!" Calvin shouted at her.

"This is a dream, isn't it?" she said, her voice soft and sweet as music. "You're not really here, are you, Calvin?"

"I don't give a shit about you, go away!" Calvin shouted, taking a half-step back for every full step of hers.

"Why? Why do I still dream about you like this when you're so terrible to me?" she said, biting her lower lip to keep it from trembling.

To Rune's surprise, instead of backing up, Calvin took a step forward and grabbed her wrist, stopping her gentle gesture with violence before she could touch him. The fawn cried out a little in pain but didn't retreat from it.

"Why are you here?!" The desperation on his haunted face gave his harsh words an even sharper edge.

"It's not okay. This is not okay!" the fawn shouted back. "It's not okay to hurt me."

"Calvin, let her go, you're hurting her," Rune repeated, grabbing his hand to try to pull him back.

The fawn seemed to see Rune for the first time, looking at her quizzically. "Who are you?"

"Get away from me," Calvin repeated, this time in a desperate whisper. Contrary to his words, he pulled her even closer, setting his forehead against hers and closing his eyes. His face twisted again in pain as he bowed his head, hiding his eyes. "Clara, I'm so sorry," he whispered.

"Calvin," Clara whispered back.

He raised his head again to look down into Clara's pleading eyes. "You don't love me, you fear me. I scare you." As he said it, the dark miasmic smoke erupted around him, spearing out like daggers.

"Calvin! Back off!" Rune screeched and got a grip on the back of his rumpled suit jacket, hauling him back with both fists. As they both moved, the apparition melted into the miasma. Then Rune's back hit a door.

She turned to look at the door that had appeared out of nowhere. Rune's blood went cold in her veins. It was a metal door, painted a clinical off-white. A small window was cut at head height, and it was covered like it always had been with a matching off-white metal cover. There was no handle, only a flat silver metal disk where the handle should be, keeping those inside unable to escape.

"Let me guess, there's a scary well-dressed woman behind it," Rune said, trying to sound flippant.

The door didn't answer her.

"I don't have time for this. Calvin, we should..." For a second, Rune didn't see him. Her heart jumped in fear that he had been an apparition the whole time, and she was the one going crazy. To her relief, she found him, sitting on the ground, staring down at something between his feet, as if he was trying to figure out how to sink into the turf without having to dig a hole first.

"Alright, no help from the peanut gallery. What is a peanut gallery, anyway? Never mind, focus." Rune stopped in her tracks when she realized that her thoughts were being said out loud.

"Okay, why would that be happening? Is this a trick of the Faerie Court? Come on, Rune, what do you know about the Faerie Court? It obviously doesn't have the same rules, but it was so stable before, now it's in absolute chaos. What's changed? Why am I hearing this out loud?!"

"Can you hear that?" Rune asked Calvin.

"She hates me. I see it every time I go to her," Calvin started talking.

"Who? Clara?" Rune asked, glancing at the door behind her.

"We need to find St. Benedict and get out of here. No wait, we're the ones in danger, right? I mean, obviously, I can't even think... I was..." the voice of Rune's thoughts, or were they Anna's, continued echoing from the mist all around.

"Okay, it's official, I hate this place," Rune said.

"I don't know why I keep going there. I can't help myself. I can't even come up with reasons anymore," Calvin's voice said from the mist as actual Calvin dropped his head into his hands.

"Why don't you just ask her out on a date like a normal person? Or better yet, just take no for an answer and stop harassing her?" Anna snapped.

Then there was a knock.

"Anna!" a young man's voice called from the other side of the door.

Rune's heart began to pound her ears. The higher-pitched, musical sound of the man's voice. It sounded like Justin...

"But, she was so real!" Calvin yelled again. "I could feel her with my hands."

"Calvin...get up. We've got to move," Rune said. She couldn't believe this was happening again. Maybe she really was going crazy and developing a split personality. "Calvin, get up!"

"Huh?"

Rune started rifling through Calvin's pocket.

"Hey! What... what's wrong with you?" he demanded. Rune finally found what she was looking for inside the front, inner pocket.

"The miasma, it's starting to get to us. Cover your mouth and breathe shallowly," Rune said, slapping the handkerchief she found over Calvin's face. He stared at her, his eyes red-rimmed like a drug addict's, then set his fingers over the cloth to hold it.

"You're still going to run away from him? After all of these years, waiting for him to come through the door?" Anna asked.

"Damn straight. This isn't real. He isn't real, and I..."

"It's because you're fifty pounds heavier. You don't want him to see how you've changed."

"BMI index can kiss my ass!" Rune shouted, to the voice coming from the fog.

The knocking continued at the door.

"We should stay away from that door," Anna said. "We can't let him see us like that."

"Don't listen to her, don't listen to her," Rune whispered to herself, trying to focus on Calvin as he got to his feet. Everything about this seemed wrong.

"Please, Rune, let's leave," Anna begged. A huge bang came from the door as if something heavy had been slammed into it.

"You're keeping me away from the door," Rune whispered.

"I'm afraid. I am. I always have been. I don't want to open the door. I like being afraid. It's comfortable. It's safe. He'll come for me someday. I know he will. Justin. Justin. Justin," the voice whispered, repeating his name over and over, a cascade of sound.

"Okay, I'm not doing this." Rune slashed her hand at the door with finality, cutting off the voice as it tried to speak. "Unlucky for you, I have already had a talk with myself earlier today. I know what I sound like. I am Rune Anna Leveau and you are not me!" The miasma visibly retreated from Rune. With complete confidence, Rune grabbed St Benedict's necklace in her hand. The line appeared, leading straight into the door.

"Anna, where are you?" Justin's voice called through the door again.

"I see what you're doing. The well-dressed bitch doesn't work anymore, so you're trying something new. This is a Faerie Court door, isn't it? You don't control it."

"Anna, answer me. Please," Justin's voice said, but that was starting to sound fake to her too.

"Yeah, I am afraid to see him again, but he isn't here." Rune laid a hand on the cold handle of the door. "But I know who is. I know who you're trying to hide from me by using Justin's voice."

"You could be wrong," the voice that had sounded like Anna warped away, deepening into the Poh. "He could be beyond that door."

"I know who's beyond this door."

Rune opened the door.

St. Benedict skidded down the hallway, coming to a stop when his back hit the wall. The hallway seemed to spring up around him out of the mist. He barely registered it as he tried to scramble to his feet. With his hand plastered to his side, trying to keep the blood inside him, he managed to stay upright as he looked around.

The lights hanging above flickered and danced, casting eerie, blinking shadows in between the pools of light. It could have been a hallway in a prison complex or some kind of creepy mental facility for the insane. He knew it wasn't. He'd never seen those places billowing the black mist from under the doorways.

St. Benedict tried to look back the way he'd been flung to see if one of those doors Rune talked about was standing open. That was when he saw them.

A circle of monochromes stood watching him at the end of the hallway. It was like they had emerged from the shadow and the smoking mist, their creepy, black-and-white faces, and pupil-less eyes almost glowing.

Before he could say anything, one of them crossed the space in an instant to kick him hard in his gut. They were all around him at once, attacking. Knowing he was outnumbered, he fought his way free and out into the hallway.

The doors flew past, each closed and ominous with chipped paint and decaying stenciled numbers. It appeared as if no one had used the place in years, except for the fact that there were scattered illuminated lights. There had to be a way out of here. He was sure he was still in the mist, and this was some kind of illusion magic or something to do with the Faerie Court that Rune had talked about.

The first attack came when he passed from one of the circles of light into utter darkness. A monochrome appeared in front of him, manifesting out of the shadow as if he had been standing there waiting. If it wasn't for St. Benedict's augmented sight and trained reflexes, he would have been laid out right there. Instead, he ducked, the man's fist passing so close over his head it brushed his hair. St. Benedict whipped out his own fist, right into the other man's solar plexus. He heard a grunt and brought the palm of his other hand up through his opponent's guard to slam it into his chin. There was a sharp clack as his opponent's teeth snapped together and left a bright white blood mark on his black face. Then St. Benedict ducked to the side, rolling away to get more space between them, except, when he gained his feet, the monochrome was gone.

Before St. Benedict could turn around, another monochrome man, skinnier but no less strong, came up from behind him to grapple him. He struggled a second, then stopped when he saw something impossible happen in front of him. Facing a darkened wall, he swore he watched as three more monochromes formed out of the shadow, raising their heads as one, their white faces glowing in the darkness. The hairs on the back of St. Benedict's arms rose at the eerie sight.

Then St. Benedict stomped down hard on the foot of the one behind him. Immediately, his opponent let go, and St. Benedict didn't hesitate to take off down the hall, throwing himself full body against a pair of double doors midway through the hall. Gratefully, they were not locked or barred in any way and he continued his escape. He ran without stopping. His side bled where he had been impaled and the blood loss was taking its toll. Rune's magic burned inside him like a fever, trying to heal this newest injury and his clothes were damp with sweat. Before he realized it, he slammed through another set of double doors.

These opened into what looked like an abandoned common room, with bits of furniture throughout the space left over from some lost 70s showroom. There was a little light in the room, coming from the floor-to-ceiling windows on the far wall. Their blinds were pulled, but gray, bleached light streamed through the even slats across the floor. There didn't seem to be any other doors.

His pursuers did not seem to be immediately behind him. Opening his palm, he flexed his fingers and activated the screen augmentation. It flashed to life and showed him with a quick glance a pie graph he had slapped together; an idea of how much time he thought he had before the augmentations could no longer keep up with the metabolic overload his body was taking from the spell. The pie graph was almost full.

"Got to keep moving," he told himself.

He almost fell over the yellow-green couch as he tried to get to the window. Not even looking for the cord, he violently pulled down the blinds.

Outside, he saw nothing but gray swirling mist.

Growling in frustration, St. Benedict turned back to the room, expecting to see the monochromes standing behind him now that he was cornered.

But they weren't there.

"No, please stop. Why are you doing this to me?" a familiar woman's voice came from nowhere. It was muffled, but the sound of it made St. Benedict's heart stop. He whipped his head back and forth, trying to locate the source of the voice. "No. No, it can't be."

A TV he hadn't seen before clicked on in the corner of the room. Its screen was the black and gray of a CCTV. His heart pounded harder as he crossed the room to stare at the screen. He had seen this before, years ago.

A woman sat at the table, chained to the top. Her hair was a mess, and her bottom lip was swollen with a cut in it that still looked shiny with wet blood. Suddenly, she screamed and her whole body contorted. Helpless, he watched on the side of the screen, screaming with her as her body writhed with electricity shot through the cuffs.

"Anna!"

The screen went dead. He hit it once, but it remained off, tendrils of black smoke curling from the back of the set.

He closed his eyes, covering his face. Slowly, he remembered to breathe and then to think.

"That was years ago. I saw that years ago. That isn't real. They're messing with you, St. Benedict," he said to himself out loud. "What the hell is wrong with you?!" he shouted at the nothing. "You like playing your cat-and-mouse game? Gives you the jollies, is that it?"

He waited, counting the seconds. Nothing happened. No one came for him, and he didn't spy any monochromes staring at him from the shadows.

What he did spy was the candy machine on the other side of the space, tucked in an alcove. He didn't think twice about it. He didn't really think at all, just rushed across to it, picking up a bent-wire chair on his way past from one of the empty tables. He threw the whole thing at the smooth glass surface of the candy machine. It shattered spectacularly.

It wasn't stocked well, but the few packages in there were more than welcome. He barely remembered tearing into them, devouring old chocolate and stale crumbling cookies as fast as he could get the packages open with his numb, shaking hands.

"Ha, ha. My last meal," he finally said to himself partway through the fourth package of imitation peanut butter crackers. He flipped open his hand and took a look at the meter. The pie was mostly filled, but a sliver thickened as he chewed until it was about an eighth of the pie. "A little more time."

The monitor came on again.

"In your testimony here," came the disembodied voice of a man St. Benedict had killed a long time ago, "it says that it was your wife who was responsible for all of this." St. Benedict approached the monitor, his eyes hooded.

"Yeah, something like that, whatever," his own voice said, tinny through the TV speakers. St. Benedict shook his head. Someone was messing with him.

"What the fuck is going on?"

He heard the sound of the double doors near him wobble open and shut. Light, real honest-to-god, warm light spilled over the ground as the lady in orange entered the room. At first, he thought her hand was burning, but that wasn't possible either. She had to be holding a lantern. He shielded his eyes against the brightness. It truly looked like her hand was on fire. His overstressed mind was interpreting things oddly.

"Why are you chasing me?" he asked.

She turned to him, almost as if she was floating. Before, the woman seemed like a goofy and harmlessly hippie, but now her gaze was like stone and just as eerie.

"I thought you were allies," he continued, taking up a reasonably sized shard of glass from the ground as a makeshift weapon. It was going to cut his own hand if he used it but needs must when the devil is DUI.

"I am his obedient child," she answered. "We are all his obedient children."

St. Benedict nodded as if that made perfect sense, trying not to antagonize her.

"Can the condemned ask a final question?" he asked.

The orange lady walked to the center of the room, holding out her light so that it cast long dark shadows of the furniture all around.

"Ask it, warrior," she said.

"Did Rune make it out?"

A small smile crossed her lips. "I pushed her through the door myself."

The tightness around his heart loosened a tiny bit. St. Benedict cracked a smile.

"Thank you," he said, bowing his head slightly to the orange lady in acknowledgment.

The orange lady gave him one last look, a moment of pity, before turning her head away to stare resolutely out the window. From the shadows, St. Benedict watched as the monochromes appeared. At first, it was just an arm sliding through, as black and inky as the shadow, followed by the rest of his body. Other shadows soon filled with other forms, as they entered the room from nowhere.

St. Benedict tried to fight, but they surrounded him too fast. Too many hands grappled him, and he lost his improvised weapon. They picked him up to slap him against a wall. He screamed in pain and panic, his eyes seeing stars as two monochrome men held him to the wall while the others clawed and hit. After a few passes, they stopped to let him hang there like a rag doll.

"Father comes," his tinny ears heard one of them say.

He tried to lift his head to see this father, but instead, he began to fall backward through the wall. His bleary eyes blinked at the strange sensation, and some part of his brain noted the looks of shock that crossed the white faces of the monochrome men as he passed through. Then arms, smaller and more gentle, caught him from behind and pulled him through, like pulling him through a waterfall.

Immediately, he tried to fight the arms.

"St Benedict! St. Benedict! It's me!"

CHAPTER 26

Rune tried to shout, but it didn't make any difference. He just kept thrashing.

The last thing she had expected when she opened the door was the sight of St. Benedict's back, pressed against the invisible wall in the space of the doorframe. In front of him, the monochromes pinned him against it and were obviously attacking him.

"Calvin! Help me!" she shouted as she rushed to wrap her arms around St. Benedict's waist and haul him through the door. It felt like pulling a twisting anaconda through water and he landed hard on the ground. Rune backpedaled, just managing to keep her feet.

Something was wrong with him, she could tell right away. He was splattered with blood and wasn't responding as she called his name. It was like before when he had gone wild. Before she could shake him awake, St. Benedict started to thrash, pushing her away, his eyes mostly pea-soup green as her spell took hold. Then the monochromes were on her, pouring through the metal door, even as St. Benedict crab-walked out of her grasp.

"Let me go!" she shouted at them, but two took hold of her arms despite her protests.

Whatever tenuous grasp St. Benedict had on his own mind snapped. The black smoke was on him, forcing its way into his mouth and nose, choking him for a moment, the taste like acid in the back of his throat.

"You fucking bitch. Just do what I say and don't argue," he heard his own voice shout, followed by the sound of the slap and her cry of shock and pain.

Somewhere in the back of his mind, the small sliver that was the sane, rational St. Benedict knew that what he was seeing and hearing was a hallucination of things that happened long ago, but the hunger inside didn't care. It wanted blood. It wanted someone to suffer for attacking her, to take the pain he felt and visit it upon his enemies.

The black miasma cleared, and he saw them; the woman on the ground, calling his current name and the dark figures of men pouring through the open door, rushing to grab her.

Like an animal, he growled and launched himself at the men attacking her. Attacking his wife. They were here to arrest them. He had to protect her. This time, he had to save her.

Rune saw the monochromes holding her fly sideways. Before she could register what happened to make them do that, St. Benedict tugged her toward him, her back against his front and just in time to miss getting smacked across the face.

"Stop!" she shouted at the monochromes. "Faerie Friend!"

This time, the title didn't slow the Faeries' steps.

Rune plastered herself against St. Benedict to shield him as best she could from the encroaching monochromes. Despite St. Benedict's best attempts to push Rune behind him, she stayed glued to his front. The monochromes were doing exactly what she thought they would, creating a wary circle around them in an attempt to flank. It made for a very awkward rescue attempt.

"Keep in the dark, they can't attack us if there is no shadow," she said to the Saint behind her. "They need the shadows. It's the source of their power. They won't risk attacking us on neutrally lit ground."

"Damn straight," Lady Trella said as she emerged from the doorway, her hand burning brightly. The light burned away the mist, revealing the trees. The trees, in turn, created long, slashing shadows on the ground.

"Oh, I liked this place better when it was a garden," Rune said as the shadows appeared on either side of her and St. Benedict, new portals for the monochromes to use to get to them.

"As do I," Lady Trella agreed as she stepped serenely forward. "But your sacrifice is for a greater good. I am sorry it went this way, kiddo. All things must change when the new king is crowned."

"A new king?"

"Yes, a new king," the well-dressed woman's voice cut through like a buzz-saw.

She appeared out of the blackness, grinning cruelly. Her once-pristine clothes now caked in dirt and blackened with smoke. She was standing beside Calvin, who was whimpering, still on the ground. With more strength than her small body should have, the well-dressed woman lifted him up by his blonde hair, extending her arm entirely straight to do it. Though conscious, Calvin hung there like a limp ragdoll, lacking even the will to move. With a vicious yank, the well-dressed woman tore open the last of his buttoned shirt. Then she grabbed the top of his undershirt and pulled it down to reveal his chest.

As one, the monochromes knelt to the ground before Calvin. Rune stared wide-eyed at the symbol burned into the flesh over Calvin's heart.

"Oberon," she said in awe.

"Yes, it seems to be the only way to control these creatures. Get some idiot to put on the necklace, and then the creatures follow the idiot's orders 'til the day that idiot dies. The only downside is the idiots all die too fast." She dropped Calvin contemptuously and he collapsed with a moan to the ground.

"Oh, Calvin, what have you done? You've made yourself a changeling," Rune said regretfully.

On the ground, black smoke rose out of Calvin and Rune finally put together what was going on. The Poh morphed into existence, rising out of its cloud of black smoke. The black horn and clawed feet promised death as its form swallowed Calvin's whole. Its whinny-roar cackled through the air, amplified again by the miasma all around.

"You should have left, Pure One," the Poh said. "He's mine now. I shall have my revenge on you."

"How exactly? I'm innocent, remember? You can't touch me!" Rune shouted back, defiantly.

"You care for that one, the evil one behind you. His death will be my revenge on you both," it said.

Rune forced herself not to look back at St. Benedict. She had to force the focus away from him. "This is about Calvin, isn't it? Your rage at me is his rage..." Rune started to say. The Poh bucked his head and stomped.

"Bitch witch. Bitch witch. You shall suffer for his pain," it roared.

"Calvin! Calvin, you don't have to do this. I can help you!" Rune shouted, hoping it wasn't a lie.

The Poh charged straight at them. St. Benedict used everything he had left and threw Rune to the ground.

"Calvin, stop!!" Rune shouted and tried to stand up. The aim of the Poh's horn was not true, and it missed driving its point into its prey, whooshing past St. Benedict's body. He sidestepped the Poh and threw an arm over to try to grip the beast by its horn and head. Instead, it carried St. Benedict back several paces, using its head as a battering ram.

"Stop! Stop fighting! Calvin! Calvin, can you hear me?" The Poh swung its head, dislodging the Saint, before prancing around, preparing to charge again. St. Benedict roared in response.

To Rune's horror, St. Benedict now bled more, the front of his shirt completely covered in his blood. His face was pale, assumedly from the blood loss, but his eyes were solidly green and dead.

"Oh, gods, no," Rune cursed as she saw her spell completely take over his body, turning him into a feral creature. He would fight now until he was dead.

"The wizardess and warrior will save us," Lady Trella's voice came from just over Rune's shoulder.

"Never mind your best efforts to stop us," Rune shot back. "I'm trying to save you."

Lady Trella gripped Rune's shoulder, turning her to face her. "We must obey our Father," she said. "You must save our King."

Rune blinked, trying to process what the orange Faerie was saying over the roar of battle. The monochromes stood about watching the fight. Their black-and-white faces were stoic, yet something in their postures seemed anxious, fearful, and resignedly sad. "You mean Calvin?" Rune asked, unsure of what the Faerie was trying to tell her with her eyes.

"Our King," she repeated. "Please, we beg you, save our King." Rune looked back at Calvin-turned-Poh. He was a terrible human being and totally unworthy, but he was the only king these people had, and if Calvin died now, the Company would just start the whole cycle all over again. How many times had the Faerie Court been thrown into chaos because the kings were constantly changing? She knew every one of these Faeries felt it, and while Rune didn't fully understand the Faerie Court, it was suffering too, like her House had without Maddie. Calvin may not have been the king they deserved, but he was the king they had. Even if she wasn't the wizardess they needed, she was the one they had. She had to do something.

St. Benedict bellowed, and the Poh trumpeted. It had made another pass and scored a hit. To her horror, Rune watched as St. Benedict crumpled to one knee, grasping at his side as more blood poured from his fingers.

"Rune, no!" Lady Trella shouted, but she barely heard it. Her legs pumped as she rushed to St. Benedict and placed herself again between them, flinging her arms out as wide as they would go.

"Stop, now!" she commanded. The Poh's eyes couldn't see her. It only saw the warrior. It lowered its horn again and charged.

She felt St. Benedict stand up behind her, wrapping his blood-covered arms around her middle. She knew his pressure was meant to haul her away from the horn coming straight for her. The world slowed down. Rune smelled sulfur and the metallic taste of blood in her mouth. A strange deafness muted the world around them, and she felt the horn's point contact the middle of her chest over her heart.

Instead of piercing pain, power shuddered through her, reverberating out like invisible waves. The horn crumpled, dissipating back into smoke. Everything stopped; the Poh halting in its tracks. Like a chain reaction, the Poh faded out of existence and floated away from Calvin's form. The man stood there a moment, staring at her with haunted eyes, and then they rolled up into his head as he collapsed to the ground, unconscious.

At first, Rune stood there, amazed by what just happened.

As soon as Calvin hit the ground, the monochromes rushed around him, encircling him in a protective ring. They muttered collectively over him until Lady Trella entered the circle and knelt beside her unconscious king. After she touched his blonde head gently, she smiled a small smile and nodded. A bit of the apprehension pooled out of the group, and the tough, stoic monochromes all breathed a sigh of relief.

"What the hell is going on?!"

Everyone turned to look at the forgotten, well-dressed woman.

"Do as you're ordered! Capture them," she shouted at the group of Fae around their king, pointing at Rune, her face twisted in rage. They all stared at her for one long beat.

Rune was the first to organize her thoughts.

"Uh, Calvin is probably going to need medical attention. We need to get him to a hospital…"

"Our people will care for our King," Lady Trella said, nodding once to Rune.

"We better all get out of here then," Rune agreed, forcing herself not to look at the well-dressed woman.

"I order you to stop and seize them!" the well-dressed woman continued to scream.

"They won't do that, ma'am," Rune said, turning the woman's attention to herself. "They obey their King and he is unconscious. Their first priority and fealty are to his safety."

"Safety. What the hell are you talking about? He just commands them, they are owned by the Kodiak Corporation."

"You put that talisman on Calvin, naming him their next Oberon. That's not a fluff thing."

"Oberon is dead," the well-dressed woman scoffed.

"Oberon is a *title*, you idiot, for the Faerie King. All hail Caesar," Rune said, shaking her head at the well-dressed woman. Suddenly, six years and all the changes and healing it brought came together for Rune at that moment as she continued her explanation, "and conveying upon him the very real power of the Oberon. It's not a Faerie talisman that you can use to control Faeries. You just bequeathed them their *freedom*, and now they are leaving with him." Rune smiled as the woman's face turned from confusion to panic.

The Faeries took that as the signal, and four of their number lifted Calvin amongst them, the rest forming a loose circle about them as guards. Lady Trella, her skirt of orange spinning about her, took point.

"The doors are open now for a while longer as the King parades, but once we leave, they close again," Lady Trella said to Rune.

"Except my door," Rune said with a smile.

Lady Trella returned the smile. "Always, Heir of the Magdalene."

"How dare you talk back to me, you insignificant..." the well-dressed woman started to say belatedly.

"Rune, help me," St. Benedict cut in, before dropping down to his knees behind her. She spun around as he wrapped his arms around himself.

"St. Benedict," she said. "Oh, god!"

"I can't control it," he muttered, the sound coming out of him like a growl. He was covered in blood. Rune pulled at the edges of his shirt to look at the gash in his side. To both her horror and relief, the wound was sealed.

"Look at me. The fact that you can talk at all is a good sign. Come on, raise your head and look at me." She tugged at his face, but he refused, tucking it even harder to his chest.

"I can't," he said, his voice dark and heavy, almost inhuman. "I'm afraid if I do, I'll..."

"You won't, I know. Look up at me," she assured him, brushing her hands down his arms soothingly.

Just as he inched his head up a little bit, the well-dressed woman sank her fingers into Rune's hair. With a vicious yank, she dragged Rune backward, tearing her away from St. Benedict.

As Rune landed on her back and reached to grab the woman's hand, a knife flashed above her. The woman's eyes were manic with delight as she said nothing further, but started to bring the knife down across Rune's exposed throat.

I'm going to die, Rune thought.

A blur of motion erupted above her. The well-dressed woman screamed as teeth sank into her neck, ripping out her throat. Rune's whole body reacted in shock. The momentum of St. Benedict's lunge forced the woman to the ground.

"St. Benedict!" Rune shouted, but it was already too late. The magic inside him had taken complete control. Without hesitation, she rushed to him, grabbing at the back of his shirt to try to pull him off his prey but it was useless. The woman struggled beneath St. Benedict, unable to scream. She put her hands on his face to push him off, her blood coating his chin and throat.

He growled harder and tried to lunge again, but Rune got her arms around his neck and pulled him back. Then there were other hands, black ones, helping her. With the aid of three monochromes, she got St. Benedict off of the moaning, well-dressed woman.

"Get him down on the ground!" Rune shouted, and they pinned his arms and legs in place as he thrashed, continuing to fight. "Oh, god, oh, god."

Rune turned back to the well-dressed woman, trying to think of what she would need to do to save her, but the Lady Trella was already at the dying woman's side. She peered down at the blood-covered mess, a twist of a smile on her lips.

"All debts are paid," she said and then, without looking away, took the knife the well-dressed woman had wielded only moments before against Rune and plunged it into her heart. The well-dressed woman went instantly still. Then Lady Trella turned to Rune, her eyes unapologetic.

"You killed her," Rune stated.

"Yes. She forfeited her life long ago. No Fae will take the life of an innocent, whether from the touch of love or the touch of death, by decree of the last King. She was a taker of life, so do not weep for her. See instead to your warrior or you shall lose him as well."

It took every bit of her willpower to turn back to St. Benedict again. He wasn't fighting; instead, his eyes were closed and he was breathing hard. Even though he wasn't resisting, the monochromes kept him down. Rune knelt beside him and tried to touch his face lightly.

Instantly, his eyes, so green they looked black, snapped open. He snarled and tried to lunge at Rune.

"Food! He needs food!" Rune said desperately, scrambling into the pockets of her belt for something. She pulled out one of Maddie's homemade bars from one of her belt pockets. She shucked it from its wrapper and fed it to St. Benedict. He almost choked on it as he tried to gobble it down too fast.

"It's not enough," one of the men holding him down asserted.

"It is enough. It has to be. Okay, okay," Rune said, and she tapped two of the men on shoulders as her plan formed in her mind. "When I give you the signal, you're going to let him go. I'll lead him away so you can escape." From around her neck, she spun the chain with St. Benedict's box on it and unclasped it.

"What are you going to do?" Lady Trella asked.

Holding the chain out over St. Benedict's face, Rune dangled the little silver box, trying to catch his eye. It worked. Almost instantly, his green-filled eyes seemed to lock onto the silver, and he went deadly still, but no less tense.

"Okay, give me a head start. Then I'm going to get him to chase me. Right, St. Ben?" she said sing-songy to him as she slowly took a few steps back. "Then get out of here, all of you." When she stepped out of St. Benedict's sight, he started thrashing against his captors, trying to get free.

"Can we let him go?" one of the monochrome men called out.

"Yeah, let him go!" Rune shouted as she turned on her heel and took off at full speed into the clearing mist of the forest.

She didn't look back to see if he followed her. She focused on one thing and one thing only. The way to the Lucky Devil.

The pull toward her destination was the clearest it had ever been in her whole life. It was only twenty feet away. She could make it. She dodged trees and picked her way quickly over exposed roots. The first confirmation that St. Benedict was right behind her was when he crashed into the first tree.

The noise forced Rune to look back at him.

He looked like an insane, wild man. His hair was sticking up with twigs and undergrowth bursting out of it. There was hardly anything left of his shirt. There were great rents in his pants. If he sprouted fur or turned green at that point, she wouldn't have been surprised.

He growled in frustration and scratched at the tree as he clambered around it.

Rune tried to pick up her speed, but the tree growth had gotten denser, and the last thing she needed was to fall and break her ankle.

"Come on, St. Benedict, try and catch me!" Rune cried back at him, laughing maniacally to stave off her fear. "Fun. We're having fun right now. This is just a game."

His momentum didn't slow. She felt him closing the distance between them. Up ahead, she burst through the tree line and saw the mausoleum shaped like her bar. Now she could flat out run through the clear space surrounding it, but he could as well, and he was right on her tail. Surprisingly, she heard him laughing.

Looking behind her, she saw his face light up with a familiar smile. Her half-turn tripped her up just short of the imitation Lucky Devil. St. Benedict was so close behind that he stumbled over her, and they fell down, one on top of the other. They reached out toward each other in reaction.

"Ow! Ow!" Rune said as he landed on her, squishing her into the turf. She wrestled to get out from under him, while he tried to pin her arms. "St. Ben-edict!" she gasped out, but it was no use. He had her. Looking up into his face, which was now inches above her own, Rune saw his wild green-black eyes roving over her face. A knot twisted in her stomach. One hand was wandering up her arm to clasp the hand that held his Saint box.

She stopped resisting him then, but instead met his hand with her own, cupping the box between them and lacing her fingers through his. "Caught you," she said.

Something shot through him. His whole body bucked up for a moment, and Rune found herself gripping onto him tightly. He went up on all fours, their hands still clasped. Rune saw green light appear throughout his skin, coming from him like his sweat. Then it traveled, pouring down his arm, and with a burst, the energy entered her through her own hand. She gasped at the rush of it. It was warm and for a moment, Rune felt much like she had when she first opened her sight, like it was too much. Then the power equalized. With a great contented sigh, she relaxed into the turf, feeling warm and satisfied as the magic tingled. "Wow! Well, that works, I guess. No clue what just happened but I'll take it."

"Rune?" St. Benedict asked, unsure.

"See. I told you, you wouldn't hurt me," she said to him. He was still above her, but his eyes were normal green again, ringed with blue on the outside iris, just simple, clear, human eyes, confused and still unsure.

He looked down at his naked chest and her position underneath him, all the way up to their still clasped hands.

"Please tell me that I asked for consent for this."

Rune laughed.

CHAPTER 27

The bar was alive with patrons when Rune and St. Benedict walked through the door. Immediately, St. Benedict crossed his arms to cover his bare chest. His necklace was back around his neck, but otherwise, he was a mess of dried blood and dirt. Rune wasn't much better. At least she managed to keep her shirt on, even if it was torn and ruined.

"Oh, my gosh, what happened to you?" Ally exclaimed, coming straight up to Rune, but not able to tear her teenage eyes from St. Benedict.

"You know...daring feats, corporate insurrection, a romantic adrenaline-filled moment, the usual," St. Benedict quipped, the higher pitch in his voice the only suggestion that he was at all uncomfortable.

"Where's Alf? And what are you doing here?" Rune asked, looking Ally up and down. The teenager looked refreshed, like she had gotten to sleep for a month. She was dressed in nice black slacks with a white button-up blouse that was just a little too "flattering" and an apron wrapped around her perfect waist.

"I start work tonight. Where have you been? It's been like two days," Ally informed them. Rune and St. Benedict exchanged surprised glances.

"Hey, is everything okay?" Liam called from the bar. Relieved to see him, Rune waved over Ally's head. A parade of expressions passed over Liam's face: recognition, surprise, concern, and then shock, the last reserved for St. Benedict's state of dress.

"Ally, we need to go to my apartment for obvious reasons," Rune said as other customers at the bar turned to follow Liam's gaze.

"Oh, yeah, okay. Should I send Alf up to you, milady?" she asked, stepping out of the way to let them pass.

"Yeah, you should, definitely, and don't call me milady. Only Alf has to do that." Rune led the way past the bar to the doorway between the Lounge and Main Bars, looking neither left nor right as people turned to stare. She left it to St. Benedict to follow her, and he did, waving casually at a few of the gawkers.

At the far end of the bar, Rune spotted Franklin in his usual spot. That, more than anything, ran home for her what she had done and left undone. She hadn't saved her bar. Guys like Franklin wouldn't have somewhere to call "their usual spot." The elation she had felt earlier petered away. Two days? She had completely missed the deadline for the payment.

They passed through the doorway between the two bars, making a straight line for the door that led upstairs to the apartments.

The Main Bar was much the same, filled with the sports crowds, but in the Back Bar, another bridal party was in full swing. This one looked calm, though, and everyone seemed to be having a good time.

All of this would be gone soon because of her choice.

Alf called out to Rune from the Main Bar just as she ushered St. Benedict up the stairs and out of everyone's immediate sight. She almost waved him off and went up anyway, but the sight of Deputy Blakely sitting at the bar stopped her in her tracks.

"I'll be right back," she said to St. Benedict, "My apartment is the one at the top of the stairs. Go ahead and take a shower."

"Is everything okay?" St. Benedict asked, leaning down the stairs to look in the direction she kept glancing toward. She planted her hand in his face and pushed him back.

"Yes, I have to take care of some business, and you're still covered in blood. Go on up, I'll be right there."

He looked like he wanted to say something more, but instead gave her a soft smile that went right to her core, warming her and making her ache at the same time. Immediately, she shook it off and gave him another little push up the stairs.

She felt jittery as she crossed to the bar, which she told herself was because of Deputy Blakely's appearance. That became truer the closer she got.

As she approached, Deputy Blakely tipped his out-of-place cowboy hat reflexively. Alf's lips pursed together, and he looked fit to burst. Rune's dread was compounded when she saw the envelope in Deputy Blakely's other hand that he tried to hide, tucking it under his arm when he leaned with both elbows on the bar.

"Leveau, you look like hell," Deputy Blakely said without pre-amble.

"Hello, Deputy Blakely. Are you off-duty tonight?" Rune asked, trying to come off pleasant.

"No, on duty. Have some business to clear up with you, Ms. Leveau," he said, eying Rune up and down. "What have you been into?"

"She's got a new boyfriend," Alf cut in before Rune could answer. "Damn idiot's into wild stuff, adrenaline rushes."

Rune thought about objecting, but other than the boyfriend part, what Alf was saying could be considered true.

"Practicing for the five-k zombie run, through the forest preserve," Rune concurred.

"Looking at the state of you, it was more like a romp," Alf said, pointedly picking a broken green leaf out of Rune's hair.

Deputy Blakely grunted noncommittally. "I understand you had some more trouble a couple of days ago. Anything you would like to put in a statement?"

Rune about had a heart attack. What was it Blakely could be referring to exactly? So much had happened in the last couple of days.

"We are consulting our attorney," Alf piped up, which drew Rune and Deputy Blakely out of their impromptu staring contest.

"Attorney?" Blakely said, his surprise bordering on effrontery.

"It was a dispute with our mortgage company that got a little out of hand, no thanks to," Alf glanced indicatively at Rune, "but we are getting it sorted out. They wanted to claim we were late with our payment, and things got heated."

"Uh, yeah," Rune said. She met Alf's eyes. How could she tell him that she didn't make it in time?

"Especially considering we have a receipt and everything," Alf said, slapping the piece of paper down on the bar.

"You have a receipt?" Deputy Blakely asked, straightening up.

Alf stared at the deputy dead on, not even exchanging a glance with Rune when she slid the receipt closer to herself to read the printed words. The mortgage company's logo was printed in the corner with the address underneath, along with the title line in big, bold letters reading "Transaction Receipt."

Deputy Blakely narrowed his eyes at Alf. Alf returned the look, un-blinking.

"So, do you want to file a report about the incident?" Deputy Blakely asked Rune, tucking the envelope hidden in his hand into his pocket. Rune feigned not noticing.

"No, no. I think it would be more trouble than it's worth. I still have to work with them after all," Rune said.

Deputy Blakely grunted and nodded once, his eyes still narrow as he looked between them. Then he tipped his hat the tiniest bit in good-bye and took his leave. It wasn't until he was gone that Rune pounced on the receipt to examine it thoroughly.

"How…what?" she stammered, "Is this real?"

"What? Of course, it's real," Alf said, unimpressed.

"But the payment. I didn't make it in time," Rune said.

"I know. Some idiot left all the money in Lucky Devil's booth, so I took it to the mortgage company before they closed."

Rune was around the counter before he could say anything more, hugging him with all of her might.

"Let me go! What…don't…don't lift me up!" he screeched, but she paid him no mind. It caught the attention of the other patrons in the bar. Without knowing why, they all broke out in cheers and claps, which made Alf's cheeks burn hotter. "Okay. Okay, that's enough," he said, this time more gently, batting her away. Rune released him but continued to beam at him.

"Don't tell me you're going to frame it or something. You're looking at that thing like it's your first-born child. You know we got to make the next one, next month, right?" Alf continued, pouring himself a drink to cover up his embarrassment.

Rune beamed. "I know, isn't it great? It's not over."

Alf rolled his eyes. "Yeah, well, we have a slew of other problems between here and there…"

"Excuse me, madam, can I fetch you something?" asked a little voice from the bar. Standing next to the basket with peanuts was a little brownie dressed as a devil.

"Acorn?" she said, blinking at the brownie. Acorn gave her a bright smile. "What are you wearing?"

The brownie was still small and brown, but its large mushroom-like hat was gone, replaced by a pair of red horns and a little tie under the chin.

"Look, I'm a lucky devil!" Acorn declared, turning on the spot to shake its attached red-barbed tail.

"Someone left a mess of Faeries running amuck in the bar, so I put them to work," Alf stated matter-of-factly.

"All of them?" Rune looked around the Main Bar, and to her shock, there were little devils everywhere. Each table had one and the patrons seemed enamored with them. A couple of women were taking pictures with theirs. A row of Faerie-Devils sat in front of a group of guys at the bar, watching and cheering the game together. One flew past Rune's head straight to Alf.

"Hey, Alf! Table four needs a refill of Bud, Holtzen, margarita, a round of whiskey shots, another basket of buffalo wings, and a house salad," she piped up like an old diner waitress.

"We can't afford to pay all of them as wait staff! That's…" Rune looked around, but it was hopeless to begin counting them all.

"We don't have to pay them. They are Faeries," Alf said as if she was slow-witted or something.

"Alf! They're not slaves!"

"They're just taking orders. I had to give them something to do. They were tearing the place apart, and now we don't have to buy those infernal computers you wanted for taking orders. Besides, they are eating more than enough to cover their work."

"We want to do this for you, Lady Wizard!" Acorn chimed in its two cents. Rune stood there, at a loss.

"Okay, okay. This is not okay, but I can't deal with it right now. We'll talk further in the morning," Rune said, though the second half of what she said was cut off by the cheers of both man and Faerie when something exciting happened on the sports TVs.

"Get out of here, kid. You look like crap. I've got work to do," Alf said, and he jumped down from his box to go into the bar to serve his customers.

No one seemed to take any more notice of Rune, so she withdrew back toward the stairs. The cheers and chanting immediately died to a dull, distant rumble after she shut the door behind her. Rune stood there listening to it for a moment longer on the dimly lit stairs.

The Lucky Devil was safe. Maddie's legacy was secure and Rune had done everything she could to make it so.

But this wasn't over, not by a long shot.

She waited to the count of three and started up the stairs, her legs feeling unbelievably heavy.

"I hope St. Benedict took his shower already," she muttered to herself and tried to push away the thought of him in said shower, touching his muscled torso as water spilled down on him from above…Rune coughed to herself and hurried up the second flight of stairs.

To her surprise, St. Benedict was sitting on the top step, decidedly unshowered, staring at something in the palm of his hand.

"What are you doing? Why didn't you go in?" she asked as she slowed to a stop a few steps below him.

"Couldn't. Door was locked," he said, giving her a tired smile.

"Oh. Sorry." She shook her head a little at her own stupidity. She should have sent him up with the keys. She dug them out of one of the pouches on her belt and let them both into her apartment. It felt strange to let him into her space like that. Other than Maddie and Ally, and maybe Alf a few times, no one else had ever been in her apartment. She looked around quickly, scanning everything to see how clean or tidy it was.

"Wow, this is nice," St. Benedict said, nodding his approval.

"No, it isn't. I mean, I like it, but..." She twisted her fingers through her snarled hair and shut the door too quickly, locking everything automatically.

He waited calmly, not daring to go any further into the space without permission.

"Um, the shower is... it's this way," Rune said and indicated for him to follow her. She reached around the doorway of the bathroom and flipped on the light. "There should be towels there." She pointed to the side of the shower. He leaned in, his bare back exposed to her gaze as he looked inside. Across its surface, she could see small scars, making him seem more human.

"Thank you," he said and brushed past her to enter, before turning to look at her, his green-blue gaze with its accompanying half-smile ratcheting the tension up inside her even more.

"I'll, um... when you come out, I'll have the medkit ready," she said before returning to the safety of her living room.

Disgusted with herself, she ducked around the counter that separated her living room from her kitchen to go to her fridge. Just as she reached for the handle, she heard the shower start.

"Come on, Rune, stop it," she said to herself and stuck her face into the colder world of the refrigerator. "What do you think is going to happen?" Her mind went several places, most of them involving her bedroom.

Frustrated with herself, she shut the fridge door, having taken nothing out. Instead, she went to her bedroom, by herself, to find her smaller medkit on a shelf in her closet. She set it out on the table, opening it to check that everything she might need to patch him up was still in there. Since it only took five minutes to do that, she tried to sit down and wait for him to finish his shower.

She couldn't sit still. What was taking him so long? Maybe he had passed out in the shower and was slowly drowning under the falling water? How long should she wait before checking? Would he think she was making advances if she checked? Another eternal minute passed, and finally, she pushed herself to her feet. Just before she arrived at the bathroom door, she realized that when he came out of there he would only be in a towel. An easily removed towel, probably wrapped around his waist.

"I should get him some clothes," she said and veered from the door to go back into her own bedroom.

"What?" St. Benedict called from the bathroom.

"Oh, nothing!" Rune said, cursing herself for talking out loud. She went to stand by the door that connected her bedroom to the bathroom. "I'm just going to find you some clothes."

"Thank you," he called back. Rune waited a few seconds to see if he would say more, but he didn't. "Are you doing okay in there?" There was no response. She chewed her lower lip nervously. Before she could decide what to do, the shower kicked off.

Almost falling over her own feet, Rune scurried away from the door to go straight for her dresser. She dug inside, tossing clothes onto her bed looking for something suitable for him to wear. She came up with a pair of men's black athletic pants that she wore because they were comfortable and an oversized white t-shirt with a black moon in the center, the symbol of the band Night Moon Revival. Gripping the clothes in her hand like a lifeline, Rune turned to see the mess of her other clothes strewn over the bed.

Just then, the door of the bathroom opened out toward the living room.

"Crap!" Rune whispered, and dropped her chosen clothes on the floor to grab up armfuls from off her bed. She stuffed them in a heap into her dresser. Glancing up in her rush, she saw the side of him coming out from the shower exactly how she pictured, his waist wrapped in one of her oversized, dark-raspberry towels. "Crap, crap," she reiterated and tried to move faster, stuffing the last bit into the drawer. As she spun around to pick up the dropped clothes she froze at the sight of him, leaning in her doorway, watching her.

It was as delicious a sight as she thought it would be. He leaned with his arms braced shoulder-level on the doorframe. Across his chest, she saw where the Poh had attacked him, along with a few other cuts, but they were all pink, covered with new skin, like they were several weeks old. He had the towel wrapped several inches under his navel, as low as it could possibly go before things got really interesting. His hair was tousled in wet waves from the shower. The look was even more appealing on him than his signature hair gel, along with the half-smile and wicked look in his eyes.

"Just give me a minute," Rune covered, trying to sound unaffected as she stooped to pick up a missed bra from the floor.

"It's a wonder your hair isn't burning, your ears are so red," St. Benedict said, his voice full of laughter.

Rune didn't answer that, just picked up the chosen clothes to chuck them at him. "Here. It's the best I got. Go ahead and change in here, then I'll dress your wounds," she said.

"There aren't any wounds to dress," he said, looking down at his own body. "And I don't feel... weird anymore."

"The spell is gone. You won't speed-heal like that anymore."

"Where did it go?"

Rune held up her hand. "I took it back, I think."

"Ah, I see. That's why your black eye is all gone," he said, nodding toward her.

"It is?" Rune asked, touching under her eye, which was no longer tender. She tried to walk past him to go look in a mirror, but he caught her hand. Her heart started to beat out of her chest.

"What are you doing?" she asked softly.

"Go take a shower yourself. I'm fine, thanks to you," he responded.

"Are you sure?"

He laid her hand on his chest, where the Poh had slashed him, "Don't you think so?"

She stared at that hand. *What am I doing?*

"When I went mad there at the end, why weren't you afraid of me?"

"You weren't going to hurt me. Don't ask me how I knew, I just knew," she said simply. She withdrew her hand from under his, her palm burning. "Go ahead and help yourself to my kitchen. You must be hungry," she added and went into her bathroom, shutting the door safely between them.

Across from her, she saw the steamed bathroom mirror above her sink reflecting a misty version of herself. Walking to it, the reflection grew and grew until Rune Anna Leveau's face filled the whole surface.

She stretched out her hand to wipe away the cloud, and a thought passed through her. This was the face of someone who was whole. She smiled and nodded to herself, satisfied with what she saw.

Instead of wiping it clear, she stripped off her clothes quickly and showered. The mud, blood, and forest detritus shed from her like another skin, leaving her feeling completely new when she stepped back out. This time, she swiped away the cloud on the mirror without a second thought. She studied her face checking for blemishes that weren't there. Then with a resolute nod, she turned to use the door that led to her bedroom, leaving her towel behind. She had nothing to hide anymore.

CHAPTER 28

The bedroom was empty. The door was open to the main room, and she heard the clinking of pans coming from her kitchen. Nodding to herself, she left the door as it was and went to her now devastated dresser to pull on fresh underwear and a clean pair of jeans. She had to dig a little more to find her softest shirt, a dark, midnight-blue one, freckled with stars on the print. It hugged her with warmth, even though it was still summer and she had just come from a hot shower.

Barefoot, her hair uncombed, she knelt down beside her bed and reached for the invisible box tucked underneath. She felt it exactly where she kept it, the Disregard spell that Maddie had engraved into it years ago still as powerful as ever. Over the top, Rune felt a layer of dust that she brushed away. The box appeared only when she did so. Then, taking another fortifying breath, she laid her hand on the top.

"Anna Michelle Masterson," she said resolutely. The spell dissipated to reveal the wooden box, clicking as it unlocked. Rune didn't lift the lid.

Instead, she stood up and went out to the main room.

What she found surprised her.

St. Benedict was in her kitchen, cooking up a storm. He had two pans and a pot going on her stove. Two plates were set out on the counter and the table was already set with silverware and cups. Wielding a spatula like a weapon, he worked on something pink and green inside her largest pan, flipping it like a professional as his other hand held the pan hovering over the heat.

He didn't look up at her until Rune sat down on one of her stools at the other side of the counter.

"Feel better?" he asked. He set the pan down and lowered the heat so he could stir what was in the pot next to it.

"Much." She watched him for a few more minutes. In short order, he pulled out spaghetti from the pot to set on the plate, followed by shrimp and asparagus from pan one and pesto sauce from pan two. Once he had plated the food, he grabbed something from a bowl and dusted it over the top, his fingers dancing in the air. The holographic screen of his hand activated suddenly when he did that.

"Ah, crap," he said and flipped up his hand to make a fist to close it. "Sorry."

"Occupational hazard?" Rune asked as he plated his own food.

He half-shrugged. "Technology isn't perfect, but I'd rather have it than not. Your plate, milady, spaghetti, shrimp, and asparagus with pesto. I assume this is all alright since it was in your kitchen."

Rune took her plate to the table. "Does cooking like a chef come in handy in your line of work?"

St. Benedict had set a bottle of wine at the table. It was pretty much the only bottle Rune had in the whole apartment, and she doubted it paired well with a spaghetti dinner. He didn't seem to mind and poured out the already opened bottle into a pair of flutes on the table— also the only two she owned. "Absolutely."

Rune took a bite. "It's really good. You know, I think this is the first time a man has ever cooked for me."

"Your husband never cooked for you?"

Rune almost choked on her next bite. "How… how did you know I was married?"

"Didn't you mention it?" he asked, raising an eyebrow at her reaction.

"Did I?" Rune couldn't directly recall; so much had happened.

"I take it things ended really badly," he offered.

"You could say that. My… my husband was not a very good man," Rune said, before looking at him guiltily.

"I'm sorry," St. Benedict said, laying a hand on hers.

"Don't be. It was just the usual stuff, and no, he didn't cook for me. This is great," she said, trying to avoid going further into it. What brought this up? Why was he asking her about Justin all of a sudden?

"So, he hit you?"

"No, he didn't hit me or anything like that. I mean, just once and that was very near the end. He was just… he was a dynamic guy, you know? One of those that everyone wanted to be friends with and women always wanted to be with. He probably would never have noticed me if it hadn't been for our parents." She glanced at St. Benedict again, and he only watched her quietly, his face unreadable.

Rune took another big drink from her glass. "Sorry. Other than Maddie, I've never really spoken about Ju-" she winced again, "about him. It's not very good dinner conversation."

He chuckled. "It's fine. I don't mind if you don't. How I see it, you've seen the worst of me today, so I think we're beyond any of that."

"Does that make us friends, then?"

He licked his lips as he chewed on his next bite, giving himself time to think a moment. "No," he said, following his words with another sip. "I don't mean it the way it sounds, though. I like you, Rune. You're amazing, but I wouldn't be a friend you would want to have."

"So, you can't be my friend, and it's for my own good?" she asked teasingly. "Okay, then how about for tonight? At least for the length of this dinner? I think, like you said, I've earned that much at lea—"

"Okay, okay. You win." He threw his hands up to show his surrender.

Rune chuckled but sobered too soon.

"My parents were so proud. We were well-to-do enough, but my mom wanted to conquer the social ladder. It was practically an arranged marriage, but I didn't care. I thought I was so lucky. He was so handsome, in a rock-star kind of way. I, at least, was in love. To be honest, I don't know why he married me."

"Maybe because you're pretty wonderful yourself," St. Benedict said, leaning back in his chair, his plate empty.

She smiled indulgently and shrugged at the idea.

"No, you listen to me, Rune," he said leaning forward, taking her hand. "Until the end of this dinner, we are friends, your words, right?"

"Yes," she said, meeting his eyes.

"Yeah, right, and friends, real ones, tell you the truth no matter how hard it is for you to hear." He paused a second as he struggled with something, but didn't dare look away unless he undermine what he was trying to tell her. "You watched me rip the throat out of another human being."

"It wasn't your fault. You were under control of a spell. My spell, actually. So, really it was my fa—" she started to say, but he stopped her.

"If our places were reversed, I would have given you up for lost and shot you dead. I would have without hesitation. But you, how did you know I wouldn't have killed you? Why would you do such an insane thing as let me chase you? You weren't even afraid…"

"It's not for the reason you think. I'm not in love with you or something." Rune furrowed her eyebrows. She hadn't meant to say that. "It was just... I had already made my mind up about something before I came to find you, to ask you for your help." She pulled her hands from his and looked over at the box, waiting on the counter. "Now is as good a time as any," she breathed and pushed away from the table to stand. "Thank you for the dinner and for being my friend. Now it's time to get down to business."

"Rune..." he said, but she didn't stop, only went to the counter and pulled the box to her as she headed out to the balcony.

"Where are we going?" he asked when she pushed open her backdoor on the city night.

"I'm taking you to Anna Masterson, like I promised," she said, holding the door open with her elbow, so she could look back at him. "That's what you wanted, right?

"Yes," he said skeptically.

She smiled and indicated her head outside. "Then come on."

Out on her balcony, in the distance, Rune heard the rumble of the city as cars, ambulances, and music harmonized with the strange thrum that all cities had and were only noticeable when one left them. Above her, the sky was blank, the stars wiped out by the overwhelming city light. Her porch was a platform made of treated wood atop a small tower of porches attached to the building. The stairs zigzagged back and forth to the alley below.

Above the alley, Rune's porch was an oasis. She had two lounge chairs, one beside the other, where she and Maddie would sit on cool afternoons drinking iced tea. Rune sat in hers, with its unusual retro pattern of burnt-orange and sage-green paisley over a hot-pink background, and put her feet up as she settled the box on her lap. The umbrella she had perched between the chairs was open, shading them from the alley light just behind her head. When it was collapsed, it could block the face of the person next to her, and tonight she wanted to be able to see her companion's face clearly.

St. Benedict stood at the back door and looked at her cautiously through the screen slider. Then he deliberately opened it and came out with a wary swagger.

She smiled again, knowing that what she was doing seemed strange to him. "Come, sit down," she said.

"What's going to happen?" he asked, eyeing the empty lounge chair next to her, which was a blue-and-purple-striped number. "Are we going to blast off or something? Or go through another dimension?"

"We're going to sit," Rune said, laughter in her voice. "Nothing magical will happen, I promise."

"Then… but you're taking me to Anna…"

She nodded.

He took her word for it and sat in the lounger next to her, putting his feet up on the extended end. He had put his shoes back on, and Rune now wished she had done the same. She wasn't sure what was going to happen after she opened the box, but it was too late to be more prepared now. Her stomach twisted hard with nervousness. Carefully, she flipped over the lid and handed him the first thing on top. It was an ID card.

St. Benedict stared down at the card, trying to make sense of the lines of numbers and words. It had a picture of Rune on the front, but a much younger Rune; her face had been slim and much less mature. He doubted he would have recognized the image as her if she wasn't sitting right next to him.

"I was blonde then, but not natural. I stopped dying my hair years ago," Rune said as if that explained everything.

"Anna Masterson," St. Benedict read the name on the card out loud as if that would cause what he was looking at to make more sense.

Rune took another set of documents from her box and unfolded them gently, looking over the names on them.

"This is my marriage license," she said and held that out to him as well, which he took. "My maiden name was Anna Wainwright, and then I became Anna Masterson when I married Justin Masterson."

She took out the newspaper clippings from the box. "Justin got caught embezzling and stealing corporate secrets from his company. We were arrested by that same corporation's internal police. Justin had implicated me in his scheme as an accomplice. I think they told me he had used my Federal ID number, and he must have forged my signature on a few documents to cover his tracks. He also opened several accounts and safety deposit boxes in my name. He knew all my numbers you see, everything. He could just keep things like that in his head and," she smiled through the tears that started to thicken in her eyes. "I never argued with him about it, so when they took me away too, it was a shock. Our families pretty much abandoned us. My mother didn't want to be associated with criminals and they applied for transfers away from us. Then we disappeared into the corporate prison system."

Rune fell quiet then, as the memory of her mother's final words to her echoed in her head. "You made your bed, now lie in it. I've never been so disappointed in you. You should be ashamed." Simple, cliché words that still cut like an obsidian knife.

St. Benedict stared at all of the documentation, going back and forth amongst the pieces.

"I don't understand," he finally said, staring at the living, breathing woman next to him, trying to match it with the young girl he looked at in the news clippings as she was stuffed into a corporate police car.

"My real identity. Rune Leveau is not the name I was born with. It was the name my Aunt Maddie gave me. So, I guess it was the name I was reborn with. Maddie came for me after Justin left me." She swallowed and rubbed her eyes. "Sorry, that part is probably just as confusing. Um, after six months in the system I think, I'm still not entirely sure, Justin made a deal with the corporation and he divorced me. I hadn't seen him that entire time. They wouldn't let us talk to each other at all. They just kept asking me questions I couldn't answer."

"You're Anna Masterson?" St. Benedict sat up, placing his feet on the ground on either side of his lounger like he needed to feel the ground underneath him. "*You* are Anna Masterson."

Rune nodded. "Yes. That's why I couldn't take you to her. I... I don't really know what else to say other than that, for obvious reasons. I know you wanted to find her, but she is me. In fact, because of you, I finally came to terms with who I used to be. I've decided to go by Rune Anna Leveau now. Seems appropriate, so..." she blinked and swallowed. "I don't know where Justin is. I'm sorry. I know you hoped that she would know, or that I would know, but I don't. I haven't seen him since the day we were arrested."

St. Benedict stood up then, dropping all of the proof from his lap onto the lounger. It clattered loudly at his sudden movement. He took several steps across her porch toward the entrance of the stairs leading down. For a moment, Rune thought he was going to leave, and she sat up straight. Instead, he paced back and forth a couple of times, his head working a million miles a minute. On the third return trip, he stopped completely and looked at her again, really looked at her hard.

"You're Anna," he said again, his face looking haunted.

"Yes, I am Anna Masterson," Rune repeated. "For the last six years, I have been Rune Leveau and living with my great-aunt Maddie Leveau, who not only took me in, but mortgaged everything she owned to bribe someone at the corporation to set me free, and to buy me a new, and very illegal identity."

He turned away again and went to the far end of the porch to lean both his hands against the railing, hanging his head between his shoulders. "Oh, god."

"St. Benedict?" Rune asked. This wasn't the reaction she was expecting. She wasn't sure what this reaction even was.

A shudder went down his spine at the sound of her voice.

"I almost killed you," he said to the ground. Then he turned to her, to look at her face again. "So many times, I almost killed you. Oh, god." His legs lost all strength, and he dropped to the ground.

"St. Benedict!" Rune jumped up from her chair and went to him, but before she could touch him, he threw his hand out to stop her from coming too close.

"You're lying to me," he said viciously.

"No, no, I'm not," Rune said. Her confession was not going well.

St. Benedict picked himself up, crossing the short distance between them and drove Rune backward until he pinned her against the rail on the other side. His body pressed so closely, trapping her there. "Anna Masterson was never a Talent. She was a normal woman."

"That was actually a lie. My family didn't want the world to know their daughter was a Talent. I wasn't allowed to ever express my magic," Rune explained quickly. "But I was registered as the law required. My aura imprint is still in the system. That's why I'm terrified of being scanned. It's the only way my false identity would ever be discovered. Justin didn't even know."

St. Benedict loosened his grip on the rail, and a breathing space appeared between them. He took a step back, saying nothing, only stared at her. Rune felt compelled to continue.

"Rune Leveau is legally not a Talent, though because of my close relationship with the magical world's most powerful wizardess, there are constant rumors. I don't know exactly what Aunt Maddie did, but she hid my abilities from others. Between the two of us, we got pretty good at disguising it. Finding things is a fairly subtle magic."

St. Benedict backed off completely then, putting a few feet between them.

"Why didn't you tell me?"

That made Rune arch one eyebrow. "I am telling you."

"No, before, when I first met you, why didn't you just tell me?"

"I... well... because I was technically in hiding, you know. I can't tell you how much I peed my pants when you first came asking about Anna. I thought, with Maddie's death, that I was finally going to be discovered, and then you went and put all those rumors out there, drawing everyone's attention to me." Rune crossed her arms and went back to the box. It was almost empty except for a strange crystal in the bottom that Rune didn't recognize. She reached in to pull it out.

"If you have any other questions, I'll answer them all. I know you've said that we aren't friends, but I hope that maybe you'll be at least a little merciful..." She stopped and shook her head. "Never mind, I'm not going to ask for mercy. Not from you. It's not your fault that I am a criminal and a fugitive." She smiled warmly at him. "Thank you, by the way, for making me find myself."

"You're going to run?"

"No, no. I'm assuming you are going to take me away, right? To find Justin's missing files or sell me back to the Kodiak Corporation, or at least tell them where I am, and they'll come get me. I don't know. At least it's over, right? That part is not so bad." She sat down on her lounger again and slipped the yellow crystal over her head on its black silk cord. It sat perfectly in the hollow of her throat, reminding her of Maddie and she smiled, feeling at peace.

Silence stretched between them. Rune looked out into the dark alley, seeing nothing, just staring at the past in her mind. He came closer, and she tensed. When he bent down and retrieved the documents on his lounger, she looked sideways at him, not daring to look all the way until he picked up the wooden box and dropped them back inside before shutting the lid. Then he sat down on the edge of his lounger, facing her, and offered the box to her.

When she took it, he cupped her face, looking at it deeply, like he was still looking for something and it eluded him.

"You are Anna Masterson," he said again, sounding dumbfounded. "I've looked for you for so long..."

Something passed through Rune. Something tickled at her brain, tickled in her mind. The way he was cupping her cheek, the way he was looking at her, it made her pause. He seemed both calm and not calm at the same time. Gently, he turned to look out at the darker city, his face half in shadow.

"If you could find Justin, would you?" he asked.

The question jarred her. "I... I never wanted to. I have no idea where he is..."

"But could you? With your magic?" he pressed, urgently.

"I don't know. I don't want to..." she stared at him harder. Something familiar was being revealed to her, something she couldn't believe she hadn't seen before.

"What are you going to do to me now?" she asked.

He chuckled and looked at the sky before turning again to look at her, as if it was the hardest thing he could possibly do. "Nothing," he said and rose, letting go of her face. Without another word, he headed down the stairs.

Rune jumped to her feet. "Wait! Where are you going?"

He paused. "I'm leaving. I got what I wanted."

Rune furrowed her eyebrows and bit her lower lip. "But... just like that. That's all?"

"That's all."

"But what about Justin? You wanted to find him, right? You wanted to find his work."

"Don't concern yourself with that."

"Then, it was never about Justin's work?" Rune asked, cocking her head to the side.

St. Benedict huffed, "Not entirely. My owners do indeed want the Masterson files, and they aren't the only ones, but that is no longer your problem."

"But I don't... I don't understand..." Rune was at a loss. It was all happening too fast, and she couldn't keep up with it. St. Benedict started to move down the steps again. Hurriedly, she swung around the rail until she was at the top of the steps herself, following him down.

"But why? You wanted... If you want me to find him, I will. I mean, I promised you another favor, right?" He didn't stop. "I don't understand. Why did you put me through all that to find me?"

That stopped him on Alf's landing. Rune halted a few steps away like she was afraid to get too close. He stuck his hands in his pockets and turned to her, imitating the same attitude he had when he had first arrived in her bar.

"I have no intention of bringing Justin back into your life, Anna," he said. "Or Rune. I suppose. Live out your life in peace." Then he started walking again, his shoes clacking on the boards in a measured, unhurried pace.

Frozen to the steps, something in Rune cried out, cried out for him to stop, to wait. It was the voice, the tiny one in the corner of her mind that always wanted Justin to come back for her. To come back and explain himself to her. To tell her yes, despite everything he had done or said, yes he had, in fact, loved her.

"Wait," the little voice said with Rune's voice, then louder, "Wait!" She rounded the corner of the stairs. He stopped at the top of the next flight, his hands still in his pockets. He waited politely for her to speak.

"It's you, isn't it?" she asked, her heart pounding out of her chest. He didn't move or even seem to breathe. "Are you him? Are you Justin?"

The question stretched for an eternity.

"No. No Rune Anna Leveau, I'm not."

Rune was stunned. "Then... who are you?"

"I suppose if I say just another monster in the night, that would sound like I was actually saying I was Justin, right?" he joked, cracking his smile. Then he took a deep breath and sighed, letting the mask go. "I'm exactly who I said I was, Rune. I'm a corporate spy. I was recruited, though that's a generous word for it, to become an elite corporate dog called a Saint." His face was all in shadow, but then he took two steps forward into the light from the alley lamp. "You don't have to worry about me. There is no profit in me ruining your life any further."

"Is that really all?"

He hesitated again, then offered, "Do you remember how I said that St. Benedict is a code name, a signal to those in the know about who and what we are?"

"Yes," she said cautiously.

"My real name is Aiden. A long time ago, I worked for the Kodiak Company, but as a computer engineer, and like your husband, I broke corporate law. I went against the corporation, and they took everything from me for my disloyalty. I sought you out because I thought..." he hesitated again, swallowed and continued speaking, this time a strain in his voice, "I thought you might be my wife."

The sentence hung in the air between them like a bubble waiting to pop.

He broke it first. "But you're not, are you? If you were, you would have recognized me on sight, right? Did you recognize me, Rune?"

Rune found herself shaking her head, no.

He mimicked her. "No, you're not her, and I'm not Justin."

"What was your wife's name?" she heard herself asking, her heartbreaking for him.

"Ironically... Anne," he said and tried to smile as a tear rolled down his cheek. "They're so close, right? When I saw the transfer order, I thought, maybe they made a mistake. It's just one letter, right?"

Silence hung between them a moment.

"You must have loved her very much," Rune said, then winced, hoping it didn't sound like a cliché platitude. "I really mean it, I mean. You sound like you loved her very much."

"Not enough. Not in time. Not before I lost her," he said.

"You're smiling," Rune said her thought out loud.

"What?"

"You smile all the time. I'm starting to think you smile to cover your pain."

He kept his smile but took a step back like he was afraid that if he didn't put more distance between them, the facade would crack and he would lose the control he was struggling to maintain. "Well, as you can see, you are not my wife, and we have no further need for each other. So, I will go and get out of your life forever. Also, don't worry about anyone else bothering you about any of this. I can redirect attention away from you, don't worry. Fairly easy for a talented guy like me."

"Why would you do that?" she asked.

"Call it just a tiny sliver of redemption for a monster in the dark." He nodded once. If he had his fedora, he would have taken it off and clutched it to his chest. Instead, he made the same gesture with his empty hand. "Have a wonderful life, Rune Anna Leveau."

And with that, he went down the stairs. Rune thought she would never see him again.

She saw him again two months later.

About the Author

Megan Mackie is a writer, actor, and playwright. She started her writing career as an indie author and had such smashing success in her first year with her inaugural book *The Finder of the Lucky Devil,* that she made the transition to traditional publishing. She has become a personality at many cons, recognizable by her iconic leather hat and engaging smile. She has recently joined Bard's Tower, a mobile con bookstore, and has sold her books next to great authors such as Peter David, Melinda Snodgrass, Dan Wells, Claudia Gray, John Jackson Miller, and Jim Butcher, to name a few.

She has written four novels including: T*he Finder of the Lucky Devil, The Saint of Liars, Death and the Crone,* and *Saint Code: Lost* all of which will be re-releasing through eSpec Books. She is also a contributing writer in the role-playing game *Legendlore* soon to be published by Onyx Path Publishing.

Outside of writing she likes to play games: board games, RPGs, and video games. She has a regular Pathfinder group who is working their way through Rapanthuk. She lives in Chicago with her husband and children, dog, three cats, and her mother in the apartment upstairs.

CPSIA information can be obtained
at www.ICGtesting.com
Printed in the USA
JSHW050957120920
7746JS00005B/19